IN THE PALE LIGHT

WESTLEY SMITH

Also By Westley Smith

Along Came the Tricksters
All Hallows Eve
Some Kind of Truth
In the Pale Light

IN THE PALE LIGHT

WESTLEY SMITH

Published by Watertower Hill Publishing, LLC
www.watertowerhill.com

Author's Note
All character and names in this book are fictional and are not
designed, patterned after, nor descriptive of any person, living or
deceased.
Any similarities to people, living or deceased is purely by
coincidence. Author and Publisher are not liable for any likeness
described herein.

Library of Congress Control Number: 2024943274

Hardback ISBN: 979-8-9902033-8-9
Paperback ISBN: 979-8-9902033-9-6
eBook ASIN: B0D6M8BZZS

Printed in the United States of America
10 9 8 7 6 5 4 3 2 1

For Clay Cambell.
A friend, big brother, mentor, and father – to a kid who had none
of these.

December 25th, 2015

The emergency lights from the Hickory Falls Sheriff's Department Ford Interceptor flashed across the snow when it pulled into the Graham Video store parking lot.

The sheet of white should have been untouched by tires at 6:45 a.m., and the snow-covered green Jetta, sitting in the far left-hand corner of the parking lot should not have been there.

Two different sets of tire tracks cut through the pristine snow. One set belonged to the Jetta. The other set made a large circle in the snow before making its way back toward Main Street.

The officer brought the SUV to a stop about five feet from the Jetta; its headlights bathed the car in the frigid darkness. Unable to see past the Jetta's frosted snow-covered windows, a building sense of unease began to crawl over him, tightening the flesh to his bones.

The officer's shift had been easy that night. He had not responded to any emergency calls, nor had he had to pull anyone over. A Christmas miracle itself. But all that had changed fifteen minutes ago while he was patrolling Broke Run Road, when Sheriff Will Daniel's voice came over the radio.

"Call just came in. We got a report of shots fired at the Graham Video store. Caller says they saw a man running across the parking lot, carrying what appeared to be a shotgun. The suspect reportedly got into the passenger side of a blue sedan before it took off with two others inside. Need you to check it out," Daniel had said.

Why the hell is the sheriff in at this hour? the officer had wondered. *Shouldn't Susan be on the call desk? And what's going on at the Graham Video store?*

Now on scene, with the first cracks of gray sky beginning to materialize through the night horizon, he radioed back into the station.

"I'm at the Graham Video store. I've located a V-dub Jetta. It's an early 2000s model. No sign of anyone else, including the reported blue sedan. Though there are two sets of tire tracks in the snow, indicating another vehicle was present."

He glanced at the video store's entrance. There were no broken windows and no ajar door to indicate a robbery had occurred. The place appeared buttoned up tight.

"No signs of a break-in, Sheriff. Getting out to inspect the vehicle."

"Ten-four," Sheriff Daniel's voice came back over the line. *"Proceed with caution."*

Again, the officer thought it was strange that the sheriff was in at that hour, and on Christmas morning. Where was Susan Green? She usually worked the overnight shift; she should still have been at the station, working the dispatch desk.

Still, the officer knew, she could have gone home for any number of reasons—the holiday, the storm, or maybe a family member had fallen –ill—and the sheriff had filled in for her. Pushing the thought from his mind, the officer returned to the pressing matter at hand.

Stay focused. Stay sharp.

Stepping from the SUV, the blowing snow and driving wind bit at the officer's exposed skin, penetrated his clothes. Zipping his jacket up to his chin, he started toward the car, trudging through the shin-deep snow.

As he neared the Jetta, pelted with snow and ice so hard it stung, he noticed a set of footprints leading away from the passenger-side door toward the second set of tire tracks before vanishing.

The tracks were nearly filled in with fresh powder, but it was unmistakable what they were. He assumed this was where the person had gotten into the second car—*an old blue sedan.*

Looking back to the Jetta, he saw something smeared along the top of the passenger-side door. Whatever it was had frozen to a hard, ruby-colored substance.

He eased in for a closer look.

Blood!

A frozen bloody handprint.

A strange tightness gripped the base of the officer's neck as if Death had wrapped a cold, boney hand around him and begun to squeeze. His heart rate quickened.

He placed his right hand on his sidearm and identified himself.

"This is the Hickory Falls Sheriff's Department. If there's anyone inside the vehicle, would you please step out?"

There was no reply. The car was dead still. The only sound across the parking lot was the howling wind and the ice pebbles hitting the closest metal lamp post.

Not wanting to disturb what he believed to be blood on the passenger-side door, the officer lumbered through the deepening snow, around the front of the Jetta, to the driver's side. Reaching down, he took hold of the handle and pulled.

The driver's side door was locked.

He took a deep breath of cold air, sending what felt like ice daggers into his lungs as he tried to steel himself for what he might find inside. His teeth began to chatter, and an internal shudder tremored in his core and quickly expanded to the rest of his body.

"I'm asking anyone inside to identify themselves and step out." He waited, but when no one replied, he said, "If you do not comply, I will be forced to inspect the vehicle. Last warning."

Silence.

No movement came from within. The car's stillness bothered him—like it was dead. But that was impossible. Cars could not be deceased like humans or animals. So why was he getting the dreaded feeling that death emanated from it?

Placing his gloved hand on the window, he brushed the light dusting of snow away and bent down to look inside.

The officer recoiled at what he saw or who he saw staring back at him.

His feet slipped out from under him, and he went down onto his backside, hard. Snow kicked up when he hit the ground, and for a moment he was cocooned in falling white powder, protected from what he had seen.

But when the snow settled, the officer was again gazing at the driver's-side door of the Jetta. There, he saw a man's pale face pressed against the glass, the muscles twisted and tightened in agony. His eyes were open and locked directly on the officer with a vacant, lifeless stare, pleading with him, even in death, to save him.

Too late. I'm too late to save you.

The officer shot to his feet; snow fell off his uniform in large patchy clumps. And though the temperature was in the teens, he felt sweat break out across his back and forehead.

Moving gingerly toward the Jetta again, the officer realized he knew the dead man looking back at him.

Clay Graham—the owner of the Graham Video store.

He removed his Maglite from his belt and turned it on. Bending, he shone the beam through the ice-crusted driver's-side window and began to scan the car's interior.

That's when he saw them.

He pressed a gloved hand over his lips, suppressing the scream that wanted to leap from his throat at the horrific sight of carnage and death inside the Jetta.

It wasn't just Clay Graham dead inside the car but also his wife, Claire, and their teenage daughter, Sidney.

<u>ONE</u>

Nine Years Later
July 21st, 2024

Terry Graham was in the den when he heard the slam of car doors outside. He looked up from the desk where a .20-gauge shotgun lay disassembled in front of him.

Brushes, rags, and gun oil sat beside it, waiting to be used in the cleaning process. Unwanted visitors, he thought, concerned whoever was outside was either there to harass him or vandalize his property. *Maybe both?*

Standing, he rounded the desk and went to the window facing the front lawn and stone driveway that led back to Route 30. A Pennsylvania State Police cruiser was parked in front of the porch steps.

Two Pennsylvania Troopers, who Terry did not recognize, stood by the passenger-side door, squinting through the hot morning sun at the farmhouse.

What the hell are you guys doing here?

He'd spoken to Troopers Allen and Quigley of the Major Case Team six months ago about the murder of his younger brother Clay, his sister-in-law, Claire, and his niece, Sidney in the pre-dawn hours of December 25th, 2015. Allen and Quigley had been on the case since the beginning.

Their yearly conversation (or interrogation) had become routine for Terry after nine years with nothing to show except frustration and continued harassment from those in Hickory Falls who believed him to be their murderer.

The case was chilled, but not cold, according to Allen and Quigley, especially since Terry had not been cleared in their murders. He suspected the troopers' surprise visit might mean they had found some new lead or evidence, hopefully clearing Terry's name once and for all.

What Terry didn't understand was why Allen and Quigley had not been the ones to come to talk with him.

He turned back to the room and grabbed a quilted blanket off his father's pipe-smoking chair; the leather still smelled of McLintock Cherry Tobacco.

Terry threw the blanket over the desk, covering the disassembled shotgun from sight. He walked to his gun cabinet, locked it, and stuffed the key into the front pocket of his jeans.

Terry did not need the troopers to see the open gun cabinet or the .20 gauge on the desk.

He had been out in the fields clearing out the small game like he did every day, morning and night. Rabbits, groundhogs, and squirrels all posed a threat to the crops and gardens. *Goddamn varmints! The only good one is a dead one,* Terry's father, Danby, used to say.

But cops, Terry knew, despised seeing guns lying around a house. Guns made them edgy, even a dissembled one that was only good for pest control.

As Terry approached the front door, he saw the troopers starting up the porch steps. He pulled it open just as the lead trooper was about to knock.

"Mr. Graham?"

Terry nodded. The lead trooper looked vaguely familiar, but Terry could not place where he knew him from. Maybe the trooper had pulled him over at some point, back when he was speeding or drag-racing fellow motorheads out on Route 30 in his black 1977 Pontiac Firebird, the same model Burt Reynolds drove in *Smokey and the Bandit.*

"I'm Trooper Henry Miller with the Pennsylvania State Police Major Crimes Team."

Miller was around forty, six-foot, lean, and muscular. He was ruggedly handsome with dusty blond hair and sharp blue eyes. He wore a white button-down shirt with the sleeves rolled up to his elbows. The collar was open; even at ten in the morning, the heat was too oppressive to keep it closed.

Heavy-duty tan work pants met a pair of brown thick-treaded boots. Terry's eyes lowered to the gun holstered high on Miller's right hip. From the shape of the grip, he could tell it was a Sig P227—he remembered reading about the Pennsylvania State Police adopting the weapon for duty in *Guns & Ammo* a few years back.

Miller held a file and a notepad in his right hand.

Miller turned to the man beside him and said, "This is my partner, Trooper Jason Ross."

Terry shifted his gaze to Ross. Terry was not a little man himself, standing at six-one and weighing two hundred and eighty-five pounds.

He had a barrel chest, large thick hands, arms, and legs. His powerful frame and physical strength came from working around the farm since childhood, a body built from manual labor.

What fat he did have was held in his midsection, caused by a poor diet of too much fatty fried foods, beer, and a pack-a-day cigarette habit.

Ross, however, stood at least six-six and weighed a good three hundred pounds, mostly made of muscle from hours spent in a gym throwing iron.

He wore a dark blue polo with the Pennsylvania State Police emblem embroidered on the left side of his chest. The shirt was so tight that it looked like it was about to explode off him. A shaved head reflected the hot sunlight as if his dome had been polished, and his face seemed to be fixed with a constant sneer.

The black briefcase in his large hand looked tiny, like something a child would use as a toy. He had the same model gun as Miller, only Ross wore his weapon in an under-the-arm shoulder holster.

Ross was an intimidating presence, and it was the first time in a long time that Terry felt small.

"We were wondering if we could speak to you about the murders of your brother and his family, Mr. Graham?" Miller asked.

Terry wondered what Miller and his partner believed they could get out of him. He had no recollection of the night of the murders until he was startled from his drunken slumber by Sheriff Will Daniel pounding on his front door the following morning.

What details he had known were that Clay, Claire, and Sidney were found inside Sid's Jetta parked in the video store parking lot. Clay was in the driver's seat. Claire and Sidney were in the back. They had been executed inside the car with a .12-gauge shotgun. *It was like shooting ducks in a barrel for the killer.*

Terry felt a familiar rage awaken and course through his veins at the thought, warming him in the already hot farmhouse.

"I had the yearly evaluation on the case with Allen and Quigley in January," Terry replied.

"They told me there was nothing new to report."

Miller nodded.

"I understand that. But Trooper Ross and I have taken over the investigation from them. We have a few questions we'd like to ask you."

Terry studied Miller closely. He felt Miller was keeping something from him—like the real reason they were there.

"I don't understand. What happened to Allen and Quigley?" Terry asked.

"They've been on this case since the beginning."

Miller's eyes grew heavy with compassion.

"Allen had a heart attack in February and passed away in March. Quigley retired last month. The case was transferred to us two weeks ago."

"Oh," Terry said, shocked to hear of Trooper Allen's passing.

"I didn't know. I'm sorry about Allen. He seemed like a decent enough guy… for a cop."

Miller glanced at Ross as if he had expected such a reply. Terry thought he heard a disapproving grumble deep in Ross's giant chest.

"Don't take it personally. The lawman and I have never seen eye-to-eye," Terry added.

Neither of them seemed to take it personally. Miller asked if they could go inside to talk.

Terry stepped back from the door, allowing the two troopers to enter his home. He led them to the kitchen, where they sat around the table.

Miller placed the file between himself and Ross, opened the notepad, and retrieved a pen from the breast pocket of his shirt.

"So, what really brings you all the way out here? I'm sure a simple phone call to tell me you were taking over the investigation would have been sufficient."

"We just want to clarify a few details." Ross spoke for the first time, his voice a soothing baritone that did not match his intimidating presence.

Terry sat back in the chair. His eyes flipped from Ross to Miller.

What are they up to?

He reached into the breast pocket of his blue t-shirt, pulled out a cigarette from the pack, and popped it into his mouth. He fished a lighter from the front hip pocket of his jeans. He lit the cigarette and coughed when he inhaled the smoke.

A wet, raspy gurgle came from deep inside his lungs and kicked phlegm into the back of his throat. Terry was sure the cough had started Christmas morning of 2015.

I really need to go see Doc Polis.

"You okay, Terry?" Miller asked. A look of concern crossed his face.

Terry nodded. He cleared his throat and asked, "Why are you here?"

"Since we took over this case, we're reviewing all the evidence again and conducting new interviews with everyone involved, including you."

"Am I still a suspect?" Terry asked, staring down the trooper.

Miller looked at his notepad, ignoring the question. With Miller's silence and avoidance of his gaze, Terry suspected the state police were still treating him as a person of interest.

"The night of the murders, you went to see Clay and Claire at their home, correct?" Miller asked.

"I did."

"And you got into an argument with your brother, is that also correct?" Ross asked.

"We did."

"What was the argument about, Terry?" Miller asked.

Terry drew a tiny puff on the cigarette. Small inhales didn't seem to irritate his lungs and allowed him to continue getting his nicotine fix.

"I wanted to run a business proposition by them—an idea I had been toying with for a few years," Terry replied after blowing the smoke out.

"My goal was to start a microbrewery. You know, one of those places that makes craft beers and serves food. The old hardware store in the square had just closed in November of 2015 and the building was up for sale. I thought it would be a perfect spot to open something new and trendy."

He paused and took a small puff.

"It was an opportune time to pull the trigger and make my idea a reality."

"Why was that?" Ross asked.

"Thanks to corporate farming, most multigenerational farms are unable to compete. I knew if I wanted to keep my parents' farm, and a roof over my head, I would need to do something else. That's when I came up with the microbrewery idea.

"I was going to sell some of my land to housing developers—which I eventually did in 2017, and they built Valley

View Condos on it—hoping I could get enough capital to start up the business, renovate the building, and buy the needed supplies.

"My plan was to bring Clay and Claire into the business and help me run it. Their video store had fallen on hard times since high-speed internet came to Hickory Falls in 2014, killing their business. But they didn't share my vision. The conversation turned heated. I left."

"What was said, Terry?" Miller asked.

"I don't remember," Terry lied.

He remembered every word of their conversation. But if he shared it with the troopers, he knew their suspicion of him would only deepen their resolve that he was their murderer.

"Okay." Miller made a notation in the notebook. "What happened next? Where did you go?"

"I went to Red's."

"You mean Red's Bar, in Hickory Falls town square," Miller clarified.

"The one and only," Terry said, bringing the cigarette to his lips. Red's was the only bar in Hickory Falls; a shithole that had always catered to townie slime.

"What happened at Red's, Terry?"

"I had a few beers. Then headed home and drank a few more here."

Irritation flooded Terry's entire being. *These questions are bullshit.* He had gone over his whereabouts that night so many times with detectives that he had lost count.

It was getting old, but Terry knew what they were trying to do—look for holes in his story, identify inconsistencies they could pick apart, and lay the blame solely on him.

"How many?" Ross asked.

"Somewhere between more than a few and not enough, given the circumstances of what I woke up to that morning," Terry replied.

"According to your original statement to Sheriff Daniel, you said you blacked out and had no recollection of that night after 12:30?" Ross said.

Admitting to Daniel that he blacked out from drinking had made him look suspicious. It had also opened his statement and his whereabouts the morning of the murders up for scrutiny.

But the truth was the last thing he remembered was sitting on the sofa, watching a re-run of *Wings* on Retro TV before falling asleep. Miller and Ross were digging around that same hole in his story, as everyone else had. He knew he had to be careful how he answered.

"I fell asleep on the sofa," Terry said, stubbing the cigarette in the ashtray.

"So, you didn't blackout then?" Ross asked.

"I fell asleep on the sofa," Terry repeated.

"But you said in your statement that you blacked out and had no recollection of what happened after 12:30 that night," Ross shot at Terry.

"Now, you say you were asleep on the sofa?"

"I didn't kill them!" Terry slapped his hand down onto the table, making the ashtray jump. He had been living with the stigma of being a murderer for nine long years.

He was tired of being accused of something he believed he was incapable of no matter what crass words he had shared with Clay and Claire that evening.

But you're not really sure you're not responsible for their murders, are you? Admit it, at least to yourself, that your temper could have gotten the best of you. You could have easily returned to Clay and Claire's, and in a drunken, black-out rage you...

"Easy, Terry," Miller said in an even tone, breaking Terry's thoughts of where his temper, clouded with booze, could have led him without recollection of his actions. It had happened before. It could have happened that night, too.

"We're just trying to get to the bottom of this. I know it's hard."

"Do you?" Terry asked.

"More than you realize."

Terry wondered what Miller meant but the thought fell to the wayside when Ross spoke.

"You were taken down to the sheriff's department the morning your family was found. Is that when you were informed about the murders?"

"Yeah. By Sheriff Daniel."

"That's also when Sheriff Daniel questioned you?" Miller asked, looking up from his notebook.

Terry nodded.

Ross opened the file and began paging through it. He stopped when he found the page he was looking for, ran a finger down to the middle, and tapped at something written there.

"It says here that gunshot residue was found on your hands. Can you explain that?" Ross asked, lifting his eyes to Terry.

"I go out twice a day, morning and evening, to clear pests from the fields with a shotgun. That evening was no different, so of course, there was gunshot residue on me."

Terry thought back to the shotgun on the desk, hoping the troopers would not question him about what was under the blanket.

"All my shotguns were checked and cleared. None of my fingerprints were found inside the car, nor on the bodies. My clothes, which I had slept in, were blood and gunshot-residue-free. I don't understand why you're going over this again."

"We just have a few more questions, Terry," Ross said.

"Do you have any enemies in town?" Miller asked.

"Now? Or before the murders?"

"Before the murders."

He had a plethora of people who disliked him. Jeff Lincoln and Colin Baker, two townie punks he had gotten into a fight with two days before the murders, came to mind.

His reputation to speak his mind—right or wrong—had not scored him points with the community, and his hot temper, especially if he was intoxicated, brought the ire of the sheriff's department.

Then there was Melissa. But he didn't want to think of that horrible night when he crashed his beloved Firebird. Those memories needed to stay locked away.

Melissa needed to remain there too.

"No," Terry finally replied, not offering up anything of his past for them to pick apart, to twist into something untrue, just like the sheriff's department had tried to do to him after the murders.

Pack it away, Terry. Don't think about it.

Miller studied him for a long moment, almost like he knew Terry was lying to them. But if he did suspect Terry wasn't telling them the truth, he kept it to himself.

"What about your brother Clay? Did he have any enemies?" Ross asked.

"Are you kidding? Everyone in Hickory Falls thought Clay shit ice cream," Terry said, almost too smugly.

He instantly regretted his choice of words and needed to course-correct himself. He cleared his throat and sat up.

"Look, Clay was a good man, a loving husband and father. Most people knew him since he owned the video store. And, as far as I know, everyone spoke highly of him. If he had any enemies, I didn't know about them."

"What about Claire or Sidney?" Miller asked.

"Sid was eighteen and away at her first year of college. What enemies could she possibly have? And Claire was a sweetheart—I don't know of anyone who ever spoke a harsh word about her."

Miller made several notations in the notebook. When he was finished, he said, "Terry, we want you to listen to something."

Miller sat up, placing his elbows on the table. "A piece of evidence that was thought lost has come into our possession. Something that could help us identify the shooter."

Terry studied Miller closely, looking for any sign that he was working an angle in hopes of tripping Terry into saying something incriminating. But he saw something else in Miller's eyes—conviction.

Whatever Miller and Ross had uncovered must have been something tangible that they believed could help in their investigation.

"What is it?" Terry finally asked, hearing a slight quiver in his voice.

He wondered if the quiver stemmed from the mention of new evidence or because it could implicate him directly to the murders, which he had no memory of committing.

"What do you have?"

Miller looked to Ross and nodded. Ross picked up the briefcase, set it on the table, and opened it. He pulled out a laptop from inside, booted it up, and searched the internal files. When he found what he was looking for, he nodded to Miller.

"The morning of the murders, an anonymous caller phoned the Hickory Falls Sheriff's Department. Until recently, that call had been thought lost."

"According to the Sheriff's Department, the system that logged all their calls had a malfunction shortly after the murders," Ross added.

"Every nine-one-one call for the past decade was erased."

"But the call resurfaced." Miller leaned forward; the table creaked.

"And we have a copy. Terry, we came here today because we want you to listen to the call. I want you to pay close attention to the caller's voice and tell me if it sounds familiar to you."

Ross clicked the mouse pad, and the call began to play.

OPERATOR: *Hickory Falls Sheriff's Department, what is your emergency?*

FEMALE VOICE: *You need to send someone down to the Graham Video store right away!*

Terry instantly recognized the frantic voice as Ruby-Lee Huckster's, a one-time friend.

The fight inside Reds on the twenty-third of December with Colin Baker and Jeff Lincoln was over her. But he would keep that to himself.

The more the troopers knew about his past violent outbursts, sometimes fueled by beer, sometimes not, the more they would focus on him for the murders of his brother, sister-in-law, and niece.

OPERATOR: *Who am I speaking with, ma'am?*

FEMALE VOICE: *Listen, I was sitting at the light at Main and West Fifth Street when I heard gunshots come from the Graham Video Store parking lot. I also saw a large man get out of a green Jetta, carrying a shotgun, and run across the parking lot, and get into the passenger side of an old blue sedan and take off. As the car pulled out, I saw two other men inside with him.*

Ruby-Lee sounded hungover, maybe still drunk by her slurred speech. A chill passed through Terry's body so sharply that he thought it would cause him to have a heart attack.

He knew he needed to remain calm, collected, and not tip Miller and Ross off. He waited nine years for answers. Now, he would get them from Ruby-Lee herself.

> OPERATOR: *Can you describe the man you saw for me, ma'am?*
>
> FEMALE VOICE: *I'm just letting y'all know something hinky is happening at the Graham Video Store. You should get someone down there right away to check it out.*
>
> OPERATOR: *Ma'am, could you tell me your name?*

There was an audible click of the line disconnecting.

Ross hit the STOP button on the computer. The room filled with a muggy stillness. Terry looked down. His thick, hairy arms glistened with beads of sweat.

He willed himself from balling his large hands into fists and slamming them down on the table. The unbridled fury that had consumed Terry for so many years, had ruined so many relationships, started to uncoil from its slumber.

Stay cool. Keep calm, Terry reminded himself. *Don't lose it.*

But angry thoughts swirled in his head regardless. Why had Ruby-Lee not told him that she saw someone that morning? She was supposed to be his friend.

"Do you know the voice, Terry?" Miller asked.

Terry could feel Miller's sharp eyes boring deep into him, penetrating through his flesh and into his soul. Finally, he shook his head but did not meet Miller's strident gaze.

"You sure?" Miller asked after a moment of silence.

Terry nodded but remained stoic, trying to keep the lid on the storm brewing inside. He lifted his heavy eyes to Miller and once more thought he knew him. *But from where?*

"I was hoping you could pin the voice down and we could find out who she was. Maybe go and talk with her about what she saw that morning," Miller said.

"Sorry," Terry replied, careful not to let his emotions show in his voice.

"I don't know who the caller is."

"That's okay." Miller gathered his things together and signaled to Ross that he should do the same. When he was finished, he looked back to Terry.

"We'll keep digging." He paused and leveled his eyes directly on Terry.

"I promise you we're going to solve this."

More empty promises. Terry wanted them to leave.

"I wish I could have been more helpful," he said, standing.

The two troopers rose from their seats. Terry shook their hands, his own large paw engulfed in Ross's catcher's mitt of a hand. He then led them back outside to the porch.

The troopers started down the steps toward their car baking under the late July sun while Terry leaned against the left porch roof post by the steps.

He pulled another cigarette from the breast pocket of his t-shirt and lit it.

"We're going to catch the persons responsible for the murders of your family, Terry," Miller said, turning back to face him, while Ross climbed in the car and started it up.

"Let me ask you something, Miller. Why do you care so much?"

"I'm not sure I understand?"

"Sure you do. Allen and Quigley were clinical in their response to this case. Just like your partner over there. To them, it's just another day on the job. But you…" Terry pointed two fingers at him; the cigarette smoking between them circled off the cherry tip.

"You're different. You have more compassion for what happened to my family. There's an eagerness wafting off you to solve their murders. Why?"

Terry watched Miller contemplate something, as if he were unsure that he wanted to admit his reasoning for making sure Clay, Claire, and Sidney's murders were not swept up in the endless number of cold cases stored in the bowels of the State Police Major Crime Team's basement, forever lost, forever forgotten.

Finally, Miller answered.

"I was the responding officer who found your brother and his family that morning."

That's why I know you, Terry suddenly realized. Strangely the years begin to melt off Miller's face, and the resemblance to the young officer Terry used to see around town, on patrol, came into focus.

If Terry's memory served him correctly, Miller wasn't with the sheriff's department long, maybe six months to a year, tops, before he transferred.

"I thought you looked familiar. You used to work for the Hickory Falls Sheriff's Department."

Miller nodded.

"I transferred a month after the murders of your family to York PD. Worked there for six years, before joining the State Police in 2019."

Terry drew too deeply on the cigarette. He coughed and spat a pinkish-colored phlegm into the dirt.

Miller turned away, heading to the car, but stopped when his eyes fell onto the barn about twenty-five feet from the house.

LEAVE TOWN MOTHERFUCKER was spray-painted in black across the front of the white barn doors in large, paint-run lettering.

"I see the harassment hasn't ended," Miller said, looking back at Terry.

"Yeah. I'm real popular around town."

Miller nodded like he understood. He didn't. Terry was positive about that much.

Miller had no idea what life was like living in a town where most believed he was a murderer. To prove their beliefs, they vandalized his home with harassing vulgarities, destroyed his crops and gardens, or threw rocks through his windows with notes attached, telling Terry he needed to leave town.

But Terry wouldn't be run off. He would stand up to these shadow people, whoever they were. This was *his* home, and he would go down fighting to keep and protect it from harm, if it came to that.

"You sure you didn't recognize the voice on the nine-one-one call?" Miller asked, once again.

Terry brought the cigarette to his mouth, slowly inhaled, and shook his head. His lungs cramped and burned. He coughed and tasted that familiar coppery mucus on the back of his tongue but swallowed it away as he had been doing for the last three months since the cough had worsened.

"Okay. I'll be in touch."

Miller turned and headed toward the car and got in. Ross was behind the wheel with the A/C running; the collar of his black polo shirt lifted from the cool blowing air. Ross slipped the car into gear, and they drove off.

Terry stood by the post until they were out of sight, with the kicked-up dust cloud from the stone driveway floating in the humid, thick air; the only reminder that the state police were there.

Then he flicked the cigarette angrily into the dirt.

Why had Ruby-Lee not come to me with what she saw that morning? Terry wondered.

Why had she kept it to herself for all these years?

Terry didn't know, but he was damn sure going to find out.

<u>TWO</u>

Miller and Ross had spoken little in the car after leaving Terry Graham's place. Having been partners for two years, they had built a rapport.

Ross knew when Miller wanted to talk about a case and when he'd rather sit quietly and mull things over.

"What's on your mind?" Ross finally asked. "You're quiet over there."

Miller had been thinking about the morning he found the Graham family slain inside the car. The sheer brutality of their murders haunted his memories, forever etched there like pictures chiseled into stone.

What the .12-gauge shotgun did to their bodies was nothing short of horrific.

Claire Graham had been sitting upright in the backseat. A large, black hole in her chest gleamed wetly with blood as Miller shined his flashlight over her body that cold and snowy Christmas morning.

Her head was craned backward, over the rear seat's headrest, and her left hand was still wrapped tightly around Sidney's—her last motherly act of love.

Miller couldn't help but think of his own daughter, Luna, and what he would have done to protect her, to keep her safe from harm.

The shotgun blast had opened up Claire's down jacket, scattering feathers throughout the car. Some had gotten stuck on the blood spatter that painted the interior.

Sidney had been shot in the upper chest and was bent at the waist with her head between her knees; a large pool of blood had soaked into the carpet between her feet, and feathers from Claire's jacket rested on top, absorbing the blood, turning them pink.

Clay Graham had taken a round in the side, just below his right armpit, and his body had come to rest on the driver's side door with his face pressed against the window; his eyes were still open when death collected him.

They look like raw hamburger was how Deputy Bob Peterson, Hickory Falls' second-in-command, described them once he was on the scene that morning and poked his head into the Jetta to get a look. A sharp chill passed through Miller at the thought of Peterson's unapologetic yet accurate depiction of the bodies.

"I was just thinking about the morning I found them," Miller replied with a blink of his eyes, snapping him from the gruesome images clogging his mind.

"I have never seen anything so ghastly, Ross."

Miller swallowed and found his throat dry. He picked up his water bottle from the center console, unscrewed the cap, and took a swig.

"What do you think about the brother? Think he pulled the trigger? He had a lot of weapons in that house. You notice the gun cabinet in the den and the blanket over the desk as we passed? Looked like he was trying to hide something he didn't want us to see."

Miller nodded.

"What do you think it was?"

"Don't know. It could've been anything. Could've been nothing."

"Then why hide it?"

Miller didn't have an answer for that. There were several reasons why Terry could have chosen to throw a blanket over the desk. Still, he didn't believe that if Terry had pulled the trigger he would have kept the shotgun in his possession.

During Allen's and Quigley's time on the case, they had focused a lot of their attention on Terry. They believed, as did Ross, that Terry was fully capable of murdering his family in a drunken, blacked-out frenzy, along with two accomplices.

As far as Miller was concerned, this theory had several problems. The murder weapon had not been found, and none of Terry's clothing, which he was seen wearing the night before at Red's Bar and the following morning at the sheriff's station, had signs of gunshot residue or blood on them.

However, when a swab was taken the morning of the murders, trace amounts of GSR were found on Terry's hands and face.

According to the forensics report, the Grahams were murdered inside the Jetta, point-blank with a .12-gauge shotgun. It was believed the killer was either sitting in the passenger seat or bent into the car, over the seat when the shots were fired.

Only small amounts of blood spatter were found on the passenger-side seat. This meant that the shooter's body had blocked most of the spray, leaving the seat relatively clean.

Terry should have been covered in both GSR and blood had he pulled the trigger. But he wasn't, other than the trace amount on his hands, which he explained away by saying he was out shooting varmints the evening before the murders.

It doesn't make sense.

Then there was the bloody handprint on the passenger side door of the Jetta.

It was confirmed that the print was of the left hand of the shooter, but it had been so smeared that forensics was unable to lift fingerprints.

Miller remembered how the blood had frozen and crystallized in the cold, making it look like rubies stuck to the paint.

The hand had taken most of the blood spray since it was closest to the end of the barrel, on the stock, supporting the gun when fired. When exiting the car, the murderer left the print when closing the car's door.

This partial print did lead to one solid theory: the murderer was most likely right-handed.

Terry Graham was also right-handed.

So were seventy to ninety percent of people, Miller knew.

This brought up another question.

"Say Terry did murder his family. What were the reasons?" Miller asked.

"Terry said he had an argument that night with Clay and Claire Graham. Since he wanted to open a microbrewery, maybe he went to them for money. When they wouldn't give it to him, words were exchanged, tempers flared, and he stormed out of the house.

He went to Red's, tied one on, returned to the Graham house later, fueled by booze, and shot them. After, he returned home and drank himself into a blackout over guilt."

"But why go to them for money when his goal was to sell his land, hoping to get enough capital to fund the business entirely by himself?"

"Hoping," Ross said, holding up his index finger. "Hoping to get more money, is the key word there. Maybe the developers didn't offer him enough to fully fund the business, so he went to his brother and sister-in-law for the rest and tried to sweeten the deal by offering them a partnership."

"We know Clay and Claire had nothing left, thanks to their bank records. They couldn't give him money even if they wanted to. Terry even said it himself that their store had fallen on hard times.

"And why murder them in the car, outside the store, and not somewhere else? That makes no sense. He could have just done it in the Graham house. Or, if he wanted to be more discreet, taken them back to his farm and offed them there.

"He owned more land back in 2015, before selling most of it to developers. The farm was basically out in the middle of nowhere in those days, yet he murders them in a public place, in the middle of town?"

"Maybe to make it look like someone else committed the murders? Remember, the caller couldn't give a description of the person she saw, other than that they were carrying a shotgun. It could have easily been Terry who pulled the trigger, or one of his two accomplices."

Ross paused and shifted his bulk in the seat.

"Speaking of the anonymous caller, do you think Terry knew it was Ruby-Lee Huckster who made the call?"

Miller nodded. Terry had tried to suppress his astonishment when he heard Ruby-Lee's voice. But Miller had seen the tell in his eyes.

It was evident Terry knew who had made the call that fateful morning, just as Miller had, once he heard the call himself.

"If Terry knew it was Ruby-Lee, why not tell us?"

Miller shrugged. It was a good question. Was Terry hiding something?

"What did Quigley think when you talked to him Saturday?" Ross asked.

Last Friday, Miller had been at the barracks getting himself up to speed on the Graham investigation when he got a call from Tim Quigley. Miller had not been expecting to hear from Quigley.

He had tried talking to him when he and Ross first took over the case, but Quigley had not seemed interested in revisiting it since his retirement.

So, when he heard Quigley's voice on the other end, it surprised him.

"Miller. It's Tim Quigley," he had said. "I need to talk to ya. You available?"

"You can stop by the barracks. I'll be here all afternoon," Miller had replied.

"Nah. How 'bout we meet for lunch? Tomorrow?"

"What's this about, Tim?"

"Just meet me for lunch. There's a good hot dog stand, Darn Good Dogs, you know it?"

"I know it."

"Meet me there. Tomorrow. Noon."

Miller had accepted the invitation, not knowing what Quigley wanted to speak with him about or why he chose to meet at a hot dog stand rather than come to the barracks. He had wondered if it was a way for Quigley to stay in the loop on the case.

Now that some time had passed, Quigley could play a pivotal role in solving it without Lt. Garcia knowing he was still actively engaged. He had seen the bloody carnage of the Graham family first-hand.

It was hard to let such violent images go, forget what happened to three innocent people, and slip easily into retirement life.

Miller knew that from his own experience.

They met on Saturday morning. Darn Good Dogs was an open-air joint with picnic tables in front of a food trailer permanently set on a small lot between two houses just off the main drag in Emmetsburg.

"Miller, it's nice to see you," Quigley said, extending a fat, bloated hand to him.

Miller had not seen Quigley since his retirement party a month prior.

He first met Quigley that Christmas morning in the Graham Video parking lot, when Quigley and Allen had arrived after daybreak and took control of the investigation, just as the worst of the snowstorm was rolling over Hickory Falls.

The man was always dressed for work, usually a suit and tie, like he had been that first morning they met.

Now that he was a civilian, Quigley looked more like a fat boat captain in his white slacks and loafers and a light blue polo shirt. He had also seemed to have significantly aged since he retired.

The once-trimmed blond mustache was now white and bushy like a push broom. His face was red, and his nose had grown bulbous and misshapen—a sign of a man who had one too many drinks over the years.

Miller took Quigley's hand.

"How's retirement life?"

"Boring. But the missus keeps me busy with chores around the house. There seems to be an endless amount of them now that I'm there twenty-four-seven."

Miller smiled. If he and Trisha had stayed together, would she have been the same way? He assumed she would have assigned him a honey-do list of things that needed fixing. She was controlling that way.

"Let's grab a bite to eat. My treat. It's been a while since I had lunch with a cop. I miss it. The banter, I mean."

Miller nodded. But there had been little banter between him and Quigley when he first joined the state troopers back in 2019. Both Allen and Quigley were old-school investigators. They did not talk much with other officers outside the purview of their cases unless necessary.

They ordered at the window and took a seat at one of the picnic tables while waiting for their food.

"So," Miller started, "what did you want to talk with me about?"

"How's the Graham case coming along?"

"Why do you want to know?"

"It's just a question."

"It's a specific question about a specific case. One you once worked."

Quigley shrugged.

Miller studied him for a long moment, trying to get a read on the old trooper's angle of why they were actually meeting that afternoon.

"When I called you two weeks ago to discuss it, you said you were retired and wanted nothing to do with investigative work anymore. What changed?"

"Well, I…"

"ORDER 66 UP!" yelled a man from the window at the hot dog stand.

"That's ours. Be right back," Quigley said, pushing himself up from the picnic table.

Miller watched him waddle up to the stand, grab a tray sitting on a small shelf with three hot dogs and two sodas. He returned to the table and passed Miller his food and drink and then sat back down.

With a lick of his lips, Quigley greedily picked up one of his two hot dogs covered with chili and onions and took a large bite. The mere sight gave Miller indigestion.

"You were saying," Miller pushed. It was Saturday, and he was missing spending time with his daughter for the meeting.

Quigley chewed and swallowed. Before he spoke, he ran his tongue over his teeth, working pieces of hot dog meat out of them.

"I found something I believe you're going to need."

He leaned his bulk back in the seat and pushed his fat hand into his front pants pocket and pulled out a small cassette tape about the size of a matchbook. He set it down on the table and slid it toward Miller.

"What's this?" Miller asked, not picking the cassette tape up.

"That, my boy, contains the nine-one-one call that came into the sheriff's department the morning you found the Grahams."

Miller's eyes shot back to the cassette tape. He had thought the anonymous caller's recording had been lost when the Hickory Falls Sheriff's Department's computer system malfunctioned, resulting in hundreds of missing emergency calls. He had only read the transcripts but had never heard the call.

"I didn't think there was a copy," Miller said through a hoarse whisper.

"I made a backup on my microcassette recorder the morning of the murders, like I always did just to be safe. Found it under my desk drawer when I was cleaning out some old case stuff. It slipped from the Graham file when I was working at home.

"Slid between the drawer and the desk and got lodged underneath. I nearly pulled my hair out, trying to find that goddamn tape. We could've used it. Someone around Hickory Falls could have known who the caller was."

"Let me ask you something, Quigley," Miller said, leaning forward. "Do you find it suspicious that there was a system failure at the sheriff's department that just so happened to lose all the nine-one-one calls only a day after the murders of the Grahams?"

"I have always found it suspicious. But proving that it was anything other than a system malfunction will be hard. You would need an eyewitness to the tampering, which you don't have."

Miller nodded.

"What about Terry Graham? You think he was involved in his family's murders?"

Quigley reached out and picked up his soda, holding it in front of his lips for a long moment before he spoke.

"I know this." He took a sip and replaced the soda on the table. "Terry Graham has a hell of a temper. It's the one thing everyone we questioned said, and feared, about being around him."

"Having a bad temper doesn't make him a killer."

"True. But it does make him look capable of being one."

Quigley had a point, Miller knew. He picked up the small cassette tape and studied it.

"If I can pinpoint who the caller is, it might open this case up."

"I hope it does."

They were silent for a while. Miller took a bite of his hot dog, but he wasn't hungry and sat it back on the paper plate. Quigley finished off his, burped, and picked up the second dog.

"What's your angle, Quigley?" Miller finally asked.

"What do you mean?" He took a bite; chili smeared on the side of his mouth.

"Why didn't you want to come and speak to me at the barracks yesterday? Why here at a hot dog stand?"

"I like this place. Outside. Under the sun." He held up the hot dog. "Good food." He took another bite, leaving more chili on the side of his mouth.

"Bullshit! What's the real reason?"

Quigley wiped the chili away with a napkin while he chewed, then swallowed thickly as the hot dog had lodged in his throat.

"I guess I was embarrassed. Forty-two years of service, and I never misplaced evidence before. Not once. Not one single time. That tape might have helped solve the Graham murders years ago."

His face grew long, and he shook his head.

"I didn't want to come back to the barracks and have everyone ask me why I was there. I couldn't take it, knowing I would have to lie to my brothers willingly. So, I called you here today, hoping we can keep this between us."

A part of Miller felt bad for the retired trooper. He had been an exceptional investigator who had solved countless cold cases. One mistake, one costly mistake, would have undone all his good deeds, and his reputation would've been run over the coals for it. The other part of Miller wanted to slap the mustache off Quigley's face for his carelessness.

"It stays here," Miller replied.

On Sunday, after Miller returned Luna to her mother's house, he listened to the call with chills running up and down his spine.

He thought he recognized the slurred female voice, had heard it before, but it took him several play-throughs to pin it to Ruby-Lee Huckster. He knew Ruby-Lee from his time working with the Hickory Falls Sheriff's Department.

He remembered her as the town's floozy and had twice arrested her for solicitation. But Ruby-Lee's charges were dropped both times by Sheriff Will Daniel, citing insufficient evidence.

His hands were tied at that time to investigate her further. But not now.

What were you doing out at that hour on Christmas morning, Ruby-Lee?

"Does Quigley think Terry murdered his family?" Ross asked again, interrupting Miller's thoughts.

"He believed Terry capable of it," Miller replied.

<u>THREE</u>

Terry pulled his Ford F-250 pickup to a stop outside Ruby-Lee Huckster's home.

The last time he was there was Christmas Eve nine years ago when he came to drop off a present for her, and to try and repair the damage he caused to their friendship after his fight with Colin Baker and Jeff Lincoln, two of Ruby-Lee's friends.

Ruby-Lee was well-known around town. Her sexy and playfully flirtatious nature garnered her male attention that she ate up like a shark at a seal feast. There had long been unfavorable rumors that she wasn't dating most of her suitors but running paying customers in and out of the Twin Pines Motel, east of town just off Route 30.

Terry had heard these rumors, considered them many nights when he saw Ruby-Lee flirting with men. But he had never put much stock in town gossip, deciding to ignore the rumor mill.

They had crossed paths often inside Red's over the years and had developed a friendship. Still, there was a deeper reason why Terry befriended Ruby-Lee, despite the stories about her: she treated him decent, unlike so many others in Hickory Falls, especially after the accident with Melissa in '06.

Her friendship should have come with a warning label.

She was the cause of many scuffles for Terry over the years, including the one with Jeff and Colin. He stuck up for Ruby-Lee when a drunk townie or scorned ex-lover badmouthed her around town or inside Red's, saying she was a whore.

She was his friend, and he'd be damned if he stood idly by while her name was dragged through the mud.

He remembered waiting at the door of the Huckster home for it to be answered. He was in the process of kicking the snow from his boots to prevent it from tracking into the house when the door opened, and he looked into the eyes of Ruby-Lee's mother, Ethel Huckster. Ethel squinted against the dark, trying to make out the face hidden in shadows.

"Yes?" she asked cautiously.

"It's Terry Graham, Ethel." He stepped into the light coming from inside the house so Ethel could see him. He'd never address her as Mrs. Huckster, after she turned a blind eye to her daughter when she needed the support of her mother the most.

"Terry Graham! Come in!"

Ethel pushed open the door, and Terry entered the home. It smelled of stale smoke. A haze hung in the air so thick one would be excused if they thought their vision had become blurry. Ethel was a heavy smoker, putting down three packs a day, according to Ruby-Lee.

Terry pulled off his cap and held it by his waist.

"What brings you up here on a night like this?" Ethel asked. She turned away from him and reached for a pack of cigarettes on the table.

"I actually came to speak with Ruby-Lee."

Ethel nodded while pulling out a cigarette. She popped it into her mouth and said, "Ruby told me about what happened at Red's last night."

Terry nodded. He looked away from Ethel's prying eyes, unable to take her gaze any longer.

"I handled it," he finally said.

Ethel studied him closely, noticing Terry's black-and-blue right eye.

"Did they hurt you?"

"On the contrary…"

"You hurt them?" Her voice darkened.

Terry lowered his eyes to the floor. Shame washed over him. His temper, again, had gotten the better of him.

When they rose, he saw consideration for his actions pass across Ethel's face. Or was that a judgmental look? He couldn't tell.

Funny, Terry had thought, how the very woman who allowed her husband to molest their daughter, and did nothing to stop it from happening, would have the gall to judge him for *his* sins.

One night, while he and Ruby-Lee were three sheets to the wind at Red's, she had told him how her father, Carter, used to sneak into her room at night, after Ethel was asleep. At first, he just touched her. Then it progressed.

After a few years of the abuse, Ruby-Lee finally broke down and told Ethel what was going on when the lights went out and the house was immersed in darkness—how a monster came to visit her in the night.

Your daddy's a good man. Now knock off that lyin', you ungrateful snot, was Ethel's reply to her teenage daughter.

The abuse continued for another year, until Carter Huckster died of a sudden heart attack, leaving Ethel to raise Ruby-Lee on her own.

You want to know what the strange thing is, Ruby-Lee had said to Terry after telling him the story about her father's inappropriate behavior.

I still cried at his funeral. Mourned the loss of that sick motherfucker. Ain't that some strange shit?

"Terry! What… what are you doing here?" came Ruby-Lee's voice from across the room that night, snapping Terry out of his memories.

Terry looked up and felt his face grow warm. Ruby-Lee was about five-foot-eight and around one-hundred and ninety pounds. She was not heavy, but curvy. She had a round face that was scarred heavily with pockmarks, giving her a natural trashy look.

Long, wavy, strawberry-blonde hair fell to the middle of her back. Her eyes were oval-shaped and deep blue. She wore a grey and turquoise sweatsuit with PINK written across her chest.

"Sorry. It's late and Christmas Eve." A nervous laugh escaped his lips.

"Oh!" He reached into his jacket pocket and pulled out a small, wrapped box.

"I got this for you," he said, holding up the package.

Ruby-Lee's eyes shifted to her mother. They exchanged a knowing look. The room had a heaviness that had not been there before Ruby-Lee entered. Terry had gotten the feeling that there had been some discussion between mother and daughter about him.

Ruby-Lee crossed the room and snatched the gift out of his hand.

"Thanks," she muttered and hurried away from Terry as if being close to him would cause her to catch a disease.

Terry glanced at Ethel. Her eyes fell to the floor, ashamed of her daughter's reaction to Terry's gift and his presence in their home.

"You can open it?" Terry said.

"I will," Ruby-Lee replied, turning back to face him.

"But it's not Christmas yet. We never open presents until Christmas. Isn't that right, Momma?"

Terry glanced around the small house but saw neither a Christmas tree nor presents. Ethel opened her mouth, about to say something, but Terry cut her off before she could say a word.

"Well, it's not really a Christmas present."

Ruby-Lee looked back to the gift in her hand. She turned it around a few times, studying it from all angles, like trying to decide what to do with it.

"But it's wrapped in Christmas paper. That makes it a Christmas present."

"It was all I had." Terry smiled stupidly.

He remembered thinking how he should have bought another kind of wrapping paper, instead of the one with HO! HO! HO! written across the red paper in big white lettering.

"Think of it more like a peace offering." He lowered his eyes to the floor, embarrassed how he had handled the situation at Red's the night before.

"You busted those two boys up pretty bad," Ruby-Lee said.

Terry nodded.

"So what? You thought you'd give me this, and it would make me forgive you for what you did to my friends?"

"Ruby, what happened last night–"

"Thanks for the gift, Terry," Ruby-Lee said dismissively.

The room grew silent then. Terry knew she didn't want to hear his side of the story. He had seen no point in pushing the issue further, turning his visit into an argument that would dissolve what remained of their friendship.

"I'll see myself out." Terry turned to leave.

Ethel pulled open the door for him; the howling winds caused the trees to creak eerily in the dark beyond the warm comfort of the house.

As Terry stepped out into the night, he looked back to Ruby-Lee. She was irritated but forced a smile and wiggled her fingers in his direction. It was a contemptuous smile and wave.

For the first time, Terry felt a spark of irritation toward her ignite deep inside and knew he wanted to be as far from the Huckster home as he could get.

He had not spoken to Ruby-Lee since that night.

Terry opened the truck door and stepped out. The shaded trees were little help from the blistering hot sun and humidity.

He started toward the home that Ruby-Lee had shared with her mother until Ethel's death last year of bowel cancer. Terry had read about her passing in the paper.

As Terry neared the front door, he noticed the yard was patchy with crabgrass sprouting up like hair from a Troll doll's head. The rest was dead, exposing rocky brown earth soiled with canine feces.

The putrid smell lingered in the muggy air, nearly gagging him. In the driveway, Ruby-Lee's gray Hyundai Accent was parked beside the house. Behind it was a beat-up Chevy Trailblazer that had more dents and scrapes than it had blue paint left on its rusty exterior.

Once at the front door, Terry rapped on it hard enough to shake the doorframe. Inside, a large dog barked, and a man's voice boomed, which caught Terry off guard.

"Who is it?"

Was Ruby-Lee dating someone? Had she gotten engaged? Married? Was that who owned the crappy Trailblazer in the driveway?

Terry said in his most even tone, "I'm here to see Ruby-Lee."

"Go away. We're busy," the voice shot back through the door.

The dog continued to bark.

Annoyed, Terry rapped on the door once again, harder this time.

"I really need to speak to Ruby-Lee," he said through the door.

Footsteps approached the front door. He steeled himself to see Ruby-Lee for the first time since 2015. He had put her behind him and did not want to be back in her orbit.

He focused on the reason why he was there. She could be the key to solving the murders of his family.

But he feared a part of him would lash out at her for not coming to him sooner. Terry liked to think that he was incapable of violence upon a woman, no matter what the town accused him of. Still, he knew somewhere inside lived a dark, violent man.

The door flew open, and a thin, wiry-built, dark-haired man with features that resembled a rat stood before Terry. He wore only white Jockey shorts and socks that allowed Terry to see the scabs covering his arms, chest, and legs. He was erect, the Jockey shorts sticking up like a tent. But the rat didn't seem to be embarrassed by his arousal.

"Wait your fuckin' turn, pal," the guy snapped angrily through rotting black teeth. He rolled his eyes and went to slam the door in Terry's face.

Terry's closed fist snapped up from his side, and he slammed it against the center of the door, preventing it from shutting.

"I really need to see Ruby-Lee. It's important."

Their eyes met, and Terry saw something work across Rat-Man's face that he didn't like—a look he had seen before in men who were thinking about throwing a punch.

"Look, pal. I paid her for da hour. You can have her after dat."

Paid her for da hour? Terry knew the pay-to-play stories. This guy, this wiry, malnourished, scabby rat was one of her tricks. He guessed Ruby-Lee was bringing her customers back to her house now that her mother was dead, instead of the Twin Pines Motel.

"Tell you what," Terry said. "You give me ten minutes, and your time with her is on me."

The rat considered Terry's proposition. Finally, he decided. "No."

"That wasn't a suggestion," Terry said, sharpening his eyes.

"Look, pal…" Rat-Man popped him in the chest with his forefinger, hard enough that Terry winced.

"Get the hell out of here before I get furious and I—"

Terry had enough. His temper took over, as it had so many times in his past, and he came up with a right hook that caught Rat-Man on the jaw.

The slug was hard enough to spin him around into the cabin's doorframe, where he bounced off it and fell back into the yard, his head squishing into a pile of dog shit.

Rat-Man lay in the yard, out cold, with his arms stretched over his head and his legs spread, making him look like a human X.

"Ruby-Lee!" Terry called as he looked away from the unconscious man and stepped through the threshold into the cabin.

The familiar smell of stale smoke brought back memories of the night he had visited. It was dark inside and warm as the pits of Hades. Whatever large dog was in the house was locked up somewhere, barking and pawing at an unseen door, its claws scratching against the wooden surface.

"Ruby-Lee!"

Ruby-Lee appeared from the hallway to Terry's left; shock played across her face at seeing him. She wore a sheer robe that left nothing to the imagination. She had gained a substantial amount of weight. Her face was puffy with splotches of red in her cheeks that accentuated the scarring.

Her belly was large and flabby and hung over her thick, cellulite-dimpled thighs, almost covering the patch of dark pubic hair between her legs. The sight of her disgusted Terry, not from the weight gain, but for what he truly saw her as now—*a fat, bloated whore*.

"You were the anonymous caller," Terry said, pointing a giant finger at her. He could feel his blood boiling, and that old familiar rage fully reawaken.

"What?" She was confused. "What anonymous caller? What the hell are you doing in my—"

She looked past him to Rat-Man outside.

"What the hell did you do to Mac?" She moved for the door, but Terry grabbed her by the elbow as she passed him and pulled her back with enough force that she flew across the room and tripped into the sofa.

"Sit down. You and I have a few things to discuss."

He leaned down, hands on his knees, and looked her directly in the eyes.

"I heard a recording this morning. It was the voice of the person who called the police the day my brother and his family were murdered. That caller… was you."

The anger and dismay from Terry's sudden appearance at her home fell from Ruby-Lee's eyes. They softened with a mix of fear and realization that her time in hiding was up.

Memories came flooding back and played across her face, causing the muscles in her forehead to jump spasmodically.

"Why didn't you tell the police who you were? Why didn't you give them more details of what you saw that morning? Why, for the love of God, did you not tell *me*?"

"Because… because I didn't want to get involved. It wasn't my business. How was I supposed to know?"

"But you found out!"

Terry hollered, his face only an inch from hers.

"You knew after the fact that my brother and his family were murdered, and still, you kept your mouth shut. You could have helped solve this."

"Terry…"

"What did you see?" Terry asked.

He coughed and tasted blood in the back of his throat; the physical exertion and his flared emotions had upset whatever was wrong inside. Behind him, he heard Mac stirring on the ground.

Terry turned. Mac was returning to the land of consciousness. He rolled over on his side, groaning. The dog shit sticking to the back of his head slowly began to peel off and fell to the ground.

Terry looked back to Ruby-Lee.

"Tell me what you saw, Ruby-Lee. I want every detail that pops into that small brain of yours." Terry popped her in the forehead with his index finger.

"Think, Ruby-Lee, think!"

"Okay!" She slapped his hand away.

"I went out and had a little too much fun. Ended up staying at Red's place above his bar. I was heading home that morning when I stopped at the red light by your brother's video store. I heard three loud booms.

"When I looked over, I saw a man carrying a shotgun, running away from a car and jump into this old blue sedan. They hightailed it out of there like their ass depended on it."

She paused and licked her lips nervously.

"I suppose it did, after what happened. As the car got back onto Main Street, I noticed two other guys inside, along with the shooter. One was in the backseat. The other was behind the wheel, driving."

"Did you get a look at them?"

"Just a quick glance at the one with the shotgun."

"You see his face?"

"No. He wore a black jacket with the hood pulled up over his head. But he was a big guy… like you."

She studied Terry carefully.

"Maybe… it was you."

Terry thought it possible, too, and he hated the fact that he knew how unpredictable he could be, especially while upset and driven by alcohol. Anything was possible.

Terry had a friend, Karl Preston, who could have easily hooked him up with shotgun, a car, and maybe even helped him pull off the murders.

The thought fell away when Terry heard Mac enter the trailer. He turned.

Mac stood in the doorway, using it to keep himself upright. His eyes were watery and floated inside his skull—the look of a man who was no longer on planet Earth but some far-off distant galaxy of his own sloggy mind.

41

"You… want… to… try… that again?" Mac asked, his speech a slurred mess.

Terry turned back to Ruby-Lee, ignoring him.

"After they left the parking lot, which way did they go?"

"East."

The closest town was Jamesburg, but it was fifteen miles away. That morning's worsening roads would have prevented them from traveling too far from Hickory Falls.

Terry suspected there was a good chance that they could have taken shelter at the Twin Pines Motel and ridden out the storm there. Had Ruby-Lee offered this information to the police, it might have made a difference.

Terry stood and coughed. That coppery tang filled his mouth, so strong and repugnant even mouthwash could not cleanse it from his taste buds. He knew he should go see a doctor before it worsened.

Still, if he just ignored the cough, the blood, the shortness of breath, and the fatigue riddling his body, it would all eventually go away. Right? Terry wasn't so sure anymore.

He headed for the door. He had thought hearing what Ruby-Lee saw would somehow ease his anguish, but it only provoked him further. Then again, what did he expect? For Ruby-Lee to give some detailed description of the people she saw that morning? He guessed he had. *Foolish of you.*

Mac was still standing in the doorway as Terry neared him. His eyes were heavy, and when he blinked, his eyelids looked like they were weighted down with iron.

Terry reached for a chair by the table and slid it in front of Mac.

"Sit. Before you fall."

Mac did not register what Terry was saying, so Terry reached out and guided him into the chair as if he were a baby. He moved back into the kitchen, pulled a glass from the metal strainer beside the sink, filled it with water, and put it in Mac's hand.

"Sip it."

He looked for Ruby-Lee. She had gotten up from the sofa and moved back into her bedroom as Terry was filling the glass of water.

When she reemerged, she was dressed in a pair of shorts too short for her meaty thighs and a Kid Rock American Bad Ass Tour t-shirt. There was something in her hands, something Terry recognized as she crossed the room to him.

She threw the object at him. It hit him in the chest and bounced onto the floor.

"Take your peace offering and get out!"

Terry looked down at the object between his feet. It was the gift he had given her, hoping to gain her forgiveness. It was still in the Christmas wrapping paper with HO! HO! HO! written across the front.

He saw the irony in his choice of wrapping paper and almost smiled. But the pain slicing its way through his heart prevented him from smiling.

She had never opened it. Then, he saw the tag taped on the outside with his handwriting that read:

TO: RUBY-LEE
FROM: TERRY

He raised his boot, and brought it down, smashing the box flat. He looked into Ruby-Lee's eyes scornfully as he ground his boot into the present.

Terry turned away and headed back out the door to his truck. He jumped in, fired the truck up, and spun out, the tires throwing dirt and rocks into the air.

FOUR

The next step for Miller and Ross was to confront Ruby-Lee Huckster about the call with a surprise visit at her home, deep in the hills east of Hickory Falls.

But it was going on twelve, and Ross asked if they could stop for lunch before going to her residence for the interview.

Miller protested until Ross said, *I do my best work when I'm not thinking about food.* Miller relented, and they pulled into a place called the Treat.

Sitting three miles outside Hickory Falls on Route 30, the Treat oozed 1950s charm complete with working carhop ordering stations under a low steel canopy.

A large sign in a soft-serve-ice-cream-cone shape was atop the brown and green building. The sign lit up in bright neon at night and could be seen up to a mile away in either direction.

The Treat was a local hot spot. It was common to see the place parked full in the evening and on the weekends, especially June through September.

Miller had taken Trisha and Luna there a few times while still living in Hickory Falls.

They parked in one of the stations. Ross cut the engine and rolled down his window just as a voice came over the speaker to take their order. He ordered a grilled chicken sandwich on wheat with no mayo.

No greasy, fried, or sweet food touched his lips. Ross was a man of routine, dedication, and hard work. His muscular body showed his lifelong commitment to living healthily.

Miller ordered the chicken Caesar wrap with dressing.

Sitting in the car, they decided to go over the Graham case file while they ate, splitting its contents between them. Miller took the transcripts and witness testimonies. Ross would focus on the crime scene photos and the forensics reports.

According to the case file, Allen and Quigley interviewed four people: Terry Graham, Red Keller, Karl Preston, and Jenny Taylor.

The first interview with Terry was conducted the morning of the murders at the Hickory Falls Sheriff's Department, after Terry was brought to the station by Sheriff Daniel.

Miller read over the transcripts.

Most of Allen's questions were similar to what Miller and Ross had asked Terry earlier that day. Terry's story had not changed in nine years.

Allen had noted at the bottom of the transcript: *See Hickory Falls Sheriff's Department Interview of Terry Graham (transcript copied from police video footage of interview) - Page 5. Video evidence in Box 2.*

Miller flipped to page five.

The interview by Sheriff Daniel happened before Troopers Allen and Quigley spoke to Terry that morning. Daniel was a small-town sheriff and his only job was to make sure Terry knew what happened and bring him to the station so the state police (who were in charge of the investigation) could question him.

Daniel had no business grilling Terry. *So why did he?*

Miller recalled Sheriff Daniel being on the dispatch radio that morning, informing him to check out the suspicious activity at Graham Video.

He had never gotten the details of why Sheriff Daniel was in that morning instead of Susan Green, who normally worked the radio.

Nine years later, he still found it odd. He looked at Ross, whose forehead was wrinkled with three deep wavy lines, intently studying the crime scene photos.

"Do we have the copy of the Hickory Falls Police Department's video interview of Terry Graham on the computer?"

"Yeah."

"Let me see it."

Ross laid the photos on the dashboard. He turned and picked up the black briefcase from the cruiser's back seat, retrieved the laptop from inside, opened the computer, found the video file, and passed it to Miller.

"What are you looking for?" Ross asked, reaching for his chicken sandwich on the seat beside him, inside the red plastic basket it had been delivered to the car's window in.

"I'm not sure," Miller replied, his fingers working the arrow across the screen.

Miller clicked the PLAY button on the screen, and the video began. The camera angle was pointed directly at Terry Graham, who sat at a table in a small room. Next to him were an unopened bottle of water, a pack of cigarettes, and an ashtray.

His right eye was bruised, swollen, and discolored. Miller wondered how he had gotten the black eye.

Tears wetted Terry's puffy, red face, and he looked pale, like he was going to be sick.

Miller guessed by Terry's sullen and haggard appearance that he had just found out about the murders of his family, while nursing a hangover. Miller couldn't tell if the tears were an act, put on for the camera and the police, or if they were real.

At the bottom right-hand corner of the screen was the timestamp and date that read: 08:36. 12/25/15.

The door opened, and Sheriff Will Daniel entered the room with a cup of steaming coffee in his right hand. He slowly placed the coffee on the table, pulled a chair out, and took a seat.

"I have a few questions to ask you, Terry. Is that okay?" Daniel started.

He kept a sympathetic but understanding tone to his voice, a tactic law enforcement often used when investigators tried to get suspects to talk to them.

Terry nodded. A tear rolled down his cheek. He pushed it away with the back of his hand and sniffed.

"Where were you last night, Terry?"

"Where was I?" The question seemed to catch Terry so off guard that it was like Daniel had delivered a right hook to the jaw that rattled his brain.

"I was at home. Why?"

"You didn't go over to your brother's house last night?" Daniel asked.

Miller could see Terry thinking about the question carefully before he spoke.

"Yes. I went to see Clay last night."

"What did you go see him about, Terry?"

"A business proposition."

"What kind of business proposition, Terry?" Daniel asked.

"I had an idea I wanted to run by him."

Daniel sat forward and put his arms on the table.

"You're going to have to be as clear as possible here, Terry. I need to know everything you did last night. What did you and Clay discuss?"

"We—Clay, Claire, and I—talked about opening a bar in the old hardware store in the town square."

"What did Clay and Claire think about that, Terry?"

"They weren't interested."

"Why not, Terry?"

"Look, would you quit addressing me by name over and over? It's irritating. You know who I am, and I know who you are, Will Daniel. We went to high school together for fuck-sake, so cut the shit. Why are you asking me all this?"

"We're just trying to put the events of last evening into perspective."

"Just like you guys were trying to put the events the night I had my car accident in '06 into perspective?"

The sheriff remained quiet.

Miller wondered what Terry was referencing. He had not known about an auto accident Terry was involved in 2006. He made a mental note to check into it later, see what he could dig up. Back on the computer screen, Miller saw Terry's irritation flare and he sat forward, his eyes boring into Daniel with fiery contempt.

Finally, after a long moment of silence and intense staring between the two, Terry sat back and threw up his hands as if defeated.

"Do you think I have something to do with... with what happened to my brother and his family?" Again, Daniel said nothing. The silence seemed to tell Terry everything he needed to know.

"Oh, fuck you, man! You can't honestly think I would do that."

"I don't know what to think right now, Terry. Why don't you tell me what happened that caused you to storm out of your brother's house last night? Did you guys have an argument?"

"We exchanged a few words."

"What was said?"

Terry lifted his shoulders.

"This and that."

"You need to be more specific, Terry. I know you don't believe this since you have zero faith in cops, but I'm on your side."

"Until you're not."

Daniel sat back as if offended.

"That's not true."

"The fuck it isn't true. This town, and its police force, have been after me since the accident. Since… Melissa."

Terry's voice broke and Miller saw agony work its way across his face. Terry looked away, tried to collect himself.

"And whose fault is that, Terry?" Daniel sat up and pointed at him.

"Yours. You were lucky to walk away from that accident. Melissa, not so much."

Terry's head snapped up. His eyes grew into thin slits.

"You know what happened to Melissa wasn't my fault, Will."

"Explain that to her parents, Terry," Daniel said with a heaviness in his voice that was almost touching.

Miller wondered who Melissa was to Terry. A friend? A lover? He assumed from the conversation that what happened to her was a result of Terry's car accident.

But what made Terry believe the sheriff's department and the town in general was out to get him?

Daniel cleared his throat and collected himself and his thoughts. When he spoke again, his voice was calmer, and he seemed more in control.

"We're just trying to find out what happened to your brother and his family. If your story checks out, you have nothing to worry about."

"I have nothing to worry about."

"Good. Then what happened between you, Clay, and Claire last night?"

"We talked. I left."

"Don't you mean argued?" Daniel asked. "I have a witness saying that's what they saw."

Terry looked at him quizzically and asked, "What witness? Who?"

"I can't tell you who, Terry. I can tell you this: the witness says they heard you and Clay shouting at one another on the sidewalk. You then got into your truck and hauled ass down the street. Said you looked pretty upset. Were you upset, Terry?"

Terry put his face in his hands. He spoke through them, his voice barely audible, but Miller could make out what he said.

"I wouldn't say it was an argument. More of a disagreement."

"About opening the bar?"

Terry let his hands fall away from his face. He nodded.

"So why didn't Clay and Claire jump at the opportunity to go into the bar business with you?"

Terry shook his head.

"I don't know. They didn't give me a reason. That was the end of it."

"If that was the end of it, why the argument? Why'd you storm off?"

"I was frustrated."

"Frustrated enough that you came back later that night and murdered them?"

Terry studied Daniel; his face flushed so red it had turned purple.

"Why would I murder my brother and his family over a disagreement, Will?"

"You tell me."

"I'm telling you." Terry jammed his finger into the table three times so hard it made a *bump, bump, bump* sound loud enough that Miller could hear it on the recording. "I would not murder them."

"Where'd you go after you left your brother's house, Terry?"

"I went to Red's. Had a few beers."

"Anyone see you there?"

"Yeah. The place was packed with locals. Red was throwing his annual Christmas Eve party."

"Give me a few names of people you saw at Red's or spoke to?"

"Well, I saw Red himself—he was working the bar. And I shot the shit with Karl Preston for a while."

"What time did you leave?"

"Around nine-thirty or so, I guess. I wasn't feeling very merry, so I left."

"Where'd you go after you left Red's?"

"I went home."

"Did you have more to drink?"

"I had a few more. At some point, I blacked out on the sofa."

"What time do you think that was, Terry?"

"Had to be around twelve-thirty. I remembered *Wings* was coming on Retro TV."

Miller paused the video there. He looked at Ross.

"Terry has been interviewed countless times over the years. This is the only instance where he says he 'blacked out' that night."

"Which is why I brought it up in our questioning today," Ross said.

"I know. And, again, Terry stated that he fell asleep on the sofa, not that he blacked out."

"So?"

"There's a difference between falling asleep and blacking out. You ever been so drunk that you blacked out?

"No. You?"

"Once. At my bachelor party. I have no memory of some of the stuff my buddies told me I did, like getting up and singing karaoke. They told me I belted out 'Living on a Prayer' in front of a packed bar as if I were Jon Bon Jovi himself. I don't remember it, but there are pictures of me."

"What's your point?"

"If Terry was blackout drunk, he could still have committed the murders and would have no recollection of doing it. But in the interview with Daniel, Terry specifically says he blacked out around twelve-thirty but remembers that *Wings* was coming on. So, did he misspeak and use the wrong term? Or was he so blackout drunk that he doesn't remember anything after that?"

Miller hit PLAY, and the video started again. There was a knock on the door of the interrogation room. Both Daniel and Terry looked up as it opened. Troopers Allen and Quigley entered the small room.

"Sheriff, a word outside," Allen said.

Daniel stood, snatched up his cup of coffee, and exited the room, closing the door behind himself. Miller wondered what Allen had said to Daniel outside the room. He would need to call Quigley and see if he remembered. On the screen, Miller watched Terry pull a cigarette from the pack. He was about to light it but stopped and replaced the cigarette back in the box.

"Why did he not light the cigarette?"

"Huh?" Ross looked over.

"Terry didn't light a cigarette the entire time Daniel was interviewing him," Miller said.

"He had two when we were at his house this morning, but here, nothing. And when he went to light one, he changed his mind. Why do you think that is?"

"That's easy. He didn't want to leave his DNA behind."

After leaving The Treat, Miller and Ross headed north on Route 30 and stopped at the red light where Mountain Road and Main Street intersected.

The town of Hickory Falls lay before them—a small, quaint village one hundred miles southeast of Pittsburgh, nestled in a valley of the Allegheny Mountains. To their right was Shaw's Grocery.

The store was a staple for everyone who lived in Hickory Falls and the surrounding area, unless they wanted to drive twenty-five minutes to the nearest Walmart for groceries.

Across the intersection, to their left, was Lincoln's Gas and Garage. What was once a small service station with one pump and a one-car garage had been updated to a six-car bay, four pumps, and an added convenience store.

The place was packed, with customers inside the store and outside filling up their tanks. Behind the gas station was the new condo development called Valley View. Miller guessed its name came from seeing nearly the entire complex while coming down Mountain Road and back into town and the valley for which it sat.

Nine years ago, the land had belonged to the Graham family, part of their sixty-acre spread. Terry had told them he sold it to developers in 2017.

The light changed and Ross took a right onto Mountain Road, heading up into the twisted, secluded forest roads above the town.

As they drove higher into the mountains, homes began to become sparse, and soon they were surrounded by dense forest that let little sunlight pass through the plentiful green foliage.

Continuing on Mountain Road, it brought them parallel to the Ottawa Creek, which, if they followed it on, would lead them to a fifty-foot waterfall that became known colloquially as the Falls.

Miller had been to the Falls with Trisha and Luna, back when his daughter was still little and had to wear floaties on her arms to prevent her from drowning.

Outsiders and townspeople alike flocked to the Falls in the summer months to either take in their grandeur or to swim in the cool Ottawa Creek which pooled under the falling water before it continued on, snaking its way back down the mountain into the Hickory Falls reservoir.

Ross turned off Mountain Road onto Bank Hill. They drove for another two minutes on a narrow, bumpy dirt road before arriving at Ruby-Lee Huckster's home, where they found the front door hanging open.

Stepping from the car and moving to the house, with the smell of dog shit and piss hanging in the air as thick as smog, they looked through the open threshold.

Inside, Ruby-Lee and a dark-haired man dressed only in his underwear and socks sat at the table in the kitchen. The man held a pack of frozen peas to his jaw.

When Miller knocked, the man with peas on his face looked up with glassy eyes, like a drunk might have when the lights were finally turned on at the bar. *Last call.*

From somewhere in the house, a dog barked to be let out. Ruby-Lee stood from the table and came to the door. She looked annoyed, and her round, pockmarked face was flushed with irritation.

"Yeah?" she said, putting her hands on her ample hips.

Miller and Ross identified themselves and asked if they could speak with her.

"I ain't got nothing to say to either of you."

The troopers looked at each other.

"You don't even know why we're here," Ross said, turning back to Ruby-Lee.

"Doesn't matter. I know my rights, and I ain't saying nothin'," she said, snapping her head back and forth to emphasize her point.

Miller quickly became annoyed. Ruby-Lee had played the 'I know my rights' card – a staple response for every dumb redneck hick he had ever met around these parts.

"Cut the shit!" Miller spat. "We know you were the one who called the police the morning the Grahams were found murdered. Why didn't you come forward, Ruby-Lee?"

She studied him for a long moment. A nervous tic began to dance in her right eye. *What are you hiding?* Miller wondered.

"I know my rights! You can't talk to me—"

Miller stepped forward and slammed his hand on the green siding hard enough that paint flakes came loose and see-sawed to the ground. The man with the pack of peas on his face snapped from his stupor and began to watch closely.

"You saw a man in the Graham Video parking lot get into a blue sedan. According to your call that morning, two other people were in that car. Did you get a look at them?"

Ruby-Lee studied Miller again, inspecting every nook and cranny of his face before she spoke.

"I have no idea what you're talking about, but I know you." Miller stiffened. He hoped she wouldn't recognize him now that some time had passed. "You're that cop from a few years back."

Miller said nothing.

"Yeah, I remember you. You picked me up twice outside of Red's. Tried to pin those sex charges on me. Luckily, Sheriff Daniel saw what you was tryin' to do and cut me loose."

"And what was I trying to do, Ruby-Lee?" Miller asked.

"Make a name for yourself." She looked Miller up and down slowly with a sneer. Her lips pulled tight, and her nose wrinkled as if she had tasted something foul.

"I guess it worked, now that you a big state po-lice man. Wonder how you sleep at night."

"Ms. Huckster, if we could speak to you about the call you made that morning—" Ross began, but Ruby-Lee cut him off.

"I already told you: I ain't got nothin' to say. You want to talk, you come back with a warrant."

"That's not really how—"

Ruby-Lee slammed the door in their faces. More paint chips fell from the siding. Miller pulled out his card and wedged it between the door and the frame.

Once back in the car, Ross said, "She's keeping her hole shut... for once."

Miller nodded. He figured Ruby-Lee wasn't going to talk to them. She had kept what she saw that morning to herself for this long. She wasn't about to come forward now, especially to Miller, who she felt wrongfully arrested her.

"That true?" Ross asked.

"Is what true?"

"What she said. That your arresting of her was a bullshit charge?"

Miller turned and looked at Ross, sharply. His hackles raised with annoyance that his partner would take Ruby-Lee's word over his own.

"If you believe I would do something like that, maybe we shouldn't continue to be partners, Ross."

"Hey, I got to ask."

"Do you?"

"I want to know you're on the level with this case, Henry. You have a history in this town, with the victims, and after what just happened, you obviously made a few enemies along the way. I just want to make sure you're not trying to settle some old scores."

"You know I'm on the level, Ross."

"I hope so. For both of our sakes."

"What—"

Miller's cell phone vibrated on his belt. He pulled the phone from its holder and looked at the caller ID. Trisha was calling. *Shit!*

He hit the cancel button, and the call went to voicemail.

"You need to take that?"

"It's just my ex," Miller said. "I'll call her back later."

"Where to now?" Ross asked.

"Sheriff's Department. I want to know why Sheriff Daniel interviewed Terry." *And why he was working the dispatch desk the morning of the murders.*

<u>FIVE</u>

Terry was heading east on Route 30, toward the Twin Pines Motel. He was alone on the road, surrounded by thick, untamed forest on both sides. A haze hung in the air, making the distant mountain ranges look faded.

A piercing blue sky with a white-hot sun burned above. It warmed the interior of the pickup uncomfortably, causing Terry to sweat.

The air conditioner no longer worked in his old truck. The warm air coming through the open window did little to cool him, and it did nothing to blow away the troubling thoughts racing through his mind since the troopers' visit.

Many people around Hickory Falls believed him guilty of his family's murders. And, in a strange way, his arrest for the murders of his brother, Claire, and Sidney would also serve as justice for what happened to Melissa in the town's eyes, especially Pastor Gary Garland and his wife, Pat, Melissa's parents.

Did he have a temper? Yes. A bad one that, if provoked, could scare someone's hair white. It had gotten him into a lot of trouble over the years with family, friends, and with the police, especially after consuming too many beers.

Alcohol made him unstable and unpredictable. He was like nitroglycerin; one hard shake and it was over. Where this anger manifested from, Terry never knew. But it was there. Strong. Controlling. Powerful.

A festering beast who wanted to consume him entirely, feeding off the fear of others.

He might have had his anger issues, and they had led him down some unsavory paths in life, but could it have led him to murder Clay and Claire?

He wanted to be optimistic and continue to tell himself that he would never hurt them, and he certainly would never have harmed Sidney—he had loved that little girl since the day she was born. He had held her as a baby. Had bottle-fed her. Had played dollies with her on the floor while they giggled and laughed. She was his *little buddy,* as he had always called her.

He couldn't have killed her, no matter how mad he was at her parents.

But there was doubt in his head. Was it possible that he had intentionally drunk himself into a blackout so he would not remember pulling the trigger? It was unimaginable. But not impossible.

He had been upset with Clay and Claire. During the argument, outside on the sidewalk, Terry balled his fist and considered slugging Clay in the mouth. But he had not. He kept his beast under control.

Or so he believed.

You didn't kill them, Terry reminded himself. *You couldn't have. Despite all the times you and Clay butted heads, deep down, you loved and respected him.*

Then why didn't you ever act like it, Terry? Clay's voice asked inside Terry's mind.

I don't know. Too proud. Too stubborn. Too…

Too late for it to matter now, Clay's voice spoke again.

Ruby-Lee said she saw a large man running across the parking lot that morning carrying a shotgun.

Could it have been me? Did Karl hook me up with what I needed that night to commit the ultimate sin?

Not me. It couldn't have been me… could it?

He honestly did not know anymore.

Terry came out of his troubling thoughts when he saw the Twin Pines Motel ahead on the left. He slowed the truck and pulled into a parking space in front of a door marked OFFICE.

He had been to the Twin Pines Motel once before when he brought Melissa there for a romantic evening, unbeknownst to her parents. Unfortunately, the evening was a bust when they found cockroaches in the room, killing his planned romantic endeavors.

That was the same night as the accident.

He swallowed the memory away before it fully blossomed in his mind. The motel was eventually shut down for health violations and was foreclosed on shortly thereafter.

The current owners, the Kellys, had purchased the property cheaply from the bank in 2012 and had renovated the façade and the rooms. The motel now held a mountainy charm, with a pine exterior, dark green wooden shudders, and peaked roofs that made it look like a ski lodge sitting at the mountain base.

When Terry entered the office, a bell inside the door dinged.

The room was spacious, with a small waiting area to his right that had two chairs and what appeared to be the most uncomfortable sofa he had ever seen, rigid and stiff from nonuse. A coffee table was between the chairs and sofa.

Fliers were scattered across it with suggestions on things to do in the area, like hiking the mountain trails or swimming in the Falls above Hickory.

"Can I help you?" a female voice asked, pulling Terry's eyes away from the coffee table.

A middle-aged woman with long silver hair, a pleasant smile, and the soft eyes of a grandmother stood behind a chest-high counter.

Terry presumed she was Mrs. Kelly, the owner of the Twin Pines Motel.

"Perhaps. I'm looking for someone. I believe they might have passed through here a few years ago, maybe even stopped and spent a night or two."

She eyed him suspiciously. Terry didn't know how far he would get with her, but he had to try. The worst she could do was throw him out, or maybe call the police, and they could do nothing to him for asking a few questions. *It's a free country.*

"I cannot give out customer information. That's against the law, sir," Mrs. Kelly said.

"I wouldn't think of asking you for names or personal information, ma'am. Besides, I don't have any names to go on."

She grew even more suspicious, the skin in the center of her forehead pinched taut. She studied Terry closely, like a mother might a child, trying to figure out a secret being kept from her.

"Who are you?" Mrs. Kelly asked.

Terry decided to come clean and tell her why he was there.

"My name is Terry Graham. My brother and his family were murdered nine years ago. I just discovered some new information that led me to believe those responsible might have passed through or even stayed here."

"Oh, my God." Mrs. Kelly covered her mouth with her palm.

"I heard about what happened to your family. I am so deeply sorry."

Terry just nodded. He was not used to hearing anyone say they were sorry for his loss, and the sentiment surprised him. He had grown accustomed to the snide remarks, the hateful glances, the harassing threats, and the vulgar vandalism of his home.

The sweet gesture was disconcerting to him.

"Would you remember if anyone checked into the motel around December twenty-fifth, 2015?" Terry asked.

"My husband would have been working the front desk back then."

"Is your husband around? Maybe I can speak with him."

"He passed away three years ago." Her voice grew sullen, and her eyes, heavy with pain, drifted to the floor.

Terry wanted to say something but decided to remain quiet and wait for her internal moment of grief to pass.

"Anyway, I was told three men had been seen heading east, away from Hickory Falls. It was snowing that morning, and the roads had become impassable; they would have had to pull off. I believe they may have taken shelter here."

"I remember that Christmas morning. It was horrendous. The snow was coming down so fast and hard that my husband and I barely made it in ourselves."

"Do you remember if anyone showed up that day?"

Mrs. Kelly thought for a moment. Again, her eyes drifted to the floor. When she looked up, Terry thought he saw a memory race across her face.

"I don't remember anyone checking in that day. However, I do remember Room 12 was occupied that morning when we came in, which I found strange and questioned Dan, my husband, about it."

"Why would that be strange?" Terry asked.

"We don't rent out Room 12 to guests, not since 2013. But Dan told me he made an exception the night before. We were booked full for Christmas, as I recall, and he said he made the exception because of the storm coming in that evening."

"Why don't you rent out Room 12 to guests?" Terry asked.

Terry believed he saw Mrs. Kelly turn a shade lighter. She brought her arms up and wrapped them around herself, as if some otherworldly chill had just crept over her skin.

"We found a dead woman in there once. Poor thing committed suicide—slit both of her wrists in the bathtub and bled to death. Left a note on the dresser saying she couldn't live with her torment. God only knows what she meant.

Terry's throat went dry. He tried to swallow but his mouth felt like it was filled with a wad of cotton, sucking every last ounce of moisture from his throat.

"That's horrible," Terry croaked out.

"Yeah…" She looked out the window to the west side of the motel. Her eyes shot back and forth, replaying something in her mind. Something she wanted to forget but was unable to, no matter how hard she tried.

"We found her a few days later."

She looked back at him. "That's why we no longer rent it out to customers. Because of what happened. I know that girl was only in there a few days, but no matter what I do, I can never seem to get the smell of death out of the air."

Terry cringed.

He had slaughtered enough animals in his life, both as a hunter and a farmer, to know what death smelled like, how it clung to you like glue and got in your clothes, hair, and skin.

If the room was closed up and the body began to decompose, that smell could linger for hours or days, even after it was cleaned. But years?

He had a feeling that Mrs. Kelly was just imagining the smell of death, her brain's strange way of continuing to remind her of what happened in that room.

"Has anyone else been in there since you rented it out that night?" Terry asked.

Mrs. Kelly shook her head.

"No. It's used for storage now."

"Do you know how many people stayed in Room 12 or when they checked out?"

"I'd have to check my logs to be sure."

Terry felt his pulse quicken. If Mrs. Kelly could confirm that three men had, in fact, stayed there, it could possibly validate his assumption.

"Would you mind checking your records for me?"

She nodded and jabbed a finger at him.

"But I can't give you any names. Laws and whatnot."

Terry understood.

"While you do that, would you mind if I look around in Room 12?"

"Don't know what you think you're going to find, but you're welcome to it."

She was probably right, Terry presumed. Looking through the room was only going to fix his personal curiosity. His chances of finding anything substantial, pointing him in the right direction to who murdered his family, were next to nothing.

And, even if he got lucky and did find something, what was he going to do with it? Hand it over to the state police who would sit on it for another year until the case came up for review, and then maybe they would check it out. *What a joke.*

There was no justice for people who really needed it.

"If it's okay with you, I'd still like to look at the room," Terry replied.

Mrs. Kelly turned around, plucked the ROOM 12 key from the wall rack, and handed it to him. He went to take it, but she held onto it with a firm grip.

"I hope you find what you're looking for, son. I really do."

Outside, Terry started down the walkway. The slanted metal canopy overhead kept the sun off the sidewalk, making it at least ten degrees cooler, which felt good on his overheated skin.

He slowed when he came to room nine. That was where he and Melissa were going to spend their romantic evening until they found the cockroaches.

His mind shot back to that night, back to how he behaved after their evening had been ruined by those goddamn bugs. Had he not lost control, blinded with outrage at the motels' nonexistent upkeep, he might have realized there was something wrong with his car.

Had he not lost his temper, he would not have lost Melissa.

Terry turned away, not wanting to relive any part of that night, and continued to Room 12 where he slid the key into the lock and spun it. The latch clicked, and he pushed the door open.

From inside came the pungent tang of mothballs, which hit him like a punch to the chest. The strong odor choked him. He covered his hand over his mouth and nose and stepped back as if trying to dodge the odor.

He figured Mrs. Kelly used the mothballs to help mask the decay she claimed lingered in there since the girl's suicide.

Inside it was dark. He searched for a light on the wall, found it, and flicked it on.

The carpet was torn up. The walls were stripped of wallpaper leaving ugly patches of paper residue and yellowed glue behind that made the room look like it was melting.

The bed had been disassembled and was stacked against the wall, along with three other tattered mattresses and box springs.

A few old mops and buckets were also in there. Two long mirrors shot Terry's reflection back at him.

He wasn't sure he recognized the man in the mirror. In fact, he was sure he didn't know that man at all anymore.

The smell of the mothballs came to him again, but fainter now that the door was open, and the fresh air could clear the room of the bitter stench. But Terry didn't smell decay, as Mrs. Kelly claimed.

Terry coughed. He did not taste blood this time.

Good.

He moved through the room, but there was nothing that stood out to him. He wondered what he expected to find. Surely there wasn't going to be some smoking gun that pointed him in the direction of those who murdered his family.

He crossed the room to a dresser that held an old tube TV and began going through the drawers. They were all empty. Moving on, he headed to the small closet and opened the door. It, too, was empty.

This is useless.

He turned and opened the bathroom door. Flicking on the light, he found the bathroom covered with a layer of dust. He pulled the shower curtain back and looked inside the tub. There was no sign that a body had ever been discovered there.

He saw enough.

Back outside, Terry closed the door and placed his back on it, then drew a breath of fresh air, sweet with pine. But the pine scent was nearly expunged by the smell of the hot macadam that stung his nose.

"You find what you're looking for?" Mrs. Kelly asked, suddenly next to Terry like a specter materializing out of nothing.

"No."

She looked at him. No, she looked through him into the room. Into the past, where the memories of finding that woman still lingered.

"There's a heaviness to the room. Did you feel it?"

She met Terry's eyes now.

He had felt no *bad juju* in the room, as if father, Rodney, would have said. He was beginning to think Mrs. Kelly's claims were a psychosomatic manifestation because of finding the dead woman in there.

"Did you check your registry books?" Terry pressed.

Her face took on a strange, twisted look. She must have found something in her records that concerned her.

"What is it?" Terry asked.

"Four people checked into that room on the twenty-fourth of December in 2015. A woman…"—she met Terry's eyes–"…and three men."

Terry pushed himself off the door. Ruby-Lee had not said anything to him about a woman. Could this woman have been with the three men seen fleeing Clay's video store that morning?

Or did the people who stayed in Room 12 that night have nothing to do with the murders? Terry felt his heart begin to sink with his last thought. His suspicion about the three men taking shelter there could be wrong.

Then another idea popped into his head that might help him prove his theory.

"When your guests register with you, do they have to supply you with the make and model of their cars?"

"Sure. How else would we know who is supposed to be here from who isn't?"

"Was their car listed in your register?"

"Yes. Of course." She said this as if Terry had asked her a stupid question.

"What kind was it?"

"An Oldsmobile."

"A blue... Oldsmobile?"

Mrs. Kelly's face grew tight with surprise.

"Yes, it was. But how do you—"

"Thank you for your help, Mrs. Kelly."

Terry shot past her, jumped into his truck, and sped out of the Twin Pines parking lot.

<u>SIX</u>

Coming back into town from Ruby-Lee's place, Miller and Ross stopped at the red light where Mountain Road and Main Street intersected.

Miller had said little to Ross since leaving the Huckster home. He was upset with his partner for the accusatory question about unjustly arresting Ruby-Lee.

Miller had worked his tail off to get where he was in his career, putting in his time as a patrolman for nine years with Belford P.D. He transferred to the Hickory Falls Sheriff's Department for a year before moving to York City PD.

There he worked for another two and half years, beating his feet on the street until he made detective. After another year and a half with YCPD working as lead detective, he transferred again to the state police when a position opened up in the Major Case Team in 2019.

He wasn't an overnight success in law enforcement by any means. He had sacrificed a lot in his nearly twenty years of public service, including his marriage to Trisha and time with Luna, whom he now only saw on the weekends.

Ross's insinuation that he would have arrested Ruby-Lee on two bogus solicitations of sex charges to help advance his career indescribably irritated Miller.

Still, there was that one time...

But Miller didn't want to think about what he had done. It was in the past. He was an honest cop now, who would never again bend the law for his, or anyone else's, gain.

The light changed, and they turned right onto Main Street and headed down through the center of town.

Miller felt like he had been transported back in time. Little had changed since he left Hickory Falls. Main Street was filled with row homes and small, locally owned shops, mostly named after their owners—Ann's Sewing Shoppe or Harry's Shoe Repair.

They passed a fantastic coffee and doughnut shop called Cup O'Joes on Main Street and East 4th made the best doughnuts he had ever tasted.

Pulling to a stop at the light at West Fifth and Main, the building that used to be Graham Video sat to Miller's right. It was now a thrift store.

Where movie posters and standees used to advertise upcoming releases in the large windows facing Main Street now hung used, faded clothing and a faceless mannequin dressed in a yellowed wedding dress.

He recalled taking Luna to rent DVDs on Friday and Saturday nights and how the store had been set up backward inside. The entrance was in the rear of the building, and a long driveway ran from Main Street to the parking lot behind.

Since the front of the store faced away from Main Street, and the windows were covered with advertisements, no one could see what was going on inside from the street. Miller knew it was a perfect place for a crime.

"Miller," Ross said, bringing him out of his memories.

He turned back to Ross. The big man's eyes were on him, heavy with guilt.

"I think I owe you an apology. I shouldn't have doubted you back there. You're an honest guy, an honest cop. I've worked with guys who weren't and others who hid behind the blue curtain when they should have done the right thing and not protected those bad apples. I know you wouldn't falsify an arrest to advance your career. You're not the type."

Miller knew the type, too; he looked at one in the mirror every morning, but he was not that guy anymore.

"I'm sorry, man."

Miller nodded. He stuck out his hand and Ross took it.

"Water under the bridge, my friend." Ross gave him a wide, toothy smile that somehow was scarier than his usual stern gaze.

"But you're buying lunch next time."

"Deal." A hearty laugh came from somewhere deep inside that bounced Ross's large chest up and down.

The light turned green, and Ross stepped on the gas.

The next block was called Old Town. On this block were homes that had been there since the town's formation by Sir John Hickory in 1751. The ones that still stood, including Sir John Hickory's house, had been restored for future generations to enjoy.

Miller opened the Graham file and began to read.

The first assumption in the case was that Clay was made to drive himself and his family, along with the shooter in the passenger-side seat, to the video store so they could rob it.

However, according to the file, there was no break-in of the video store the morning of the murders. Inside a safe in Clay's office was three hundred and fifty dollars in cash and coins.

Miller recalled that snowy morning when he pulled into the parking lot. He had not noticed any signs of a robbery; the doors were secure, and the windows were undamaged.

"Why was Clay Graham made to drive his family to the video store in the first place?" Miller asked.

"There was still three hundred and fifty dollars inside Clay's safe, and the store showed no apparent signs of being broken into. Why was it still in the safe if they went to the video store to get money?"

Ross shrugged.

"If we're going with the robbery angle, and not that Terry Graham pulled the trigger out of spite, maybe something happened inside the car. Maybe one of the Grahams tried to wrestle the gun from the shooter, causing an accidental discharge of the weapon.

"With no other choice now that there were witnesses to a murder, the shooter offs all of them, runs to the waiting blue sedan, and they hightail it out of there. But if money wasn't the motivation…" Ross trailed off, becoming lost in his theories of what could have happened.

Miller turned back in the seat. Ross's question mirrored Miller's own about the motivations behind the killings.

They entered Hickory Falls Town Square, which sat on a roundabout interchange.

The roundabout's center was grassy, with inlaid white brick walkways leading to a large pavilion and strategically placed benches. Most of it was hidden under large green maple trees, creating shade for people to sit and enjoy themselves.

Early twentieth-century brick buildings made up the first quarter of the circle, housing the Beckman Real Estate Agency, a bookstore, a computer repair service, and Hinkle's Pharmacy and Café.

As they approached the first bend, Miller noticed a police-issue Ford Interceptor parked in front of the pharmacy. The door opened, and Deputy Bob Thompson stepped out.

He looked the same as Miller remembered, but grayer and older. Otherwise, he was still big and fat, with a double chin and a thick mustache, resembling a walrus.

Thompson adjusted his utility belt under his ample belly and headed toward the pharmacy.

"You know 'em?" Ross asked, catching Miller gawking at the cop out of the corner of his eye.

Miller nodded.

"Yes. Bob Thompson. I switched shifts with him that night."

Miller felt Ross's eyes lingering on him, expecting more to the story.

The truth was that there wasn't much of a story. Miller had asked Thompson if they could switch shifts that Christmas Eve so he could be home with his family Christmas morning. Thompson didn't have kids, and wasn't married, so the switch had been fine with him.

They exited the first bend and passed by School House Road, which led back to Hickory Falls High School. The lights from the football field were visible over the trees and buildings in the square.

Red's Bar, a converted three-story house that had served as an Inn and Tavern for westward travelers since 1802, made up the second quarter of the circle and was beside the post office.

As they passed the bar, Miller saw it had undergone a facelift. It no longer looked like a scary, haunted house with neon beer signs in the windows that attracted vampires.

Now it appeared inviting, with its fresh coat of paint, new windows, door, and a sign that said RED'S BAR in stylish bold letters across the front.

"Red finally cleaned up the place," Miller said with a touch of disdain in his voice.

"You don't like this town much, do you, Miller?"

Miller shook his head.

"Hickory Falls is the kind of place people come to visit for its small-town appeal. To peruse its shops or see the Falls and swim in the cold waters of the Ottawa Creek before moving on to bigger towns and cities. But the majesty of Hickory Falls is a façade.

"Through all its small-town elegance and charm, an ugliness dwells just under the surface. I've seen it firsthand. People in this town don't like those who are different, and they don't like outsiders, other than for their money.

"There are a lot of dark-hearted people, with warped, small-minded views that are best left in the past.

"So, to answer your question: it's not the town I dislike, it's what it represents that I despise."

They continued out of the square, heading past large Victorian homes that made up the north end of town.

Next came the Shady Pines development—or as it had become known to locals, Shitty Pines. Clay and Claire Graham had called Shady Pines home until their deaths.

Miller had heard about how the development of the land had brought much contention with locals back when it was being built in the late 1990s. Fires and vandalism plagued the construction for months, stalling production and preventing people from moving into their homes. There were never any arrests made, as far as Miller knew.

Still, everyone in town understood these crimes were being committed by people who didn't want the town's old ways to change, nor for new people with different beliefs to infiltrate their community.

Miller wondered how the town reacted when the Grahams' land was sold to build the Valley View condos, bringing more outsiders into a town that didn't really want them there.

Ross turned on Plum Run and drove down a secluded, overgrown road until they came upon a dark brown building on a patch of cleared land in the middle of the forest.

HICKORY FALLS SHERIFF'S DEPARTMENT was written in bold yellow lettering across the side of the building.

Ross parked the car in front of a sign that said VISITOR PARKING and killed the engine.

Inside the sheriff's department, Miller spoke to a young woman working the reception desk. He did not recognize her. He told her who they were and that they needed to talk to Sheriff Daniel.

She picked up the phone and called the sheriff's direct line. She listened intently to whatever the sheriff was saying, her eyes glancing up at them every so often.

"I don't know what they want. They just said that they needed to speak to you." She listened. "Yeah, yeah, okay." She looked back at Miller and Ross.

"Sheriff said he'll be out in just a moment."

"Thank you," Miller said.

They stepped back, and Miller scanned the small squad room behind her. There were no officers inside except the sheriff, who had an office in the right corner of the building.

Hickory Falls only had enough money in the town budget for four officers. One for the day shift. One for the evening shift. One for the night shift. And the sheriff, who floated between the three shifts to fill in if someone was sick or on vacation.

The shifts were rotated every two weeks, so no one was always stuck on the same shift.

Miller thought back to that night.

Thompson would have gotten the call that morning if he had not switched shifts with him. Miller wondered, if he had not seen what happened to the Grahams, would he still have the drive to find the person, or persons, responsible for their deaths?

The hypothetical question went unanswered when Sheriff Daniel appeared behind the receptionist.

He had put on weight, mainly in his belly, and his brown hair had grayed at the temples. When his deep-set brown eyes fell on Miller, he could have sworn he saw Daniel turn ashen. Something had spooked Sheriff Daniel at seeing him there that afternoon. He quickly tried to mask his alarm and act surprised instead.

"Look what the wind blew back into my department. Henry Miller, how the hell are you?"

He came out from a door to the right of the receptionist's desk, his hand coming up from his side to shake Miller's.

"Been good." Miller shook Daniel's hand. It felt clammy.

"How's Luna?"

"Luna's having a little trouble with some bullies right now." The question reminded Miller that he needed to call Trisha back and see what she wanted.

"Bullying can be rough on a kid," Daniel said with a nod as if he had experience dealing with a child who was being harassed.

But Daniel couldn't understand. He had no wife or kids and lived alone in a cabin past the Falls.

"Especially now with all those social media sites; kids can't escape the provocation. Social media is the worst thing mankind ever invented, if you ask me, which no one does."

"I can't disagree with you, Sheriff," Miller replied.

"And Trisha. How's she?"

"We're not together anymore."

"Ah, hell. Well, that sucks. I'm sorry to hear that, Miller."

Miller nodded. He wasn't.

"So"—Daniel looked from Miller to Ross and then back to Miller—"What brings you in today? I know you didn't come here just to chit-chat."

"We're investigating the Graham murders."

Daniel studied Miller closely as if he were waiting for a punchline of the joke to follow. "Really?"

He looked away and nodded as if he had accepted some internal agreement with himself. "Well, come on back to my office. I don't know how much help I will be, but I'll help any way I can."

"We appreciate that, Sheriff," Miller said.

They took seats in Daniel's office in front of his desk. Daniel sat down, picked a rubber band from a tray full of them, and circled it around his left and right index fingers.

Miller's phone vibrated on his belt. He checked it and saw Trisha was calling him again.

What the hell do you want? He dismissed the call.

"How can I help?" Daniel asked.

"I was wondering if you could tell us why you decided to question Terry Graham the morning of the murders," Miller said, getting right to the point. Daniel was right; they were not there to *chit-chat*.

"That's easy. I was trying to get him to confess."

"Confess? You had no reason to believe he committed the murders," Miller said.

"But I knew Terry. I'd seen his temper firsthand. I knew what he was capable of."

"So, you believed he murdered his family?" Ross asked.

"And I still believe that. Terry's a drunk with a hot temper. He's been downstairs so many times because it gets him into trouble that I've lost count. And, from what Red Keller told me, Terry was spouting off all kinds of things that night that made him look suspicious as hell."

"And which night are you referring to?" Ross asked.

"Christmas Eve of 2015. Terry had gone to Red's—just like he said he had—but what he didn't say, what he never admitted to either me or the state police, was that he was running his mouth to Karl Preston while downing beer after beer. Typical Terry."

"And when did you speak to Mr. Keller?" Miller asked.

"That morning, when I brought Terry down here, after putting him in the room for those state boys to talk to, I came back out, and Red was in the waiting room when I returned. He said he needed to talk to me."

The file did not mention Red's statement about overhearing Terry's conversation. Normally, it would have sent up a red flag.

However, Miller knew it would not have been out of character for Red Keller to withhold information from the state police when they questioned him.

Like many folks born and bred in Hickory Falls, Red was suspicious of the government and most likely only talked to Daniel because he was the local law and could be trusted, unlike the federal or state authorities.

"How did he know what was going on?" Ross asked.

"Everyone by that point knew what was going on. Hell, the Graham Video parking lot was lit up with emergency vehicles, state police, and forensics. The news made its way back to Red that the Grahams had been murdered, and he came to see me. Told me that he had overheard Terry talking to Karl Preston the night before."

"Do you know what was said between Terry and Karl Preston?" Miller asked.

"I'd advise you to speak to Red. He would be able to give you a detailed recount of the conversation. But the one thing I do remember, and this was what made me believe Terry committed the murders, was that Terry said to Karl Preston: '*My brother's dead to me now.*'"

"That cemented your belief Terry Graham murdered his entire family?" Ross asked.

"Because he said his brother was dead to him after the two just argued?"

"No. What cemented my belief that Terry murdered his family was finding Clay, Claire, and Sidney Graham murdered, after Terry said those words.

"Look, it was a shock to me too. Everyone in town knew about Terry's legendary temper, which was worse when he was drinking. I thought if I were the one who questioned Terry—since we knew each other and went to high school together—he would feel more comfortable opening up to me. That he would tell me the truth.

"I was hoping he had a better alibi, I really was, but when he told me he had 'blacked out,' I knew right then and there he was responsible."

"Have you ever seen Terry blackout drunk before?" Miller asked.

"Sure. He'd wake up the next morning in the drunk tank downstairs and ask me how bad he had been. Had no memory of what he'd done the previous night. But Terry didn't really need to be drunk to mix it up with someone who made him angry."

"Give us an example," Ross said.

Daniel thought about the question.

"Well, the one that sticks out in my mind is when he got into a fight at Red's with Jeff Lincoln and Colin Baker. Gave Jeff a concussion and broke Colin's right arm."

"When was this?" Miller asked.

"December twenty-third of 2015."

Two days before the murders. Miller felt a spark warm his blood.

He remembered Terry's black eye in the interrogation video he'd watched earlier, wondering how he had gotten it. Now, he believed he knew.

"No charges were filed against Terry?" Ross asked.

Daniel shook his head.

"People went to Red's to get drunk, have a good time, and maybe fight. Back then, Hickory Falls was a small, boring town with little to do. It was how locals blew off steam."

Again, Daniel looked to Miller.

"You know that as well as I do, Miller. How many times were you at Red's to break up a fight when you worked here?"

Daniel paused, waiting for Miller to reply, but when he remained quiet, he continued.

"Anyway, Terry was looking for a fight that night. Jeff and Colin said the wrong thing at the wrong time."

"Do you know what was said that caused the altercation?" Ross asked.

"Jeff and Colin had been talking trash about a friend of Terry's. Terry confronted them, words were exchanged, and the fight broke out."

"Who was the friend?" Ross asked.

"Ruby-Lee Huckster."

Miller felt a jolt of energy leap into the back of his throat, pulling it tight. Had they just made a connection to why Terry had not told them he knew it was Ruby-Lee's voice on the nine-one-one recording?

If Terry was willing to fight two men just to defend Ruby-Lee from some trash-talking, then what else was he willing to do for her?

Or, more importantly, what was Ruby-Lee willing to do for him?

"What came of it?" Ross asked.

"Nothing. Though Red did call me the next morning, asked if I would speak to Terry about paying for the damages he had caused in the fight."

"Why'd he do that?" Ross asked, looking up from his notebook where he had been writing.

"Red and Terry shared words after he threw Terry out of the bar. He thought it was better if I handled it. I did. And Terry, reluctantly, I might add, paid for the damages after I spoke with him—not that I left him with much recourse, since I threatened to arrest him if he didn't square up with Red."

"What about Baker and Lincoln? They didn't want to press charges on Terry?" Ross asked.

"My guess is they just wanted to drop the issue, for the moment. Knowing how those two were back then, I'm sure they would get back at Terry in their own way."

"Maybe by killing his family," Miller said matter-of-factly.

Daniel said nothing. And his face showed no signs that he believed anyone other than Terry Graham could have possibly committed the murders.

"What about Red?" Miller continued.

"Wouldn't he have wanted to press charges on Terry for damages to his bar?"

Daniel smiled.

"Are you kidding? Red was okay with the fighting. As long as he was repaid for the damages, and no one was killed inside his bar."

"Was he?" Miller asked, but he already suspected he knew the answer after seeing the renovations made to the bar when they passed through town square.

"Red's went through a complete overhaul, clientele and all. It's a much safer place to grab a drink than it used to be. Red really cleaned the place up. And, doing so, brought in all those millennials that live out in Valley View—they love all that microbrew shit that Red now offers."

"And what about you? You could have pressed charges on Terry for fighting," Miller said.

"Too much paperwork for a misdemeanor."

Now Miller pounced.

"Is that why you let Ruby-Lee Huckster off when I arrested her for soliciting outside Red's?" Miller asked.

The words sprang from his mouth before he could stop them.

"Too much paperwork?"

Daniel put the rubber band back in the tray and sat forward.

"You lacked any real evidence on Ruby-Lee. She was right to complain." He sat back with a smug smile.

"You should really be thanking me."

"Oh? Why is that?" Miller asked.

"Because Ruby-Lee wanted to file a complaint against you."

He waved his forefinger at Miller like he was scolding him.

"That wouldn't have looked good on your record. But I talked her out of it."

You son of a bitch. Miller wanted to give Daniel a piece of his mind but bit his tongue.

"I saw her take money for sex, Sheriff," he replied instead.

"Yes. You saw her take money, but it wasn't for sex. Like I explained to you then: Don Lemming owed Ruby-Lee twenty bucks for a few drinks she bought him at Red's."

"And you believed the town strumpet?"

"Didn't have any reason not to. And Don backed her up. So did Red. You overstepped, Miller."

"What about when I caught her with her hand down Lee Charles's pants in his car behind Red's Bar? What would you call that?"

Daniel lifted his shoulders.

"They were a couple then. It might be indecent, but they were inside Lee's car. Not out where some kid could see them."

"Lee Charles is a married man," Miller said.

He felt himself growing agitated. Daniel had a way of putting the blame back on him.

"How could he and Ruby-Lee have been a couple when he was married?"

"Just because Lee Charles is married doesn't mean he couldn't have a piece on the side. But that's his business. You cannot arrest someone for their infidelities."

Daniel had Miller there.

"You were a patrolman back then looking to do good. But your eagerness to prove yourself made you blind to the facts. And besides, you never actually saw her take money from Lee Charles, did you?"

Miller said nothing.

"I think we're veering off track," Ross said, breaking the tension in the room.

"Let's get back to why we are actually here, gentlemen."

Miller took a breath and nodded.

"That's fine with me," Daniel said, sitting back in his chair.

"What else can I help you with?"

"In the interview you conducted with Terry the morning of the murders, he brought up something about an accident in '06 and someone named Melissa. Can you explain what that was about?" Miller asked.

Daniel studied Miller with heated intensity as if he'd been asked about some awful memory he didn't want to revisit.

"Melissa was with Terry that evening," Daniel's voice filled with heavy emotion.

"Terry lost control of his car and it careened off the road, down an embankment, and into a tree."

His eyes grew sad, and they lowered to the desk; he ran a hand across the surface as if to brush some unseen dust away.

"Melissa was ejected through the windshield and died at the scene. That son of a bitch walked away without a single scratch. Not really fair, is it?"

"How's that?" Miller asked.

"That no harm comes to Terry, but a wonderful woman like Melissa Garland ends up dead."

He paused as if calculating something in his mind. "Seems like anyone who's around Terry for too long falls into his trajectory for bad luck."

"Melissa Garland? Any relation to Pastor Garland?" Miller asked.

Daniel nodded.

"She was his daughter."

He knew of Pastor Garland and his wife Pat but did not know they had a daughter. He and Trisha were not church-going people and they had never set foot inside the Zion Methodist Church in the year they lived in Hickory Falls, nor had they ever spoken a word to the Garlands.

"What was the pastor's daughter doing with a man like Terry Graham?" Ross asked.

"That's what we'd all like to know," Daniel said with disdain.

"Was Terry drinking the night of the accident?" Ross asked. "Is that how he lost control of the car?"

"No. He was stone-cold sober. We don't really know what happened that caused the accident."

"Did Terry say what happened?" Miller asked.

Daniel shook his head.

"What about a post-accident inspection of the vehicle?" Ross asked.

"Did it yield anything out of the ordinary—bad brakes, steering, balding tires?

"There was nothing wrong with the car." Daniel's face darkened and his voice took on a heavy tone.

"Can we get the accident report?" Ross asked.

Daniel nodded.

"I'll have Ashley, the girl you met at the front desk, pull the file for you. And, unless you have anything else you'd like to discuss with me, I really need to get back to work."

Miller felt there was little else they could get from Sheriff Daniel.

"Thank you for your time, Sheriff," Miller said, standing.

"We appreciate your assistance in this investigation."

Ross and Daniel rose to their feet, as well.

"We'll be in touch," Ross said.

They turned and headed to the door, with Ross leading. But before Miller walked out, he had one more question—a question he had held off on asking until this very moment.

"Were you here when the nine-one-one call came in reporting the activity at Graham Video?"

"No. Susan Green took it. If you recall, she was the overnight dispatcher back then."

"I remember. But you were the one who radioed me that morning? Shouldn't Susan still have been here to do that?"

"I came in early to send her home because it was snowing. I was going to take over dispatch until Andy Thompson came in for his normal shift at eight. I wanted her home before the roads really turned bad. Susan's eyesight wasn't great, and she hated driving in bad weather."

"So, you didn't hear the caller's voice?"

"No. I got here just as Susan was hanging up the phone. She told me about the call. I radioed you to check it out. The rest, as they say, is history."

Miller thought about that morning.

The wind. The snow. The bitter cold. Clay Graham's dead eyes staring back at him. The feathers. And the blood. *So much blood.* The lost 9-1-1 call with Ruby-Lee's voice on it.

"What happened to cause the system to lose all the calls? Including the one that morning?" Miller asked.

"Hard drive failure the following day. The damnedest thing, really."

"Shame. It could have been helpful. Maybe to identify whoever reported the call that morning to your department."

SEVEN

Terry was lost in thought as he drove back to the farm that afternoon.

There was an exhilaration inside that he had not felt in years, maybe since the first time he had tracked a twelve-point buck through the woods and tagged it from fifty yards away with a 30/6.

But tracking humans and tracking wild animals were two different things. An animal was dumb enough to leave its trail behind: footprints in the dirt, a broken branch here, droppings there, allowing a man to get close enough to fire a kill shot.

Humans, on the other hand, were intelligent and tried to hide their tracks. And these men had hidden their tracks well.

Still, Terry felt confident he was on the right trail. Three men in a blue sedan (an Oldsmobile) had stayed at the Twin Pines Motel that night.

However, he had one concern: Ruby-Lee had not said anything about a woman being present at the time of the murders.

Yet Mrs. Kelly confirmed that a woman and three men had checked into Room 12 on December 24, 2015. Was it possible that there was a woman inside the car that Ruby-Lee had not seen?

There was no way to be sure, useless he located those who stayed in Room 12 and asked them.

Terry shifted his thoughts to why Clay, Claire, and Sidney were chosen that night.

Was it money?

But there was no money.

Danby and Winfred, Terry and Clay's parents, were the sole inheritors of Clay and Claire's estate. Claire's parents had passed away, and she had no siblings.

This meant Terry's parents had access to all their information, including personal and business bank accounts. From what his father told him, twenty-five hundred dollars remained between their checking, savings, and business accounts at the time of their deaths.

The video store had become an archaic business that most around the world had abandoned years ago. Clay and Claire had been lucky to have survived and thrived for as long as they had.

They had some credit card debt amounting to about ten thousand dollars, a mortgage with seventy-five thousand dollars left, and they were paying for Sidney's college tuition.

Their only saving grace at the time would have been to sell the building along with the inventory, giving them at least three hundred thousand dollars in equity.

Terry knew most of this even before Clay's death. His brother had brought up his concerns with Terry in November of 2015, at Danby's seventieth birthday party.

Terry had desperately tried to convince Clay and Claire to sell the building and the inventory, which they could then put into savings, getting them by until they got steady jobs, while continuing to put Sidney through college.

Instead, the sale of the building went to settle their debt and burials, leaving only about one hundred thousand for Terry's parents, which eventually went to cancer treatments once both became ill a few years later.

But the video store was locked the morning they were discovered, and what money was inside was still in the safe in Clay's office.

So why had they made Clay drive down there if the only intentions were to kill them in the parking lot?

Maybe because whoever murdered them had not known Clay's business was in its final plunge into the abyss? That was possible.

If those men in the blue Olds had been from out of town, they would have no knowledge about Clay's financial troubles. When they forced their way in, possibly threatening to harm Claire or Sidney, Clay could have told them he had cash at the store, money he could give them if they spared his family.

But why didn't they go inside the video store for the money? And why not the bank where there was twenty-five hundred dollars?

These thoughts bounced around in Terry's skull like ricocheting bullets. He only had snippets of the trail he was following. What was he seeing but not seeing at all?

Or was he just seeing what he wanted to see?

The thought materialized in his mind again that he could have murdered his family in a drunken blackout. He could have gone back over to Clay's, armed, and ordered all three of them into Sid's car and then made Clay drive to the video store where he executed them at the very place Clay loved.

Terry could ask Karl Preston about those missing hours from his memory, if he acquired the shotgun, help, and a disposable car that could not be traced back to him or anyone else for that matter. But did he really want to know?

Terry wanted to tell himself he was incapable of murdering his family. But even he could not deny that he had blacked out before when intoxicated, or when in a fit of blinding madness, and had done things he had no recollection of doing.

But murdering his family?

No. No, you couldn't have. You wouldn't do that. Not to Clay. Not to Claire. And certainly not to your little buddy.

If there was one person in Terry and Clay's relationship that helped mend their differences, it was Sidney.

From the moment he first laid eyes on his niece, he had felt a connection to her in a way he had not been connected to his own brother.

It was said that siblings share a bond. But Terry knew that wasn't true for him and Clay. The rift between them started when they were young, and the divide only widened when Clay returned from college.

College had changed Clay's outlook on the world, both politically and socially. A liberal viewpoint that Terry would never concede to.

Their relationship had become so frayed that they refused to speak to one another for a few years because of Terry's beliefs, behavior, and insidious reputation around town.

That was until Sidney was born.

Her birth had not fixed what was wrong between him and Clay, but they began talking again. Sidney's birth had, to a degree, softened his and Clay's disagreements. Kids had a way of doing that, Terry realized later on.

Sidney had cast a spell over their family, and he would have done anything for her. *Anything.*

That was the bitch of it all. Not knowing if he had actually committed the unspeakable. Or if his family had been chosen, at random, and murdered in cold blood.

Not having answers was sometimes worse for Terry than living with the memories of his slain family.

And if he got to the end of this trail, and Terry did find out that he *was* responsible for their deaths, what then? Would he be a man and turn himself in? Or would he take the coward's way out?

He replayed the events of December twenty-third and twenty-fourth in his mind.

Nine years had not made his recollection of those days foggy; he remembered nearly every detail clearly, vividly, as if it had just happened.

It was the night of the murders, and the following days, months, and years he had trouble recalling.

He had killed many of his brain cells after the murders with his beer consumption to keep the memories from resurfacing. *To repress them? To keep me from knowing the truth about what I had done?*

He pushed those thoughts away as soon as they came.

You need to focus on what you do remember. Maybe the truth lies somewhere in your memories, but you just forgot about it.

On the twenty-third, Terry had gotten into the fight at Red's. As he recalled, he had just arrived at the bar that evening around six. Jeff and Colin were already there, sitting at a table to Terry's left. They were two pitchers deep, buzzing on the beer, and growing rowdier by the moment.

They had been talking loudly, making sure everyone in the bar noticed them. That was typical, as Terry recalled. Both loved the attention.

He had strolled up to the bar and ordered a beer from Red. He remembered asking Red if he had heard if anyone was interested in buying the old hardware store across town square. Red had always been reliable when it came to town news; the man was in the know about everything going on.

"Not that I know of," Red had told him. "Why you askin'?"

"No reason," Terry responded, taking a sip of beer, avoiding Red's eyes burning a hole in him.

"Just wondering."

It was then that he had overheard the conversation.

"Man, let me tell you, Ruby-Lee can suck a cock like a pro porn star. Seriously, man, it's the best twenty bucks I ever spent."

Terry had looked over his shoulder and scowled at them. Neither Jeff or Colin had noticed his scornful gaze, and Jeff continued to expand on his sexual exploits with Ruby-Lee, growing increasingly louder, drawing attention to himself from others in the bar.

Terry had felt his face grow warm, his jaw had clenched, and his hands had started to tremble; he had to ball them into fists to keep them still. Yet, he had been willing to ignore Jeff's crude remarks, brush them off, since they were friends of Ruby-Lee's.

That was until he turned back and caught Red snickering. Then he saw others at the bar laughing while Jeff continued on with his story. It wasn't right.

Terry pushed himself away from the bar and started toward the table.

"Leave it alone, Terry," Red called from behind. "Just leave it alone."

As Terry neared the table, he overheard Jeff say, "For an inspection sticker on her car, she let me stick it up her ass. She'd had it before, too. Slid right in with no problem."

He tried to recall what he said that inflamed Jeff, but it was buried somewhere deep in his subconscious. Whatever words they had shared had caused Jeff to shoot to his feet, kicking his chair to the floor in the process, and take the first poke at Terry's face.

Had he been a few beers in, Terry knew he would have had his lights turned off by the jab; it was thrown hard and accurately by someone who knew how to throw a punch.

Luckily, Terry had sidestepped Jeff's swing and countered with his own right hook, catching Jeff across the right side of his face as he followed through on the punch.

Terry's blow knocked Jeff to the floor like a bag of rocks, hard enough to shake the place. Before Terry knew what was happening, Colin Baker lunged at him, drove his shoulder into his midsection, and pushed him back into the bar.

Bottles and glasses were knocked to the floor in loud crashes of broken, shattering glass and the sound of splashing liquid.

Terry remembered hearing a few women scream, which surprised him because he had not realized there were any women in Red's that night.

He hit the lip of the bar hard enough that it sent a shot of pain straight up his back and into his neck. His body had seized with fiery agony, just long enough to allow Colin to land the blow to his right eye that would leave him with the bruise he'd wake up with the following morning.

The slug to the face had taken him off guard, and he'd gone down to one knee, his head a jumbled mess of murky disorientation.

When the cloudiness of his mind began to clear, enough so that he could form irrational thoughts and decisions, Terry looked up and saw Colin standing over him.

Colin's chest rose and fell with each gasped breath, fuming like a madman. His fists were tightly balled, and spittle flew from his mouth when he had yelled, *Come on,* motioning with his fists for Terry to get up.

Not out of the fight, not out of the fight by a long shot, and it would take more than a love tap from Colin Baker to knock him out, Terry had obliged.

He remembered nothing of what happened next, not how he broke Colin's arm nor the damage he had caused to the bar. Terry guessed, if he were honest with himself, he *had* blacked out in a rage-fueled fury.

The next thing Terry remembered was Red pulling him toward the door and throwing him out into the cold night air.

"Get the hell out of here!" Red shouted. "Go cool off, you animal."

"Fuck you!" Terry screamed back, his voice echoing across the quiet town square.

"This town needs a better bar, with better clientele than the trash this place attracts."

"You're part of that trash, Terry. A big part."

"Yeah? Well, you see the old hardware store over there? My brother and I are going to buy the fuckin' place, and we're going to open our own bar, a better place than this shithole. A place that Hickory Falls will be proud of and everyone will want to come to, hopefully putting you out of business."

"Whatever, Terry. Go home."

Red turned away and went back inside to clean up the mess. Terry had returned home to drink and sulk in his own wrath until he passed out on the sofa.

On the morning of December 24th, 2015, Terry had woken with a headache and was in the bathroom studying his swollen black and blue eye in the mirror.

When he lightly touched the bruised right eye with his fingertips, he winced. The skin was tender and hot to the touch. Colin had landed a solid punch.

The phone in the kitchen had begun to ring.

Terry remembered taking one last look at the bruise before turning away from the mirror and heading downstairs to answer the phone in the kitchen—he only used landlines.

"Hello," Terry said, answering the call.

"Terry, it's Sheriff Will Daniel. I have a few things I need to discuss with you."

"This about last night, Sheriff?"

"Yes, sir. Red said you started quite the ruckus with Jeff Lincoln and Colin Baker at the bar."

"I didn't start anything, Sheriff." *I finished it,* Terry had thought.

"It was just a misunderstanding, is all."

"You broke Colin's arm. That doesn't sound like a simple misunderstanding."

"You arresting me? Or are you askin' me to turn myself in?"

"Neither. Colin's not pressing charges. God only knows why after what you did to him. However, you damaged some property at Red's last night…" The sheriff trailed off.

"Well, Red came in this morning and spoke to me about what happened. He's upset and wants to be reimbursed for the damages. Red's willing, like always, to forgive and forget as long as you pay for the repairs. If you don't, well then, I'm going to have to arrest—"

"What about the other two? They started it. Shouldn't they have to pay something?"

"That's not how Red tells it. He says you started the fight."

"That's a goddamn lie. Jeff threw the first punch. I was just defending myself."

"You stickin' with that story, are ya?"

"Not a story. It's the truth. I don't care what Red Keller tells ya. Jeff took the first shot, and I reacted appropriately. Did I share words with them for the shit they were spewing? Sure. But that's not a crime. Not my fault they took it the wrong way."

"What were they saying?"

"Just running their mouths. I suppose it was the booze talkin'. They needed an equalizer."

"Did they, though?"

"Yeah. They did. Look, you tell Red, I'll pay for the damages, but I will not take responsibility for that fight. I didn't start it, and the blame will not be put on me. But you tell him that I'll be down at his place this afternoon."

"That's all he's asking for."

"I'll square up with him, Sheriff. You have my word on that," Terry said and slammed the phone down.

Terry remembered stopping later that afternoon, at the red light at Main Street and Mountain Road. Traffic was backed up at the intersection in all directions as well as down through town. Shaw's Grocery parking lot was filled with cars and people trying to finish last-minute Christmas dinner shopping before the big day arrived.

Terry had looked across the intersection to Lincoln's Gas and Garage Station. Jeff Lincoln was outside pumping gas into a blue sedan. *Fuckin' grease monkey.*

He had wanted to pull into the station and kick the shit out of Jeff right there for the trouble he caused. It would have served him right after spewing that vomit about Ruby-Lee.

But Terry had shaken the thought off.

As much as he had wanted to bury his thick fist into Jeff's jaw again, doing it outside of Red's would surely get him arrested. He didn't need that. This wasn't Terry's first go-around with the police in Hickory Falls, nor with a smart-mouth townie-punk like Jeff Lincoln.

No. Terry would wait for the right time when he and Jeff would cross paths again inside Red's, and the dance would start all over. Such was life in a town that had little to offer in the way of excitement.

The light turned green, and traffic started to move. The lamp poles lining Main Street had been decorated with red and white fabric, making them look like candy canes. On top of each light was either the Christmas Star or a Christmas tree. He had passed row homes with wreaths on their doors and Christmas lights around the porches, windows, and gutters.

Some of the locally owned shops were also decorated for the holiday and advertising Christmas deals. Cup O'Joes, he vividly recalled, was selling coffee or hot chocolate of any size for just a quarter that morning.

As he neared Graham Video, Terry thought about stopping in and speaking with Clay. But he figured it best to deal with Red before getting sidetracked. He could talk to Clay afterward.

He continued into Old Town before coming into the town square.

Like the rest of Hickory Falls that morning, the square was filled with activity. The middle of the court was decorated with a Christmas tree, along with a small Christmas Village that was meant to resemble Santa's Workshop.

A sign had been placed across the front of the gazebo, behind Santa's faux shop, that read NORTH POLE.

Mr. and Mrs. Claus (Pastor Gary Garland and his wife Pat in costume) were out that morning, waving to motorists as they made their way around the square, shouting *Merry Christmas* when someone blew a horn.

Seeing them for the first time since Melissa's passing gave Terry a moment of pause.

He didn't need to get into an altercation with the pastor and his wife in the middle of town on Christmas Eve. Pastor Garland had already done enough to harm Terry's reputation with *his* twisted version of the truth, turning a lot of people, especially those inside the Zion Methodist Church, against him.

He quickly turned down School House Road to avoid them and pulled into the small parking lot behind Red's that was used for staff.

He remembered how, when he stepped out of the warm cab of his pick-up, the wind had brought with it tiny flecks of ice and snow. The storm was fast approaching. The weather forecast had called for over twenty inches by the end of the following day, making for a white Christmas.

It had been several years since Hickory Falls had snow on Christmas and Terry had been looking forward to spending the day at Clay and Claire's house with his parents and Sidney, who was coming home from her first semester of college that afternoon.

He was excited to hear about Sid's first year away from home and catch up while the snow fell outside.

Terry made his way into the bar through the side entrance, without Pastor Garland or Pat seeing him.

It was dark inside the bar, and the smell of old smoke and sour booze that had soaked into the porous wooden walls was horrifically noticeable that morning. The scent had turned his stomach and solidified the feeling that Hickory Falls needed a better, upscale establishment to wet its whistle.

It was quiet as a library that morning; the usual music coming from the jukebox was silent. The local news was on the TV over the bar, but the sound was barely audible.

The weatherman was talking about the approaching storm and the original predicted twenty-plus inches of snow had increased to over thirty inches by the time the storm ran its course.

Listening to the weather that morning, Terry had worried about Sidney.

She was traveling home from school that day. Her Jetta had not been the best in the snow; it sat low and slid easily when the roads were wet or snowy.

He had prayed that she made it home without incident.

He remembered looking around the bar but saw no one. It was Christmas Eve, and Red would have been busy getting ready for his party.

For as long as Terry could remember, Red had thrown a yearly Christmas Eve party, where drinks were half price from five to ten, and for fifteen bucks, one could get an all-you-can-eat catered buffet.

The crowd turnout was modest in years past, mostly filled with regulars who scrambled to get one last drink and say Merry Christmas to their fellow barflies.

"Red!" Terry called. "You here?"

"Back here!" came Red's voice from the kitchen entrance behind the bar.

Terry moved until he looked through the open doorway into the kitchen. Two of Red's employees were washing dishes while Red was drying them.

"I come at a bad time?" Terry asked.

"Nah. Just finishing up." Red cleared the rest of the water from the plate, stacked it in a rack above his head, and then dried his hands on another towel.

"Let's talk out front."

Red walked from the kitchen, kicking the door stopper at the bottom to allow it to swing closed. He wiggled his index finger for Terry to follow him away from his employees' earshot.

Once they were away from the staff, Red said, "You really tore up the place last night. I need compensation for the damages."

"The sheriff called me about it this morning. Why I'm here."

"I hate calling the sheriff. You know that. I like to handle this kind of stuff myself. But last night, after what you said..."

"Yeah. I get it," Terry replied dryly. "How much?"

"Let me see." Red brought a finger to his mouth and tapped his lips.

"There were four glasses broken, two glass pitchers, and the table."

Terry watched Red calculate the charges in his head, before looking at the TV. The weatherman was still talking about the incoming storm.

"Five hundred should cover it."

"Five hundred dollars?" Terry's eyes shot back to Red.

"For a few glasses, two beer pitchers, and a thirty-plus-year-old table that was as wobbly as one of the drunks in here?"

"Well... this could have been avoided. You didn't need to go over and confront them."

"They started it!"

"Sure, they did," Red replied matter-of-factly.

"Then why ain't Colin and Jeff paying for the damages? They caused this mess; they should have to pay for it."

"I only see it as fair, since you actually caused the damages when you choke-slammed Colin through the table like The Undertaker at a WWE match. You broke his damn arm, man."

Terry's left eye twitched with irritation. A few glasses and an old rickety table didn't cost five hundred dollars to replace.

Red was shaking him down for cash, in exchange for not pressing charges.

"They should learn to keep their mouths shut," Terry said.

"And maybe you should learn to control that temper of yours." Red looked Terry up and down.

"Just because you have fists as hard as anvils don't mean you have to use them every time someone pisses you off."

Terry said nothing.

A breaking news alert appeared on the screen, drawing Terry's and Red's attention. An anchor said there was new information about the robbery of a convenience store in Mercersburg.

"A manhunt is on for those who robbed and murdered two people at the Quick Fill in Mercersburg two nights ago..."

"Besides," Red continued, turning back to face Terry, "I don't understand why you stick up for Ruby-Lee. She brings this talk upon herself."

"If that was your daughter, would you want some jackass telling an entire bar of drunks about how she sucks cock like a pro porn star?"

"They were just saying what everyone already knows."

"That's bullshit. Ruby-Lee isn't like that. And it doesn't change the fact that they were spreading rumors about her."

"And you smashing Jeff across the face and putting Colin through a table does?"

"It helps."

"You're the one who's full of bullshit, Terry. The problem is that you can't see Ruby-Lee for what she really is."

"She's my friend, Red."

"You should get a better friend."

Terry ignored the insult.

"Look, five hundred dollars is a little steep. Think we could work something else out? It's Christmas."

Red smirked. He shook his head and crossed his arms over his chest.

"Awww, that's sweet, you trying to get on my sympathetic side. But no dice, buddy-boy. You fucked up. Now, pay the piper. Or I can call the sheriff back and let him handle this the legal way."

After Terry cut Red a check for five hundred dollars, he left annoyed and headed back to speak with Clay at the video store.

Entering, Terry saw Clay was in the process of moving DVDs around the store. When Clay turned, Terry realized by the surprised look on his brother's face that he had not expected to see him standing there.

He understood why.

It was the first time since the grand opening in 2000 that Terry had been in the store. He did not share his brother's love for films.

He found Hollywood, in general, to be pretentious and patronizing to ordinary folks like himself.

"What brings you by?" Clay asked, putting down the stack of DVDs.

"You're not the movie-watching type."

"I prefer to fish or hunt to pass my time rather than let the Hollywood machine ruin my brain."

Though *Smokey and the Bandit* was the one exception to this rule. It was Terry's favorite movie, and why he had bought a black 1977 Firebird.

"Hollywood didn't ruin your brain. You were born with that mess." Clay pointed at the center of Terry's forehead and made a circle with his finger.

Terry had no witty retort.

Though he and Clay disagreed on almost everything, there was no denying they were brothers, bound for eternity by blood. He remembered studying Clay that afternoon, thinking how similar they looked even though Clay was leaner, clean-shaven, and an inch shorter.

They shared the same mop of thick red hair and green eyes—a trait they inherited from their mother. Both had their father's nose and chin, including the dimple, though Terry's was hidden under his thick, red beard.

"Everything all right?" Clay asked.

Terry nodded.

"Yeah. Nothin's wrong. But I have something I wanted to talk with you about."

"Sure. What's up?" Clay crossed the room to where Terry stood by the register.

Terry shook his head.

"I'd rather not discuss it here, in the middle of the store, where people could hear."

A dismissive grunt came from Clay's throat before he said, "Look around, Terry, it's dead in here. Who's going to overhear our conversation?"

"Be that as it may, I'd still like to talk at your house. And besides, what I want to talk about includes Claire, so I'd like her to be present."

Clay's face pinched with confusion.

"What's this about? Are you sure everything's okay?"

"Everything's fine. Trust me."

"Trust you? The last time I trusted you resulted in my ass being beat by Dad."

Clay was talking about the time Terry stole their father's '75 Ford pickup.

The truck was untagged and used exclusively for work around the farm. Terry had the bright idea to take it for a spin and talked Clay into going on the joyride with him one evening when their parents went into town for dinner.

Trust me, Terry had told Clay. *No one will see us.*

Terry was wrong. They were pulled over, and their parents were called to pick them up.

"I got it worse than you," Terry said.

"My ass was so welted and bruised I could hardly sit down for a week."

"You deserved it for stealing Dad's truck."

"Look," Terry said, changing the subject before it ballooned into something bigger, "I might have an idea that could help you and Claire out. I just need a few minutes to run it past you guys."

"We don't need help."

Terry leveled his gaze on his brother.

"So, you're going to try and make this place work, even with Netflix and Amazon chipping away day after day into your profits."

"That's none of your concern."

"You're my family. That's my concern."

"I know your concern, Terry. You just want to talk me into falling in line. Come and work the family farm with you. You're still upset that I went my own way. Did my own thing and succeeded at it, even after you told me…" Clay shifted his voice to sound more like Terry's.

"Opening a video store is a stupid idea."

Terry felt a prickling of anger surge across his body. The conversation had not gone the way he had hoped. Looking back on it now, he guessed that it was a sign of the argument to come later that evening.

"My feelings about your business have nothing to do with this. But the stupidity of your continued denial that this is a rapidly failing venture does concern me. If you don't get out from under it soon, Clay, it's going to drag you down."

"That's our problem. Not yours."

Terry held up his hands. He had not come there to fight.

"I just came to say I have an idea. I know we don't always see eye to eye—"

"That's an understatement."

"—but, if you'd give me a few minutes of your time this evening, I believe what I have to say will benefit all of us."

Clay's eyebrows had nearly touched with puzzlement, and Terry remembered seeing a little fear dance through them—fear of Terry's unpredictability.

"What are you up to, Terry?"

Before Terry could answer, the door opened and two women in their late forties entered. They were laughing and carrying on, their cheeks pink from the cold and filled with Christmas cheer.

Clay greeted them with a smile, pointed them to a few sales he had going on for the holidays, and directed them to the DVD horror section when one asked if he had the horror film *Black Christmas* to rent.

Terry had remained quiet until they were out of earshot.

"What time are you going to be home tonight?"

"Well, Claire and I are attending Christmas services in Bakersville this evening…" Clay and Claire had not attended Pastor Garland's church since Terry's accident.

They were guilty by association and no longer welcome.

"What time?" Terry interjected.

"Services start at six. They usually last two hours with the music, so we should be home around eight-thirty."

"I'll be at your house around eight-thirty."

"Can't this wait until later? Sid'll be getting in around that time."

"Good. I can say 'hi' to her then."

Clay blew out a long, irritated breath that puffed out his cheeks like a chipmunk filled with nuts.

"I really wanted to spend Christmas Eve with Claire and Sid. It's not that I don't want to hear you out, I do, but whatever it is can wait until tomorrow when you, Dad, and Mom will be at the house for dinner."

"I don't want to talk about it in front of Dad and Mom."

"Why? What's so damn important that you need to speak with us tonight, alone?"

"Trust me," Terry said again.

"Oh, trust you," Clay threw up his hands but finally relented.

"Fine. Come over around eight-thirty. But don't get pissed off if Claire isn't too happy to see you."

Terry knew better. Claire never got upset with anyone. She was the most level-headed, understanding, and sympathetic person he'd ever met. She had to be, to have him as a brother-in-law and allow him to be close to her only daughter.

"She'll be fine. Just tell her I'm stopping by. It'll only take up a half-hour, forty-five minutes tops, to hear me out."

"Hear you out? You sound like you're leaving us with little options in the matter."

"You're out of options, Clay. Time too," Terry said, staring hard into his brother's eyes.

"If you want to continue to run a business, to make money, have a roof over your head, and make sure Sid can stay in school, then you need to listen to what I have to say."

"I guess we'll see you tonight."

Terry nodded and left without saying goodbye.

When he stepped back outside into the cold, windy, gray morning, an old blue sedan drove slowly by.

The sudden recall of the blue sedan shot across his brain with such intensity that Terry had to pull the truck over to the side of the road.

Holy shit! Holy shit!

Had he just made a connection from his memories? He had seen an old blue sedan at Lincoln's garage that morning and again outside Clay's video store.

Though he could not remember the make and model of the car, nor who was inside, he distinctly remembered seeing that same blue sedan twice that morning. And then there was the BREAKING NEWS report on the TV while Terry was at Red's.

The police were looking for those who robbed and murdered two people at the Quick Fill gas station in Mercersburg.

Terry's heart rate shot up like a rocket. His lungs began to burn, like a swarm of angry wasps repeatedly attacking him.

He began to cough, a raspy gargle that bubbled up from inside with such intensity that his stomach became unsettled.

When the coughing fit finally subsided, he sat wheezing, trying to catch his breath as spittle dripped from his lower lip onto the truck's seat.

He was covered in a clammy sweat and felt like he'd just been hit by a Mack truck and dragged across the concrete. All he wanted to do was go home and crawl into bed. Sleep would make him feel better.

When he woke, he'd be his usual self once more.

But you can't stop. Not now. You're on the trail; you're on the hunt. You have to keep going. You have to prove someone else murdered your family.

Terry sat up in the seat, and this time he pulled a full breath. The hot, muggy air was sweet on his tongue like he'd just licked a sugar cube. He ran a hand over his wet lips, and when he pulled it away, he saw dark blood smeared across his palm.

Never mind that now. Pack that shit away.

Terry reached up, put the truck in gear, pulled onto the highway, and headed back toward town. He had a few stops to make before he could rest.

<u>EIGHT</u>

Miller and Ross stopped at Jenny Taylor's home in Shady Pines, but no one was home.

They had hoped to catch Mrs. Taylor before heading back into town to speak with Pastor Garland. Now, they would have to circle back to her later to get her recount of the events she witnessed between Terry and his brother on the sidewalk.

Coming back into the town square, they passed by Doctor Polis's office, a large yellow Victorian on the corner. Beside Polis's office was a restaurant called Keller's Family Dining. Miller couldn't stop himself from seeing the zemblanity of the situation.

It was apparent, at least to Miller, that Red Keller had purchased what used to be the hardware store and converted it to a restaurant, almost as an act of thumbing his nose at Terry, since it was the very same building Terry had wanted to turn into a microbrewery.

Passing by Colonial Run Road, which led west to the interstate, the Zion Methodist Church took up the final corner of the roundabout. It was the only church in Hickory Falls.

The large white steeple stood above the tree line, making it easy to spot no matter which direction one came into town from. Ross took a parking space in front of the church.

They entered the church through the front doors into the sanctuary, which was empty at that hour of the day.

"Is there anyone here?" Ross asked, looking at Miller as if he had the answer.

"I don't know."

Miller started up the center aisle. The pulpit loomed large and pastor-less over the empty pews stretched out before it. He glanced up to a large gold cross mounted above the stage and in front of a stained-glass window.

"C'mon, we'll see if we can find someone."

"Can I help you?" came a voice from the left side of the sanctuary.

Miller turned. A middle-aged woman stood by two white double doors. One door was open and led to a hallway that, Miller guessed, contained the church's offices.

"Perhaps," Miller said. "We're looking to speak with Pastor Garland."

"And you are?" the woman asked, eyeing them skeptically.

Miller studied her for a long moment, trying to understand her concern about them being inside the church. *Weren't the church's doors open to everyone?*

She was small and thin. Her short, permed hair was unnaturally dark for her age; it had obviously been dyed. She wore a dark green dress and a white blouse. A small gold cross hung from a necklace and rested on the loose skin just below the V of her throat.

"We're with the Pennsylvania State Police," Ross said.

Her concern deepened the lines on her face.

"And who are you?" Miller asked.

"I'm Ellen Hardy, Coordinator of Lay Ministries here at the Zion Methodist Church."

"And what exactly is that?" Ross asked, his left eyebrow raising.

"I'm an assistant to the church, the pastor, and our congregation." She folded her arms across her small chest.

"Now, how can I help you, gentlemen? I'm busy scheduling this year's mission trip."

"Is Pastor Garland around?" Miller asked.

"No. But he should be back soon. We had a funeral service this morning. He's with the deceased's family at the Mount Hope Cemetery."

"Do you know how long he'll be gone?" Ross asked.

"Shouldn't be more than a half hour. It was a small funeral."

"Would you mind if we waited?" Miller asked. "We really need to speak with him."

The inner workings of Ellen Hardy's brain traveled across her face, trying to figure out why two state police officers would want to speak with the church's pastor. She opened her mouth to ask but thought better of it.

"You can wait in the conference room for him," she said instead.

"Thank you," Miller replied.

She told them to follow her and led them through the double white doors to the hallway beyond. Along the top of the hallway were signs telling which door led to what room.

They passed under an EXIT sign that opened into the alley beside the church before turning into the conference room.

"I will let the pastor know you're here as soon as he returns," she said, closing the door.

They only had to wait a few moments before the door opened and Pastor Gary Garland entered the room.

Garland was a tall, thin man in his mid-sixties. His gray hair had thinned long ago, revealing a liver-spotted skull. His face was short and stubby, with a beak-like nose and a small chin that was barely noticeable.

Miller and Ross introduced themselves.

"Sorry to keep you gentlemen waiting," Pastor Garland said with a smile, pulling out one of the chairs at the conference table. "Mrs. Hardy said you needed to speak with me?"

"We do," Miller began, watching Garland slip into the seat across from him. "It's about your daughter, Melissa."

Garland's eyes locked onto Miller's with an intensity that worked its way under Miller's skin.

"My daughter? What about her? I don't understand. She died eighteen years ago."

His eyes shifted from Miller to Ross, then slowly drifted to the table. Miller thought he saw tears moisten the pastor's eyes.

"We're actually interested in your daughter's relationship with Terry Graham," Miller said.

Garland's head snapped up. Whatever hurt Miller had seen in Pastor Garland's eyes just a moment ago was gone, replaced with a hatred he had never expected to see in the eyes of a man of God.

"Don't you speak *his* name," Garland spat, his face twisting with indignation.

"The mere mention of *him* is not welcome inside these holy walls."

"We understand this is hard for you, Pastor Garland, but we're investigating the Graham murders—I'm sure you remember them."

"Of course, I do, Detective Miller," Garland said with a nod, but his face still held the contempt he felt in his heart, in his soul, for Terry Graham.

"Then you understand why we're here," Miller said. "Why we need to ask you these hard, but possibly relevant, questions."

Garland's eyes held a defiant gaze, and his demeanor was rigid. He sat stiffly in his seat as if trying to prevent his emotions from bursting through the mental dam he had built in his mind. Finally, he nodded.

"Ask your questions." He checked his watch. "Make it quick. I have a meeting to attend shortly."

Miller saw through Garland's act. He didn't want to talk to them.

Whether that was because he wanted to keep the memories of his daughter's death pooled away, or because his hatred for Terry Graham was so intense that he'd rather avoid saying or doing anything to cause a flood of unholy wrath to be unleashed in front of the police.

Or is it something else?

"Was your daughter seeing Terry Graham?" Miller asked.

"No. She would not have dated *him*."

"But she *was* with Terry the night of her death, correct?" Ross asked.

"I suppose so." Garland sat back in the chair, the defiant gaze still fixed on his face. It was almost like he didn't want to admit to himself that his daughter was with Terry.

"Do you know why Melissa was with Terry that night?" Miller asked.

"I don't know how she ended up in *his* car. I didn't even know that Melissa was acquainted with… *him*," Pastor Garland's upper lip rose in disgust.

"She kept her relationship with Terry a secret from you?" Ross asked.

"Melissa wasn't in a relationship with *him*," Garland shot back.

"Then what was she doing with Terry?" Ross asked.

"I have no idea. What I do know, what I'm positive of, is that my daughter would not have gotten into a car with a man like that."

"Are you implying that Terry forced her into his car?" Miller asked.

"Anything is possible. He was a dangerous, violent man."

"You saw his violence firsthand?" Ross asked.

"No. I heard things about him over the years."

"About his drinking? His fight—"

"His temper," Garland said, cutting Miller off.

"What do you know about his temper?" Ross asked.

"Enough to know I didn't want *him* anywhere near my daughter."

That really wasn't an answer, Miller realized.

He decided to press him further.

"So, you only heard about Terry's temper, his fighting, and his drinking. But you never saw any of this with your own eyes?"

Garland said nothing. And it was his silence that betrayed him.

"You believed the rumors about Terry and decided to judge him from town gossip alone."

"I don't judge people. That's for God to do."

"I'm sure you don't," Miller replied sardonically.

Pastor Garland's eyes sharpened like arrowheads and his lips pursed into a tight pucker. He was about to reply to Miller when Ross asked, "Did you speak to your daughter before the accident?"

Garland pried his gaze off Miller and looked back to Ross. He took a moment to collect himself, and then another to recall his last conversation with Melissa.

"I did. She called me that morning."

"When was that, Pastor Garland?" Ross asked.

"March tenth, 2006."

Ross nodded and made a notation in his notebook. "What did you and your daughter talk about?"

"She called about the church fundraiser. We collect cans of food every March and donate them to a local food bank in Bedford. We had just collected nearly five hundred cans and she wanted to know if she should drive them to Bedford, or if someone from the foodbank was coming to pick them up like they had last time."

"Anything else?" Ross pressed, lifting his eyes from the notebook.

Garland thought for a long moment.

"She might have mentioned something about wanting to talk to me," Garland finally answered.

"Do you know what was on your daughter's mind?" Ross asked.

"I don't know. She died before we could speak again."

"Could it have been that she was seeing someone? Maybe Terry Graham?" Miller asked.

"No!" Garland nearly shouted this time.

His sharp eyes shot back to Miller with a scornful gaze. "I already told you, Detective Miller, my daughter would not be caught dead with him."

She was literally caught dead with him, Miller wanted to say, but kept the heartless thought to himself.

Ross picked up the line of questioning again.

"Did your daughter ever mention dating anyone?"

"No."

"From what we understand she was well liked. Were there any men interested in her?"

"Like you said, she was liked, and pretty. So sure, there were men interested in her."

"Who?"

Garland hiked his shoulders.

"Todd Bowmen—he was a member of this church, recently a widower, father of two. I know he had his eye on Melissa because she told me he had asked her out. She politely refused and that was the end of it."

"You said Mr. Bowmen *was* a member of the church. Should we take that to mean he's not anymore?"

"It's not because of anything deceitful, I assure you, Detective Ross. Todd Bowmen moved back to Pittsburgh to be closer to his parents a few months before Melissa was…" He trailed off, suppressing his agony with a grunted cough that forced it back into its unseen place.

"Was there anyone else who was interested in your daughter?"

Garland nodded.

"Sheriff Daniel."

Miller perked up. He remembered how Daniel had responded when he brought up Melissa earlier. It was now apparent why the sheriff had been so distraught—he'd had feelings for Melissa, feelings that were crushed with her death.

"Was Melissa interested in Sheriff Daniel, too?" Ross asked.

"I liked him. He's a valiant member of this church, and our community. I thought he would've made a good husband for Melissa."

"Did you tell her that?"

"I voiced my opinion on the subject."

"And what was Melissa's response?"

"She laughed. Said it wasn't God's plan for her."

"Could she have said that because she was already seeing Terry Graham?" Miller cut in.

"Absolutely not! Look, I don't know why Melissa was with *him* that night, but I know for sure it wasn't because she was seeing *him*."

Garland shook his head, as if shaking away the idea that his daughter could have been in a relationship with someone he clearly despised.

"I can't accept that. I won't accept that she could love such a man, especially after what we now know he did to his family." There were tears in Garland's eyes and pain warped his face.

When he spoke again, his voice was harsh, just above a whisper as if he did not want God to hear his sinful words.

"He could have made an advance on Melissa, and when she rejected him—and she would have rejected that swine—he could have lost his temper and forced her into his car, just like he forced his brother Clay and his family into a car before murdering them. Her car was still here, ya know, in the parking lot. They could have argued and fought. Melissa would not have let him lay a hand on her without putting up a fight. It could have been the reason he lost control and crashed."

Miller studied Pastor Garland. His face was so puffy with resentment that he looked like he was about to explode. He firmly believed that Terry Graham was capable of forcing his daughter into his car that night.

The problem, Miller assumed, was that there wasn't proof to back those claims up.

Had there been, Terry would have been arrested and charged, locked away long before the murders of Clay, Claire, and Sidney.

Miller lowered his eyes to the pastor's hands. They were balled into tight fists. Garland caught Miller's gaze, slipped his hands under the table, and quickly composed himself.

"I really need to be going. Is there anything else I can do for you two?"

"I think we have enough," Ross said.

For now, Miller thought.

<u>NINE</u>

The Hickory Falls Public Library was housed in Wallic Haylee's converted Victorian mansion on the outskirts of town.

Haylee had been a construction tycoon who played a significant role in developing Hickory Falls following World War Two.

The mansion had been converted to a library sometime in the late 1960s, after Haylee's death. Since he had been a vigorous reader and collector of books, Haylee's final wish was that his home be turned into a public library for future generations to enjoy.

Terry visited the library once a week to use the internet, check his email, and contact buyers who purchased produce from him far outside Hickory Falls' reach. He did not have a computer at his house and had no particular interest in buying his own.

Today, he was at the library for a different reason.

There was a connection, Terry believed, between the robbery of the Quick Fill in Mercersburg and what happened to his family. He needed proof that the three men who robbed the Quick

Fill were the same people responsible for the murders of his family. Proof he could find on the news websites, thanks to the internet.

Inside, the mansion's foyer was the central hub for the library's day-to-day operations. Books lined expensive handmade shelves from floor to ceiling, covering most of the walls.

Angie Corman, the librarian, was sitting at her desk behind the checkout counter, typing something into the computer.

"Hey, Angie."

Angie resembled the cliché librarian with her red hair pulled back into a tight bun and a pair of pointy glasses that made her look like a cat. She was dressed in a floral, long-sleeve shirt with a lacey collar. A dark skirt fell to her ankles, just above white socks and her Mary Janes.

Terry had always thought Angie was pretty in a homely sort of way.

"Terry! How are you?" Angie said, standing and coming around the desk to the front counter where Terry stood.

"Need to use the computer. One free?"

"Sure. It's Monday, so the place is dead."

Terry reached into his pocket and pulled out the required five dollars to use the computer.

"It's okay. Just go on up. No charge."

"Nah." He put the five on the counter and slid it to her.

"Only fair to do my part to keep this place operating and you employed."

Angie lowered her eyes, pulled her bottom lip between her teeth, and smiled bashfully. Her light skin turned pink.

When he began working with produce buyers outside Hickory Falls after the murders, since local stores would no longer do business with him, Angie had helped him navigate his way around the computer and set up an email account.

She was kind and nonjudgmental, unlike others in town, and they often struck up conversations about their day-to-day lives.

He wondered if Angie treated him well because she was an outsider like him. Only in her case, she was lost in a world of books and dreamlands, unable to relate to what most would perceive as acceptable social norms, especially in a town as closed-minded as Hickory Falls.

He had always felt that there was a spark between them, just waiting to be lit. But Terry had never pursued a relationship, fearing his labeling as a murderer would taint Angie by association.

Angie's green eyes rose. She studied Terry closely. A worrisome gaze deepened the lines around her eyes, as if she saw something on Terry's face she did not like.

"You feeling okay? You look awfully pale." She went to touch his face but caught herself and lowered her hand back to her side.

"I'm just a little tired. It's the heat."

"Okay. I can bring you some water."

"No. I'll be fine," Terry said, starting away from the desk.

"Just need to use the computers. I won't be too long."

"Okay." Her voice was filled with concern now. "But there's no hurry—your five dollars gets you an hour."

Terry knew he wouldn't be on the computer for an hour. He thanked her and took the steps to the second floor.

By the time he got to the top, he was out of breath, the wheezing amplified in the quiet. He paused to catch his breath on the landing. Glancing down, he saw that Angie had returned to her desk. He prayed she could not hear his labored breaths nor ask him further questions.

Once his lungs seemed to be fully refilled with oxygen, Terry began down the hallway to the computer room.

Turning the corner, Terry saw four computer terminals in the center. Between each computer were pencils and scrap paper in a plastic tray.

Terry walked to one of the terminals facing the far wall so that if anyone came into the room that afternoon, they would not be able to see what he was doing.

He didn't want anyone catching wind of what he was up to, and he wasn't sure who he could trust.

Sitting down, he opened the Internet.

He typed QUICK FILL ROBBERY, MERCERSBURG, PA in the Google search bar and hit the enter button. The screen loaded, and he began to scroll down through the listings.

Terry stopped when he came to a link that read:

ROBBERY/HOMICIDE AT QUICK FILL IN MERCERSBURG

A jolt of excitement tingled his fingers as he clicked the link, which led him to an article written in the Mercersburg Daily Record on December 23rd, 2015.

ROBBERY/HOMICIDE AT QUICK FILL IN MERCERSBURG
By
Adam Whelan

Mercersburg, Pa -- Two people are dead and one critically injured after a robbery of the Quick Fill gas station in Mercersburg, police say.

Tamika Jackson, 32, was shot dead while entering the store. A second victim, Caleb Winter, 30, an employee, was shot behind the counter. The third victim, Horace Gillbanter, also an employee, was critically injured and airlifted to the Mercersburg Hospital for gunshot wounds.

According to an eyewitness, two ski-masked men entered the Quick Fill just after midnight on December 22^{nd,} 2015, wielding shotguns and demanding that the cash registers along with the safe be emptied into a duffle bag. When the employees informed the robbers that they could not open the safe—they were not given the safe's combination by the store's owner—they were both executed. Mr. Winter was pronounced dead at the scene. At the time of this writing, Mr. Gillbanter is still in the Intensive Care Unit at the Mercersburg Hospital, fighting for his life. Ms. Jackson is believed to have been shot as she entered the store, while the robbery was in progress. She was also pronounced dead at the scene.

"We are still processing the crime scene," said Sgt. Dan Harper of the Mercersburg PD. "These men are armed and extremely dangerous. We believe they may have been the same group of individuals responsible for the robbery of the First National Bank of Gettysburg last month."

According to an eyewitness, the two men fled the store to a waiting blue sedan, where a third individual was behind the wheel. The make and model are unknown at this time. They were last seen heading west.

If you have any information, you are to contact the Mercersburg Police Department at...

Terry felt his heart hammering in his chest. *This is it. It has to be the same car.*

Though he had no explicit proof it was the exact car that he'd seen in Hickory Falls the day before the murders, nor the one Ruby-Lee claimed she saw that morning, he still felt confident he was following the right path and that it would soon lead to his salvation.

Pulling a piece of scrap paper and a pencil from the tray beside the computer, he jotted down the phone number and the officer's name quoted in the article.

He also wrote down Horace Gillbanter below it. Had Gillbanter survived his injuries?

He backed out of the article and began to scroll and click his way through the following several pages but found nothing further on the robbery of the Quick Fill nor on Gillbanter.

The story quickly faded from the headlines and was most likely forgotten, except to the victims, their family members, and those who pulled the triggers.

He typed into the search bar:

GETTYSBURG FIRST NATIONAL BANK ROBBERY

The screen loaded, and several articles on the robbery filled the page. Terry clicked on a link that read:

POLICE NEED HELP IDENTIFYING THREE MEN WHO ROBBED THE FIRST NATIONAL BANK OF GETTYSBURG

The link took him to a website called PA CRIME STOPPERS.

Here he found a blurb describing the events:

Gettysburg Police responded to a 9-1-1 call on 12/6/2015 at the First National Bank of Gettysburg. Around 5:00pm, just as the bank was about to close for the evening, two men, armed with shotguns and wearing ski masks, entered the building and demanded the tellers to open their drawers.
Surveillance video shows the men going behind the counter and pulling cash from the drawers—around $2000 in total was stolen.
They were then seen getting into a blue sedan, where it is believed a third person was waiting behind the wheel.
If you have any information…

Beside the blurb, a series of scrolling screen grabs from the bank's surveillance cameras showed the crime in process. The images were grainy, and Terry couldn't identify the individuals under their masks.

Still, Terry felt the car used in the robberies matched the one he saw that morning at Lincoln's garage and again outside his brother's store. If these men were in Hickory Falls that morning, then there was a good chance that Jeff Lincoln had gotten a look at them.

But would Jeff remember that day, let alone what they looked like?

The thought ground around like a stone wheel. Though he did not want anything to do with Jeff Lincoln, he knew there was only one way to find out what Jeff remembered about that morning.

He would have to ask him.

Terry returned to the front desk to talk to Angie.

"Can you find someone on the internet?"

"You can find everyone on the internet, Terry." She put her hand over her mouth and snickered at her own joke.

"Do you think you could locate a Horace Gillbanter for me?"

"You know where he's from?"

"Maybe Mercersburg."

"Let me see what I can do."

Terry nodded and began to write his phone number down on the paper he'd taken from beside the computers.

"If, and when, you find him, you can call me at this number."

He tore off the piece with his number and handed it to her

"Okay," Angie said, taking the paper from him.

"Thanks," Terry said as he turned to leave.

TEN

When Miller opened the door to Red's Bar, the hot July sun cut a sharp angle of light across the polished wooden floors.

Stepping inside, Ross let the door slam shut behind him, soaking them in a cold dimness that caused chills to race up Miller's arms. It felt like he had just stepped out of a sauna and into an industrial freezer.

Red had not only remodeled the exterior, but the entire bar interior had also had a makeover.

The old bar stools and tables had been replaced with upscale wooden booths and high-top tables. The bar was a long, elegant-looking piece of polished walnut that gleamed under the lights with plush, comfy bar stools in front.

Behind the bar, where liquor bottles once sat on lopsided bracket shelving, was now a customized unit with ornate trimming. The liquor bottles appeared to glow under the inset lights, attracting the eyes of everyone who entered.

Instead of just two beer taps—Coors and Budweiser—there were now eight different varieties of beer; something to suit everyone's tastes.

Miller remembered the place had always had a sour smell that reminded him of bile. Now, the air was scented with superb cuisine and sugary, alcoholic drinks.

Red had done well for himself over the past several years, Miller realized.

The bar was empty.

But Miller figured that would change when the hungry lunch crowd ventured in to grab a bite to eat and maybe a drink or two.

Red Keller stood behind the bar, reading a newspaper.

He was a stout man. A pair of glasses sat low on the bridge of his nose, and a toothpick stuck out between his fish-like lips. What hair he had left on his head was grey and horseshoed around his skull and connected to bushy, wild sideburns.

His pale face was pudgy, loose in the jaws and wobbly, causing his chin to disappear in the folds of flesh. Dark, purple bags hung under his eyes from too many years spent in the murkiness and living his life mostly at night.

The night takes its toll on you, Miller knew.

"What can I get you?" Red asked, not looking up from the paper.

"We're not here for a drink, Mr. Keller," Ross said.

"We're with the state police, and we'd like to ask you a few questions," Miller added.

Red looked over the top of the paper. His eyes shifted between the two troopers as they neared the bar. Irritation at their presence came off him like radiation. He lowered the paper, pulled the toothpick from his mouth, and placed it on the bar beside him.

"I know you." His eyes settled on Miller, giving him yet another chill, this one deeper than when he first walked into the bar.

"Didn't you used to work in the sheriff's department a few years back?"

"I did."

"Now you work for the state po-lice, huh?"

Miller ignored his taunts.

"We're from the Major Case Team, investigating the Graham murders, and we have a few questions we'd like to ask you."

"This town not thrilling enough for ya?" Red asked.

He did not appear to hear or care about what Miller had just said.

"The town was plenty thrilling for me," Miller replied—a lie. He had hated living and working in Hickory Falls.

Red looked confused.

"So why leave?"

"I wanted to pursue other endeavors."

"Like becoming a state po-lice-man with the Major Case Team." Red said this with a smarmy tone as if he were trying to get under Miller's skin.

It was working.

"Something like that."

Red picked up the toothpick and brought it to his mouth but did not put it between his teeth; he held onto it as if it were a cigarette while contemplating something.

"So, is this about Terry?"

"What makes you think that?" Ross asked.

Red shrugged.

"No other reason you two would be in here if it wasn't about Terry."

He put the toothpick between his teeth and wiggled it back and forth with his tongue for a moment before he spoke.

"You know those other two state-boys—I forget their names—they were in here askin' me what I saw that night, too. Isn't my statement already logged in a case file somewhere? Why do we have to do this all over again?"

"We're just doing some follow-up questioning," Ross said.

"Ah-uh."

Red glanced between the two of them again. He pulled the toothpick out of his mouth.

"Yeah. Terry was here that night."

Red looked down the bar to the end, where it made an L shape, and pointed a chubby, hairy finger in the direction he was looking.

"He and Karl Preston sat at the end of the bar, chatting."

"And what time was that?" Ross asked.

"About nine, I believe it was."

"What was Terry like that night? Do you remember?" Miller asked.

"Yeah. He was irritated when he came in. I could tell. I'd seen that pissed-off look in his eyes before. He sat there brooding into his beer until Karl slid onto the stool beside him.

"I didn't think much of it—other than Terry being his usual self and bringing his problems in here to drink them away.

"That was until after I heard what happened. Then it made sense—I believe he was thinking about killing his family even then."

"About how many beers did Terry have?" Miller asked, ignoring Red's blatant finger-pointing and assumptions of Terry's guilt.

"I know he had a few; enough to get a buzz going anyway. I could see it in his eyes; Scary Terry was about to make an appearance."

"What do you mean?" Ross asked. "Scary Terry?"

"Terry was a different man when he got drunk. It was strange to watch the process.

"At first, he could be having fun: laughing, playing pool, talking to his friends. But the more Terry drank, it was like this other personality slowly took over.

"He even looked different—a real Jekyll and Hyde thing. We had a nickname for him around here when he got like that: Scary Terry."

"How often did this happen?" Miller asked.

"A few times. Not every time, not even once a month, but enough that all of us around the bar had seen Scary Terry come out a time or two."

"What was he like when he got like that?" Ross asked.

"Sometimes, he would shoot his mouth off and end up getting into a fight. Then again, Terry really didn't need to be drunk to get into a fight; say the wrong thing about him or Ruby-Lee, and that temper of his went off like TNT.

"Other times he was quiet. Would sit alone, sulking into his beer, staring straight ahead, his eyes glassy and black—that thousand-yard stare look, ya know—kind of the same look he had that night he came in before the murders."

"According to Sheriff Daniel, you came to see him after you learned about the murders. You believed Terry might have been involved because you overheard him speaking with Karl Preston. Do you remember what was said?" Miller asked.

Red slipped the toothpick between his teeth and began moving it back and forth with his tongue again, thinking carefully before he spoke.

"I remember Terry pissing and moaning to Karl about his brother. He and Clay had had words before he came in here that night. I don't know what it was about. But I overheard Terry say something like, 'Clay's a pretentious college boy who doesn't think I can do anything other than sling shit, eat dirt, and drink beer.'"

"And did you hear Karl Preston's reply?" Ross asked.

"No. I had moved away from the bar by that point. You'd have to ask Karl; he might remember. But he hasn't been the same since his accident.

"Poor guy. The man was just working around his house when a tree came down on him, broke his neck, paralyzed him, and gave him some brain damage. Ain't that some shit?"

Some awful luck indeed, Miller thought.

"What else did you hear Terry say?" Miller asked.

"*My brother's dead to me now*—they were Terry's exact words," Red replied.

"And you took that to mean that Terry murdered him?"

"Well… not at the time. I just figured it was some brotherly spat they were having. They never really got along.

"Terry used to whine about Clay sometimes when he had a little too much to drink. He'd boo-hoo and bawl to anyone who'd lend an ear about their contentious relationship."

"What do you mean?" Miller asked.

"Ya know, he'd say things like—Clay's the good son. He has the perfect family. The pretty wife. Clay can do no wrong in my parents' eyes.

"Which was probably true, given that Terry was a bastard and had caused Danby and Winfred nothing but heartache since he was a kid."

"Let's go back to the night Terry got into the fight with Colin Baker and Jeff Lincoln on December twenty-third. Do you remember the fight, Mr. Keller?"

"Sure. Terry put Colin through a table right over there and broke his arm."

"What was the disagreement about?" Ross asked.

"Aw, hell. It was over Ruby-Lee. My take was that Jeff had screwed her and was bragging about it to Colin. Terry overheard, lost his cool, and confronted them. A fight broke out, and I threw Terry out of the bar."

"The next morning, you went to see Sheriff Daniel, correct?" Ross asked.

"I did."

"You're pretty chummy with the sheriff," Miller said. "Seems like you go to him about everything."

"I wouldn't say that."

Red seemed annoyed that Miller would accuse him of being friends with a *po-lice-man*.

"But I go to the sheriff when I need him. That morning, I wanted Terry to pay for the damages he caused. The sheriff's more of a *boys-will-be-boys* guy. As am I. So, I figured if I talked to him, the sheriff could speak with Terry about the damages.

"And as long as Terry paid for what he broke, I wouldn't press any charges."

"You didn't care that people fought in your establishment?" Ross asked.

"I do now since the renovations. But back then, this was a small town. There wasn't much else to do except farm, fight, or fuck. As long as no one got killed, I didn't care all that much. I'd break 'em up and throw 'em out for the night. When I see 'em again, it's like nothing happened."

"Doesn't seem like that was a smart idea," Ross said. "Letting the troublemakers back in."

"Look, if I had barred everyone who got into a fight in here back then, I wouldn't have had any customers. But since all the new housings have gone up around Hickory Falls, it's brought a much better class of people in."

No thanks to Terry for selling his land to bring in those new, upscale customers, Miller thought.

"Did you know that Terry was thinking about opening a bar with Clay, directly across the street from yours—in the old hardware store?"

"I heard 'bout it. Didn't worry me a bit, though."

"Why not?" Miller asked.

"One brother was a mean drunk, and the other was a failed businessman. Could you imagine those two trying to run a bar together? Terry would drink them out of business. And Clay would lose all their investment money on bad business decisions. What did I have to worry about?"

"I'm not sure 'failed businessman' is the correct term for Clay Graham," Miller said. "He owed a successful video store for fifteen years."

"Then why was Clay about to close his store?" Red asked.

"How do you know he was about to close his store?" Miller asked.

"Terry. He came in one night—sometime in November of 2015. After a few beers, he started shooting his mouth off 'bout Clay's troubles. Later, he started berating everyone for turning their backs on Clay and not supporting the store once Hickory Falls got the high-speed interwebs."

"What was Terry and Ruby-Lee's relationship like?" Ross asked.

"They were friends."

"Friends with benefits?" Miller asked.

"Hell, no. Terry's temper and his ability to fly off the handle and hurt someone scared Ruby-Lee. She'd never leave the bar alone with him. That, and because of what happened with Melissa back in '06."

"What do you know about that?" Ross asked

"I heard…" Red leaned over the bar, closer to them. When he spoke his voice was low as if he didn't want anyone to overhear him.

"…that Terry and Melissa were secretly an item so her holier-than-thou pastor daddy didn't find out his perfect angel was fuckin' the town drunk. I also heard Terry beat the shit out of Melissa and crashed his car into a tree to cover up what he did."

There was a pause in the conversation. Even if what Red said was just a nasty town rumor, it still held some weight in the realm of possibility.

The thought of Terry hurting an innocent woman and covering up his crime by steering his car into a tree darkened Miller's mind. He considered his next question carefully. It could unspool the interview and their goodwill with Red, causing him to close up like a vice grip and refuse to speak to them anymore.

"By the name across the front, I take it that you own what used to be the hardware store, and turned it into a restaurant?" Miller slowly asked, making sure Red heard every word.

Red leveled his dark eyes on Miller, and his face tightened.

"I do," he replied gruffly.

"I bought it about a month after the murders. Made the renovations needed and opened the place up as a family restaurant, a place those who don't like the bar crowd can go and get a good, homecooked meal, just like my momma used to make."

"Interesting," Miller replied, hearing his accusatory tone.

"What are you suggesting?" Red asked, his voice a low, scary whisper.

"Nothing."

"Your *statement* makes the hairs on the back of my neck stand up, Mr. Miller. I don't like when cops give me that feeling."

"It was just a statement."

"A statement that makes me believe you think I had something to do with what happened to Terry's family that morning."

Miller had expected Red to react this way. But he felt he still had control of the interview and could save it, as long as he treaded carefully with what he said next.

"I was simply curious because my partner and I saw the building was now a restaurant with your name on it when we came through the square."

Red's eyes flicked to Ross and back to Miller.

Finally, he said, "Hey, Terry had a good idea about opening a microbrewery. I'm not going to say he didn't—he saw where Hickory Falls was heading before the rest of us did. Why I made the improvements to this place.

"But it's not my fault I was in a position to buy the hardware store in 2015, and Terry wasn't. It sucks for Terry. However, I had nothing to do with what happened that morning to the Grahams."

"Well, since you brought it up. Where were you the morning the Grahams were found, Mr. Keller?" Ross asked.

"I was here. My place is directly above the bar."

"Can anyone verify that?" Miller asked.

"I live alone. But my staff and I were in the bar past four that morning, cleaning up the place. A few of them still work for me, so they can vouch that I was here all night."

Red paused. Miller believed he saw a light of remembrance turn on in his eyes, something he had forgotten until that moment.

"Karl Preston was also in here until closing time that night, and so was Ruby-Lee. I remember she was with three other fellows. So, they all would have seen me, too."

"Ruby-Lee Huckster was in here that night?"

"Yeah." Red nodded.

"She didn't come in until later, past ten, which was unusual for her, but she was with these three out-of-town guys. I never saw 'em before."

"Do you remember what these men looked like?" Ross asked.

"Or if they left with Ruby-Lee?" Miller shot at him.

"Fellas, you're asking me to remember details going back nine years. It was packed in here that night, and I saw many faces, some I recognized, others I didn't.

"You want to know what these guys looked like, and if Ruby-Lee left with them, then you'll have to ask her. I'm sure she got an up-close and very personal look at them." Red winked.

They left the cool darkness of the bar and returned to the bright, hot sun baking Hickory Falls. Miller felt sweat instantly break out across his body. He wanted a shower, not just to wash the stickiness from his body, but the grime he felt had gathered on his skin from being back in Hickory Falls.

"The call came in at six that morning," Miller said as they headed back to the car.

"I arrived on the scene at six-forty-five. If Ruby-Lee left the bar around two-thirty that morning, as Red claims, where did she go for four hours only to later be in town to make the nine-one-one call?"

"She could have gone back to her place with those three guys, or they could have known someone in town, who they were shacking up with, and took her back there."

Miller was about to disagree with Ross about Ruby-Lee going back to her place since she lived with her mother at the time of the murders when he felt someone tap him on the shoulder and say, "I thought that was you."

Miller turned and looked into Deputy Bob Thompson's steel blue eyes. His plump face was lit with a smile.

"What brings you back to town?" Thompson asked. "Last I heard, you were with York PD?"

"I was. Transferred to the state police two years ago. My partner and I are looking into the Graham murders."

"Oh?" Thompson's eyes shot to the big man beside Miller. He quickly assessed his size and hard demeaner. He turned back to Miller with a disconcerting look, as if the sight of Ross both angered and frightened him simultaneously. "Well, I wish both of you luck."

"Thanks, Bob," Miller replied.

Thompson nodded, put on a too-friendly smile that made Miller's skin prickle with unease, and was about to turn away when he decided against it.

"If I were you two, I'd watch out for Terry Graham. He's going to do everything in his power to keep the truth about what really happened to his family from getting out."

Miller considered this.

"You think he's a killer?"

"I know he is."

"How do you know?"

"Because he did it before."

"I don't follow," Miller replied, but he felt he knew where Thompson was going.

"He killed a girl. Back in '06. Do you guys know about that?"

"Melissa Garland? It was a car accident."

"Car accident, my ass!" Thompson nearly shouted, his face turning beet red and shiny from the sweat suddenly running down his brow.

"I was there the night of the accident. There were no skid marks on the pavement, no signs of a mechanical malfunction, and he didn't hit ice. He drove that car off the road and into that tree, killing Melissa.

"And that begs another question: how did Pastor Garland's daughter end up in a car with Terry Graham?"

He waited, and when Miller didn't respond, he continued.

"There's no logical or rational explanation for a girl like Melissa, a girl who was revered in this town by many, to be with him that night. Unless…"

"Unless Terry forced her into the car," Miller finished Thompson's thought for him.

"So you think Terry caused the accident to cover up his crime?" Ross finally spoke up.

"Bingo."

Thompson ran his hand across his brow, slicking the sweat off his head.

"Like I said, watch yourselves. Terry's a wolf hidden is sheep's wool and he's just waiting to take his next bite."

ELEVEN

The heat of the day was upon Hickory Falls by the time Terry pulled into Lincoln's Gas and Garage.

He felt like he had come down with a fever and the sweltering afternoon humidity made him feel like he was sitting in the middle of Hell. *Maybe you are.*

Every joint in his body ached with each movement, and his muscles felt like thin rubber tubes, nearly unable to support his weight when he stepped out of the truck's cab.

He steadied himself on the pickup's door and closed his eyes. He wanted to go home. To be in the cool darkness of his bedroom, with the fan blowing on his overheated body, the soothing sound of its white noise to comfort him.

There were no memories of the past in sleep. Only a still blackness wrapped around him like a blanket. *Peace.*

Terry knew he would have to call the doctor in the morning. He had been pushing off the inevitable for far too long.

What had started as an annoying, repetitive cough had morphed into something much worse over the past three months. The blood. The shortness of breath. The wheezing.

Fear of the unknown, fear of knowing the truth really, was a hell of a deterrent. If he just ignored the problem, it would go away on its own. Did that thinking ever work for any man? Terry supposed not.

His eyes snapped open when he heard the sharp blast of an impact wrench. He looked up to the six open garage doors in front of him. Inside, mechanics were busy working on auto repairs—one man to each bay.

The sounds of clanging metal, air guns, and compressors echoed off the concrete block walls. A radio was on in the rear of the shop. Creedence Clearwater Revival came through the speakers – "Have You Ever Seen the Rain?" The song made Terry think of Clay, Claire, and Sidney.

Sharp pangs of guilt and sadness passed through his heart, twisting his chest into a tight knot. He forced the sorrow and hurt back into that dark place where he had kept it buried for all these years.

Stepping away from the pickup, Terry approached the first open garage door.

Jeff Lincoln's business had thrived in the last nine years, most likely due to the surge of people moving into town once Valley View Condos were built.

He had added five more bays to his garage and hired a crew to work on the auto repairs. He also added a small convenience store and had replaced the old pump with four new ones that could read credit cards.

I guess you're not the grease monkey I always took you for, Jeff.

He came to the first bay. A young guy was working under a Camry jacked up on the lift, cranking a wrench back and forth to loosen the oil pan bolt.

"Excuse me?" Terry said.

The young man looked over his shoulder at Terry.

"Be with you in a sec," he said, just as the bolt broke free and a black streak of oil shot from under the car as if it were bleeding out like a stuck pig.

The mechanic turned, picked up a rag from his toolbox, and began wiping his hands on it as he neared Terry.

"Can I help you?"

"I'm looking for Jeff Lincoln. He around?"

"Yeah. He's in the office."

The mechanic turned and pointed to a door beside the first bay.

"Go through there, and just before you get into the store, Jeff's office will be on the right-hand side."

"Thanks."

He walked past the mechanic and into the hallway. The door automatically closed behind him; the sounds of the shop were instantly cut off.

Terry started for the office, thankful to be out of the heat, even briefly. His knees screamed with each step, begging him to stop, but he pushed forward.

The convenience store was in front of him. A few people stood by a counter that said HOMEMADE SANDWICHES above it, waiting for their dinners to be made.

He came to the office on the right. The door was open. When Terry rounded the corner into the office, he found Jeff Lincoln sitting behind his desk. He was speaking in hushed tones to someone on the phone.

"...we'll deal with it."

Jeff's eyes rose when he felt a presence in the room with him, and his face went white as if he had just looked a ghost in the eyes.

"I need to call you back," Jeff quickly said and hung up.

"We need to talk," Terry said, entering the office and closing the door behind himself.

"I don't think we have anything to discuss, Terry."

"No, we do, Jeff." Terry turned and crossed the office to the desk. "I need your help."

Jeff cocked an eyebrow.

"Christmas Eve of 2015, you were outside pumping gas into an old, blue sedan. Do you remember it?" Terry asked.

Jeff thought about the question, carefully, as if he were deciding how to answer while keeping his eyes trained on Terry. What's that look about? Terry wondered.

"Not off the top of my head," he finally said.

"You were. I remember because I saw you that afternoon. I was coming into town to pay for the damages at Red's from our fight the night before."

"If you say so. I can't say I remember that far back." He paused, and a perplexed look crossed his face. "What's this about anyway, Terry?"

"You're a car guy, right?"

"Look around. What do you think?"

"When you see a car, especially a model you haven't seen around town before, you'd remember it, right?"

"Yes. But that doesn't mean I remember the car you're talking about. It was nine years ago."

"Around that same time, a convenience store robbery occurred in Mercersburg. Do you remember that?"

He thought for a moment. Then nodded slowly.

"I believe so. The Quick Fill, right. Whoever did it shot the place up, killed someone as I recall."

"Two people, actually. Eyewitnesses reported seeing a blue sedan fleeing the scene."

Jeff straightened in his chair as if he had just got a jolt of electricity to the spine.

"Are you saying they were here that day? That I…" He trailed off and swallowed thickly, understanding how close he might have come to possibly being their next victim.

"I believe so. But I need you to remember what type of car they were driving and if you got a look at them."

"Why does it matter?"

"I have good reason to believe they were the same people who murdered my family. Ruby-Lee reported seeing a blue sedan with three men inside to the police the morning of the murders."

"Ruby-Lee?" Jeff asked, his voice rising.

"How did you find out Ruby-Lee made the call?"

"Troopers showed up at my house this morning. Let me listen to the call. It was Ruby-Lee's voice."

"You heard the call? I thought it was lost?"

"Yeah. Me—" Terry's words choked in his throat, and he began to cough. He bent at the waist and covered his mouth until he was finished.

"Jesus Christ, Terry. Are you okay?"

Terry thought he detected a hint of fakeness in Jeff's cadence, but it could have been his own self-pity seeping in. *Like you give a fuck,* he thought, nonetheless. He stood and pulled a breath. The air tasted of metal and car oil from the garage.

"I'm fine."

"You don't look fine. You should go see a doctor."

Terry ignored him.

"Do you remember that day or not, Jeff?"

"Look, as much as I would like to help you, I can't remember. Hundreds of cars are in and out of this place daily, including those getting worked on. I see so many cars and faces that I don't try to commit them to memory."

"But not back then. Back then, you were a one-car garage. You did everything alone—pumped gas and worked on cars."

"I'm sorry. I wish I could help." He gave Terry a *what-are-you-going-to-do* look.

Disappointment washed over Terry like a wave of hot magma, burning away any hope that he might get the information he sought from Jeff. He was at a standstill for the moment. He could not beat the memories out of Jeff, even if he wanted to. *This is a dead-end.*

"Okay. Sorry to have bothered you."

Terry turned and opened the door.

"Terry," Jeff called to him.

Terry turned back around. Jeff looked distraught as if there had been something weighing on his mind.

"I know you and I have had our differences in the past. But I'd like to put all that behind us."

He stood and came around the desk, extending his hand to Terry.

"And maybe we can be friends."

Terry looked down at the outstretched hand but did not take it.

"Are you seeking my forgiveness for what you said about Ruby-Lee?" Terry asked.

"Step five of AA is: 'Admitting to God, to ourselves, and to another human being the exact nature of our wrongs.' I've done some bad things in my life and hurt many people—myself, my family, my friends—because of my substance abuse.

"I even hurt you that night by what I said. I knew you and Ruby-Lee were friends. I should have kept what happened between us to myself. It was wrong of me, and I want you to know that I'm terribly sorry for the trouble I caused."

Terry studied Jeff closely, looking for any sign that he was pandering to him for his own mental well-being. But he found only sincerity in Jeff's eyes, where the pain of his past behavior seemed to linger, longing for forgiveness.

"I should have come out to your farm a long time ago. But I couldn't find the strength because…"

"Because you thought I murdered my family."

Jeff's eyes met his again. This time, Terry saw that was precisely why Jeff had stayed away. Terry understood.

Had Jeff come out to the farm, word would have gotten around town. His business would have suffered, maybe even been vandalized if he was caught socializing with Hickory Falls' equivalent of Frankenstein's monster.

Even now, Terry might have put him and his business in danger just from being there.

Terry took his hand.

"I'm sorry, too."

A warm smile eased onto Jeff's face.

"You know Red got me for five hundred bucks for a few broken glasses and that rickety table."

"Red's a piece of work. Doesn't surprise me. The guy's a liar and a cheat."

"Let me ask you something else. You ever hear about Ruby-Lee hooking up with Red?"

Terry thought back to that morning at her home when she told him that she had spent the night of the murders with Red.

"Look, I don't want to upset you with what I know."

Terry waved him off.

"I just want the truth."

Jeff nodded.

"It was believed, though no one could prove it, that Red was pimping Ruby-Lee out around town."

"To whom?"

"To anyone who wanted it. Even the sheriff and his deputies. Ruby-Lee told me once that she did it with Bob Thompson in his squad car. Said he was the kinkiest person she'd ever been with and did things to her that made even her uncomfortable."

Terry felt his skin begin to crawl. How could he have been friends with someone who would demean themselves to such an extent? How had he missed the signs?

Or had he always seen them? Willingly looking the other way in hopes that he could save her from herself, show her that he was always there for her, that he would always have her back no matter what she did or what anyone said?

You're so stupid, Terry. So, so stupid.

"But back to your original question: yeah, old Red was banging her too back then."

"Back then? He doesn't anymore?"

"No. They had some falling out a few years back, shortly after the murders."

"You know what the fallout was about?" Terry asked.

Jeff shook his head.

"I don't know the real reason. You'd have to ask Red, but I doubt he'd give you the truth anyway—the guy's slippery as a fish.

"But the scuttlebutt was that he was using Ruby-Lee to gain leverage on a few powerful people around town.

"From what I understand, Red had a bunch of dirt on people, thanks to Ruby-Lee's services, giving him a lot of pull when it came to getting his way. Know what I mean?"

Terry nodded.

"But you didn't hear that from me, understand."
"It stays between us."

<u>TWELVE</u>

Pennsylvania State Police Troop G was in the Borough of Hollidaysburg. Miller and Ross were exhausted by the time they arrived at the barracks.

It had been a long, hot day spent riding around in an uncomfortable police cruiser from one interview to the next. Ross was eager to hit the weights. Miller, the sofa.

But there was more to do before they could call it a night.

Miller had talked to Lieutenant Michael Garcia on the way back, wanting to get his take on the case before any further move was made. Like bringing in Ruby-Lee for questioning.

If they could get her to the barracks, they'd be able to grill her in ways they had been unable to at her home that morning.

Inside Lieutenant Garcia's office, Miller began to lay out their day and their theories about the case. Garcia listened enthusiastically, nodding with approval. Miller took it as a good sign.

Garcia agreed that they needed to bring Ruby-Lee in for questioning, find out where she went after leaving Red's Bar, who the three men she was seen with were, and what they were doing in Hickory Falls the day of the murders.

After the conversation ended, Miller and Ross parted ways, with Ross heading straight to the barracks' gym. Miller took the Graham case file and the accident report from the Hickory Falls Sheriff's Department and headed back out.

He wanted to go over both files, at home, alone, where he did his best thinking.

When he got home, he popped the top of a Tröegs IPA beer and threw a frozen dinner in the microwave.

As his dinner nuked, Miller moved into his living room and began going through his extensive record collection.

Since he was a kid, he had been collecting vinyl, and his collection had grown to well over one thousand albums with everything from classic rock and country to blues and jazz to comedy albums like Cheech & Chong and George Carlin.

It was the one thing in his divorce that was nonnegotiable; he had made sure he got out with all his albums—everything else could be replaced.

He settled on Fleetwood Mac's *Rumors*.

Pulling the record out, he ran a microfiber cloth over its surface to catch any dust or debris before placing it in the record player. He lifted the arm and gently touched the needle to the record.

That familiar first scratch of the needle to record was its own music to Miller's ears, a part of the experience of appreciating vinyl.

The microwave *beeped*.

Miller sat down at the kitchen table and dug into his food, alone, like most evenings. He tapped his foot to the beat of "Second

Hand News" while attempting to shift his thoughts from the day and focus on the music, to let it take him away even if for only a moment.

But the thoughts lingered like a fog across a moor, common for him when he was deeply involved with an unsolved case.

He finished eating just as "Dreams" began to play.

Stevie Nicks' weary, road-worn voice felt as vulnerable as it was filled with pain and torment. It seemed to match Miller's somber mood.

He dumped the plastic tray into the trash and picked the files up from the kitchen counter, took them back to the table, opened the accident report, and began to go over it.

The fill-in-the-boxes police accident report was divided into twenty-two sections. The first section wanted officers to log their name, date, time of dispatch, and arrival on the scene.

Right off the bat, Miller saw Bob Thompson had been the responding officer the night of the crash. That concerned him after talking with Thompson earlier.

The man had been quick to point out that Terry was the direct cause of the crash. Miller wondered what evidence Thompson had found that led him to this theory.

Sections two through seven were dedicated to the location and time of the accident:

Crash date: March 10th, 2006.
Crash time: 2340.
Number of Units: 01.
People: 02.
Injured: 00.
Killed: 01.

Miller paused and studied the 01 scribbled in the little box. Melissa Garland had been reduced to a number.

He knew this was a formality for the state, but it bugged him nonetheless that victims become nothing more than a digit in the clog of government paperwork.

The eighth and ninth boxes were the traffic control portion of the form, where an officer would fill out if a broken traffic light or a road closure was the cause for the accident. Since they were blank, Miller figured there was nothing to note.

The following two sections, ten and eleven, centered around the vehicle's driver. This section had been filled in with Terry Graham's personal information, such as his address and date of birth.

Toward the bottom, there was a section labeled: Alcohol/Drugs Suspected. Below it was a series of blank bubbles next to what illegal substance the officer suspected the driver of being under at the time of the accident.

The alcohol bubble was colored in.

Next came the Alcohol Test Type. Here the bubble beside the word BREATH was filled in. Under it was the Alcohol Test Results. Terry had passed with flying colors: 0.00.

With Terry's substance abuse history, it was possible that Thompson had assumed Terry might have been drinking and administered the breathalyzer test as a precaution.

But if Terry was not intoxicated, as the breathalyzer test showed, then what caused him to crash?

He moved on to section twelve.

In this box was the make and model of Terry's car and his insurance information.

But Miller was interested in the section marked Direction of Travel and the large N written there, indicating that Terry had been headed north when the accident occurred, back toward Hickory Falls.

Miller felt the juices in his stomach bubble and pop like hot liquid in a cauldron. Where had Terry and Melissa crossed paths that night? The church?

Pastor Garland said her car was still in the parking lot, so it's possible he could have met her there. But how did Melissa end up in Terry's car?

If what Pastor Garland believed was true, that Terry had forced Melissa into the car, then why would he be heading back toward town and not away from it?

Something's not adding up.

Section thirteen was dedicated to victims taken to a hospital or treated by EMTs. Here he found Melissa Garland's name for the first time.

Below her name and address, there was a list of pre-written text that could be circled in this section. Passenger. Ejected through the windshield. Head-on impact. Not wearing a seatbelt. All had been circled.

Miller moved on to sections fourteen through nineteen then.

These boxes contained more fine-tuned, pre-written details about the accident that Thompson had to circle. Miller was particularly interested in the questions of section nineteen.

First came Weather Conditions. Beside it, Thompson had circled: No Adverse Conditions.

Next was Road Surface Conditions. Thompson circled: Other. Meaning the surface road conditions could not be verified or be excluded as the possible cause of the accident

Miller moved on to section twenty.

Here there was a line graph where Thompson had drawn a crude rectangle with a sideways V at the front of the box, indicating where damage had occurred to the car.

Miller knew, just from looking at the drawing, Terry was lucky to have survived the crash, let alone walk away unscathed.

Miller had been to dozens of accidents where people hit trees or telephone poles head-on and had not survived.

The next two sections contained Thompson's final written report. This was where Miller would learn what the police believed happened.

On Tuesday, March 10th, 2006, @2340 hrs, the Hickory Falls Sheriff's Department received a report that a vehicle was spotted along Route 30. The vehicle was reported as a black 1977 Firebird. Upon arrival, police found the car off the road, down an embankment, and in the woods. The car had impacted a tree after it left the road, and a female passenger was ejected through the windshield and found ten yards away from the crash site.

Melissa Garland (34) was pronounced dead at the scene. The driver, Terry Graham (36) was unharmed.

Preliminary investigation showed that Ms. Garland was not wearing a seatbelt. but Mr. Graham was. The cause of the crash is undetermined at this time.

Miller did not see anything out of the ordinary with the report, other than Thompson administering the breathalyzer, most likely because of Terry's reputation alone, and even that was handled properly.

Was that why Terry had believed the sheriff's department were trying to railroad him for the accident? Because of a breathalyzer test?

Yet, something else concerned Miller: why Terry was wearing his seatbelt and Melissa wasn't. Did it prove that Melissa was trying to get out of the car when Terry lost control?

Then again, if Terry forced Melissa into his car, she would have fought back against him, so when would he have had time to put on his seatbelt?

He thought back to what Red Keller said about Terry beating Melissa up and running his car into the tree to hide his crime. It was a stretch, given the likelihood that Terry would have either been killed or severely injured himself. But it was not out of the realm of possibility.

People did all kinds of things to cover up their dastardly deeds.

Next Miller looked for the Claims Adjustment Report. This was the insurance agency's investigation of what caused the crash. But the report wasn't in the file. *Odd.* It should have been there. A troubling thought entered Miller's head.

Had someone removed It?

Multiple fingers were pointed at Terry for the murders of his family primarily because of his past behavior, and Miller suspected partly because of the mystery surrounding Melissa's death.

He had gotten slight variations of the same story from Sheriff Daniel, Pastor Garland, Bob Thompson, and Red Keller about what they believed Melissa was doing with Terry and what had caused the crash. All of them felt Terry was responsible in some way.

The problem was the stories did not match the facts in the accident report. If something foul was at play when Melissa was killed, Miller was sure it would have been noted on the report.

The sad fact, Miller knew, was that the people were shocked and heartbroken when news about Melissa Garland's death became public knowledge, and rightfully so since she seemed to be a beloved member of the Hickory Falls community.

They wanted answers to why Melissa was with Terry that night, why she had to die, and if they couldn't get them from Terry, then it deepened their resolve that something reprehensible was at hand.

And then, when Clay, Claire, and Sidney were found slain, it instantly made a town that was already prone to spreading and trusting gossip believe Terry murdered his family that Christmas morning.

Miller wasn't sure he liked this thought. It brought up a slew of new questions, which he had no evidence pointing to. Still, it was there, seeded in his brain. If he fed it, he knew it would grow, flower into a rational idea. He had to stick to the facts of the crime.

The facts would lead him to the answers he sought.

And the facts, at least in the Graham case, leaned heavily in Terry's direction.

He sat the accident report aside, picked up the Graham file, and flipped to Jenny Taylor's witness statement.

Taylor was fifty-three and married. She worked at Beckman Real-Estate Agency. Her address and phone number were in the file. Miller decided to give her a call.

He stood and turned down the stereo—Lindsey Buckingham had taken over vocals on "You Can Go Your Own Way"—and dialed Jenny Taylor's number on his cell.

"Jenny Taylor," a sharp female voice answered. "How can I help you?"

Miller introduced himself.

"I'm sorry for calling so late, my partner and I stopped by your house this afternoon, but you weren't there."

"I was at work. How can I help you?" Miller detected a discreetness in her voice, like she didn't want anyone to overhear her conversation.

"I'd like to ask you a few questions about the night you saw Terry Graham and his brother, Clay, arguing on the sidewalk."

"I really don't have the time at the moment. I'm in the middle of going over a settlement contract with clients right now. Could we possibly do this later?"

Miller understood why she was being discreet. He kind of felt bad for interrupting her work. *Kind of.*

"Sure. Could I meet you tomorrow sometime?"

"My schedule is free until noon; after that I have several showings. I will be at the agency until then, we can speak there, if that works for you?"

"Yep. What time will you be in the office?"

"I usually get in around eight. Do you know where the office is?"

"I do. I'll meet you there. Thank you, goodbye."

Miller disconnected the call. *One thing down.*

But there was still the unanswered question of how the 9-1-1 calls had been lost from the Sheriff's Department. A hard drive failure was Sheriff Daniel's story.

Yet, Miller had a difficult time accepting that. Susan Green, the overnight dispatcher back then, might be able to fill in some of the blanks. Daniel had sent her home that morning, just after the call came in.

Maybe she knew more about what happened to the call logs and would be willing to talk to him about the failure.

Miller stood and walked over to the small desk in the corner of his apartment, where he kept his computer. Opening up the internet, he found Susan Green's home phone number within moments of typing her name into the White Pages internal search engine. He picked up the phone and dialed.

"Hello," a male voice answered the phone.

Miller identified himself and that he wanted to speak with Susan Green. There was a hesitation on the phone, and Miller thought for a moment that the line had gone dead.

"Hello?"

"Hold, please," the male voice said without a stitch of emotion.

Miller heard the phone being transferred and voices faintly speaking to one another through the open line, but he could not determine what was said.

"Yes. This is Susan Green," a female voice answered, hesitantly.

"Hi, Susan. I don't know if you remember me or not. My name is Henry Miller. I used to work for the Hickory Falls Sheriff's Department."

"Yes. I remember. What can I do for you, Mr. Miller?"

"I'm working with the state police now, investigating the Graham case. I was wondering if I could ask you a few questions about that morning. Is that okay with you?"

"I don't know how much help I'm going to be. The sheriff took over for me that morning. I really didn't have much to do with it, other than taking the call. I didn't learn what happened until later that afternoon."

She sighed as if a great burden rested on her shoulders.

"Well, that's really what I wanted to discuss with you, Susan. What time did Sheriff Daniel come in?" Miller asked.

There was a momentary pause.

"I know it was minutes after the call, so I'd say just after six."

"Six?" Miller felt adrenaline shoot through his body. "Are you sure?"

"Positive."

A deep concern began to rise internally and warm Miller's body. Why had Sheriff Daniel waited a full half hour before radioing Miller?

"Why did the sheriff send you home that morning, Susan?"

"Because of my eyesight. The roads were getting bad, and the snow was coming down hard. The sheriff knew I had trouble driving in bad weather, so he sent me home and took over the dispatch desk until Andy Thompson arrived."

"He told you that?"

"Well… no. He didn't come directly out and say it. But I knew when he came in that was why he was there. I told him about the call, and he took over for me."

This all seemed logical enough to Miller, but it didn't answer why Daniel had not contacted him until six-thirty that morning.

Miller thought of something else.

"How long did it take you to gather your belongings and leave the building?"

"I would have no idea."

"Approximation."

She exhaled, thinking. "If I have to put a time on it, I'd guess… three minutes, five tops."

Not enough time to make a difference.

"Did you and the sheriff chat before you left that morning?"

"Only about department stuff, like the call that came in that morning, but we did that while I was gathering my stuff to leave."

Miller ground his teeth while thoughts pecked at his brain like a buzzard to dead meat. Approximately forty-five minutes had passed between the call coming into the department and when he arrived on the scene at six-forty-five.

Those forty-five minutes could have made a difference in apprehending the murderer.

Why had Daniel waited to call him, Miller wondered angrily.

Stay focused. Stay sharp.

"The second question: do you know what happened to the nine-one-one call log?"

"I was told there was some kind of hard drive failure."

"When did you find this out?"

"A day after the murders."

"Who told you?"

"I believe it was Sheriff Daniel."

"How long were you with the Sheriff's Department, Mrs. Green?"

"Twenty-five years."

"In that time, was there ever a hard drive failure that lost the calls?"

"No."

"Did you find it strange that the hard drive failed so soon after the murders occurred?"

"Not really. You can never trust computers to be reliable. Pen and paper, now that's reliable."

Miller couldn't argue with her there.

"So you didn't see anything suspicious? No one tampering with the computers or anything like that?" Miller asked.

"Son, if I would have seen something like that, I would have reported it."

"Thank you for your time, Mrs. Green."

Miller disconnected the call and sat at the desk, his thoughts mulling around.

The intoxication to solve the Graham murders was like an alcoholic's need for a drink; it drew him in and wouldn't release its hold. There were so many variables, so many unanswered questions and loose ends; it was like a jigsaw puzzle without a clear picture to figure out how the pieces fit together.

He was thankful when his cell phone rang. He needed a break to clear his head.

Looking down at the caller ID screen, Miller hoped Susan Green was calling him back with something important that she had forgotten to mention a moment ago. But that hope quickly sank.

Shit!

Trisha was calling. Again. Miller had forgotten to call her back. The thought of ignoring the call, and letting it go to voicemail, crossed his mind. He could deal with whatever Trisha wanted in the morning when his head was less cluttered.

Instead, he decided to answer it. The call could be about Luna, and he didn't want to be accused by his ex-wife that his job was more important than their daughter, which wasn't true, and never had been.

"Hey, Trish. Sorry I didn't return your calls. What's up?"

"Luna got into a fight today, Henry!" Trisha screamed at him, with a shaky voice.

"Is Luna okay? Is she hurt?" Miller's concern for his daughter rose.

"She's fine. But the other girl, Regan McCall, isn't."

Miller leaned forward with his jaw set. Fire rose inside him, traveling from his feet to his face, instantly warming his entire body.

He suspected Luna had had enough of Regan's harassment and cold-cocked her.

They had talked about the issue last weekend. He had not known Luna was having trouble with a bully until she brought the subject up.

Luna explained that Regan McCall had been picking on her for most of her junior year and spreading rumors about her around school. Luna's slim, lean frame, short sandy blonde hair that she styled like Megan Rapinoe—Luna's hero—and her physical ability to outplay and outperform most male and female students on the soccer field, put a mark on her head for girls like Regan McCall.

A pretty, preppy-bitch, Luna had called Regan when describing her to him.

The harassment started when Regan found her boyfriend speaking with Luna in the hallway, by her locker, after a pep rally. The pair had just been chatting, according to Luna.

Ms. McCall, jealous, began calling Luna *booger queen* (which his daughter had explained to him was a slang term for an unattractive drag queen) to her friends.

Later, Regan started a rumor around school that Luna was secretly a boy. The rumor had begun to take hold, and Luna was facing harassing text messages from so-called friends and Instagram DMs from kids she didn't even know.

"What happened?"

"According to Luna, Regan showed up down at the soccer field—you know, the one just down from the house." Miller did.

"Luna was there practicing. Minding her own business. Anyway, Regan was there with a few of her friends, and she started picking on her. Saying Luna's shoes—those new ones you just bought her—"

"The Jordans?"

"Regan kept saying they were boy shoes." They are boy shoes, Miller thought. *What did it matter? That was the pair Luna wanted.*

"And that only a *booger queen* would wear boy shoes. Henry, there were other kids there. They all were laughing at her."

Miller dropped his head, disgusted by what he heard. The hatred for those who were different was embedded in the bone marrow of people like Regan McCall.

"Evidently, when Luna was getting ready to leave, she was changing out of her cleats and back into her sneakers. Regan grabbed her sneakers from her bag and was going to dump a bottle of soda inside." Trisha continued.

"Luna said she went to stop her, and the next thing she knew, Regan was on the ground, bleeding. Jesus, Henry. She broke that girl's nose."

Good job, kiddo.

"Now, the parents are looking to press charges. Henry… they're thinking about suing us, too. You need to do something."

That caught him off guard.

"W-what would you like me to do?"

"Go and have a talk with this Regan girl and her parents."

"I can't do that!" Miller nearly shouted, even though the father in him wanted to find out where Regan lived and pay the snot a visit that evening.

Give the little twerp a taste of her own medicine and maybe her parents too. The critical-thinking cop in him stopped him from reacting emotionally though.

"Why not?"

"Let me see if I got this straight. You want me, a state police officer, to go to someone's house and intimidate them not to press charges after Luna slugged their daughter in the face, breaking her nose.

"Do you know what that kind of interference would do to Luna's credibility? And to my career?"

"This is your daughter, Henry. You need to protect her."

"I will. But this is my life, Trisha. What you're asking me to do could cost me my job."

"You didn't worry about your job when you falsely testified to protect one of your brothers-in-blue from being prosecuted, did you? But now you pull the moral high ground when it comes to our daughter's future."

What had happened wasn't as black and white as Trisha made it sound. Yes, Miller had falsely testified to protect his partner at the time, Officer Kane Lauver, when forty-five seconds of video was leaked to the media from Miller's bodycam by someone within the YCPD.

The leaked video showed the physical altercation between Lauver and a known gangbanger, Louis Gomez, who was wanted for a drive-by shooting that resulted in the death of a ten-year-old girl.

In the footage, Lauver was seen using excessive force.

Gomez's hands were already cuffed behind his back but Lauver continued kneeing him in the side. The media blew it out of proportion.

They labeled Officer Lauver a racist and his actions a hate crime, blaming systemic racism within the YCPD.

Never mind the fact that moments before, Gomez had resisted arrest by any means necessary: biting, spitting, punching, kicking.

But the fact was, Lauver had continued to knee Gomez when he was down, cuffed, and under control. Was it wrong? Sure.

But when you were fighting for your life, adrenaline kicked in, and it was hard to stop it from controlling you, from taking over—fight or flight, and most cops would always continue to fight.

So, Miller lied for Lauver.

He told the jury that Gomez continued to resist arrest, even while cuffed, and that Officer Lauver was well within his rights to continue to view him as a threat that needed to be subdued until backup arrived on the scene.

It had not been the most honest thing to do. Miller knew that.

Once Gomez was cuffed, Miller should have pulled Lauver off before it escalated further. Miller's testimony helped keep Lauver out of a jail cell.

And Gomez got life in prison for the drive-by shooting. He had to live with what he'd done. Had to look that man in the mirror every day, knowing he enabled Lauver's behavior, putting him back out there – *a bad apple*, as Ross had called officers like Lauver – to do it all over again.

"This is my job, Trisha. I can't just interfere in a local dispute."

"Your job. Your job. Your job. I've heard that so many times that it makes me sick. Your *job* cost you your marriage. Your *job* cost you a home. Is your *job* going to cost your daughter's future too?"

"That's not fair."

"I think it's plenty fair, Henry. Do something about this."

The line went dead before Miller could respond.

THIRTEEN

Terry felt terrible by the time he got home. He was positive he was running a fever.

Making his way to bed, he stripped his clothing and had just climbed under the covers—thralled with sweats and shivers that came in waves—when another coughing fit gripped him.

He had inhaled water once when he and Clay were playing at The Falls. Terry had slipped on a rock and went down, sucking in a mouthful of cold, slimy creek when he went under. Water filled his lungs. Agonizing pain gripped his body like he had just breathed in molten metal. All rational thoughts eluded him and panic set in as he sank deeper into the murky water.

When he was pulled to the surface by Clay, he instantly began to expel the water from his lungs with painful heaves that tightened and twisted his abdomen.

What he faced now was a similar feeling, only he could not oust entirely whatever was inside.

171

The coughing fit continued until Terry's stomach became upset, and he vomited on the floor. Afterward, he was so exhausted that he fell back onto the bed with bile stuck in his beard.

He lay there in the dark, trying to pull a full breath, wondering what was wrong with him. Was the muscle soreness, the fever, and the cough related to whatever was going on internally?

Were these the symptoms of some incurable disease? He didn't know.

He kept his eyes closed in the dark, cool room, with only the blowing fan to keep him company. He tried to focus on his breathing—in through the nose and out through the mouth—slow and steady, he told himself.

At some point, he drifted off to sleep.

Terry awoke coughing.

He sat bolt upright in bed, as his body tried to purge fluid buildup from his lungs. His chest heaved while his back arched as the hacking fit gripped his body, paralyzing him.

He looked like a silhouetted hunchback in the dim morning light coming through the windows. He tried to draw a breath but was unable to, and the room began to spin, slowly at first, and then faster and faster.

The coughing continued.

Terry felt his underpants grow wet and a shameful embarrassment washed over him, even though he was alone in the bedroom. He coughed one final time, feeling something thick and slimy that tasted of tar and copper dislodge from his chest and shoot into the back of his throat.

Only then could he pull a full breath. Lightheaded he fell back onto the bed, gasping for air and soaked in sweat.

His chest, back, and abdomen hurt from straining. The taste of tar and copper was so strong on his tongue it was like he had been sucking on a mouthful of ash-covered pennies all night.

When he swallowed, his throat was raw like it had been scraped with a razor blade, and that thick, slimy, warm, and wet thing that he coughed up slid down the back of his throat slowly, like a slug.

Congealed blood?

He lay on his back, staring at the bedroom ceiling, following the lines of plaster that looked like a raised road map above his head. His heart rate slowed, and his breath came in shallow pulls. Except there was a new concern.

A wheezing from deep inside his chest seeped through his lips, which sounded like a baby's rattle.

It had not been there yesterday.

He continued to follow that white plaster roadmap above. *My life in a nutshell. If I had only chosen the right road, things could have turned out differently.*

Terry knew his life choices had led to this very moment, alone in his bedroom, with no one to care whether he lived or died. A deep, unsettling worry was settling in.

You're on borrowed time.

Pulling himself up, he felt lightheaded again and the room started to tilt. But thankfully, the sensation quickly passed. A bottle of water that Terry had let sit from the previous night was beside him on the nightstand.

Terry snatched the bottle, unscrewed the cap, and took a long pull. The water tasted like gun oil. He nearly spat it across the floor and would have, had he not been so thirsty.

It was hard to swallow—a feeling like talons digging into the soft meat on either side of his throat—but he managed to get a quarter of the bottle down before returning it to the nightstand.

Terry had his suspicions about what was wrong, but he was not a doctor, so to assume was stupid.

He had been feeling bad for about a year now. His symptoms had started with fatigue, joint soreness, and headaches. Beer and pills—aspirin, Tylenol—seemed to take the edge off for a while, and he continued on with life as usual.

Then the cough, which had come and gone over the years, worsened to a daily occurrence about six months ago. He had tried to quit smoking, hoping it would stop the coughing fits, but that only lasted a day before Terry was back puffing them down.

About three months after that, he first saw blood when he coughed.

This usually happened after too many cigarettes and late nights of drinking or when he overworked himself around the farm. It was just a little blood that initially tainted the saliva a light pink color.

But soon, the cough became a wet, raspy gurgle, and deep red, almost black-colored phlegm came up from his chest like his lungs were filling up with some kind of viscous reddish-black liquid.

Climbing out of bed, Terry stood on joints so stiff it was hard for him to move. He shuffled to the bathroom. His entire body felt hot. *Am I still running a fever?*

Sweat dampened his clothes, and the soiled underwear and puke chunks still in his beard made him smell like a bag of soured onions. He desperately wanted a shower to wash the sticky sweat, vomit, and urine from his body.

He felt better after he was done showering. Not great. But better.

He dressed slowly, taking his time not to cause another attack. Once finished, he cleaned up the bile on the floor beside his bed, made his way to the kitchen, and put on a pot of coffee.

While waiting for the coffee to brew, he called Doctor Polis's office in town. He disliked doctors and steered clear of them as much as possible. But he needed to go. He *needed* to know what was going on inside.

On borrowed time.

The nurse set the appointment for eight that morning. That gave Terry an hour to do a few small chores around the farm before he left.

Terry worked for an hour, pushing through his bodily discomforts by concentrating on completing his tasks, like feeding the chickens and checking the tomato plants for bugs. He saw a few rabbits, thought about getting his shotgun, but put the idea aside.

Free pass, you furry bastards. Eat up. This offer is only good for today.

He returned to the house, changed shoes, and headed out the door for his doctor's appointment in town.

Arriving at the doctor's office in the square, Terry slid slowly out of the pickup.

He had not been to town since his mother's passing four years ago. There was nothing in Hickory Falls for him except hatred. It always felt like everyone was watching him, judging him, dissecting him as if trying to figure out what made a monster like him tick.

There he is, or *that's him,* or *that's the guy who murdered his family,* people whispered as he passed by.

The stench of being labeled a murderer stuck with him like the smell of pig shit on a hot summer's day.

His eyes fell onto Keller's Restaurant directly in front of him. It was hopping with hungry breakfast eaters, and he watched several waitresses run from table to table with coffee pots, to eagerly-awaiting customers for refills.

Irritation fluttered his insides.

Terry had come into town about a year after the murders to pick up medication for his father, who by that time was suffering from stage four melanoma cancer, and had seen the restaurant up and running. He'd had no idea that Red was interested in the building, let alone starting a restaurant.

Stole the building right out from under me, Terry thought bitterly. *But it wasn't like you were in any position, or state of mind to buy it.*

Inside the doctor's office, Terry gave the nurse working the front desk his name. She made no indication that she knew who he was. *Must be new in town.* She picked up his file, placed it in a basket next to her, and told him to have a seat.

He only had to wait a few minutes before his name was called by another nurse and he was taken back to an examination room. Once there, she took his blood pressure—155/94—and stuck a thermometer under his tongue.

He could feel her eyes penetrating his flesh with contempt. It was obvious she knew him, had heard the rumors, and believed everything she'd been spoon-fed; her loathing feelings toward Terry pulsated off her skin.

When the thermometer *beeped*, the nurse ripped it out of his mouth; the metal tip clicked off Terry's central incisor, sending a small jolt of pain into his gums.

"You're running a low-grade fever," she said, reading the digital readout.

"I figured as much," Terry replied, rubbing his mouth.

"The doctor will be right in," the nurse said and exited the room quickly, without an apology; she did not want to be alone with him.

Terry guessed he understood.

Doctor Polis came in a few moments after the nurse's exit. Polis was a short, bald man in his fifties.

"Terry, how have you been?" Polis asked, shaking Terry's hand. A handshake was Polis's way of greeting all of his patients. If there were any harsh feelings or opinions about Terry's guilt, Doc Polis kept them to himself and remained professional.

"I've been better," Terry said.

"Tell me what's going on."

Terry went over his symptoms. Polis listened to his heart and lungs. After Polis was finished, he began to feel around Terry's neck with his fingertips, driving them deep into his fatty flesh, searching, probing for something.

He moved his hands down and searched spots just above Terry's collarbone. Terry watched Polis's face closely as he continued his examination. He saw something worrisome in the doctor's eyes that he didn't like.

"Terry, I want to send you to get an X-ray," Polis said, stepping back.

"An X-Ray. Why?'

"There's a rattling in your lungs and slight enlargement of the lymph nodes. You're a smoker, right?"

"Most of my life."

"Mmm-hmmm."

"What…" The right words were hard to find, and they felt jumbled coming out of his mouth, like he was trying to talk underwater.

"What does that mean, Doc?"

"Nothing, yet. We need to know more. Let's get the X-ray and see where we are. In the meantime, I'll prescribe you a vaporizer. That should help with the inflammation in the lungs and keep you from coughing constantly."

"Is this something I should be concerned about?" *More concerned than I already am?*

"Let's get the X-ray done this week, and I'll see you back here next week. We'll know more then. Okay?"

Terry nodded, but his head felt heavy, like it would fall off his shoulders if he moved it too much.

"In the meantime, no smoking or physical activities that can irritate your lungs."

Polis said the prescription would be called in at Hinkle's Pharmacy and sent him on his way.

That was that.

Terry stumbled out onto the sidewalk in a daze of confusion and fear. He had gone to Doc Polis for answers, a solution to his problem, but left with more questions and without a resolution.

What's going on inside me? What's wrong?

The air smelled hotter than it had before Terry entered the doctor's office, and the world around him seemed surreal. He had overlooked its majesty his entire life, taking it for granted. There was always tomorrow to catch a glimpse of the setting sun or tell someone you loved them.

But tomorrow isn't guaranteed. Terry knew that better than most, and even still, he had not really understood at all. Until now.

Searching for his family's murderers wasn't Terry's only problem. He was ill. How ill he was, he would not know until the follow-up visit with Polis, after he got the X-ray done. *What's it going to show?*

Terry knew his excessive smoking might have led him to this exact moment. Hell, the warnings were written all over the packages and crammed down the public's throat with TV ads. But Terry, the red-blooded American he was, ignored all that. *It won't happen to me.*

But it is happening to you.

He had thought about the *what-if* scenario of becoming sick from smoking over the years. How would he react? How would he handle knowing his time on earth was limited? How would he approach what came next: chemo, needles, weight loss, slowly dying from the inside out until he was nothing more than a skeleton under a thin veil of flesh?

He had watched what cancer did to his parents, slowly eating them away day by day. What was the point of going through all the discomfort, the pain, and the prodding from doctors if only to get a few extra months at best? And for what? For whom?

He knew he could speed the process up. He had a .357 with hollow points that would take care of everything.

He pushed that thought from his mind. He wasn't quite ready to go there, not yet at least. But that topic was very much on the table.

Terry knew himself well enough to know that he would not wait around while he slowly wasted away, and his body gave out.

Fuck that!

He made his way around the square to the Hinkle's Pharmacy. When his parents fell ill, both diagnosed with stage four melanoma a year and a half apart, he had picked up their prescriptions from the pharmacy. It was one of the only reasons he came into town over the last nine years.

As he entered the building, he found it strange, like returning to a crime scene. The smell of plastics and powdery medications was strong and still oddly familiar, all these years later.

The medicinal smell took him back to those long days and nights nursing his mom or dad. He had watched them slowly wither to skin and bones as cancer ate away any semblance of who they had been, with pain so unbearable it would have been easier to die than continue fighting like they had.

He had been with his parents in their final days. Terry had held their hands, told them it would be all right, told them they would make it through, even as death inched closer and closer.

Death had a way of doing that—it crept slowly over a person, sucking what little dignity they had left day after day before they succumbed to Death's will.

His father had called this moment *in the pale light*—where the body was in limbo between life and death.

And when his mom and dad took their final breaths, Terry was glad, for once, that he could do right by his parents and be there for them when they needed him the most.

Yet, Terry understood he would not get the same treatment if whatever was going on inside turned out to be a death sentence. There would be no one to hold his hand, to keep his spirits up, to urge him to continue to fight on to the next day and the day after that.

No one was going to be there for him in those final few moments of his miserable life. He would die alone. No tears would be shed.

Terry gave his name to the pharmacist at the counter. He watched her closely, wondering if she recognized him or his name. With a smile, she told him that his prescription would be ready in about thirty minutes.

Another newbie, Terry thought.

With some time on his hands, he decided to go to the pharmacy's café and order something to eat and drink, even though he wasn't all that hungry.

The café was separate from the pharmacy, walled off with access through a single door.

As soon as Terry entered, the smell of fresh coffee, cooking eggs, and bacon flooded his senses.

A few people were in the café, but no one glanced up from their meals as Terry slid into the small round stool by the counter. The café still retained its 1950s decor, right down to the milkshake maker on the counter and the miniature coin-operated jukeboxes at every booth.

"Terry Graham?"

A female voice drew his attention back to the bar where Alma Preston stood in front of him. A half-smile was fixed on her face, almost like she didn't want anyone to notice that she was happy to see him.

Hard to be friendly to the resident leper.

Terry had been close with her husband, Karl Preston, before the murders. They used to drink together at Red's and go hunting and fishing on the weekends when they were both free.

Karl was also the one person Terry knew who could have gotten him an unregistered shotgun, fixed him up with a car, and maybe even helped him murder his family. He had spoken to Karl that night at Reds. *What did we talk about?*

Terry couldn't remember a goddamn word of their conversation. A freak accident had left Karl a paraplegic with some minor brain damage after a tree came down on him while working around his yard one day.

The years since Karl's accident had not been kind to Alma. She was deathly thin and –frail-looking—her Hinkle's uniform, old, faded, stained with grease and foods, hung off her bony body. Her once-round face was now narrow and long, with eyes sunken so far into her skull she resembled a skeleton.

She reminded Terry of his own mother when the cancer was attacking her, eating her away—caught in the pale light.

"Alma?" Terry heard his voice lift. It was nice to see a friendly face in town for once.

"How are you? How's Karl? I've meant to call." A lie.

"I'm getting by," Alma said. "You should come out and see Karl. It would really lift up his spirits."

Terry nodded but said nothing. He wasn't sure he wanted to see Karl confined to a bed, unable to move, with tubes and wires hooked to him, keeping him alive but in more or less a vegetative state.

"I should," Terry forced himself to say. "I should have at least called after the accident. I'm sorry."

"I'm sure you had your reasons," Alma replied.

Terry met her gaze and saw compassion softening her eyes. It had been a long time since he had seen someone from town looking at him that way. He pulled his eyes away before he started to tear up.

"How… how's Karl doing?"

"He has his good days and bad." She swallowed, and her throat made a pop. "Sometimes, I know he wishes that tree would have killed him."

"It must be tough for him. He was always such an active person."

"He talks about hunting and fishing with you sometimes." She paused and studied Terry. "You should really come out and see him, Terry. It would help."

"I don't know, Alma." Terry shook his head. "If someone sees me—"

"Who gives a…" She looked around to see who was watching or listening to their conversation. When satisfied that no one was, Alma continued by whispering, "…shit? Neither of us believe you did what they say you did—never did."

"Thanks." Terry looked away from her.

Alma was the first person to admit to believing he was innocent. It was good to hear, but it did little to repair the damage done to his already fragile reputation around Hickory Falls.

"Karl and I should have been there for you when all that went down. We should have had your back, and we didn't."

Is that because Karl knows the truth about what I might've done?

"It's not your fault, Alma. Sticking up for me would've just made your lives hell. It's better that you steered clear like you guys did. I don't hold it against you."

"Fuck this town and what they think. They wanted to pin the murders on you because of your reputation and the accident with Melissa."

"Maybe."

Melissa's terrified scream shot across Terry's mind, cutting a sharp centralized pain in his forehead. He remembered how frightened she had looked, her face aglow in the dashboard lights, as the Firebird careened off the road and down the embankment, heading toward a large spruce pine.

There was nothing Terry could have done to stop the out-of-control car, to stop the inevitable from happening.

"Maybe hell! They did." Alma's voice snapped him out of his memory.

"They wanted to pin Melissa's death on you, and when they couldn't do that, they tried to nail you for your family's murders. You think anyone in this town cared whether you were innocent?"

Maybe I'm not so innocent. Maybe I'm exactly the monster that everyone thinks I am?

He saw Clay, Claire, and Sidney's headstones at the Mt. Hope Cemetery. *Did I put you there?* He couldn't help but wonder.

"Karl can still communicate?" Terry asked, forcing the gravestone images away.

"Sure. He's lucky that way—some paraplegics can't even do that. Though his speech can become jumbled from time to time. Why?"

Terry thought for a moment. Maybe Karl could fill in some of the blanks in Terry's own memory of that evening. Questions Terry wondered about himself.

"When's a good time to stop by?"

"Terry Graham, your prescription is ready to be picked up," a voice announced over the loudspeaker.

Terry sunk inward as the feeling of being watched by every eye in the café worked its way over his body, making his flesh crawl. He had wanted to keep a low profile.

Now everyone, in Hinkle's at least, knew, and they would surely start to spread the word that the boogieman was back in town. He needed to leave.

"You can head on over now if you want. The day nurse is there. I'll phone and let her know you're on your way."

Terry nodded.

"Can I get a to-go cup of coffee and one of those glazed donuts by the register?"

With his vaporizer, coffee, and doughnut in hand, Terry started back to his pickup, which he had left in front of Polis's office before walking around the square to the pharmacy.

As he came to his truck, while fishing for his keys in his pocket, he heard the heavy rumble of a diesel engine entering the traffic circle. Terry paid it little mind, until the rumbling grew closer, and a black GMC pickup pulled into the space next to where he had parked.

Terry unlocked the pickup's door and sat his bag down on the seat.

He was in the process of putting the coffee in the cup holder when a voice called out from the GMC, "You have a lot of nerve showing your fat ass in town."

Terry didn't need to turn around to know who the voice belonged to. Colin Baker. He had not seen Colin since the fight inside Red's. He wasn't looking for trouble and just wanted to get on his way.

"Look at me when I'm talking to you, fat boy," Colin said sharply. His voice held a tone that was meant to invoke fear in Terry if he did not comply.

"I ain't got no business with you, Colin," Terry replied, not bothering to turn and face him. Terry heard the truck's doors open—all four of them. His body began to buzz. Colin wasn't alone.

"I just came into town to grab a few things. Don't want any trouble."

"Yeah? Well, looks like trouble found you," Colin said, coming around the front of the pickup and into Terry's line of sight.

He pointed at himself with his right thumb. Terry saw a long scar running from his right wrist up to the middle of his forearm. It was the arm Terry had broken in their fight. He guessed Colin needed surgery to fix it.

"And I'm trouble."

"You're something," Terry grumbled, locking eyes with Colin.

Colin reached out and gripped the pickup's door with a massive hand, causing the muscles and tendons in his huge forearms to flex like rubber bands.

He was no longer the pipsqueak Terry had put through the table—thin and malnourished—but a man who spent massive amounts of time and energy focused on his physique.

His black hair was slicked back over his head; the sides were shaved down to small black stubble. He wore a form-fitting white-and-blue striped tank top that allowed him to show off his lean midsection and tanned and toned cannonball-shaped shoulders. A pair of tan cargo shorts matched the pair of flip-flops on his feet.

"You might want to watch what you say, fat boy. I give the word, and my dogs will bite." His eyes shot past Terry to the three men behind him.

Terry turned and looked at Colin's buddies. Ike Arnold was to his immediate left.

Ike was short and stocky, with a mop of wild sandy-blond hair. A pair of thick-rimmed black glasses, that looked too small on his round face, rested on a sharp pointed nose. Terry had run-ins with Ike a time or two over the years inside Red's, but nothing that ever amounted to anything other than a few crass words. Ike liked to talk a big, tough game, but his ass couldn't back up what his mouth delivered.

Travis Kope was dead center. He was the tallest and fattest of the four. His budging belly was hidden beneath a blue T-shirt tucked into his jeans. Travis wasn't the brightest bulb around town, and that was saying a lot in a town filled with dim bulbs.

The third guy to his right, Terry did not know. He was about the same height as Terry. A trucker's hat with a Confederate flag rested high on his head. He wore a cutoff, button-down western shirt and a pair of jeans with cowboy boots.

The wannabe tough guy appearance almost made Terry laugh; he resembled Larry the Cable Guy.

"I got things to do," Terry said, turning back to Colin. "I don't have time for this."

"What's the hurry? Got someone to kidnap…" Colin looked past Terry to his buddies and lifted his eyebrows, Groucho Marx style. "Or murder?"

Terry didn't bother to reply. He wasn't going to give this prick the satisfaction of getting worked up. When Colin realized this, he tried another route of antagonization.

"What? No smart comeback? No tough talkin', tough walkin' Terry Graham retort? You didn't go all soft on me, did you, fat boy?" Colin poked Terry in his belly and snickered.

The men behind Terry laughed too.

"I've got bigger fish to fry than a minnow like you, Colin," Terry shot back, slapping his finger away from his stomach.

This snickering stopped suddenly behind him. Terry felt the hair on his neck rise. He might be able to take Colin in a fight, even with his health issues, but not all four of them at once.

He would have to play this smart if he wanted to walk away with all of his teeth in his head.

Colin stepped around the pickup's open door and pushed out his chest, as if he were getting ready to throw down right in the middle of town square.

"Don't push your chest out at me, Colin, unless you're prepared to have it punched in," Terry whispered just loud enough so Colin could hear.

Colin's lips pursed and his jaw worked around in circles, almost like he was desperately trying to think of something clever to say but was unable to come up with a witty remark.

"What'd he say?" Terry heard Travis say behind him, closer now.

"Don't know," the unknown guy replied. "You hear him, Ike?"

"Naw!"

"Don't push it, Colin. I'm not in the mood," Terry said, again just loud enough that Colin could hear.

"I'll fuck your world up. And then, I'm going to fuck theirs up."

"You hear 'em that time?" Ike asked. "Travis? Brent?"

"No. Not me," the one named Brent said.

"He sounds like he's talking with a mouthful of cock," Travis added.

The three laughed at the joke. Colin did not. He was locked in a stare-down with Terry, weighing what he was going to do next.

Still, Terry hoped his tough talk bluff and his past reputation for not being afraid to slug it out would save his bacon and avoid a fight in the middle of town, where everyone and their brother could see.

"You talk a tough game for a guy who looks like he's just gotten out of a hospital," Colin finally said, his eyes traveling up and down Terry's pale face. "Christ, you look like shit."

"Yeah. Like ghost shit!" Ike remarked.

The three laughed again.

Terry felt himself tense and his right fist balled tight. He might not look as healthy as he once did, and rightfully so, but he was pretty sure he could still put a punk in the dirt if it came to that.

"Look, I don't got all day. If you and your boyfriends are going to do something, then let's get to it. If not, get the fuck out of my way."

Colin didn't move a muscle, except those in his eyes, which flipped to his buddies behind Terry, looking to make sure they had his back no matter what happened next.

But Terry saw a change in Colin's hard demeanor; he must have seen something in his buddies' reactions that he did not like, and his shoulders slumped slightly.

They didn't want to fight, Terry understood.

"Move," Terry said, pushing past Colin and climbing into his pickup. He slammed the door closed and fired it up.

"I still owe you for my arm," Colin said, stepping up beside the Ford's door. Terry again noticed the large scar.

"Don't think I won't come to collect one of these days when you least expect it."

"Me and my shotgun will be waiting," Terry said defiantly, as he backed out of the parking space, before taking off with a squeal of the tires, leaving Colin and his crew standing in a cloud of white smoke.

Twenty-five minutes later, with the vaporizer working its way through his system, helping to keep the coughing to a minimum, Terry pulled into the Preston driveway.

He saw a curtain pull back, and an attractive, raven-haired nurse stuck her face in the window. She smiled and waved at Terry. Terry waved back. He stepped out of the truck and started up the walk.

The front door opened as Terry approached, revealing the nurse's full-bodied figure and a busty chest that was hard for Terry, for any man, to miss.

"You must be Terry," she said. "Alma called and said you would be stopping by. I'm Maggie, Mr. Preston's nurse."

"Pleasure."

"Mr. Preston's in his bedroom. He just woke up from a nap. I told him you were coming."

Maggie turned and led Terry into the house and down the hallway. The smell of sour body odor and rotting flesh, masked by a flowery powder, stunk up the air, creating a repugnantly indescribable hybrid smell.

They rounded the corner into a small bedroom on the right.

Karl Preston lay in the middle of the room, in what Terry assumed was some kind of special bed for paraplegics. There were all kinds of buttons to manipulate the mattress on the side of the bed.

Karl was on his back, the covers pulled up to his chest, his arms at his sides. Wires and tubes - a trach tube, heart monitor, and oxygen - ran to and from his body to the machines keeping him alive. Urine and colostomy bags hung off the side of the bed.

The smell of flowery powder and rotting flesh was more pungent in the room. Terry figured Karl was suffering from bedsores, just as his father had when he became too ill to get out of bed. He had no doubt that the nurse was treating the wounds, but it was a losing battle. The sores would not heal.

The powder was there to simply mask the smell the sores emanated. Karl's eyes were closed until Maggie spoke.

"Mr. Preston?" Maggie said, coming to his bedside. Karl's eyes slowly opened. "Mr. Graham is here to see you."

Karl's eyes brushed past her to Terry standing in the doorway. Maggie turned around, smiled at Terry as she passed, and closed the door behind her on the way out.

Terry stared at Karl, unable to speak. He knew the injury Karl had suffered was severe. Still, he had not entirely understood the extent of it until that very moment.

Karl's body was tiny. The muscles had long ago wasted away, the skin so thin it looked almost translucent and mummified to his bones. His face was gaunt, pasty white, and drawn.

But his eyes. His eyes haunted Terry. They were so sad and very, very tired.

His once-full head of brown hair had thinned to see-through silk that exposed his scalp. The sounds of the ventilator rising and falling synchronized with the movements of his chest inflating and deflating.

It was the only sound in the otherwise quiet room.

Terry had come there with an ulterior motive in mind but now felt like an intruder. He should not have been allowed to pass the threshold into this hell that was Karl Preston's life.

This isn't living. This is torture.

His mind flashed back to Alma; her frail body was nearly a mirror image of her husband after so many years as his caregiver.

Terry realized that death's pale light didn't just affect those about to die; its tentacles reached even the living.

"It's nice… to… see you… Terry," Karl spoke between the oxygen the ventilator provided him. A small smile creased his lips, and his eyes brightened, if only for a moment.

"Nice to see you too, Karl," Terry said, moving to the bed.

"How… have you been?"

"Good. Real good," Terry said.

Karl saw through it.

"Bullshit."

"Yeah. Bullshit."

"Pull… up… a chair. It's been a while… since… I talked to someone other than Alma, a doctor, or… Tits."

"Tits?" Terry asked, grabbing a chair by the end of the bed.

"Maggie. I call her Tits. Only in my head… mind you… never… to her face—that's not PC. See… that rack."

Terry smiled.

"How could I miss 'em?" Terry sat down.

"So, is that what all this is about? You faking it just to get the sponge bath from her instead of Alma?"

Karl's eyes glowed now, and the smile grew wider. He almost looked like the man Terry remembered going hunting and fishing with. The man he had played pool and drank until Last Call with at Red's years ago. Almost.

"I… wish," Karl said. "What… I wouldn't… do to get my hands… to feel… them." His eyes drifted off to a spot on the wall.

Terry could see something playing behind those melancholy eyes, maybe a memory of what it was like to touch a woman's soft skin.

"So… what's going… on?"

"Just came to see you. I should've done it sooner. I ran into Alma at Hinkle's today. She told me it was okay to come."

"I'm glad you did." Another smile. "Very… glad."

"Me too." Terry paused and looked around the room.

There was nothing on the white walls, not a picture, a clock, or even a TV. They were bare and sterile, like a room in an asylum.

It disgusted Terry to think his friend had to lay there in that room, day after day, waiting for the moment death finally took him away from that barren hell that had become his life.

When he looked back, Karl was staring at him—not just staring at him but looking through him to something inside Terry's soul. Those invading eyes disturbed Terry and made him feel violated.

"You… don't look… so good, Terry. You feeling okay?"

Terry nodded. He did not want to burden his friend with his health concerns.

"You… sure?"

Again, Terry nodded and quickly changed the subject.

"Hey, you remember that time you caught that twenty-five-inch bass out by Coogan's Bluff?"

Karl's eyes moved up and down as if in a nod.

"Yeah. I caught him… on… five-pound test. My heart… was pounding… and… there was so much adrenaline… coursing… through my veins. I thought… I thought my line was going… to snap… until he came up out of the water."

Terry watched as the memories washed over his buddy, wetting Karl's eyes of days when he could walk and fish. Then the haunting sadness of his eyes returned; those days were long past.

Terry wished he'd never brought the subject up.

"What's… the real… reason… you came… Terry?" Karl asked, his eyes flicking back to him.

"I told you."

"Bullshit. You didn't… come here to catch... up… on… old times."

Terry considered what Karl said. He had seen through his tough exterior, his walls, through his deception of why he was really there that afternoon.

"Karl, I have a few questions about that night at Red's. Do you remember it?"

Karl replied, but Terry was unable to understand him. He paused, closed his eyes, allowing the ventilator to fill his lungs with air, and tried again.

"The night your brother was murdered," he said fully this time.

Terry nodded. Karl had a way of getting his hands on things. Terry never asked questions. It was better if he didn't know how Karl came across some of the stuff people asked him for.

"Do you remember what we talked about? If I said or did anything that would lead you to believe that I hurt them?"

Karl studied him. Once more, his eyes searched inside Terry. A chill crept up Terry's spine. Or was that death's fingers he felt? The room was filled with death's overbearing presence.

"You did not… murder… your family," Karl said matter-of-factly.

"I'm not so sure anymore." Terry looked down at his lap.

"I can't remember that night very well. Do you remember what we talked about? Did I ask you to get me a shotgun? Or a car? Maybe some help to mur…"

Terry couldn't even bring himself to say the word out loud.

"I know you know people and can get your hands on… things."

"We talked… about… your brother."

"My brother?"

"You… were upset… with him. You told me… that you… wanted him and Claire… to start up… a business… with you. They refused… you told me."

Terry nodded as if he remembered the conversation with Karl.

He did not.

"They didn't want anything to do with it."

"Because… of your… reputation around town… you said."

"Yeah. Did I say anything else? God, I wish I could remember, but it's like there's a wall blocking my memories."

"You were… angry… that they… wouldn't help. But… you also said… that you understood… their reasoning."

"I didn't say anything about hurting Clay?"

"Of course… not."

Terry felt a slight weight lift off his shoulders with Karl's admission that he had not required his services. But would Karl admit, even to Terry, that he was an accomplice? He was wise enough not to implicate himself in anything, even in his own home.

"Let me ask you something, Karl." Terry coughed, but nothing came up. "Did you see Ruby-Lee at Red's after I left that night?"

Karl thought about the question for a moment before answering.

"She was there. Came in with three guys."

Terry sat up.

"Wait. She came in with three guys?" Ruby-Lee had said nothing about going to the bar with three men when he spoke to her yesterday.

"Yes."

"Did you know them?" Terry pushed.

"No," Karl said.

"Ruby-Lee told me she was at Red's, but not that she was there with three men."

Karl studied Terry carefully before he spoke.

"That's… always been… your problem… Terry. You've… always believed… everything that came out of Ruby-Lee's mouth. You've been so blinded… by your friendship for her… that you could not see the truth … when… it was right in front of you."

"I'm starting to get a clear picture," Terry replied through gritted teeth.

"You get a look at these guys that came in with Ruby-Lee that night?"

Karl's eyes moved up and down again.

"Yeah. One was… a big guy. Baldhead, graying goatee. Looked… like the jailhouse type I'd seen in the slammer back in the eighties. The other… was a tall, skinny… with blond hair. Third… guy… I remember… was dressed like… a cowboy—boots, hat, big belt buckle."

Who were these guys?

"Later, I was… outside… having a smoke… when Ruby-Lee, drunk off her ass, came stumbling out with them. They looked… pretty chummy to me, like… she knew them very well."

Terry stood up now, his hand wrapped around the bedside rails so tight his knuckles had turned white.

"Did you happen to see what these men were driving?" Terry asked, feeling the muscle in his throat begin to tighten with anticipation.

"Yes. A blue… Olds."

It was them. Terry was sure of it. The same men who had robbed the Quick Fill and the First National Bank of Gettysburg. *What were they doing in town that night?*

"Did Ruby-Lee go with them?"

"No. She got… in her car… and left."

"Ruby-Lee told me she spent the night with Red, at his place. Why would she lie to me?"

"The question… isn't why… would she lie to you. The question… is… why do you continue to believe she… wouldn't lie… to you?"

FOURTEEN

Miller tossed and turned most of the night.

His thoughts were on Luna and how he could help her out of the predicament she currently found herself in. But nothing came to mind while he lay in the blackness, hoping sleep would take him away from his troubles.

It made for a rough night.

By five, Miller had had enough, got out of bed, showered, and made breakfast—two eggs, toast, coffee, and coffee—and headed out the door to get a jump on the day.

He arrived at the barracks a little before six that morning. The building was quiet, and few people were in at that hour of the day as he walked to the office he and Ross shared.

He closed the door and sat down at his desk. The small number indicator on his phone flashed with a red 2. Two calls came in overnight, and both callers left messages.

He hit the play button.

The first message was from Trisha. Her voice was an irritant tone, a demeaning, put-you-down timbre that had always made Miller feel like a bug that needed to be squashed.

"I tried to reach you on your cell. Where are yo—"

He erased the call before it went any further, not wanting to hear his ex-wife's voice first thing that morning.

The next call was from Tim Quigley, surprising Miller since he was going to call him that morning anyway.

"Hey, Miller. Just called to see how things are going with the case. Anyway, when you get a chance, give me a call. Bye."

Miller felt Quigley was fishing to see if he had squealed about the tape to Garcia.

He looked at the clock and saw it was just past seven. Was it too early to call Quigley back? Miller didn't care if it was. He picked up the phone and dialed the retired trooper's number.

"Hello?" Quigley answered.

"You wanted to speak to me?"

"Miller?"

"Yeah."

"Uh. I didn't expect to hear from you this early." He paused, waiting for Miller to explain himself. When he did not, Quigley continued.

"How're things going with the case? Did the tape help?"

"We identified the voice on it."

"Oh! That's great news." Quigley sounded genuinely excited to hear this. "You didn't tell Garcia where you got the tape, did you?"

"No. It stays between us. As I promised."

"You're a good man, Miller."

Am I? Trisha had gotten into his head and made him judge his every move and decision as a cop. It was water under the bridge, he reminded himself. *You're not like that now.*

"Hey. I have a question for you," Miller said, trying to push Trisha's opinions of him from his mind.

"Shoot."

"Do you remember the morning Terry Graham was brought into the Hickory Falls Sheriff's Department for questioning?"

"Sure. Allen and I first questioned Terry there."

"What I'm wondering is what Sheriff Daniel told you. You and Allen interrupted his interview with Terry that morning. Allen asked to have a word outside—what was said?"

"Oh, yeah. I almost forgot about that. Allen chewed his ass out for questioning Terry Graham when all he was supposed to do was bring him down to the sheriff's department. Because of that half-assed interrogation, Daniel gave Terry a heads-up that we were looking at him. Dumb sumbitch!"

"So why did he interview Terry in the first place?"

"The sheriff said he believed Terry committed the murders and was hoping since he and Terry knew one another, that Terry would confess. I think he was just trying to make himself look like a big shot in front of a watching town."

"Did he tell you why he believed Terry was their murderer?

"He said the bartender—Red Keller—told him that he overheard Terry talking about how his brother 'was dead to him.'"

It fit with what Sheriff Daniel had told him and Ross yesterday.

"And what did you think about that?" Miller asked.

"I think it was weak. People say dumb things all the time, and Terry was known to shoot his mouth off when he was upset. Didn't mean shit without evidence to back it up. Daniel jeopardized the entire investigation with that interview."

"So, he wouldn't have known about Graham's neighbor—Jenny Taylor—who told you and Allen that she saw Terry and his brother fighting on the sidewalk?"

"We never said anything to him. That interview with Ms. Taylor wasn't conducted until the thirtieth of December, and it never became public knowledge."

"Then how did Daniel know a neighbor saw them arguing that evening on the sidewalk?"

"I'm not sure I follow."

"During the interview, Sheriff Daniel says a witness saw Terry arguing with Clay, outside his house on the sidewalk. If you didn't tell Daniel about Jenny Taylor and what she saw, how did he know what happened? He wouldn't. Unless someone else had already told him."

FIFTEEN

"The question isn't: why would she lie to you? The question is: why do you continue to believe she wouldn't lie to you?"

Karl's words echoed in Terry's mind until he got home.

Grabbing a beer from the fridge, Terry took it out onto the porch. He sat down on the rocker overlooking the front field, cracked the beer, and took a long pull. The beer was cold and refreshing after a long, emotional day.

He reached into his breast pocket, pulled out a cigarette, lit it, and inhaled the smoke slowly. *No smoking or physical activity,* Doc Polis had warned. It was like breathing in fire.

He coughed up a wad of bloody mucus and spat it over the railing into the dirt but didn't snub the cigarette out. The burning in his lungs seemed somehow fitting, as if it were what he deserved for allowing himself to be fooled yet again.

You could go back out and see Ruby-Lee.

As much as he liked this idea and seriously entertained it, Terry knew it was a bad decision.

He was worried from the visit with Polis about his health, worked up after running into Colin Baker and his merry crew, and after talking with Karl, who reaffirmed Ruby-Lee lied to him, he was just pissed off.

He was off-balance, walking a tightrope between keeping it together and exploding. He knew deep down he might lose his shit if Ruby-Lee didn't come clean.

Terry drew on the cigarette. He held the smoke in his lungs and let it burn. He let the smoke out with a cough and pulled a long breath that caused an ache deep in his chest cavity.

His thoughts shifted to something else Karl had told him.

Later, I was outside having a smoke when Ruby-Lee, drunk off her ass, came stumbling out with those three. They looked pretty chummy to me, like she knew them very well.

Mrs. Kelly told him that four people had stayed at the Twin Pines Motel—three men and a woman. Was it possible that Ruby-Lee had been that woman?

And if Ruby-Lee knew those men well enough that even Karl thought they looked *chummy*, as he put it, she probably knew their names too.

Again, the thought of talking to her began to metastasize in his brain. He returned inside and drank another beer while sitting at the kitchen table, hoping it would dull the thoughts of confronting Ruby-Lee again.

But the beer only worked him up further. Anger replaced worry about his actions. Frustration replaced pain and discomfort in his body.

What were you really doing that morning, Ruby-Lee?

If Ruby-Lee had not been with Red, as she claimed, then where had she gone after she left the bar? Did she go with them? Was she still with them on the morning of the murders?

Was she at the scene when Clay, Claire, and Sidney took their last breaths just before a shotgun cut them down?

I need to know.

There was a knock at the front door.

Not expecting company, Terry rose from the chair and cautiously stepped out into the hallway. Through the door's window, he saw Deputy Bob Thompson standing on the porch. His face was splotchy and slick with so much sweat that he looked feverish.

What the hell do you want?

Terry walked to the front door and pulled it open.

"Terry, we need to have a chat," Thompson said, stepping back. His voice held a gruff, authoritarian tone.

Terry stepped out onto the porch, pulling the door closed behind him.

Thompson continued. "Sheriff wanted me to come and speak with you. He talked with Ruby-Lee this morning. She said you were up at her place yesterday, pestering her. I'm here to tell you to leave her alone."

"I think she has me confused with someone else. I haven't seen her in nine years."

"Is that a fact?"

Thompson squared up with Terry, and his eyes grew skeptical. He placed his hands on his utility belt, like a sheriff in a western movie standing up to some roughneck cowboys looking for trouble.

"Yeah. That's a fact."

"That's not how Ruby-Lee tells it. According to her, you busted into her house, assaulted her friend, and roughed her up."

"Are you arresting me, Bob?" Terry asked, staring Thompson dead in the eyes.

There was no other reason for him to be there if not to arrest him, unless, Terry thought, there was an ulterior motive for him suddenly showing up. "Or are you here because of a personal request?"

Thompson scoffed.

With Thompson's quick dismissal, Terry was positive his visit wasn't official police business, but rather, maybe at Ruby-Lee's behest. Jeff had told him Ruby-Lee was banging people in the sheriff's department. Thompson was one of them. She could have contacted him to help get Terry to back off.

Thompson pulled his eyes from Terry and slowly let them travel across the yard, past the two large maple trees, where they finally settled on the barn with the words LEAVE TOWN MOTHERFUCKER spray painted across the doors.

"You should be careful, Terry. There are a lot of people in this town who wouldn't mind seeing you strung up," Thompson said with a cold, yet calculated tone, as if he'd rehearsed it before coming out to the farm.

"Is that a threat, Deputy Thompson?"

"No, sir! All I'm saying is that if something happened to your farm, or to you, because you were asking too many questions around town, it would be nearly impossible for the sheriff's department to respond in time for us to help."

Terry said nothing. His questions had ruffled some feathers. *Good!*

"I can't say I would blame them." Thompson ran his hand across his forehead, slicking the sweat off his fat face. "After Melissa. After what you did to your folks, most people wouldn't mind seeing you hang."

"You know damn well that what happened with Melissa was an accident. And I had nothing to do with what happened to Clay, Claire, and Sidney. When is this town going to accept that?"

"When you take responsibility that you murdered them—all of them, including Melissa," Thompson said, jabbing his sausage finger into Terry's chest so hard that it made an audible *pop*.

The stab to the chest with that meaty appendage hurt, and Terry felt himself stagger as a cough forced its way into the back of his throat. He gripped the doorframe to steady himself and tried his best to suppress the cough by clearing his throat, a sound he knew made him look vulnerable in front of Thompson.

"You're a disease in this town, Terry. One that needs to be eradicated to keep everyone safe."

"Get off my property, Thompson. Now! Before I get really angry."

A sly smile slid across Thompson's face, almost as if Terry's reply was exactly what he wanted to hear. And maybe it was. But Terry didn't give a flying fuck.

"Look who's the one making threats now," Thompson mused.

Terry stepped close enough to Thompson that he felt the officer's body heat on his flesh and could smell the onions he had for lunch on his breath.

"Oh, no, Bob. That isn't a threat. That's a promise."

Thompson studied Terry for a long moment, searching his eyes to see if there was even a hint of doubt in Terry's words. There wasn't.

Thompson seemed to get the picture and began backing away from Terry, down the porch steps toward the Interceptor. He did not take his eyes off Terry until he was beside the police SUV.

"Stay out of town, Terry. Stay away from Ruby-Lee. You've been warned."

Thompson pulled his fat butt up into the SUV and plopped into the seat. The springs squealed in protest from the weight of his bulk. He pulled the door shut, started it, and tore off back up the stone driveway, leaving circling dust trails in his wake floating over the tops of the corn.

Terry turned and walked into the den. He removed the key to the gun cabinet from the desk drawer, unlocked it, and lifted a stainless-steel Model 66 Combat .357 Magnum, with a 2.75-inch barrel out.

Reaching back inside the cabinet, Terry grabbed the box of hollow-point rounds. He shook the bullets out of the ammo box onto the desk, popped the revolver's cylinder, and began to load the gun.

From here on out, Terry considered everyone a threat and wasn't going anywhere unarmed.

Ruby-Lee had sent her dog after him to prevent him from uncovering what happened to his family. *What else does she know? What else has she lied to me about?* He wondered if she had dirt on Thompson, which persuaded his decision to threaten him to stay away from her.

Terry slammed the cylinder back into the gun and headed out. His mind was made up.

You're going to answer every one of my questions, Ruby-Lee. And this time, you're not going to lie.

Twenty minutes later, Terry pulled his truck off the road just down from Ruby-Lee's house. He did not want to tip her off that he was there, so he
would walk the rest of the way.

Stepping out, Terry tucked the .357 into the waistband of his jeans. *Just in case.* He began to make his way through the woods toward the cabin.

He approached the property by the side, near the driveway. A silver Prius sat in front of Ruby-Lee's dark grey Hyundai Accent. He wondered if she was with another trick. Perhaps.

Terry crept to the side of the house, pushing the smell of dog feces from his mind. He could hear Conway Twitty's southern twang singing "I'd Love to Lay You Down" coming from inside.

He ducked low, making sure to stay under the windows, and made his way along the front of the house, keeping himself out of sight. He could hear Ruby-Lee talking to someone inside, her voice louder than Conway's singing.

"You like what you see, darlin'?" her voice teased.

"Yeah. Very much," replied a male voice.

She was with another guy, just as Terry had suspected. He continued to the front door, where he knocked, then stepped aside, putting his back against the siding, giving the element of surprise when the door opened.

The dog barked from somewhere in the house.

"You expectin' company?" the male voice asked, suddenly alarmed.

"Um, no."

Terry heard footsteps approaching the door.

He readied himself.

The locked latch popped free with a loud *click*.

Terry dug his feet into the dirt, ready to propel himself forward.

The door handle began to turn, and Terry felt his insides come alive with circling butterflies.

Slowly the door started to open.

Terry sprang from the blind spot, smashed his forearm into the center of the door, ripping the handle away from Ruby-Lee's grip, imbedding it into the drywall behind. A scream erupted from her that echoed across the forest. Spooked birds took flight from their perch high in the trees above.

Terry's large hand snapped up and he took ahold of Ruby-Lee's neck. Her eyes bulged with shocked terror. Holding onto her throat while trying not to squeeze the life from her lying lips, Terry pushed Ruby-Lee back into the house, kicking the door closed behind him.

Once inside, Terry shoved her to the floor, hard. She slid across the wooden floor on her knees, peeling off flesh in the process.

From the corner of his eye, Terry saw a movement. A man sitting on the sofa, with his pants open and a hard-on resting on his belly, was reaching for something on the end stand.

Terry pulled the .357 from his jeans, swung the barrel at the guy, and thumbed the hammer back. The sound of the gun cocking made the man freeze, his hand inches away from a Benchmade Automatic knife, the modern-day equivalent of a switchblade.

No turning back now.

"Don't you fucking move," Terry ordered. He lowered the gun to the man's organ. "Or I'll blow your pathetic dick off."

The man's eyes instantly went wide. He slowly sank back into the sofa and raised his trembling hands.

"Please, man. This isn't what it looks like."

"Shut up! Stay quiet," Terry snapped.

The man nodded feverously as the dog's barking continued behind a locked door somewhere.

"Yes, sir. Yes, sir!"

Terry turned his attention back to Ruby-Lee, on the floor at his knees. He reached down and grabbed ahold of her hair and pulled her upright. She screamed and twisted in his hand, trying to flail her way from his grip.

Terry held fast and dragged her across the room. She tried to stop him by digging her heels into the floor, but Terry easily overpowered her. He threw her onto the sofa beside the man.

"You lied to me!" Terry screamed, stepping back and aiming the gun at Ruby-Lee's face. His breathing was heavy and labored; it felt like he needed to suck in twice the amount of air just to get a full breath.

"What?" She was confused.

"You lied to me, you fucking whore. I spoke to Karl Preston. He saw you that night at Red's and said you were there with three guys, outsiders who drove a blue sedan, just like the one you saw the very next morning. Who were they, Ruby-Lee? Names. You tell me their names or so help me God—"

"You really are sick, Terry. You need help."

"I want to know who killed my brother and his family. You got a look at those guys, a real good look."

He saw the fear of her exposed lie run across her face, like a child who knew they'd just been caught with their hand in the cookie jar.

"No more lies."

He stepped forward and put the .357 to her forehead. Her eyes nearly crossed trying to look at the gun, and she grew stiff as a board.

"Okay! Okay! I'll talk. Just lower the gun. Please, Terry," she pleaded with a quake in her voice.

Terry slowly lowered the gun to his side.

"I didn't know them," Ruby-Lee began, her voice still shaking.

"Not personally, I mean. I got a call from Red earlier that day. He told me there was work for me at the bar if I wanted it. I knew what he meant. So, I went down to meet them."

"So Red set you up with them? How much was his payment for this—gotta pay the pimp before they pumped the rump, right?"

"Fuck you. Pig," Ruby-Lee spat.

"Yeah. Fuck me. How'd it go down, Ruby-Lee? Red checks these guys over, makes sure they're on the level, then calls you. Once you get there, he gets his cut for pimping you out, and you take them around back and give them a quickie in the alley behind the bar?"

"No. We went to the Twin Pines Motel. I rented us a room for the evening."

A grimy feeling washed over Terry as images of what Ruby-Lee had done with these men flashed into his mind's eye, but he shook them away.

"Afterward, they brought me back to get my car, which I had left at Red's earlier that afternoon. We decided to go inside before we parted ways, have a few more drinks, while Red's Christmas Eve party was still going on."

"What time was this?"

"Around eleven."

That matched with what Karl had told him.

"The three of us hung out at the bar until closing time, drinking, bullshitting, having a good time. It started snowing pretty hard by that point, and the guys wanted to return to the motel. They were expecting a call from someone in town—someone they were there to meet."

"Who?" Terry asked.

Ruby-Lee lifted her shoulders. "I have no idea. Maybe it was you?"

Terry sneered at her.

"What happened next?"

"I was drunk. Red told me to go up to his place and sleep it off before I drove home. I walked out with the guys to their car, bid them farewell, and then got in my car and pulled it around back, to the employee entrance behind the bar.

"I took the fire escape up to Red's place and fell asleep on the sofa for the night. I woke around a quarter to six and headed home."

"And the guys you saw that morning at the video store were the same guys you'd spent the afternoon with?"

She nodded.

"I didn't see their faces when they were in the parking lot. That was the truth. But I saw their car. That blue sedan. That's how I knew it was them. You have to understand that I didn't want to get involved.

"If I came forward, I would have exposed myself and Red. We had a good thing going. It would've cost us everything. So, I called it in anonymously.

"Terry, I did not know it was your family in that car. Honestly, I didn't. You have to believe me."

Terry felt his finger involuntarily tap the trigger of the gun. He wanted to shoot her in her lying mouth. She had been the key to all of this for so long.

She knew who these men were and could have identified them to the police and cleared his name. But she had decided, without much guilt, that she would keep what she knew to herself to protect her own interests while he took the fall.

"You should have come forward, Ruby-Lee."

"I was scared, you idiot! Scared these guys would find out where I lived and come back and kill Mamma and me if I talked. I didn't know who they were or what they were really doing in town that day. I didn't find out until afterward that they might have been the same guys who robbed the Quick Fill a few days earlier and murdered two people." She lowered her head.

"What were their names?"

Ruby-Lee looked back up at him.

"Chet and Luthor Morgan. They were brothers."

"And the third guy?" Terry asked. "What was his name?"

"Stevie Boyd." She paused. "There was something wrong with him."

"What do you mean? Wrong how?"

"He had trouble speaking. Like he was retarded or something. He wanted to watch… us. Like I said, he was retarded, so I believe all he could do was watch."

Terry had what he had come there for. Now he needed to find them.

"Did you send Thompson to my place to threaten me, Ruby-Lee?" Her face tightened like she didn't know what Terry was talking about.

"What? Of course not. I haven't talked to him since… well, in years."

He didn't believe her.

Reaching out, he yanked Ruby-Lee to her feet.

"We're going to go have a chat with the state police over in Hollidaysburg right now."

"The fuck I am!" Ruby-Lee screamed and ripped her arm from Terry's grasp.

Terry leveled his stern gaze on her and said, "We can do this the easy way or the hard—"

He was cut off when the man sitting on the sofa, now with his pants buttoned up, lunged for the gun in his hand.

SIXTEEN

Just after eight that morning, Jenny Taylor emerged from the hallway inside the Beckman Real Estate building and introduced herself to Miller and Ross.

Her short, auburn hair was styled in a bob cut with layers. She was elegantly dressed in a gray pantsuit with a tie waist that fit a little too snugly over her plump frame to be entirely comfortable. A pair of black heels completed her outfit.

Miller figured she was dressed to impress her clients since she had told him she had showings that afternoon.

"We can speak in my office, gentlemen," she said with an inviting smile. "If you'll follow me."

She led them down the hallway from which she had just emerged. Miller thought he noticed a slight limp as they entered her office. They sat in front of her desk while she rounded it and gently eased herself into the desk chair. She winced as she did.

"Are you okay?" Miller asked, noticing how uncomfortable she looked trying to get into the chair.

"Sciatica," she grumbled.

"I hurt it last year when my husband and I went hiking at Yellowstone for our twenty-fifth wedding anniversary. On the second day of our trip, I stumbled on some loose rocks, twisted my back, and was laid up for the rest of our vacation. Now, I'm stuck with it for the rest of my life."

"I'm sorry to hear that," Miller replied genuinely.

"Me too. If we had just gone to the Caribbean, like I wanted to, this could have been avoided. But no. *He* wanted to go camping. *He* wanted to go hiking. *He* wanted us to get back to nature and all that crap." She rolled her eyes with a mix of frustration and annoyance.

"Anyway, enough about my back. How can I help you?"

"I'd like to refresh your memory by reading the statement you gave to the state police on the thirtieth of December. Is that okay with you, Mrs. Taylor?"

"Whatever will help."

Miller nodded. He began to re-read her statement, which she had given to Quigley and Allen nine years ago. Jenny listened closely, nodding with agreement as Miller went over the details about what she'd witnessed between Clay and Terry Graham on the sidewalk.

When he was finished reading, he looked up from the file and asked, "Is there anything you would like to add to your previous statement, Mrs. Taylor?"

"No. I don't believe so," Jenny replied, shaking her head. "That's how it happened, as I recall."

"After Terry sped away in his truck, did you see any strange vehicles in the neighborhood?" Ross asked.

"No. I didn't see anything strange. And besides, I would have heard a car come up the lane. I'm a light sleeper, and the windows in my bedroom are thin. I can usually hear any car that passes by our house, especially since it's a quiet neighborhood."

"Did you hear any other cars that night?" Ross asked.

"Just one. Sidney Graham's."

"How do you know it was Sidney Graham?" Miller asked. "And what time was this?"

"I know it was after nine-thirty that evening because my husband and I were getting ready for bed—our usual time—and I heard the car coming up the road. I peeked out just as she was pulling into the driveway. Clay and Claire came out in the snow and helped Sidney get her bags in the house."

Ross drew her attention by asking, "And you didn't hear any other cars that night?"

"Not that I recall."

"Before you spoke to Troopers Quigley and Allen, had you talked to anyone with the Hickory Falls Sheriff's Department about what you saw?" Miller asked.

"No."

"What about one of your other neighbors? Maybe one of them saw Terry and Clay's argument on the sidewalk too, and called the sheriff's department the following morning, once they heard about the murders."

"Sure. I guess. But I've lived in Shady Pines since it was built, and most folks keep to themselves and don't get involved in others' business."

Miller sat back in the chair. He glanced at Ross and could see something working around in the big man's head.

"Mrs. Taylor, you said you were a light sleeper. Sidney's Jetta was found in the Graham Video parking lot. Did you hear it start up and leave that morning?" Ross asked.

Jenny Taylor took her time thinking through the evening that had changed not only her life, but those of so many. Her eyes darted back and forth like ping-pong balls over a table. Then they stopped and she focused on a spot on the desk. When she looked up at them, Miller saw the surprise in her eyes. She had evoked a buried memory.

"Yes. Now that you bring it up, I believe I-I did," she stammered.

"What time would this have been?" Miller asked, feeling the familiar tingle he often had when a witness was on the verge of a breakthrough memory.

"Had to be early morning sometime. It was still dark outside. Jesus, I can't believe I didn't..." She put her face in her hand and sighed.

"Did you get up to investigate?" Miller asked.

Jenny pulled her hand from her face.

"Gosh, no. Not at that hour. Not on Christmas morning I didn't. We had a lot to do that day and I was dead tired."

She paused again as a tremor shook her body, almost like another memory had forced its way out from somewhere deep inside her.

"Now that we're hashing this out in more detail, I do recall hearing two vehicles start up and then pass by the house that morning, one right after the other, like they were traveling together."

"Two," Miller said, hearing the excitement rise in his voice.

Jenny slowly nodded.

"I believe so. The second vehicle had a big, heavy engine. Like an SUV or a pickup would have."

"Are you sure?" Ross asked.

"Well, like I said, I didn't get up to look. I'm just assuming what I heard was a pickup. But I never heard a car's engine, even a souped-up one, make that sound before."

Miller knew the weather conditions that morning had prevented a sulfur casting from being made of the tires and footprints; the snow was falling too hard and too fast and had covered over the impressions, burying them under several inches of fresh white powder by the time a forensic team arrived on site.

Thanks to Ruby-Lee's call, it had long been believed that the second car was a blue sedan. *But what if it wasn't?*

What if it was an SUV or a pickup? What if it was Terry's pickup?

The thought bounced around his head as he and Ross returned to the car and got in. They were going to confront Ruby-Lee next.

Miller sat quietly as Ross drove, mulling things over in his mind, which was going a thousand miles an hour.

How had Daniel known about Terry and Clay's argument on the sidewalk? For that matter, how did Daniel even know that Terry was visiting his brother that evening?

If Jenny Taylor had not told Daniel or one of his deputies what she saw, then how did he know about it when he questioned Terry that morning?

A flurry of irritation warmed Miller. They always seemed to be a step behind in this investigation. For every stone they overturned, another fell into its place, like a crumbled building being pulled away piece by piece for disposal.

It was maddening.

They came to the light at Main and West Fifth Street, directly across from what used to be the Graham Video store. Miller looked past Ross at the building when something suddenly occurred to him.

"Pull over!"

"What? Why?"

"That spot," Miller pointed to the empty parking space just to the right of them. "Pull into it."

Ross cut the wheel sharply and pulled the car into the vacant space along the road.

"What are we doing?" Ross asked, slamming the gear shifter into park.

Miller ignored Ross. He was studying the building that used to be the Graham Video store.

Though the business was no longer there, and the thrift store had replaced it, the layout of the building and the parking lot behind it had stayed the same since the murders.

"What do you see?" Miller asked, nodding at the building with his chin.

Ross followed Miller's eyeline.

"The same as you, just a building," he replied after a moment.

"Look closer."

Ross expelled a whoosh of frustrated air, but he turned and looked back to the building across the street.

"I see the building and the small driveway leading to the parking lot behind it."

"Right. Now, what can't you see?"

Ross's eyes lingered but he wasn't seeing what Miller was.

"I give up. What am I missing?"

"You cannot see the parking lot from here, can you?"

Ross slowly shook his head and said, "Not from this angle. No."

"Not from any angle," Miller corrected.

Ross's attention snapped back to Miller. Intrigue had replaced his annoyance. Miller turned in his seat, grabbed the Graham case file from the back, and flipped through it until he found what he was looking for.

"When I arrived on the scene that morning, the Jetta was parked in the far left-hand corner of the parking lot." He turned the file around so Ross could see.

A crime scene photograph of the Jetta, taken the morning of the murders, showed where the car was positioned in the parking lot.

"We've all been focused solely on what the caller had described that morning—a man with a shotgun running across the parking lot and getting into a blue sedan. But the photos taken at the crime scene do not match what Ruby-Lee claims she saw."

Miller pointed to the building. "You cannot see that part of the parking lot from the road."

Ross pointed in front of them.

"But if we move up the road, surely—"

Miller shook his head.

"The left rear of the parking lot is blocked from view in both directions by the building. There was no way Ruby-Lee could have seen what she claimed in the call."

Ross's eyes danced with excitement; he was starting to see what Miller had put together.

"Then how would Ruby-Lee know the Jetta was back there if it was out of her line of sight from the road?" Ross asked.

And then it hit him. "She wouldn't have been able to."

"Right."

"Then that could only mean…" Ross trailed off. He swallowed and his Adam's apple bobbed in his throat.

"The call was a fake."

Miller knew there was something wrong the moment he rapped on Ruby-Lee's door.

Where's the dog?

There had been a dog the last time they had been there, and it had been barking its head off, locked away somewhere in the house, scratching at the door to be let out.

But now the home was unnervingly quiet. Nothing moved inside. It reminded Miller of when he found the Jetta, how it had seemed dead.

He glanced over to Ross just as a warm breeze blew through the trees, rustling them and bringing with it the smell of something sulfurous and metallic—a scent Miller recognized instantly— gunpowder.

"Miller?"

"Yeah, I smell it."

Miller reached down and pulled his Sig out, holding it by his right side. Turning, he scanned the area, looking for anything unusual.

Besides the silver Prius parked in the driveway, nothing appeared different from when they were there last. Still, they needed to proceed with caution; they did not know who or what waited for them behind closed doors.

"Ms. Huckster, are you home?" Miller asked through the door. "This is the state police."

There was no reply. Again, no barking dog. No footsteps.

Miller looked at Ross. He was sweating profusely, with beads dripping off his forehead onto his shirt, darkening it around the neckline.

Ross, like Miller, knew they had probable cause to enter the residence. Yet the fear of the unknown scared them into a clammy, cold sweat even in the hot morning air.

Miller reached out and took hold of the door handle. He turned it slowly. The latch popped free. He let the door swing slowly open with an eerie creak that raised the hair on his neck.

"Ms. Huckster? You home?" Miller asked again.

Now Miller heard whistling, like air blowing across the top of a bottle, coming from inside the house. It was an unnerving, desolate sound. Miller felt his throat constrict and his balls wither into his body.

Peeking around the doorway into the cabin, he saw it was dark inside and he could only make out the silhouetted shapes of the furniture. Still, he didn't see any human shadows or ghostly movement that set off an alarm that someone else was there. He pulled back.

"Right side all clear."

Ross stuck his head in this time, checking the left side.

"Left side clear," Ross said, starting into the house.

Miller followed closely behind Ross; the smell of gunpowder was stronger inside the house. It took Miller's eyes a moment to adjust, but when they did, he quickly realized a struggle had occurred.

The dining room table was overturned, the chairs were on their sides, and the drywall had a large dent like a body had been pushed into it. By the open window above the sink, a hot breeze snapped the curtains.

Air blew across several empty beer bottles in the sink, creating a whistling sound. A small pool of blood on the counter dripped onto the floor and then dotted its way back across the kitchen.

"Miller," Ross said, pulling Miller's attention away from the sink.

When Miller turned to Ross, he saw a grave look on his partner's stoic face. This scared Miller, as he followed his partner's gaze to the living room.

"Shit," Miller said, lowering his gun.

Ruby-Lee was slumped over on the sofa. A large black hole in the center of her forehead leaked blood onto the cushions.

Directly behind her, the wall was decorated with her blood, skull, and brain matter. Another blood stain was visible on the front of her white t-shirt, just above her left breast.

On the floor, between the sofa and the coffee table, was a man, face down in a pool of blood. The back of his head was missing, and Miller suspected his face too.

They cleared the rest of the house, finding only a dead pit bull in the bathroom. Someone had shot the poor animal, most likely to stop it from barking and attracting attention.

They returned to the living room, holstering their weapons, and began to look over the bodies without touching anything.

"Looks like an execution," Ross said, his eyes traveling over the bodies.

"Someone shut Ruby-Lee up before she could speak to us."

<u>SEVENTEEN</u>

After he returned home, Terry stripped his clothing and jumped in the shower. When he was finished, he redressed, went downstairs, and threw his clothes in the washer.

Blood tended to stain if not washed out right away.

Moving back into the kitchen from the washroom, the phone rang as he passed it.

"Hello."

"Terry? It's Angie."

Terry had not expected to hear from her so soon. He cleared his throat and tried to shape his thoughts; he was having trouble focusing after what happened at Ruby-Lee's.

"Hey, Angie… sorry… um… I wasn't expecting to hear from you already."

"You okay? You don't sound like yourself."

"Yeah. Yeah, I'm fine. I had to rush to grab the phone. What'd you find out?" He was surprised at how well he lied, how easily he hid the truth.

"I found Horace Gillbanter. You were right. He lives in Mercersburg."

He survived! Terry felt relief that the soulless bastards had not taken Gillbanter's life too.

"That's great! Were you able to get a phone number or an address?"

"Both." She recited the phone number and address to him. Terry wrote it down. "Why do you want to find him?"

"He's an old friend from high school." Again, the lie slipped from Terry's lips effortlessly and he hated himself for it.

"Too bad you're not on Facebook. That's where I found him."

"Oh. I never thought of that. But I would have had to create an account to view his page, right?"

"Yeah."

There was no way Terry was signing up for a Facebook account. He had heard the news stories about how Facebook was manipulating its users for their own benefit, how it tracked you, listened in on your cell phone. He would have no part in that.

"Did you know he was the only survivor of a shooting?"

"I did not. What happened?" Terry tried to sound shocked but sympathetic.

Angie went over the details. Terry pretended to listen with interest and acted like he knew nothing about the robbery.

"That's terrible," Terry replied when Angie was finished speaking.

"What an awful world we live in..." she trailed off, hesitating before speaking again.

"But I guess you know that all too well after what happened to you, huh?"

"Yeah," Terry croaked out as images of Clay, Claire, and Sidney all seemed to flood his mind at once, like the dam that stored his memories had crumbled.

A mix of sadness and anger pricked his skin, reminding him of the names Ruby-Lee had mentioned.

"Hey, I'm looking for a few other friends from high school. Think you could do a search for them, also?"

"Sure! I'd be happy to help."

"Their names are Luthor and Chet Morgan and Stevie Boyd. I lost touch with those knuckleheads after high school." Terry faked a laugh, and he knew it sounded forced. He just hoped Angie hadn't noticed.

"We used to cause quite the ruckus around Hickory Falls."

"Got it. I'll be in touch."

"Thanks, Angie. I owe you one."

"You can take me out for dinner some night. How's that sound?"

Terry swallowed. Angie knew who he was and what he had been accused of. She couldn't possibly want to be seen in public with the likes of Terry Graham, could she?

"I'd like that," Terry found himself saying.

Stupid! Don't ruin her life by getting her involved more than she already is. Nothing good will come of it but heartbreak.

"Cool."

The line hung open with a heavy, black static between them that felt uncomfortable. Terry wanted to say something, but words eluded him.

"I should get going," Angie finally said, breaking the awkward silence.

"Me too."

"Talk soon?" she asked, her voice rising with more hopefulness than Terry had expected to hear.

"You bet."

Terry disconnected the call. A pang of regret instantly gripped him. He should not have deceived Angie. She was a nice girl, an innocent soul who was only trying to help. He should have told Angie the truth; she deserved that much.

But Terry had to force such thoughts from his mind. He needed to stay the course and not get sidetracked.

He had a phone number and an address for Horace Gillbanter now. Maybe Gillbanter could help him. Perhaps he would remember something significant about the men who shot him. Something that would link them to the murders of his family.

Then again, maybe not.

But Terry had to try.

He picked up the phone and went to dial the number but slowly replaced the receiver. A call would not do. He needed to speak to Gillbanter in person.

Look him in the eyes when he told him the reason he was there.

It took Terry over an hour and a half to get to Mercersburg. By the time he arrived at Gillbanter's home, it was past four.

An overturned tractor and trailer on Route 30, eastbound, had slowed traffic to a miserable crawl.

At the front door, Terry pressed the doorbell. He heard the chimes ring inside, and soon the sound of tiny feet pitter-pattering toward the door. It slowly started to pull open, revealing a little boy, around five or six, with curly black hair.

"Hi!" the child said, opening and closing his fist in a wave.

"Hi," Terry replied. "How are you?"

"Good."

"Is your daddy home?"

"Darren!" came a female voice from somewhere inside.

Terry looked past the child, into the house. A woman slowly materialized from the shadows and made her way down the hallway and into the sunlight.

Cautious observation steeled in her brown eyes. Her dark hair was pulled back into a ponytail, and she wore an apron dusted with baking flour.

"Can I help you?" she asked, stepping beside the boy.

"Hi," Terry said, putting on his best smile. "My name is Terry Graham. I'm looking for Horace Gillbanter. Is he here?"

"I'm his wife, Erin. Can I help you?"

"Maybe." Terry paused, trying to decide whether to tell her the truth or lie to her like he had Angie. He decided to go with the truth.

"I need to talk with your husband about the night the Quick Fill was robbed."

"Darren, go play," Erin said.

"But Mom!" the boy protested.

"Go. Now." She pushed him away and remained quiet until her son disappeared into another part of the house.

"What's this about?" she asked, turning back to Terry.

"I believe the men who shot your husband and murdered two other people that night are the same men who murdered my family. I was hoping that speaking to your husband could shed some insight into them for me."

The truth knocked Erin Gillbanter off balance. She had to place her left hand on the doorframe to steady herself from falling. Her right hand slipped between her breasts, gripping her shirt into a ball as if it were her heart.

"That day. It just keeps haunting us." Erin said slow and dense.

Their anguish was not lost on Terry.

Grief haunted him too.

"I know this is hard and unexpected, Mrs. Gillbanter. But I believe I'm onto the men who did this. If I could talk to your husband, maybe he could remember something that would help me find them."

Her eyes locked on Terry's, and she searched deep inside his, looking for something. But what?

"And if you find them? What then?"

Terry had thought about that question a lot over the years.

"I'll report them to the police."

The flinch in her eyes told Terry she did not believe him. She understood what he was up to, what he would do if he *did* locate them. Terry did too, but he had to find them first.

"My husband's not here, Mr. Graham. He's down at the Mercersburg First Church. He runs a support group Tuesdays and Thursdays."

"Would you mind calling him and letting him know that I'd like to talk with him?" Terry asked.

Erin nodded.

"Sure. Just give me a minute to grab my phone."

She disappeared down the hallway. Terry heard her talking to her husband a moment later but could not hear what was being said.

She returned with her hand over the speaker of the phone.

"He said if you can come after group, he'd be willing to talk with you."

"What time?"

"Five-thirty."

"Tell him I'll be there."

Terry thanked Erin Gillbanter for her time and left. He had an hour to kill before he met with Horace.

He found a bar called Webber's and went inside for a drink. The urge for a beer came on strong, but Terry thought better of it and got a Coke instead.

The smell of alcohol on his breath would not lend credibility to his story. Terry took his soda to the outside porch area, lit a cigarette, and watched the cars pass until it was time for the meeting.

When Terry pulled to the curb in front of the Mercersburg First Church, he saw a group of people exiting the side entrance.

As some of these people left the building, they paused momentarily by the door, where a short, dark-haired man with round-rimmed glasses, a blue button-down shirt, and dark slacks stood.

Some shook his hand, gave him a hug, or exchanged a few words with him before they continued on to their lives of dealing with their past traumas. Terry suspected the guy wearing the glasses was Horace Gillbanter.

He sat in the truck until Gillbanter looked in his direction. Terry waved. Gillbanter slowly lifted his hand and gave an uneasy wave in return. He started toward the pickup.

As Gillbanter neared the passenger-side door, Terry could see the man's face better, including the scarring on the right side. It was so severe that it looked like someone had taken a cheese grater to his chin, cheek, and ear; the flesh was twisted and misshapen with deep grooves and hollows in the skin.

"You Terry?" Gillbanter asked, leaning down on the passenger-side door's open window.

"I am."

"We can talk in my office."

Inside, Terry took a seat in front of Gillbanter's desk. Gillbanter asked Terry if he could get him anything—water, soda, muffin, or doughnut leftover from the group session.

"I'm good. Thank you."

Gillbanter sat down. He looked tired, weary. His eyes held a deep sadness that Terry recognized in his own when he looked in the mirror.

A sadness that would not go away no matter how much therapy you put yourself through.

The pain. The trauma. It was always there. Always picking away at you. Always in the back of your mind, weighing you down, stopping you from moving forward with living your life the way you had always intended on living it.

"My wife told me over the phone what happened to you, Mr. Graham. I am truly sorry."

Terry nodded.

"But I don't see how I can help you."

"Mr. Gillbanter, did you see the men who robbed the Quick Fill?"

"No. Their faces were covered with ski masks. I really only remember snippets of that night anyway. Everything happened so fast it was like a dream, morphing its way from one image to the next with liquid-like motion."

"Do you remember noticing anything distinctive about the men? A tattoo or earring, something like that?"

"Well, they both were fully covered—jackets, gloves, masks—there was no way to see anything unique that I could point out. I do remember one was a big, well-built guy. The other was about the same size, but leaner, and wore this giant cowboy belt buckle with a horse's head."

Big belt buckle was how Karl Preston described the one who dressed like a cowboy, Terry remembered.

"According to the news article I read, these two came in, hit the cash register, and then wanted you to open the safe. Is that correct?"

"That's true. However, the news did not report that they pulled right up to the door. Two men jumped out. The big guy came towards the registers, while the one with the cowboy buckle stayed by the door, watching the front. The big guy demanded we empty the registers and the safe. Except we—Caleb Winter and I—didn't have the combination; only the manager did."

"What then?"

"It upset him. He threatened to shoot us if we didn't comply."

Gillbanter paused, and a chill shook his body. His scarred face tightened, the twisted flesh pulled taut, making it look almost like latex movie make-up.

The memories were still there, forever circling in his mind, a wound that would never heal like the ones on his face. He blinked, coming out of the past.

"I'm pretty sure he would have shot us, too, right there on the floor, behind the counter. I could see it in his eyes—this blank, emotionless stare—calculating whether he should pull the trigger or not."

Like shooting ducks in a barrel. Just like they shot Clay and his family inside the car.

"But before he could, the shotgun went off by the front door."

"The girl who entered the store?" Terry asked.

Gillbanter nodded solemnly.

"The one at the door caught her as soon as she came in. She was looking at her phone and had not seen what was going on when she entered."

Gillbanter looked away to the trees outside his office, lost there between the present and the past.

"He shot her in the side of the face, took most of her head off. She was still holding her phone when she hit the floor. God, I'll never forget how her thumb was still moving over the keypad."

Gillbanter sniffed back tears and returned his gaze to Terry with glassy eyes.

"Did the one with the cowboy belt buckle say why he shot her?"

"Told the big guy he believed she was calling the police."

"Because she was on her cell phone?" Terry asked.

"That's what I assume."

"What then?"

"The big guy turned back to us, leveled the shotgun and pulled the trigger. A single round on both of us. I lived; Caleb didn't. He took the brunt of the blast. As you can see, I caught the rest." He paused there and ran his tongue across his dry lips.

Terry tried to swallow the lump in his throat, but it remained.

"That night, did you see what they were driving?" Terry asked, his voice a hoarse whisper.

"Some kind of older blue sedan."

"A blue Oldsmobile perhaps?"

"Could be. I really don't remember what kind it was."

"Was there anyone else? Or only two of them that night?"

"There was another guy, the driver. He waited in the car."

"You sure?

Gillbanter nodded.

Terry suddenly felt uncomfortable. The walls of the small office were closing in around him, choking his air. He needed to leave.

"Thank you for your time." Terry rose to his feet and started to the door.

"You know, Mr. Graham, you're welcome to come back and talk about your grief in the group. It helps. Getting the pain out rids the soul and mind of torment.

"To share your experience with others who are in a similar situation allows the healing to start. You look like a man who needs to heal."

Terry thought about it for a second or two and then shook his head.

"I have my own way of dealing with what happened, Mr. Gillbanter."

EIGHTEEN

The house had grown ripe by late afternoon with the thick stench of curdled blood that attracted flies and other insects.

The county coroner, Lori Dell, had arrived twenty minutes earlier and was working on getting internal body temperatures on the victims to approximate the time of death.

Lori was the first female coroner for Bedford County. She had spent twenty-five years as a registered nurse and was certified in Forensic Nursing.

Miller liked her. She worked hard and was quick to get her findings back to the police.

Elsewhere, the Pennsylvania State Police Bureau of Forensic Services took photos, dusted for fingerprints, and had a team searching around the grounds for tire tracks or footprints.

The place was abuzz with so much activity that it made Miller's head throb.

What a mess, Miller thought sourly, while standing in the doorway of the house, watching the forensic team go about their jobs.

So far, nothing had been recovered that pointed to Ruby-Lee and the unknown male's killer. A few prints were lifted from various places around the house, but Miller suspected they would belong to either Ruby-Lee or come back to the dead male.

"What now?" Ross asked, suddenly beside him.

Miller shook his head, frustrated. *This place is not going to give up its secrets easily.* Whatever Ruby-Lee knew, she had taken to her grave, just as her killer had wanted.

Dell looked up from the dead male between the sofa and coffee table and waved them over. Miller and Ross moved into the living room so she could go over her findings with them.

"I'm estimating the time of death between eight and ten this morning." Dell handed Miller the dead guy's wallet.

"I pulled that off him."

Miller took the wallet and opened it. According to the guy's driver's license, his name was Roger Kline from Mooresville, Pennsylvania.

"Run his name," Miller said, handing the wallet to Ross. "See what comes up."

Ross snatched the wallet from Miller and exited the house, back to the cruiser's onboard computer. Miller looked back to Dell, who was focused on the male body at her feet once more.

"Killer shot him in the back of the head, execution-style," Dell said, making a gun shape with her right thumb and forefinger. "Boom!"

The finger gun rose like it had recoiled.

"It was a close contact shooting from the burnt hair and skin around the entrance wound. There's also powder tattooing on the scalp. That's an indicator that the barrel was no further than a few inches away when the trigger was pulled. From the looks of the entrance and exit wounds, I'd say he was shot with a high-caliber pistol."

Dell turned her attention to Ruby-Lee slumped over on the sofa.

"Headshot was the kill shot to Ms. Huckster. The one in the pump was just for good measure."

Miller knew *the pump* meant heart.

"But unlike Mr. Kline, the killer was further away when he shot her, maybe in about the same position I'm standing now. There's no powder or burn markings on her skin or clothes." Dell looked back to Miller.

"Won't have more until they're down at the morgue."

Miller knew the drill.

"Thanks, Lori."

He turned away. Miller figured they would hear back from Dell tomorrow sometime with her findings. Forensics would also need time to work on the scene and try to recover the bullets fired into Ruby-Lee and Mr. Kline, if they recovered them at all.

Unlike on TV and in the movies, bullet recovery was not always possible. Often, bullets were never found, or they were so damaged upon impact that they were useless in lab tests to match them to the gun they were fired from.

It was rare to recover a pristine bullet unless it was a through-and-through shot into a soft target, like a bed or a pool of water, or if it was still lodged in the body, but even then, they could be mangled after striking bone.

Miller stepped out into the humid air. The smell of dog shit and piss seemed constantly present since it had been disturbed, with the forensic team walking around the house, looking for evidence.

He stepped away from the doorway, unable to take the smell, and moved to the driveway so he could grab a breath of fresh air.

A male forensic technician stood beside the dark gray Hyundai Accent parked in front of the silver Prius, logging his notes. As Miller neared the car, he was hit in the face by the bitter tang of marijuana emanating from within—the summer heat had made the plant's stench more prevalent.

"Find anything?" Miller asked the tech working the driver's side of the Accent.

"This was in the glove compartment," said the male tech, handing Miller an EVIDENCE baggie with a dime bag of marijuana and a pipe inside.

"Anything else?" Miller asked, unsurprised that marijuana had been found after smelling its earthy scent coming from the hot car.

"Not yet," The tech said, sitting down in the car and reaching for the driver's side sun visor, about to flip it down. "If we find anything el—"

He was cut short when something fell out from behind the visor and feathered down to the floor and slipped under the seat before the tech could grab it. He groaned.

"Shit."

Stepping out, the tech got on his knees and reached under the small space between the seat and the floor, searching for whatever fell from behind the sun visor. His hand was barely able to fit.

Miller watched the tech wiggle his hand around until his fingertips fell onto something he had not expected to find.

"There's something else under here," he said, glancing back at Miller.

Miller felt his pulse quicken.

The tech inched his hand back until he pulled whatever he had found from under the seat. He held something black and rectangular up for Miller to see: a smartphone.

The tech turned the phone on. A second later, Miller heard it chime that it was fully booted up and ready to use.

"Let me see that," Miller said, snatching the phone away from the tech's hand.

There was no facial recognition lock or encryption key to open the phone; it was already on the home screen and ready to use.

Just under the Google search bar at the bottom of the screen were four icons, each indicating what they were: Messenger, Phone, Gallery, and Camera.

Miller touched the Google search bar, and the screen loaded with text from generic searches that had been preprogrammed into the phone by its manufacturer. It did not appear that anyone had used the phone to search the Internet, and even if they had, they could have easily erased their viewing history.

He backed out and clicked the green phone icon. It opened to a numbered keypad. Three words were under the numbers: Keypad, Recents, and Contacts.

Miller touched *Recents*.

The screen opened to a list of phone calls that had come into the phone. The numbers did not have names associated with them. As he scrolled down through the list, he noted that call after call had come into the phone, but none had gone out.

It's a burner phone, Miller realized.

He backed out of the screen and clicked the Message icon. There were more numbers on the Conversations page, but again, no names had been attached to the numbers.

He touched the first number at the top, 717-555-4255, which had come in at 9:22 p.m. yesterday.

Miller quickly went to the first message in the chain and began to read.

717-555-4255: *Hey, babe!*
RUBY-LEE: *Hey, handsome.*
717-555-4255: *You free tomorrow morning?*
RUBY-LEE: *Always free for you, handsome.*
 717-555-4255: *Time? Place?*
RUBY-LEE: *My place. 10:00 am. Work 4 U?*
717-555-4255: *Yup. B there.*

It was Ruby-Lee's burner phone. Miller figured the male stiff inside with his brains blown all over the hardwood floor was the same person who sent her the text message yesterday.

The next message in the chain was a picture message. In the photo Ruby-Lee was sitting in her car. She wore a low-cut top that revealed her ample cleavage, and she had pulled her long, strawberry-blonde hair across her face, seductively.

There was a text message with the picture that read: *I'll be waiting*.

Miller didn't think Ruby-Lee kept her burner phone in her car as a way of hiding it. Instead, he figured she had mistakenly dropped it under the seat before getting out of her car and had not noticed it missing.

But could her murderer be one of the numbers in the phone?

He closed that message chain and went to the one below it with the number 717-555-8585. It had also come in yesterday but at 11:15 a.m.

RUBY-LEE: *We have a problem. Need to talk. Now!*
717-555-8585: *Busy. Talk later.*

RUBY-LEE: *A certain someone came out to see me today. Was asking questions.*
717-555-8585: *I said: talk later.*
RUBY-LEE: *When?*
717-555-8585: *Tonight. When I message you.*

Miller swiped left again, bringing up the time stamp beside each message. The conversation had lasted less than a minute. Still, there were several more messages in the chain. The next one came in at 8:36 p.m. that same evening.

717-555-8585: *Change of plans. Can u meet?*
RUBY-LEE: *I guess?*
RUBY-LEE: *Where? When?*
717-555-8585: *HHS. Side entrance – 9*
RUBY-LEE: *I'll be there.*

HHS? Miller knew it was code for something. But what? There were no other messages following Ruby-Lee's reply.

He went back to the conversation page and pulled up a few more text message chains. Most of the messages asked Ruby-Lee if she was available. Others were sexting texts in which she had sent pictures of herself.

Some of the pictures were of her smiling or dolled up, trying to look sexy. And then there were the lewd pictures of Ruby-Lee, pictures that would have fit perfectly in *Hustler* magazine.

Miller's skin slithered with revulsion at the thought of people sharing her, using her, just to fulfill their twisted sexual needs. He closed the app.

Without names to accompany the numbers, he knew it would be impossible to determine who the texts were from just by looking through the messages. Unless they got lucky, and someone slipped up and used a name.

But Miller doubted that. These were deceptive people looking to get a piece on the side without anyone knowing what they were up to.

They would need to go through the phone service and trace the numbers back to their owners. That was going to take some time.

A disquiet began to slide over Miller. Who was this *certain someone* Ruby-Lee spoke of in the text message?

Miller was positive she was not talking about his and Ross's visit yesterday. Whoever she was referencing had given Ruby-Lee cause for alarm. Miller knew it was useless to speculate.

Speculation leads to mistakes.

He reopened the message chain from 717-555-8585 and read down over it again, only stopping when he got to the message that read: *HHS – 9*.

"You know what HHS stands for?" Miller asked the tech.

The tech hiked his shoulders and made a funny *I-have-no-idea* face.

There was more to be done with the phone. But it would have to be handled by professionals who had experience tracing numbers from a burner phone.

He turned the phone off and slipped it into an evidence bag the tech had, closed, and tagged it.

The tech held something out. "This is what fell out of the sun visor."

Miller took a photograph. It was a picture of Ruby-Lee and her mother, taken in front of their home. Ruby-Lee was young, late teens, wearing her graduation gown.

Her bright eyes and confident smile showed a girl who was looking forward to the future.

What a sad life Ruby-Lee's turned out to be, concluding with a violent ending. What had gone so wrong that she felt she had no other recourse than to turn to prostitution to make a living? Life was unfair that way, Miller knew.

Sometimes one had to play the shit cards they were dealt.

"Miller!" It was Ross behind him.

Miller turned.

"I ran a BG on Mr. Kline. He's married with two kids. No priors. Not even a speeding ticket. Looks like the guy picked the wrong time to cheat on his wife."

Was there ever a good time to cheat on your spouse?

"How'd he get mixed up with Ruby-Lee?" Miller asked, more to himself than to anyone standing in his vicinity.

"Mooresville is ten miles away."

"Maybe Ruby-Lee advertised her services somewhere?"

Miller knew better than that. Ruby-Lee did not advertise. She was a "bar worker." She made physical contact with men.

From the amount of phone numbers in the burner, Miller believed she was in high demand. And, if she provided her clientele with a wide range of sexual services, this alone would have solidified her reputation beyond Hickory Falls.

"No. Someone told Mr. Kline about Ruby-Lee." Miller handed the phone in the evidence bag to Ross.

"It's a burner. Filled with smut to her clients."

"Where was this found?" Ross asked, looking at the phone.

"In the car, under the seat. It looks like she met up with someone last night. There are messages to an anonymous number saying they needed to speak because someone showed up at her place asking questions."

"Where?"

Miller shrugged.

"Don't know. The meeting place was the acronym HHS. Any idea what that means?"

Ross thought for a moment, the muscles in his face contorting.

"No idea."

"We need every call and text message to or from that phone. Contact the cellular company and get the logs."

"I'll get on it."

Miller was riding high with excitement. He could feel they were getting close. But close to what? he wondered.

He was sure once a deeper dive was done on the phone and the numbers, it would link back to some prominent residents within Hickory Falls, maybe even Sheriff Daniel or Terry Graham.

"Something's rotten here, Ross. The day after we start probing into this case, the only person who claimed—falsely, I might add—to have knowledge about what happened that morning ends up executed in her home just before we're about to speak with her."

"Detective Miller," a voice said from behind. Miller and Ross turned to find another male forensics tech standing there.

"This was just recovered."

He passed Miller something already in an evidence bag.

"It was found in the trash can, under the kitchen sink."

Miller took the bag. Inside there was a box. The HO! HO! HO! Christmas wrapping paper had been torn free, and the box was busted open.

Inside, something sparkled under the hot sun—maybe a necklace or a bracelet, Miller couldn't tell.

But it was the tag taped to the paper that grabbed Miller's attention and made his blood turn to ice.

To: Ruby-Lee
From: Terry

NINETEEN

The sun had set by the time Terry returned home. He threw open the truck's door and stepped out into the sweltering evening.

Arching his back, he stretched the stiff muscles that had tightened up on the return ride from Mercersburg.

A white moon burned in the clear sky, casting its glow across the land and throwing nighttime shadows of the trees across the side of the house. The Katydids sung their *'katy-did, katy-didn't'* song from the trees, while the crickets and cicadas created a chorus through the open fields surrounding the farm.

The sounds of a beautiful summer evening, Terry thought.

Closing the truck door, the interior light blinked off, and he started toward the farmhouse. While searching for the front door key, Terry thought he saw a shadowy movement that drew his eyes to the barn, about fifty feet away.

His hand instinctively reached for the .357 tucked into his jeans at the small of his back, but he didn't pull the gun out. Terry saw nothing but the white barn walls illuminated under the moon's light.

He waited.

Sweat trickled down his back and into the crack of his ass.

He listened.

No sounds, other than the nighttime critters amongst the vegetation.

He watched.

No shadowy movements in the still, hot, and muggy air.

Terry's grip on the gun lessened but he did not remove his hand from the butt of the revolver. He started to the house again, his boots crushing on the stone driveway; the occasional stone kicked and bounced in front of him, making a *tick, tick, tick* sound.

He was about to start up the porch steps when another movement, by the cornfield this time, caught his eye.

Terry turned to where he believed he had seen the movement, scanning the moonlit land. This time, he was positive he saw a human shadow disappear into the field next to the barn, the corn masking their presence within its husky embrace.

"Who's over there!" Terry hollered into the night. His voice echoed across the tops of the corn.

There was no reply.

He kept his eyes trained on the area of corn where he thought someone ran into, where he heard the rustling of the stalks slapping at their skin as they shot into the field.

Turning his attention to the barn, the words LEAVE TOWN MOTHERFUCKER seemed to glow under the moonlight; Terry saw no signs that anyone tried to add to the hostile art.

Had someone returned to try and deface his property again, but he spooked them off before they could deface his property more?

"Get your asses off my property!" Terry screamed over the singing of the nighttime bugs. "Or I'll blow a fucking hole in you."

As Terry had expected, there was no reply.

I'm not leaving. This is my home. My home.

He stood for several more seconds searching the dark, studying the corn where he thought the shadow had entered, before turning away and heading up the steps.

If someone was on his property, he was sure he had scared them off. The people who harassed him were cowards. They did not have the balls to accuse him of being a murderer to his face.

Instead, they resorted to hiding in the veil of darkness, using graffiti to try and drive him out of his home.

It would not work. And besides, what's the worst they could do? Paint his barn with more lies and threats, hoping that would scare him away with his tail tucked between his legs.

It's not going to happen.

He would paint over the words as soon as he got to them, just like he had done so many times before.

He unlocked the front door and entered. The house was ungodly warm inside. Terry turned on the lights and made his way into the den and flipped on the air conditioner, the *hum* of the starting compressor rattling the window frame.

He gazed out the side window at the barn and the cornfield beyond. Still, he could see no one creeping around.

The long, emotional day had taken a toll on him, and he suddenly felt the stress in his joints. He turned away from the window and returned to his father's leather smoking chair, sinking down into it with a *sigh*.

The smell of cherry tobacco wafted up around him. The scent reminded him of his dad, reading the evening paper and smoking his pipe after the day's work around the farm was completed.

The room would fill with thick smoke that rose and hung around the ceiling. The burning tobacco smell had been sweet and hot to Terry's young nose.

That seemed like a lifetime ago. Maybe it was another life altogether. Terry did not believe in reincarnation or any of that mumbo-jumbo.

Still, it sure felt like he had lived two lifetimes—one before the murders and the one after.

To think about the good parts of his past was complicated; he needed to keep them at arm's length to complete his hunt. He felt he was getting close to finding the men who altered his life, who shortened Clay, Claire, and Sidney's lives.

He needed the anger and the pain their murders brought; it fueled him, unlike any drug could.

I have my own way of dealing with these things, he had told Horace Gillbanter.

And, Terry guessed, he had always known this to be true.

He had thought long and hard about how he would deal with those who took his family away from him, if ever given the opportunity. Somewhere deep down, where his anger lived, where it grew and festered into a black mass like cancer, Terry understood he had to kill them.

They would get no mercy from him. No pity. No remorse. He would feel nothing when he took their worthless lives, the same way Terry felt nothing when he shot a rabbit or a squirrel for digging up his garden.

Reaching into his shirt pocket, he pulled a cigarette out and lit it. He did not cough. The vaporizer was working.

That's all Terry cared about now; he just needed enough time to see his hunt through until the end.

Terry's thoughts shifted away from his health issue and returned to Angie. He wondered how she was making out with her search.

A sharp pang of guilt sliced into him at deceiving her again, for allowing her to believe that he would someday take her out to dinner, maybe hold her hand, or kiss her.

He wished now he could go back and tell her to forget everything—the search, the dinner talk—forget about him and move on with her life.

Still, he needed Angie's help to find the men he believed were responsible. And when she found them, when that phone rang with the information he required, a ticket would be punched for a one-way ride he was sure he would not be returning from.

And that was all right with him. It was better than the alternative of a slow, painful death by the disease he suspected was consuming his body from the inside out.

He thought back to that night at Clay's house. There had been no kind parting words, no hugs, no 'I love you' between brothers. Only anger. Disappointment. And an insurmountable amount of rage that Terry felt for Clay at that moment.

"Hi, Claire," Terry had said when the door opened that Christmas Eve.

His sister-in-law stood on the threshold wearing a bright red dress that brought out the blue in her eyes and the blonde of her hair.

Clay used to say Claire had doe eyes, and they were what stole his heart. That night, Terry saw what his brother had meant. She looked radiant, luminous with spiritual cheer. She and Clay had just come from Christmas Eve services and were eagerly awaiting Sidney's arrival.

"Hi, Terry. How are you?" Claire asked. She smiled and stepped toward him with her arms stretched out.

"I'm fine," Terry replied, welcoming her warm embrace.

All the ugliness that surrounded Terry, his drinking, his anger, his seedy reputation around town, none of that seemed to bother Claire and she welcomed him into their home with an embrace at the door and a warm smile that always made Terry feel wanted.

Even when Clay was less than hospitable, Claire had always insisted that Terry be present, at least for major family events like holidays or birthday parties.

He guessed Claire had done this because she had no living parents or siblings. She was alone in the world except for Clay and Sidney.

It wasn't a perfect family, far from it, but it was all she had, and she had long ago accepted both the good, and the bad, that came with the last name Graham.

Claire stepped back from the doorway.

"Come in out of the cold."

Clay had come around the corner from the kitchen into the hallway just as Terry stepped into the foyer. He was wearing a black suit with a red tie that matched Claire's dress. He came up beside her. They had always looked good next to one another, like their coupling was somehow predestined.

"Can I get you anything?" Clay asked. His voice sounded strained, as if Claire had told him to be polite.

"A beer. If you have one," Terry said, remembering how much he needed the drink since leaving Ruby-Lee's place.

He was still worked up, his insides jittery with mixed emotions while remembering her little dismissive wave and obligatory smile that was more of a *Fuck You* to Terry than anything else.

Looking back now, Terry realized how stupid he was. He should never have gone to Ruby-Lee's that snowy Christmas Eve, let alone gotten her a bracelet from Walmart in hopes of smoothing things over, to try and save their friendship after his fight at Red's with Jeff and Colin.

Their friendship meant nothing to her.

"You okay?" Claire had asked, sensing Terry's distress.

Terry nodded. A moment of uncomfortable silence filled the room until Terry looked at Clay and said, "Sure could use that beer."

"Oh! Right. Be right back."

Clay turned and headed to the kitchen.

"Let's move into the living room," Claire said.

They stepped out of the foyer and into the living room. A fire was burning in the hearth, and the warmth had felt good on Terry's cold skin. He'd taken a seat on the sofa, across from Claire, who took the love seat.

"What time is Sid due in?" Terry asked.

"I just got a text from her. She's about an hour away. The storm is slowing her down."

Terry nodded. He felt disappointed. He had hoped to see her that evening and give her a big hug. He needed that, after the day he'd had.

Clay returned with some British IPA beer Terry had not heard of and handed it to him.

"So," Clay said as he sat next to Claire, "what did you want to talk to us about?"

Terry took a breath followed by a swig of beer. It puckered his tastebuds.

Though he loved beer and was interested in learning how to make all kinds for his microbrewery, he could never stomach the strong tang of an India Pale Ale—which was fermented for so long the hops lost their fruity flavor and became bitter, causing the beer to taste like rotten grapefruit.

But he took another long pull. His insides were bouncing around, anticipating how Clay and Claire would react to his proposal. The beer helped take the edge off regardless of the taste.

"I know things are not looking so good with the business, Clay," Terry began, choosing his words carefully.

Clay and Claire glanced at one another. Their faces took on a strange, despondent look that made Terry uncomfortable, but he continued. "I want to help out."

"You want to help us?" Clay asked sharply. "Since when do you care about our business?"

His eyes were icy black like a shark's right before it struck and took a swimmer into the sea's dark depths.

Terry shook his head.

"It's not about your video store. There's no saving it at this point."

"Excuse me!" Clay snapped while sitting up on the edge of the loveseat.

"You come into our home and insult what we do for a living and then expect us to listen to your proposal?"

"Relax," Terry snapped back. "I didn't mean anything by it."

He paused to gather his thoughts.

"But the truth is, if you don't get out from under it, it's going to take you down like a rapidly sinking ship. You told me yourself back in November that the business was suffering since high-speed internet came to town, and if things don't turn around, you're going to be forced to close it down. It's just a matter of time."

He paused again. He could feel Clay's eyes burning a hole through him. When he spoke this time, he tried to sound more understanding.

"If it's any consolation to you both, it's not your fault the business isn't as successful as it once was."

"Oh! Well, that's nice of you to say," Clay retorted. "That makes everything better. Thanks, Terry."

Terry bit down on his lower lip. Getting through Clay's stubbornness to see the reality of his and Claire's situation would not be easy.

"I know it's tough—"

"Do you?" Clay cut him off.

More than you realize, little brother, Terry remembered thinking.

"I believe there's an opportunity for us in this town, outside of farming, outside of running a failing—and I am not trying to disrespect both of you—video store. A way to make a lot of money, while at the same time bringing something fresh and unique to Hickory Falls."

Claire and Clay glanced at one another with skepticism.

"And what makes you think this town needs something fresh, let alone will accept it?" Claire asked, looking to Terry.

"This town doesn't know what it needs until it's already here," Terry replied. "Just look at the internet. How many people bitched and moaned when high-speed internet finally came to town?"

"I was one of them," Claire said, raising her hand.

"Sure. But you had a legitimate reason. It has killed your business. There isn't anyone who wouldn't understand your reasoning for not wanting high-speed internet.

"Others in this town just hate change. That's not anything new. But change can be good. And Hickory Falls is changing, whether the old-timers want to admit it or not."

"Okay, Terry, get to the real reason why you're here," Clay shot forth.

"I want to open a bar."

The room grew silent. Clay and Claire stared at him. Their faces were blank, unreadable masks that weighed upon Terry with a heaviness that made his shoulders ache.

"A microbrewery, to be more specific." He held up the beer Clay had given him. "We would make our own beer, harvested from hops grown on our parents' land."

Clay stared at his brother for what seemed like an eternity. When he finally blinked, Terry could have sworn he heard the snap of his dry eyelids.

"You want to open a bar, a microbrewery of all things, in a town where every redneck in a ten-mile radius only drinks Budweiser or Coors?"

Terry nodded.

"Are you insane?"

"I know it sounds crazy, Clay. But I'm telling you this could work."

"It might work, but not here in Hickory Falls. No one around here wants a trendy microbrewery, and the locals are not going to want to drink in a place like that when they have Red's."

"Red's is a shithole that breeds disease every night," Terry said.

"You're part of the disease. Just remember you help spread it by continuing to patronize that place."

Terry eyed Clay with annoyance. He was not seeing things clearly; his love and loyalty to his dying business had clouded his judgment.

"That's my point, Clay. Hickory Falls doesn't have a nice place for people to go. We only have one dive bar, and there's blood on the floor in there every night."

"The rumor is that you caused a lot of that spilled blood," Clay said.

Terry looked away; shame washed over him from his past behavior. But he had expected Clay to bring up his bad reputation. It was only fair. How could Clay and Claire trust working with someone who had handled himself so poorly over the years?

"That's true. I've had my share of problems at Red's, but—"

"But what?" Clay interjected. "You come to us with this… this… idea and expect us to grovel over it. You still won't accept responsibility for how you've behaved for the last thirty-five years of your life."

"Clay… ease up," Claire said with a soft tone.

Terry shook his head.

"Of course I accept responsibility for my actions."

"But you never learn from them," Clay said.

"You remember the old hardware store on the square?" Terry asked, ignoring his brother.

"Sure."

"It's for sale. It would make the perfect place for a microbrewery. We'd have enough space to create beers in the rear and have room in the front for a bar and seating area.

"Unlike Red's, we could offer food—pub food like burgers and wings. We could create our own specials like the Hickory Falls Burger. I know that's a lame example, but you get my point.

"That's why I came to both of you. I think we can do this together, as a team."

"You want us to…" Clay swallowed, looked at Claire, and then back to Terry and said, "… be partners with you."

Terry nodded.

"I know you own the video store building. If you sell it, you could take the money, use it for bills, and pay Sid's tuition while we work on getting the bar up and running.

"I'll put the down payment on the old hardware store, pay for the renovations needed, liquor license, the fermentation tanks, along with supplies to make the beer the first year—until the hops are harvestable the following year."

"And where would you be getting this money, Terry?" Clay asked condescendingly. Terry remembered Clay looking him up and down as if he were eyeing a bum with his handout.

"It's not like you're rolling in money just to throw some at a risky business idea."

"I've been holding off telling you this for a while. Mostly because I thought you would be upset."

He paused, sipped the beer, and replaced it on the stand.

"I've been talking to land developers interested in building a new condo complex. I'm thinking about selling off some of the farmland to them."

Clay stared at him uncomprehendingly. The look was enough to have sent chills up Terry's spine.

"You're… you're selling off Mom and Dad's farm?" Clay asked slowly, fear shaking his words.

"No. I'm only planning on selling a few acres of land."

"How much is a few acres?" Clay asked sharply.

"Just thirty-five."

"Oh! Just thirty-five acres, honey," Clay said, tapping Claire on the thigh. She glanced from Clay to Terry, worry set deep in her big blue eyes.

"No big deal. Just sell off over half the land our parents worked their asses off for, so he can try some hare-brained business venture."

"It's not like that, Clay," Terry said, shaking his head defiantly.

"I've thought about this for a long, long time. Farming isn't what it was when Mom and Dad first started. I can no longer compete against corporate farming. If I don't do something now, I risk losing the farm altogether. I don't want that—for any of us. My plan is to keep the land we would need to grow our own hops, helping to cut down on the cost of creating beers."

"Oh, you thought this all out, I see," Clay spat back with a roll of his eyes.

Of course, Terry had not figured everything out. Hell, he hadn't even put together a business plan. Why would he have? Until the hardware store closed, he had only been toying with the idea, an idea he now hoped Clay and Claire would help make a reality.

Claire was less aggressive in her response, which Terry was grateful for.

"Do you know anything about creating beers, Terry? For that matter, do you know anything about running and managing a bar?"

"No. But I already know how to grow crops, and I'll learn what I don't know about hops. I'm good with that kind of stuff, always have been.

"Same with the beers—I'll learn. It can't be that hard. And you both have experience running a business. What I figure is this: if we go into this together, it would be a win for everyone."

"Not a bar," Clay shot at him. "Running a bar is totally different than running a video store."

"So what we don't know, we'll learn," Terry said, excitement rising in his voice.

"This could be lucrative for all of us. These developers are planning a sprawling complex with over one hundred fifty condos. With that comes a lot of new people to Hickory Falls—young people who don't want to go to a place like Red's."

Clay sat back on the loveseat. His face was red. Fumes of anger drifted off him and filled the room.

Terry had known in that very moment that Clay wanted nothing to do with his microbrewery, or him for that matter.

"I'm sorry, Terry," Claire said, her voice remorseful. "We just can't do something like this. Running a successful business takes more than an idea, some money, and good intentions."

"You don't think it would work, is what this boils down to."

"No," Clay sat up. "What it boils down to is you." He jabbed a finger at Terry.

"You're now feeling the pinch, just like us, and you're trying to save your own ass."

"That's not true. Not at all," Terry said honestly.

"The hell it's not. You've only ever been concerned about one person—you."

"That's bullshit!"

"Is it? Where was your support for our store in the last twenty years? I never once heard a good word come from your mouth about it. You've never supported your family, Terry, so quit coming off so self-righteous, because you suck at it.

"Now, you come in here with this stupid idea, hoping we'll go all in with you. That's low, taking advantage of our situation. You should be ashamed of yourself."

Terry had shot to his feet at that moment. He was not going to sit there and listen to his brother badmouth him.

He had come with good intentions, hoping to start not just a new business, but a new life, one where they all were included, one that would maybe fix their frayed relationship.

But Terry guessed he should have known better; his past followed him around like a bad habit, and there wasn't anything he could do to change it, not even in his brother's eyes.

"I understand," Terry said quietly. "I'll see myself out." He rose and hurried for the door.

"Terry…" Claire called after him.

Terry threw open the door and headed back down the walkway to his truck parked on the street.

"Stick to what you're good at, Terry—throwing shit and getting drunk," Clay said, suddenly behind him as he neared his pickup.

"Fuck you!"

Terry spun around, jabbing his finger in his brother's face this time.

"You want to point fingers at me for not being there for our family. Where were you, Clay? You ran off to college when Mom and Dad were struggling to keep the farm. I stayed and worked my ass off to keep it from folding to those corporate assholes while you were pushing pencils for good grades. And I'm still working my ass off to keep it."

"Save it for one of your bar friends. You know as well as I do, if it wasn't for Mom and Dad, bailing you out time and time again, including giving you the farm so you had a place to live when they decided to retire, you wouldn't have a pot to piss in or a window to throw it out of.

"And don't blame me for the decision I made to better myself. We all make our own choices in life. I made mine. You made yours."

"I don't need to listen to this." Terry turned away and rounded the front of the truck.

"Yeah. You don't need to listen to anyone. No one tells Terry Graham what to do—no one. He's Mr. Tough Guy. Mr. Big Mouth. Not listening to anyone is what got you into the situation you currently find yourself in, Terry. You're a failure as a brother and as a son. Dad and Mom both told me how disappointed they are with the way you turned out."

Terry quickly spun on his heels, flew back around the front of the pickup, and got into Clay's face. His fist had been clenched so tight that he later noticed his nails had dug into his palm, creating black and blue crescent shapes in the flesh.

He had wanted to punch Clay so badly that night, beat him until he was nothing but a bloody pulp on the sidewalk.

But Clay stood his ground. He was no longer the cowering little boy Terry could intimidate; he wasn't scared of standing up to his big brother.

Clay's eyes slowly moved down to Terry's closed fist and rose just as slow back up to meet Terry's eyes, wild with anger. When Clay spoke again, his voice was softer, measured; he was in control of the situation.

"You going to hit me, Terry? Beat me up like when we were kids? Ya'know, when I was in school, most of my friends looked up to their big brothers. Talked about them like they were rock stars. Not me, though. I was ashamed to admit I had a big brother.

"And this, this right here, how you're acting now, is why Claire and I would never go into business with you. Why we will never be closer to you than we are, why we will never be a family.

"Your anger, Terry, your outbursts, your internal rage, I don't know where it comes from, why you have it, but you have brought nothing but heartache to this family."

Clay paused, allowing what he said to sink into Terry's thick skull.

"But that's your cross to bear, not ours."

Terry had nothing to say. He turned away, rounded the front of the pickup, climbed into his truck, and drove off.

For the first time in years, he had felt the warm sting of tears mist over his eyes as he sped out of Shady Pines and back onto Main Street.

Terry's eyes blinked open. *What a way I left things.*

Tears stung the corners and his throat pulled tight with remorse, just like they had that night nine years ago.

He wanted to let the tears flow, allow them to cleanse the hurt from his aching soul, but he couldn't. Not yet.

A flicker of orange light caught Terry's attention, snapping him out of his thoughts. He slowly rose from the chair and walked to the window and gazed across the shadowy night at the barn. He did not see anyone or anything that could have made the light.

But he could have sworn he'd seen a flash near the top of the barn, almost like someone was in the hayloft striking a match.

Just then, a lick of orange flame shot out from under the barn's metal roof and curled up around the lip like a fiery mitten and took hold.

The barn's on fire!

Terry sprang from the window and hurried out into the hallway. Moving to the front door, he ripped it open and charged out onto the porch.

Something heavy and hard connected across his upper back, just below his neck, making a dull *plunk* sound of wood meeting human flesh.

Pain shot through him in a white-hot flash. A husky grunt worked its way from between his clamped teeth. He fell forward and tumbled down the steps into the gravel driveway.

He rolled a few feet from the porch before finally coming to a rest on his back. Dirt and dust that had kicked up around him and quickly settled in his eyes, causing them to burn and water.

He tasted earth on his tongue, dry and grainy, that turned his saliva into a thick, muddy paste.

Rolling over onto his side, facing the house, Terry tried to rub the dirt from his eyes when...

A movement!

A blurry, dark figure hurried down the porch steps with something long in his right hand. Maybe it was a baseball bat. Terry couldn't be sure; it was like his vision was smeared with Vaseline.

He tried to get to his feet, but the shot across the back had knocked something in his head off-balance.

Everything around him became swimmy and rippled, like standing on a boat while out fishing, and it began to teeter. He fell back into the dirt, facedown. His eyes burned so bad now that he could barely think of anything but the irritation. His cheeks were stained with tears.

Terry knew he could not stay down. He had to fight his attacker off. Despite the discomfort and slushy mind, he forced himself up onto his hands and knees, swayed to the right, but caught himself before he went over again.

Suddenly, a booted foot slammed into his left side, clipping his ribs.

Pain shot through him like a lightning strike and the air was driven from his lungs. An *ufff* sound seeped from his lips.

He went down into the rocky driveway. Dust kicked up around his face, catching in his throat. Terry coughed. His lungs screamed.

Still, he tried to push himself up, but he was knocked back onto his stomach when he was kicked dead center in the back, between the shoulder blades.

Another shot of pain erupted inside; this one traveled up into his skull, pinching the nerves with searing hotness that made his right eye spasm.

Whoever attacked him pressed their foot into the middle of his back, pinning him to the ground.

With the added weight on his back, his lungs felt as if they were being compressed into pancakes, and he was only able to pull narrow draws that barely allowed him to get a breath.

"Listen up, murderer," a male voice from above him spoke.

"You're makin' lots of folks uncomfortable in town with your recent visits. You're not wanted in Hickory Falls. Do yourself and the rest of us a favor and leave. Just get out."

"Fu-ck… y-you," Terry groaned dryly, his breath kicking out a plume of dust as he spoke.

The foot was removed from Terry's back. He turned to see who had attacked him but was met with the heel of a boot instead.

The blow to the side of his skull set fireworks of all colors and shapes off behind his eyes. He fell limp back to the hard earth with his head spinning and pounding with each heartbeat.

He could feel the sting of a laceration at his hairline and warm blood begin to run down the side of his face.

"Not so tough now, are you?" the voice said sardonically. Terry thought he recognized the voice, had heard it recently, but his mind was drawing a blank as to who it belonged to.

"Get out, murderer. This is your last chance. Next time we're going to set your goddamn house on fire, with you in it."

"We need to go!" Terry heard another voice say nearby.

"The whole barn's gone up."

He heard several pairs of feet running across the stone driveway, though he had trouble deciphering how many people were there. Maybe two. Maybe three.

Then the heavy rumble of a diesel engine firing cut across the hot air. Doors slammed. Tires peeled out. Gravel kicked up. Dust floated over him, enveloping him as the truck sped off into the night.

Terry rolled over onto his side, feeling blood running down the side of his face and into his left eye. It stung and burned worse than the dirt had.

He tried pushing it away with grimy fingers, but there was so much blood, as thick as oil, leaking from his skull that his efforts were futile.

Get up! Get up!

It hurt to think. But Terry couldn't just lay there bleeding, useless. He could feel the heat from the fire on his skin now, smell the burning wood, and hear the roaring of the flames.

Maybe you can still save the barn. There's still time. But you have to get up, Terry.

With a tremendous amount of effort, he got one knee under him. Then an elbow. Then the other knee and the other elbow until he was on all fours.

He stayed that way for a moment, watching the blood drip off his nose and form a small pool; it looked black against the orange flames that lit the entire area around him.

Slowly he sat back on his knees and looked at the barn...

And his heart sank.

Somewhere behind him, the sounds of fire sirens split the hot air.

But there was no saving the barn.

It was totally engulfed in flames.

TWENTY

Terry had been out to see Ruby-Lee, Miller thought after the gift was found in the trash. *He knew it was her voice on the 9-1-1 call. Was Terry who Ruby-Lee refenced in her text messages?*

Except the name on the tag alone proved nothing at the moment. The only way to determine who gave her the gift was to match prints.

Two sets were lifted from the box. Miller figured one set was Ruby-Lee's. The second belonged to whoever gave it to her—maybe Terry Graham.

The prints were being run through the system. Miller had yet to hear back from anyone.

He returned home around four-thirty that afternoon, completely exhausted.

Falling onto the sofa, he closed his eyes and had just begun to drift off into the quiet blackness of a nap when his cell phone rang.

Miller shot up from the sofa and grabbed the phone from the coffee table.

Maybe it's the lab with a hit on the prints, he thought, hopeful. But it was Trisha calling.

Miller sighed. He was not in the mood to deal with her right now, but suspected the call was about the fallout after his daughter's fight.

"I just got off the phone with the investigating officer. The McCall's are pressing charges against Luna. Henry, they're going to try and sue us," Trisha machine-gun-fired at him as soon as the call connected.

Miller took a long breath and slowly let it out between his teeth.

"Just try and stay calm, Trisha. We'll get through this."

"You need to do something."

And what am I supposed to do? Miller wanted to scream at her.

His hands were tied, and he had no say in the matter, even if he was a state trooper.

"How's Luna?" he asked instead.

"She's okay. Worried that this could ruin her chances at a scholarship, college—her future. You really need to do something," she repeated again as if saying it over and over was going to snap Miller into action.

Miller closed his eyes and shook his head. Trisha wasn't listening to him. There wasn't anything to stop what was coming their way.

The best he could do was find out the facts, see what the charges against Luna were going to be, and deal with them as they came. Perhaps Luna could help him understand what happened better.

"Is Luna free tonight?"

"Sure? Why?"

"I want to hear her side of the story. Think I could swing by, pick her up?"

"If you want. But I don't know how much you're going to get. She's been pretty withdrawn; spent the last two days in her room, alone. I'm worried about her."

"Let me talk to her. She'll open up for me. You know how close we are."

"I do."

Miller heard the disappointment in Trisha's voice. She had wanted to mold Luna into a miniature version of herself.

But Luna was too much like her father: strong-willed, bullheaded, and independent. No one, not even her mother, would tell Luna how she should live her life.

"I'm coming over."

Thirty minutes later, Miller pulled to a stop outside of what was once his home. The front door opened on the small stone rancher, and Luna and Trisha came out.

Luna looked pissy with a frightening inward scowl, a trait Trisha had passed onto their daughter, and one Miller was familiar with.

Miller decided not to bring up the fight. Luna needed time to decompress, to unwind from her mother's constant worries and controlling nature.

He was sure Trisha was about to come unglued. She liked to have control over everything and everyone. This situation was way out of her control—out of either of their control.

Luna opened the door of his car, got in, and slammed it hard enough that the car shook. Miller said nothing, but he saw Trisha's eyes narrow at their daughter.

He felt they might have been arguing before he arrived but decided not to ask.

He was willing to listen if Luna wanted to talk to him about home troubles with her mom. But unlike Trisha, who always told Luna how awful he was, he would not badmouth her in front of his daughter, even if she deserved it.

At the end of the day, Trisha was still Luna's mother, and Luna needed to respect and love her, the good and the very bad.

"I'll have her back before too long," Miller said.

"No hurry. I think she can use some time away from the house," Trisha replied.

"And from you," Luna mumbled under her breath.

Miller heard the snarky remark, but Trisha had not. It was an excellent time to get going.

"Okay. See you soon," he said, pulling the car away from the curb.

They drove for a half-mile in silence before Miller asked, "Where would you like to get something to eat?"

"I don't care." Luna crossed her arms and looked out the window.

"Burger King? That's always been your favorite."

"Sure."

The closest Burger King was about five miles away, so it would give Luna some time to cool off and come around to the idea of opening up to him. He wouldn't pressure her. She would talk when she was ready.

Miller parked the car in the Burger King parking lot. They went inside, ordered their food, and took a seat by the window. The restaurant was empty, so they could eat and chat in private.

If Luna wanted to, that was. If not, that was okay with Miller. Just being with her was enough for him, and he hoped some time away from home, from her mother, would at least clear her head and get her thinking straight.

Get her to open up to him.

They ate their food in silence, and it wasn't until they were nearly finished that Luna finally spoke.

"Dad?"

"Yeah?"

"Do I look like a boy?"

Miller studied his daughter and wondered why in God's green earth she would think she looked like a boy. She looked so much like Trisha that it scared him.

"Where's this coming from, honey?" Miller asked, already knowing the answer, but he wanted to get her talking.

She lifted her shoulders, and her eyes drifted back to her tray where a few fries and smeared ketchup remained. She picked up a fry, dipped it in the ketchup, bit half of it off, and chewed it slowly.

Miller realized she was stalling, trying to find the right words to express herself.

"You know where it's coming from."

"Regan McCall."

She nodded.

"They're just sneakers, Luna. That doesn't make you a boy."

Luna put the rest of the fry in her mouth and chewed.

"Besides, since when do you care what anyone thinks of you?"

Luna might have looked like her mother, but she was her father's daughter through and through. Miller didn't give a fuck what someone thought about him, and he had believed that his daughter was the same way.

But maybe he had misjudged Luna. Maybe her skin was thinner than his.

"I don't care what people think of me."

"Then why did you punch Regan?"

Her eyes rose and quickly fell back to the tray just as fast. Miller thought he saw a slight smirk wrinkle her lips, but she held it back. Luna had felt some justification for her actions.

"She deserved it."

"Did she?"

"You sound like Mom."

"Is that what you two were arguing about before I got here tonight?"

She shrugged. And with it, Miller knew he was right.

"I thought you'd be on my side, unlike Mom."

"I am on your side. I'm just trying to figure out what happened."

"Because that's your job, right? To figure out what happened."

Miller sat back on the bench but kept his stare on his daughter. Trisha's words came out of his daughter's mouth in a backhanded slap.

"I'm going to let that one slide, Luna, given the circumstances. But I'm only going to ask you one more time what really happened. Did Regan deserve to be punched? What did she do to you to cause you to lash out that way?"

Luna picked up another fry and repeatedly dipped it in the ketchup, but she did not put it in her mouth.

"You know, your mother wants me to get involved. According to her, the family wants to press assault charges on you. But here's the thing, Luna, I don't want to be involved."

Luna's face grew worrisome.

"You know why I don't want to be involved? Because this looks bad on me, and more importantly, you."

"Me? Why me?"

"You are the daughter of a state police detective. You get into trouble, Daddy pulls a few strings, and bam-o, you're free to go with maybe a stern warning and a slap on the wrist. You see how that looks to the outside world?

"It doesn't just reflect badly on me and my character, but it makes you look like an entitled brat. You want to go through the rest of your life with that stigma on you?"

"No."

"So, if you want my help, then you have to come clean—I mean the I'm-just-out-of-the-washer-and-still-sudsy-clean—with me."

A small smile cracked Luna's stone face. Miller was happy to see his daughter smile for the first time that evening, but he had not meant anything he said to be funny.

He was dead serious. If he was going to stick his neck on the line, his career, he needed to know what happened that caused Luna's outburst that resulted in a girl ending up with a broken nose.

"So," he leaned onto his elbows, "what happened, Luna?"

"I was down at the soccer field practicing when Regan and her friends came over. Regan was picking on me," Luna began.

"Calling me Booger Queen and T.B."

"T.B?"

"Tomboy. She said I was built like a boy because of... well... because I don't have..."

Miller nodded that he understood and saw the relief play across Luna's face that she did not have to spell it out to her father.

This girl, Regan, was calling Luna a boy because Luna was not yet as developed as most of the other girls her age. Instead, Luna's frame was lean and long from years of playing soccer.

And, if Luna took after her mother like she had with everything about her appearance, Miller knew she would keep that build.

"Go on," Miller said. "Tell me the rest."

"I was changing from my cleats into my sneakers—the Jordans you just bought me—when Regan tried to pour a bottle of soda in them."

"So you punched her in the face?"

"It didn't happen quite like that, but yeah."

"How did it happen?"

"I grabbed ahold of her arm, just as she was going to pour the soda into my shoes. But when she tried to pull away, she turned and slapped me in the face. It stung. My eyes started to fill with tears, not out of pain, but embarrassment, Daddy."

Luna's eyes misted over.

"I heard laughter from some of the other kids. Something snapped. And before I knew it, she was on the ground, crying, with blood running out of her nose and onto her white blouse."

"She hit you first?"

Luna nodded. A thick tear ran down her cheek.

"What then?"

"Regan started bawling. She was bleeding a lot. Her friends got her off the ground and took her away.

"By the time I got home, Mom had already gotten a call that I had been in a fight, and a police officer was coming to the house to question me."

"Did her friends back up her story?"

"Of course they did."

"Was there anyone else around? Anyone that can back up your side of the story?"

"A few other kids."

"Other kids saw what happened?"

"Yeah."

Miller sat back in his seat, thinking about what to do next. They had to play this smart if they wanted to get the charges on Luna dropped.

"What happens now? Am I going to go to jail?"

"No, honey. You're not going to jail," Miller said, reaching out and squeezing his daughter's hand reassuringly.

"I'm sorry, Daddy. I didn't mean to hit her. It just happened. I don't know what came over me."

Luna's recall of the events caused Miller to think of Terry Graham. Was it possible that he had blacked out, after speaking with his brother that evening, and murdered his entire family in a fit of drunken rage?

If Luna could hurt someone, there was no question in Miller's mind that a man with a well-known temper could easily find himself in the same situation.

The pain on his daughter's face was enough to shake Miller out of his thoughts and cause his own eyes to grow moist. Childhood was hard enough without a bully to make it worse.

Miller slid into the seat next to his daughter and pulled her into him. She wept into his chest, and he held her trembling body until the crying fit subsided.

When she was done, Miller put his fingers under her chin and lifted her face so she was looking at him.

"We're going to get this sorted out, okay?"

Luna nodded. For the first time that evening, Miller saw the brightness of her eyes flicker on.

He felt his phone buzz twice on his belt. A text message had just come through. He pulled away from Luna and opened the phone. The message was from his partner:

> **ROSS:** *Someone just set Terry Graham's barn on fire and beat him up. He's in the Bedford Memorial Hospital.*

Miller kept his emotions in check as he replaced the phone on his belt. What happened to Terry Graham needed to wait. Luna was more important at the moment.

But he needed to find a way to take care of this issue for his daughter before it went any further.

"Honey, do you know Regan's parent's names?"

"Yeah. Earl and Rose. Why?"

Sinister thoughts of ways to deal with Mr. and Mrs. McCall started to form in Miller's mind.

"What about the names of the kids that can confirm your side of the story?" Miller asked. "Did you know them?"

"Yes."

"Let me have their names."

TWENTY-ONE

Terry had passed out after the burning barn collapsed in on itself. When he came to, he was staring at the ceiling of some strange, dark room.

His head throbbed as if his skull were an eggshell, and his brain was trying to crack through with each heartbeat.

Dirt lingered on his tongue, and fine granules of sand and rock were caught between his teeth. When he tried to swallow, his throat felt like sandpaper. Something plastic was around his face, shooting air up his nose, drying his nostrils.

Where the hell...

Pushing through the discomfort, the disorientation, Terry looked around the strange room. It hurt to move his eyes, causing a stabbing pain behind them that made him wince.

Beyond the darkened wall of the room was a brightly lit hallway. He could hear a soft female voice floating through the air, but couldn't make out what she was saying or which way it was coming from.

How'd I get here?

The mere act of thinking hurt, and Terry had to close his eyes or risk vomiting. He needed to return to the comfort of the black emptiness from which he came.

So he did.

When he woke again, it was still dark in the strange room. The throbbing inside his skull remained, but it had lessened to a piercing, centralized pain. A feeling similar to having a dagger inserted into his skull, just above his left eye.

Someone stood next to his bed. A woman with long, dark hair pulled back into a ponytail. She wore nurses' scrubs and was checking something on a machine monitoring his heart rate and oxygen levels.

I'm in the hospital.

Noticing Terry was awake and watching her, the nurse turned, smiled, and rested a warm hand on his forearm.

"How are you feeling, Mr. Graham?" she asked.

Terry tried to speak, but his mouth was still so dry all he could muster out was one broken word.

"Wat-er."

She picked up a small cup with a straw and placed it between his lips. Terry pulled greedily. The cool water filled his mouth faster than he could swallow it, washing away the grit from his tongue and teeth and the dryness of his throat.

Some water dribbled down his chin and became stuck in his beard. She pulled the straw away before he had his fill and dabbed at his mouth with a paper towel.

"That's enough for the moment. You'll make yourself sick."

Resting his head back on the pillow, Terry felt a burning, stinging sensation, just below his hairline on the left side of his scalp that he had not felt when he came to earlier.

Reaching up, he gingerly touched the tender spot, but the nurse pulled his hand gently away and placed it back on the bed beside his thigh.

"You have ten stitches. Leave it alone."

The words hardly registered in Terry's mind.

"How… how I get here?" he asked instead.

"You were brought in by ambulance."

He tried to recall the ambulance ride. But he had no memory of anything after the barn's roof caved in with a thunderous crack as the thick support beams gave way.

He had felt the hot rush of fiery air on his skin, followed a second later by a gray cloud that exploded from inside the barn and began rolling toward him like a smoke monster, gobbling up everything in its path.

The cloud, filled with dust and debris, had hit him with such force that it had knocked him back onto the ground, where his head had connected hard with the earth. And as the smoke had rolled over him and began to dissipate, he stared up at a glowing orange sky filled with black smoke, just before he lost consciousness and fell into a dark void.

"W-where I am?" He found it hard to speak; his words were a jumbled mess in his mind like a Scrabble board played by a dyslexic, backward and nonsensical.

"Bedford Memorial Hospital."

His eyes drifted away from the nurse's face. She seemed to sense that he had more questions but was having difficulty processing his thoughts.

"You were brought in just after nine this evening. You have a concussion, Mr. Graham. You'll be a little out of it until the swelling in your head goes down. Someone beat you up pretty good. Do you remember any of it?"

Terry slowly nodded. If he moved too fast, he felt the water he'd just drank would come back up.

"The police will be here in the morning to question you. I suggest you get some rest."

His eyes drifted back to her.

"The po-lice? I didn't do… wrong… this time."

She looked at him strangely, but Terry had trouble understanding what her look was about.

"They want to question you about the fire and who attacked you."

She placed her warm hand on his forearm once more and patted it lightly, caringly.

"I can give you something to help you sleep, would you like that?"

Oh, God, yes, please, Terry's mind screamed out, suddenly centered. *Let me go back to the land of blackness.*

Before he knew what was happening, he was returned to the abyss.

When Terry woke for the third time, gray daylight seeped through the curtains. A dark and stormy sky hovered ominously outside.

The pain in his head and behind his eye had considerably subsided and rational thoughts began to form without feeling like his brain was being twisted around like spaghetti on a fork.

The room felt statically charged with the presence of another human being. Lifting his head slightly from the pillow, Terry expected to find the nurse who had been there when he came to earlier.

But someone else was in the room with him.

A man sat on the chair across from his bed, staring out the window, watching the storm clouds lull over the hospital. It took Terry a moment for his disorientation to pass and to recognize the figure.

Trooper Miller.

"What are you doing here?" Terry asked in a raspy voice.

Miller pulled his gaze from the window, stood, and came to Terry's bedside. He asked, "How are you feeling?"

Miller's tone was sincere. Though the trooper had a compassionate side, Terry suspected Miller's visit could be a ploy to trap him into saying something incriminating when he was not processing everything clearly. *Cops are sneaky that way.*

"Like I got my ass handed to me."

"Do you remember anything?"

Terry nodded. The assault, the blazing inferno, flooded his mind, causing the sharp pain above his eye to return.

"Someone was waiting for me when I got home. They set my barn on fire and attacked me when I came out of the house. Hit me over the back and then kicked me in the head when I was down."

"Did you see them?"

Another shot of pain. Terry closed his eyes.

"No. It was dark."

"Did they say anything?"

Terry shook his head. But he remembered every word that had been said. The pain sunk deeper into his gray matter.

"Listen up, murderer," the familiar male voice had said. *"You're makin' lots of folks uncomfortable in town with your recent visits. You're not wanted in Hickory Falls. Do yourself and the rest of us a favor and leave. Just get out."*

It had finally resorted to violence. The same people who despised him from a preconceived notion that he violently murdered his family would resort to violence themselves just to force him out of his home.

Hypocrites.

The town's vengeful nature never ceased to amaze him. But what did he expect when Pastor Garland taught his flock that *an eye for an eye* and *a tooth for a tooth* was acceptable Christian behavior?

"What do you want, Miller?" Terry asked, once the pain subsided enough that he could speak again.

"I want to know why someone attacked you and set your barn on fire."

"Isn't it obvious? I'm the town's booger-man; they want to get rid of me."

"They go from harmless spray painting one day to arson the next?"

"Looks that way, doesn't it?"

Or was it because I was asking questions around town? Terry thought, but he did not offer that information up to Miller.

"What are you really doing here?" Terry asked the policeman.

"I'm afraid I have some more bad news, Terry. My partner and I found Ruby-Lee and one of her tricks dead at her home yesterday."

Terry's eyes shot to Miller. His head screamed out from the sudden motion of his eyes, causing the stabbing pain to nearly blind him. A sickening feeling gripped his chest.

Did Miller suspect him…

"What…" Terry tried to align his thoughts, but his mind was still jaded with pain. He closed his eyes and touched his head.

"What… happened?"

"Someone shot them. Execution style. You know anything about that?"

Terry slowly opened his eyes and leveled his gaze on Miller. He tried not to think about what had transpired at Ruby-Lee's place yesterday. He had already packed it away, compartmentalized it in his mind.

"Why would I know anything about it? I haven't seen Ruby-Lee in nine years."

"You expect me to believe that?"

"I don't give a fuck what you believe or don't believe," Terry snapped.

Miller set his jaw and squared his shoulders with resolve. There was something picking away at him, something he was frothing at the mouth to bring up.

"We found a present. A Christmas present," Miller finally said.

A warmness crept up at the base of Terry's neck. *Play it cool.* He remembered Ruby-Lee throwing the present at his chest. The same present he had smashed flat with his boot, as if it were the last remaining physical attachment to their friendship that needed to be squashed like a venomous spider.

"So."

"This particular Christmas present has your name on it?"

"Does it say 'Terry Graham'?"

"No. Just Terry."

"There must have been other Terrys that Ruby-Lee knew. She got around, ya know."

"She did. But out of all of them, how many would give her a present for Christmas?"

"Are you insinuating that I pulled the trigger, Miller?"

"I'm just wondering whose fingerprints we're going to find on it, Terry."

"Get out," Terry muttered. "Get out and don't come back unless you find out who murdered my family."

Miller nodded and headed toward the door. But he stopped in the threshold and turned back.

"What happened that caused you to lose control of your car, resulting in the death of Melissa Garland?"

Terry closed his eyes again and swallowed deeply. Behind his eyes, Melissa stood in the middle of a sun-glazed field filled with wildflowers. The wind blew through her dark hair. She was smiling and motioned for Terry to join her.

Terry's eyes snapped open. *Not yet.*

"It was an accident. That's all," Terry replied, feeling the sting of tears.

"Everyone in town thinks differently. They think you had something to do with her death, just like they believe you had something to do with Clay, Claire, and Sidney's."

Terry did not bother to respond.

"Fine. Have it your way." Miller was about to turn and walk away when Terry spoke.

"I was in love with her," Terry began. "And she was in love with me."

"You were dating?" Miller asked unsurprised, almost as if he had already suspected as much.

"I knew Melissa from church when my mother used to take Clay and me on Sundays before I stopped attending and refused to believe anything that came out of that silver-tongued charlatan's mouth.

"One afternoon—this would have been in early '05— Melissa came out to the farm to buy fresh fruits and vegetables when I still ran my little stand in the summer. We struck up a conversation. There was an instant connection, a spark that I had never felt before or since with anyone.

"Her visits to the farm became more frequent. Soon we started chatting on the phone and that led to us meeting in secluded spots, away from the prying eyes of the town. We were like two teenagers sneaking off to the woods to fool around. Always made me think of the Bob Seger song 'Night Moves.'"

Terry smiled. "Our relationship became intimate..."

He sucked in a shaky breath that clicked in his chest.

"I never thought a girl like Melissa, a pastor's daughter nonetheless, would be interested in a loathsome creature like me. But Melissa saw something in me that I did not, and still do not, see in myself."

Terry rubbed his hand over his face, pushing away the tears that had begun to run down his cheeks.

"But I know this much: I would have changed every bad habit I had for her."

Terry paused again and looked up at Miller. "But that's the thing about bad habits—they're hard to break and resurface just when you believe you have a lid on them.

"That night, I met her in the small alley beside the church so no one would see her getting into my car. She hadn't told her parents about our relationship yet, and if word leaked to Pastor Garland that we were together, before she was able to tell him herself, she would've been shunned from his church and labeled a harlot by the entire congregation."

"What kind of church does that to one of their own?" Miller asked his voice nothing more than a whisper.

"The kind of church Pastor Garland reigns over. He appears holier-than-thou on the outside, but what he says is spoken with the Devil's tongue."

Terry reached over and drew the straw in the cup to his lips and took a sip of water.

"Looking back, I'm not so sure if Melissa telling her father about us would have made a difference.

"Pastor Garland disliked me, even when I was a kid. I saw how he was misleading folks, lying to them while hiding behind his misguided fire-and-brimstone sermons. I refused to blindly follow him, as so many others around Hickory Falls have."

Terry paused and touched the tender spot on his head, as if checking to see if the stitches were still there—they were. He winced, then continued.

"Melissa and I went to the Twin Pines Motel that night. I had rented us a room. I had flowers, chocolates, and champagne. All the trimmings for our romantic evening together are tucked away in the trunk.

"When we got inside the motel room, the place was filthy and filled with cockroaches. Typical me, I blew my stack and went into a tirade—remember what I said about bad habits?

"Melissa tried to calm me down, tried to tell me it wasn't my fault, and that we could go someplace else. After screaming at the motel's owner and demanding my money back—which I never got—I dumped everything in the trash can and sped out of the parking lot, angrier than before.

"Everything was ruined. I was heading back toward town to take Melissa back to the church so she could get her car. I was steaming, cussing up a storm, threatening to go back and beat the shit out of the owner for stealing my money.

"Melissa was still trying to calm me down. *'It's alright, Terry. It's alright. Just calm down,'* she kept saying. She was scared. I could see it in her eyes. She'd never seen that side of me come out before.

"And then something happened, as if God himself had come down from the sky and flicked the front of my Firebird with his finger. The wheel suddenly snapped to the right, wrenched out of my hands. The car shot off the road and went down the embankment, and..."

Terry dropped his head to his chest. Inside he felt a tremor pass through his core as the thoughts of what happened next played through his mind.

"I remember looking over at Melissa, as the car was heading down the embankment. Her eyes were wide with terror, her face pale against the dashboard's lights, cemented with the shocking truth at what she saw awaiting us at the bottom.

"I remembered thinking: *You just ruined the best thing in your life.* And then, the impact. And like that"— Terry snapped his fingers—"she was yanked from my sight. From my life. There one moment, gone the next."

Terry looked at Miller. "She wasn't wearing her seatbelt. And do you want to know why?"

Miller shrugged.

"Because she didn't believe in them. She had been taught that God would always keep her safe, that he only punishes the wicked, the sinful. Old Testament bullshit her father pumped into her head since she was a child."

"I'm sorry," Miller said thickly.

Terry fell silent for a long moment.

"Turned out the left front tie rod on the Firebird broke, resulting in the steering wheel yanking to the right and causing the car to shoot off the road and down the embankment and into that fucking tree.

"But that wasn't a good enough reason for the people of Hickory Falls. Most felt there must've been something nefarious going on, since Melissa was with *me* and in my car when she was killed. That was when the rumors began. I'm sure you heard them, or you wouldn't have asked me about Melissa."

Terry met Miller's gaze. He nodded.

"It's all bullshit. Like I said, it was an accident."

"Why didn't you just tell the sheriff's department the truth?"

"I did! But no one wanted to believe me because of my past—the temper, the drinking, the fighting, my sharp tongue, and the take-no-shit attitude. It all came back to bite me in the ass and continues to bite me in the ass now.

"So, everyone in town, including the sheriff's department, began to point fingers and accused me of things that weren't true. How outlandish and absurd to think such a thing."

Terry shook his head slowly. "Even after the Claims Adjusters report came back confirming that the accident was, in fact, caused by a broken tie rod, it was quietly swept under the carpet. They just couldn't accept the truth.

"But I know the real reason why they continued to refuse to believe, even after documents proved there was no wrongdoing on my part.

"They were constantly being spoon-fed a lie from a master manipulator high on his pulpit, and they all lapped it up like babies. It was easier to believe it than to accept the truth, that Melissa and I were actually in love."

"The Claims Adjuster's report was missing from the sheriff's department file," Miller said.

"Interesting how things go missing inside that place, isn't it?" Terry replied.

Miller nodded.

Terry could tell ideas were working their way around in Miller's brain now. He wasn't sure if that was good or bad for him, but he'd got Miller thinking, that was for sure.

"I'll see you around, Terry," Miller said and walked out of the room.

"Yeah. See you around."

About an hour later, the day nurse helped Terry out of bed and into the sitting chair by the window. He was feeling better than he had when he first woke. The headache was still there but duller than before.

However, the cut just below his hairline hurt like hell. He had a hard time not reaching up and rubbing it.

When he was settled into the chair, the nurse told him the doctor would be in to see him shortly. He only had to wait fifteen minutes before the doctor came through the door, introducing himself as Dr. Aahan Kharti.

"Mr. Graham, how are we feeling?" Dr. Kharti asked, checking Terry's chart.

"Better," Terry replied. "Headache's almost gone."

"Feeling dizzy, nauseated, anything like this?"

"Nope. Just a dull headache now."

"Look at me, please." Kharti pulled a penlight out of his white jacket and shined it into Terry's eyes.

"You have a concussion, Mr. Graham. But I do not believe you will have any lasting damage. However, you will have a scar where the laceration occurred. You're also badly bruised across your back, just below your neck, where you were struck. Ice and pain medication will help with the discomfort."

"That's positive."

"Yes." He cleared his throat, turned, and slid another chair in front of Terry, and took a seat.

"But there is another matter we must discuss."

"Oh?"

"When you were brought into the ER this morning, the doctors did not know to what extent your internal injuries were. An X-ray was done."

Kharti paused, studied Terry closely as if he were looking at a dead man walking.

"The X-rays showed a mass on your right lung that we are confident is cancerous."

Terry felt an internal shudder quake through his entire body. His eyes fell away from Kharti.

"How long do I have?" Terry asked quietly after a moment of internal contemplation of his entire life, which seemed to pass through his mind in a millisecond.

"We do not know the exact extent of the spread of your cancer from the X-ray alone. More tests will have to be done."

He had suspected something significant was wrong. Even suspected it might be cancer. But hearing what he long feared probable was something altogether different now that it was a reality.

"I know this is difficult to process, Mr. Graham—"

"If you had to guess, how long, Doc? Don't bullshit me, please?"

Kharti studied him again, searching his eyes. Maybe to see if Terry was thinking about doing anything stupid, like harming himself.

"I could not—"

"I have a few things I need to see finished. I just need a little time. How long? Days? Weeks? Months? What?"

"Well… with treatments, chemotherapy—"

"Without any of that?" Terry pushed. "How long?"

There was a look of shock on Kharti's face.

Cancer or not, he was going to find out who murdered his family.

"Without treatment, your survival rate quickly diminishes."

"How long?"

"With the size of the mass on your lung and without treatment, I would give you a few months to live at best. But with—"

"Thanks, Doc."

"Mr. Graham, I think you need to take some time and process this. It's a lot to accept."

Terry nodded. But he had already packed his illness away in his mind, just like he had packed away what he had done at Ruby-Lee's house yesterday after her trick lunged for his gun.

"When can I get out of here?"

"Mr. Graham…"

"When?"

"Today. This afternoon. But I would highly suggest you speak with your doctor and get treatments set up right away."

"I appreciate your concern, Doc. But right now, I just need you to release me."

"Very well." Dr. Kharti stood and left the room without saying anything else to him.

Terry turned and looked out the window to the overcast sky that filtered his room into a sickly gray hue.

He was the one in the pale light now.

TWENTY-TWO

When Miller got back to the barracks, Ross was on the phone. He swiveled around in his chair and shot him a thumbs-up sign.

Something good was happening. The room was charged with positive electricity.

"Hey, Lori, Miller just walked in. You mind if I put you on speaker so he can listen in?"

A pause.

"Perfect."

Ross clicked the speaker icon on his phone and laid it on the desk.

"Can you hear us okay, Ms. Dell?"

"Yes, I can hear you fine."

"We're ready when you are," Ross said.

Miller sank into his desk chair. His eyes burned from the lack of sleep and his body felt tight, like all his muscles had cramped at once.

He'd spent several uncomfortable hours the night before, tossing and turning in bed before going out onto the sofa to watch television, hoping it would take his mind off the Graham case, but more so, what was happening with Luna.

He was worried about her. Not just because of the possible charges, but what this could do to her mentally.

This thing needs to go away so I can focus fully on the Graham case.

"Let's start with Mr. Kline," Dell said. "I found defensive wounds on his hands, wrists, and arms. There were abrasions on his elbows and knees, which most likely happened during his struggle with the killer.

"His nose was broken, along with his right thumb. He was shot with a .38 Special caliber round—I pulled the same size slug out of Ms. Huckster. Like we assumed, Mr. Kline was shot in the back of the head. The bullet exited the front of the skull, just above the right eye."

"Sounds like he put up a fight," Ross said.

"Yes, it does appear so."

Dell paused. Miller could hear shuffling papers.

"As for Ms. Huckster: I found some discoloration around her throat; it appears, at least to me, that someone grabbed her by the neck, leaving black and blue marks on both sides of her throat. Whoever did it had a massive hand. It nearly tripled mine.

"The skin on her knees, and on the heels of her feet, was peeled back, and small wooden fibers were found embedded in the flesh. Those wooden fibers match the flooring of her home."

"What could cause that?" Ross asked.

"I believe whoever took ahold of her either forced her backward or dragged her across the floor before killing her. She had dug her feet into the floor, trying to stop them."

"Did you find any other defensive wounds on her?" Miller asked.

"I did not. Ms. Huckster's cause of death was the shot to the head. The one in her heart is where I pulled the .38 slug out—like I suspected yesterday, at the crime scene, this happened postmortem."

Miller was happy to hear that Dell had been able to recover a bullet. But without the weapon to match the slug to, it was useless at the moment.

"Anything else?" Ross asked.

"No. That covers everything I have."

After thanking the coroner, Ross hung up the phone and looked across the desk at Miller.

"You look like hell. You get any sleep last night?"

"Not really. I got up early this morning and drove to Bedford to speak with Terry before coming in."

"Oh? You should have called me, I would've rode along."

"Thanks. But I needed the peace and quiet, the drive, to clear my head."

"Understand."

But you really don't.

"So, what happened with Terry Graham?" Ross asked.

Miller sat back in his chair, chewing his bottom lip, lost in thought. Terry's story about what happened the night of the crash, and Melissa Garland's death, made him question everything he was starting to believe about the man.

And what happened to the Claims Report? Why wasn't it in the file? Had someone inside the sheriff's department removed it before handing it over to them?

To Miller, it was odd that not once, but twice, evidence that might have exonerated Terry went missing from the Hickory Falls Sheriff's Department.

"Miller?"

"What?" Miller blinked his eyes and looked at Ross.

"I asked how'd it go with Terry Graham?"

"He denied that the Christmas gift came from him."

"Of course he did. You don't believe him, do you?"

Miller thought about the question for a long moment before he answered.

"I don't know."

"What about the fire?"

"Said someone set his barn on fire and beat him up. Looks like they were trying to scare him out of town."

"Did he get a look at them?"

Miller shook his head.

"Convenient."

"How so?"

"The same day we find Ruby-Lee and her banging buddy murdered, Terry Graham is assaulted. It could be a cover to throw us off. Get us back on his side."

"I don't think so," Miller replied, recalling the discolored, stitched-together skin at Terry's hairline, the heavy tiredness in his eyes, and his weak body.

"Terry didn't do that to himself, Ross."

He let his words hang in the room for a moment before he spoke again.

"I did not find a Claims Adjustment report in the police file."

"That's strange," Ross said. "It should be in there. Did you miss it?"

Miller passed the file to him.

"Have a look for yourself."

While Ross was paging through the file, Miller told him Terry's recollections about the accident.

"We need to contact the insurance agency. If we can confirm Terry's story, that at least puts one piece of this puzzle into place."

Ross nodded. He closed the file.

"You're right—it's not here. Think someone removed it before handing it over to us?"

"Let's confirm with the insurance company first. Make sure Terry's story checks out. If they come back and tell us that copies were sent to the sheriff's department, we'll handle it then."

"I'll get to work on it," Ross said.

"You hear back from the cellular company yet?"

"No. They said it could take a few days to gather all the calls and texts made to or from the device, depending on how long the phone had been in use."

This was the part Miller hated most about being a cop—that waiting game.

The phone on Miller's desk rang. He picked it up.

"Is this Trooper Miller with the P-A state police?" a man's voice asked.

"Yes. Who am I speaking to?"

"My name is Mac. We met the other day."

Miller was at a loss.

"I'm sorry, I—"

"At Ruby-Lee's place."

Now he remembered.

"Oh, yes! What can I do for you?"

"I just heard what happened on the news to Ruby-Lee. I think we need to talk. I might know who killed her."

TWENTY-THREE

After Terry was discharged from the hospital, he had to call a taxi to get home.

It was the first time in Terry's life that he had been in a cab. In the TV shows and movies, the cabby was always a Chatty Kathy, asking all kinds of questions as they drove.

But his cabby was as quiet as a church mouse, which Terry was thankful for. His head still ached, and he wanted to wallow over his diagnosis in the silence.

Coming down the farm's stone driveway, Terry saw what was left of the barn: a smoldering pile of charred wood with plumes of black smoke rising into the grey sky.

"That how you ended up in the hospital, my man?" the cabby asked once they had stopped by the front of the house.

"Yes. Here." Terry slipped the cab driver a twenty, thanked him for the lift, and got out of the car.

He looked at the vacant space that had always been taken up by the barn. *It's all gone.* His heart ached, and he pressed a hand to his chest and rubbed the tender spot that suddenly hurt.

It did little to quell the loss he felt inside.

Rain started to fall. Terry turned and walked into the house, unable to look at the ruins any longer without breaking down.

Inside, Terry made his way upstairs. Each step felt as high as a running hurdle and just as tough to traverse. By the time he got to the top, he was winded and wheezing. He coughed. Tasted copper on his tongue.

Need my inhaler.

Moving into the bathroom, he slowly stripped his clothing and began to fill the tub for a hot bath. As the tub filled, he looked at the bruise across his back in the mirror.

A straight discolored line, about two inches thick, ran from shoulder to shoulder, just below his neck. There was little pain, other than some tender stiffness in his shoulders, which Terry was thankful for.

He turned around and looked at the stitches in his forehead. It was red where the gash had been closed and sewn back together, the skin around the slice swollen, black and blue. He felt ill at the sight of the injury.

After taking his inhaler, Terry sank into the warm water and sat there until it cooled. Once out, he toweled off and returned to his bed, where he instantly fell asleep.

He dreamed that he was standing over Clay, Claire, and Sidney's graves in the Mt. Hope Cemetery.

Next to where Sidney rested was an open grave ready for a deposit of human remains.

The ringing of the telephone downstairs woke him. He looked over at the clock on the nightstand. He had been asleep for three hours. It was half past six.

Throwing the covers aside, he stood and groggily made his way downstairs to the phone on legs that felt like they needed a shot of oil to keep the bones from grinding against one another.

"Hello?"

"Terry? I've been trying to call you all night. I heard what happened on the news. Are you okay?"

Terry was unsure who he was speaking with. His mind was still foggy with sleep and disorientation from the pain riddling his skull.

The pain pills must have worn off.

"Terry?"

"Who is this?" Terry asked.

There was a moment of silence.

"It's-it's… Angie." Hurt was in her voice when she replied.

"Angie?"

"Yeah."

"Sorry. I… what's up?"

"Well… I called to see if you were okay."

"I'm fine."

"That's good. The fire was all over the news. Police suspect it was arson?"

"Angie, were you able to locate the men I asked you to find?" Terry asked bluntly.

Again, there was a moment of silence. Terry knew his sharp tone had taken Angie aback. She had called to check on him, to see if he was okay, and he was short with her.

But he needed to know what she had. He no longer had time to pussyfoot around with small talk. From here on out, he had only one goal in mind.

"Sure." Angie tried to mask the discontent in her voice. "I found one of them."

"Which one?"

"Stevie Boyd. He runs a small salvage business called Boyd's Salvage."

"You have an address?"

"Yeah."

Suddenly the fog of sleep and pain lifted, and Terry shuffled to the kitchen counter where he kept a pen and pad of paper. He scribbled down the address that Angie gave him.

"Thanks, Angie."

"Welcome." Her voice still held a dejected tone.

The pang of guilt returned for how he had treated her. Terry knew he couldn't leave it like this between them. He had to say something to smooth things over.

"Look, sorry for being curt with you. I'm just a little banged up, is all. I'm not myself. Please accept my apologies."

"It's okay," she replied, her voice just above a whisper as if she had expected him to act the way he had—to use her.

Terry got the impression that Angie had been walked on, over, by too many men in her life.

"No, it's not, Angie. You did me a big favor. I acted like a jerk to you just now. You deserve to be treated better than that."

She said nothing.

"I have a few things I need to take care of. When I'm back in town, I would like to take you out for that dinner we talked about the other night. How does that sound?"

"You're leaving?"

Terry looked back to the address he had written down.

"Just for a few days. I'm going to find my buddy. When I get back, we'll go have dinner. How does that sound?"

"I'd like that, Terry. I really would." Her voice was soft and cautious, as if she didn't believe him.

"I'll call you when I'm back home. I promise."

"Okay." Her voice rose slightly this time with hopefulness.

They said their goodbyes, and Terry hung up the phone.

There was another matter he needed to attend to before he left. After Miller's visit at the hospital, Terry was positive they were looking heavily at him for Ruby-Lee's murder.

His prints would be found on the gift. With that, they would try to connect the murders of Ruby-Lee and her fuckbuddy back to him.

From there, they would try to tie him to Clay, Claire, and Sidney's murders as well.

What Terry needed to do now was throw them off his tail and make them look at who he believed was really responsible for the murders of his family.

Returning to the kitchen, he grabbed the piece of paper that he had written down Sg. Dan Harper's name from the Mercersburg Police Department on, along with the number where he could be reached.

Terry had discovered his name in the article about the robbery of the Quick Fill and wrote it down. But calling Harper from his home phone would allow the cops to trace the call directly back to him, blowing his plan before it even got started.

He would have to make the call from somewhere else.

Terry returned to his bedroom, dressed, brushed the awful death taste out of his mouth, grabbed his keys and the .357 from the den, and then hurried outside to his truck.

He drove south on Route 30 past the Treat, past the Twin Pines Motel, to a hole-in-the-wall trading post called Snake's Place, where there was still a working pay phone outside.

Fishing a quarter out of his pocket and slipping it into the slot, he dialed the number he'd written down on the scrap piece of paper.

"Sg. Dan Harper speaking," a gruff but cordial voice answered.

"I might have information about the murders at the Quick Fill and who robbed the First National Bank of Gettysburg back in 2015."

"Who is this?"

"I believe I know the names of the three men who were involved in those crimes. Luthor and Chet Morgan, and Stevie Boyd. I also believe they were responsible for the murders in Hickory Falls in December of 2015. You need to speak to Trooper Henry Miller at Troop G."

"Who is—"

Terry slammed the receiver back into place; the pay phone's ringer *dinged* from the impact.

His call should buy him some time.

Miller and Ross would be preoccupied following up on the lead Terry just handed them, giving him enough time to get to Stevie Boyd first.

<u>TWENTY-FOUR</u>

Mac wanted to meet somewhere public but secluded.

They chose Shawnee State Park, ten miles west of Bedford. They were to meet him by East Beach, a stretch of sand along the eastern side of the Shawnee Lake.

Stepping from the car, Miller heard voices, the laughter and screaming of kids playing and splashing in the water coming from the beach area.

The cool, green water sparkled under the sun and reflected off his sunglasses.

They were told to walk to the end of the East Beach parking lot to where a thick group of trees made an arrow in the landscape.

Mac would meet them there.

They headed to the trees, left of the lake and beach area, and walked into the thicket. It was cooler in the shade but did little to stifle the humidity.

"You Miller?" an unseen voice asked from somewhere in the wooded plot.

Miller looked around but saw no one amongst the trees.

"I'm Miller. Why don't you come out so we can talk, Mac?"

In front of them, a skinny, dark-haired guy who resembled a rat stepped out from behind a large maple tree.

Miller hated to judge someone by their looks, but he had been a cop long enough to know Mac was a meth user. The skinny physique. The darting eyes. The bad teeth. The trembling hands and bad, sore-ridden skin all pointed to him being heavily addicted to the drug.

He remembered seeing him at Ruby-Lee's house. He had been sitting at the table, holding a frozen package of peas against the right side of his face. Miller now understood why. A bruise discolored his cheek and left eye.

"You said you had information on who killed Ruby-Lee?" Ross said. "Spill it."

"I said I *might* know who killed her." His eyes darted past Miller and Ross to a movement behind them.

Miller turned to see what Mac was looking at, but it was only a family walking from their car to the lake.

"I think it was that big guy who showed up at Ruby-Lee's on Monday."

"There was someone else at Ruby-Lee's house on Monday? You saw him?" Miller asked.

"Sure. Gave me dis," Mac pointed at his bruised face.

"Sumbitch slugged me when I wasn't ready to defend myself. He's lucky I wasn't ready—punk-ass-bitch—I would've cleaned his clock."

"I'm sure he is," Miller replied.

Ross snorted out a small laugh at the foolish tough guy talk—Mac couldn't defend himself against a strong wind because he was so malnourished from his drug use.

"What did he look like?"

"Big guy. Six-one, maybe two. Fat—pushing three hundred pounds. Had a big-ass red beard and hair. Wild, crazy eyes, too."

Miller glanced at Ross and saw the excitement work across his partner's face.

"Do you remember what he wanted?" Miller asked.

"To speak with Ruby-Lee. Said it was important."

Mac shook his head, twitched, and scratched at a scab on his right arm. It pulled away and started to bleed. He flicked the scab from under his fingernail into the brush.

"You know what about?" Ross asked.

"Nah. When I told him to get lost, he laid me out cold before I's could overhear what was said. By the time I woke, they had mostly finished their conversin'. I'm assumin' it was about Ruby-Lee and her occupation."

"What makes you say that?" Ross asked.

"When my head cleared, I asked her who that guy was. Said he was a former acquaintance of hers—Terry-something—but wouldn't go into further detail."

"Did Ruby-Lee say what she and Terry spoke about?"

"Nah. She was quiet after dat. Scared. Nervous. Kept chewing on her nails. I got the sense, whatever they talked about was important stuff. I do remember her throwing something at him before she kicked him out."

"Throwing something at him?"

"Yeah. Something wrapped in Christmas paper—a gift he had given her years ago, a gift she never wanted. Told him to take it and get out."

"How did he respond?" Ross asked.

"Stomped on it, then left."

Mac twitched again. He ran his tongue over his rotten, black teeth.

"After you two showed up, she asked me to leave. I was happy to. I gathered my shit and hit the bricks. I didn't want to get mixed up in some domestic dispute, end up like that guy on the news who they found with Ruby-Lee yesterday. I found your card in the door; how I knew to call you."

"Let me ask you a question," Miller said. "How'd you hook up with Ruby-Lee?"

"I call her when I wants a piece."

"No, before that. How'd you find out about Ruby-Lee's services?"

"Oh!" Mac thought momentarily, again picking at another sore on his right arm. "I met her at a bar a few years back."

"Where?"

"A bar in Hickory Falls—Red's. I went to meet up with a few buddies I know from Hickory Falls when Ruby-Lee slid up beside me. Asked me if I wanted to buy her a drink. I knew what she was, what she wanted. It wasn't my first time dealing with a bar lizard, ya know.

"Anyway, she started talking about all the things she could do for me, if I was interested. And let me tell you, this broad was kinky as fuuuuck. There wasn't much she wouldn't do, like, she loved to be—"

Miller held up his hand.

"We get the picture."

"So, you paid Ruby-Lee for sex that night?"

Mac shook his head.

"Nah. I paid the bald guy."

"The bald guy?" Ross asked, his brow pinched.

"Yeah, he was the bartender. Ruby-Lee told me how much it was for what she called 'The Works,' but she pushed my hand away when I went to pay her.

"She said that there was a do-gooder cop in town, who wouldn't look the other way like the other cops did, and that I should pay the guy behind the bar instead.

"We made it look like I was ordering a drink. I passed him the money, he passed me a shot of water disguised in a Vodka bottle. I took that as a sign that the transaction was complete. We left after dat."

"When was this?" Ross asked.

"I don't remember the exact date. Was a while back."

"Did she take you back to her place, like the other day?" Miller asked.

"Nah. She was livin' with her moms back then. We went to the Twin Pines Motel; that's where Ruby-Lee took most of her clients. It wasn't until after her moms died that she started working out of her place."

"After you were done at the motel, where'd you go?" Ross asked.

"Back to that bar. Ruby-Lee had left her car there. But when we got back, the place was torn apart—a table was broken, glass was everywhere. A fight had broken out in the joint.

"The bald guy talked to Ruby-Lee about it. I don't know what was said. They were whispering to each other."

Miller knew the night Mac was refencing: December 23rd, 2015—the same night Terry was in the fight with Jeff and Colin.

Miller thought it best to check out the Twin Pines Motel to corroborate Mac's story.

As they pulled into one of the motel's parking spaces, Ross's cell phone rang. He answered the call and listened to whoever was on the other end speak.

He then looked to Miller and mouthed the words, *It's the insurance agency.*

Inside, Miller felt a flutter of excitement. Ross asked a few questions, said something about sending a copy to his email, thanked the caller, and hung up.

"According to Terry's insurance agency, the left front tie rod on the Firebird was the cause of the accident. During their investigation, they found no signs of foul play, tampering, or anything of the sort that led them to believe it was anything but a freak accident that, sadly, resulted in the loss of Melissa Garland's life."

"Did they send a copy to the sheriff's department?" Miller asked.

"Sure did. And they're sending a copy over to my email…"

Ross' phone chimed.

"And there it is."

He opened the email and began to read.

"It says here that the report was sent to the Hickory Falls Sheriff's Department two weeks after the crash. It would have cleared Terry of any wrongdoing in the accident."

Ross took a slow breath, and let it out slowly, making him look like a deflating balloon.

"I don't get it. If Terry was proven to be innocent in the crash, then why try and hide it from us?"

"Because having it wouldn't allow them to portray Terry as the bad guy to us outsiders," Miller said.

"Are you saying there's a town conspiracy against Terry Graham?" Ross asked.

Miller thought about the question for a long moment.

"Maybe," Miller said, opening the car door and getting out.

The little bell above the door marked OFFICE rang as they entered. A gray-haired woman was standing behind the desk, waiting for them with a warm smile.

"Good afternoon, gentlemen. How can I help you?" she asked.

"Are you the owner?" Miller asked.

"Yes. Mrs. Kelly," she replied.

"We're with the state police, Mrs. Kelly, and we were wondering if we could look through your guestbooks from a few years ago. We're confirming a lead."

"You have a warrant?" Mrs. Kelly snapped back.

Miller felt a hot flash of irritation warm his face.

"We were hoping we wouldn't need one," Ross replied. "We just need to have a quick look at your guest logbook for December 23, 2015; make sure what we were told was the truth, and then we'll be out of your hair."

"Hmmm?" Mrs. Kelly's face grew tight with intrigue.

"What?" Miller asked, sensing the date had resonated with her for some reason.

"I'll be right back."

She turned and went through a doorway into a small office. She was gone only a second before she returned with a logbook and laid it on the desk. *2015* was printed on the front in gold letters.

"There was a fella in here the other day asking me a bunch of questions about that same year, but the following day, the twenty-fourth of December. Said he was a family member of the Grahams. Believed three men, who might have murdered his family, stayed here."

Ross glanced at Miller.

"You remember his name?" Miller asked.

"Yeah. Terry Graham. He was asking me all kinds of questions. I didn't give him any personal information, mind you, since that's against the law."

"What kind of questions?" Ross asked.

"Wanted to know when they checked in and to see the room where they slept, which I found unusual, but I obliged."

"Do you know why he wanted to see the room?" Miller asked.

"Haven't the foggiest of ideas. Maybe he thought he'd find something. He was also really interested in what they were driving, and after I told him, he took off outta here like a lightning strike."

She found the page she was looking for and turned the book around to them. Sliding her finger to the bottom, she pointed at the registered name written in that section.

"There's what you asked me about."

Miller and Ross saw that Ruby-Lee had checked in on December 23, 2015. Beside her name it was marked +1. It confirmed what Mac had told them.

"Can you show us who checked in on December 24th, 2015, Mrs. Kelly?" Miller asked.

"Sure." She flipped the page and pointed to the name registered in the ledger.

Together, Miller and Ross began to read where her finger rested.

Ruby-Lee rented the room again on December 24th, 2015. Beside the name was a + 3, indicating there were three other people checking into the room with her.

Beside that was a car license plate number XBZ-3217, followed by the color, make, and year: Blue. Oldsmobile. 1988.

Miller looked at Ross and could not contain his smile. But his excitement was short lived when his phone began to ring. Miller answered it.

"Is this Trooper Miller?" the gruff voice on the other end asked.

"Yes. Who am I speaking with?"

"This is Sg. Dan Harper with the Mercersburg Police Department."

TWENTY-FIVE

Terry pulled the pickup into a thicket far enough from the road that anyone passing by would not be able to see.

It was hot inside and sweat seeped from his skin as if a bucket of water had been poured over his head, staining his coal-colored button-down shirt almost black.

Still, it wasn't just the heat causing him to sweat. It was the excitement. The thrill of the hunter catching up to the hunted.

Through the forest he could just make out the home that belonged to Stevie Boyd.

He ran his index finger over the crescent moon trigger of the .357 resting on his right knee, caressing it like he had Melissa's skin.

But the time for love had long passed him by. His heart was now filled with bitter hatred. He had become the bringer of vengeance. The deliverer of death.

Stevie Boyd was caught in the pale light; he just didn't know it yet.

Boyd lived in a rundown two-story brick home ten miles outside of Mercersburg. There was no redeeming quality to the home, and no self-respecting person would have lived there if they had any sense.

It was in the middle of nowhere, surrounded by densely thick forest. There were no neighbors for miles, and Terry hadn't seen a single car pass by since he began watching the place.

It was the perfect hiding place for someone to remain inconspicuous and continue to evade justice, Terry thought.

Nine years I waited for this.

Terry was so close to ending this nightmare that he could taste sweet vengeance on his tongue. His grip tightened on the handle of the .357, and his thumb feathered the hammer.

He could do it quick. Knock on the door, and when Stevie came to see who was calling—*BAM!*—one bullet worth sixty-two cents would snub out this son of a bitch's life in a blink of an eye.

But Terry pushed the impulse down into that dark place where his indignation had grown and festered. He needed to see Stevie's eyes when he told him why he was there.

The truth would be in his eyes.

Stepping from the truck, Terry stuffed the .357 into his pants and pulled his shirt over it. The smell of honeysuckle and pine reminded him of when he and Clay were kids, playing around the Falls in the summer when school was out.

A bittersweet memory of better times before Terry had ruined their relationship.

He moved through the forest toward the house, carefully avoiding the road so he would not give himself away to anyone driving by.

His stomach flip-flopped, the churning of a gut about to explode from a combination of anticipation and fear.

Coming parallel to the house, Terry hid behind a large oak tree and watched. The screen door was open, and the faint sounds of a baseball game floated across the silent woods, drowning out the natural music of the forest surrounding him.

He licked his lips and found them incredibly dry, like running his tongue across bark.

It was eerily silent in the woods, as if the wildlife sensed what was about to happen. The only sounds came from the baseball game inside the house.

A chill rose across Terry's skin, even in the sticky air. He shook it away with a circle of his shoulders and stepped out from behind the tree

As he came up the driveway, Terry saw junk strewn about the yard. Refrigerators, stoves, microwaves, and other piles of indescribable scrap metal were everywhere, some piled shin-high with weeds growing up around them.

There were several old cars jacked up on blocks, stripped of their parts and metal exteriors.

Collecting metal was how Stevie made a living, Terry knew. After stripping the metal, copper wires, and tubing from the old appliances and cars, Stevie most likely resold it at a metal recycling plant for money.

It was a job for someone who couldn't get work doing anything else.

As Terry grew closer to the screen door, a high-pitched male scream erupted from inside. He froze. His hand shot to the gun tucked into his jeans, ready to pull it if need be.

But Terry quickly realized the scream was only from someone yelling at the TV. It seemed whoever was watching the ballgame, their team had just missed an important play.

Continuing to the porch, Terry peered through the screen door into the house. He could only make out murky shapes in the darkness.

And for a moment, for one fledgling moment, Terry thought about turning around and going home.

He knocked on the door instead.

"Jabba need good away baseball game watch me," came the same high-pitched voice from inside.

"Stevie Boyd?" Terry asked through the screen door.

"Stevie Boyd you askin' cause me know you?" the voice asked.

Terry understood all the words, but they were spoken in a way that were out of rhythm.

"I'm looking for Stevie. You him?"

Terry heard the springs of a recliner release, and footsteps nearing the door. He waited for someone to appear; his hand rested on the butt of the gun under his shirt.

A tall, thin form stepped into the light spilling in from the screen door.

"I know not you baseball watch game interrupt fun time?" the guy spouted off, looking Terry up and down.

"Stevie Boyd?"

Stevie's eyes sharpened suspiciously. But Terry saw nothing else; they were empty vessels that held no life, no understanding.

"Jaybe. You askin' baseball why I game you here watch no?"

Terry remembered Ruby-Lee telling him she thought Stevie had some mental deficiency by the way he spoke.

"If you're Stevie, then I need to talk to you about a few things," Terry replied.

"End? Remember times when Ends. Jaybe you end?"

"End?" Terry asked.

Stevie nodded and pointed to Terry.

"You end mind of know you before now?" He smiled enthusiastically, exposing his badly crooked teeth.

Terry understood then.

"Oh! You're asking if we're friends?" Stevie's smile grew. "No. We've never met."

"Gone be from sight."

"We have a lot to talk about, Stevie."

Stevie waved Terry away like shooshing a fly from a plate of food at a picnic. He turned from the screen door, about to return to his ballgame, but not before Terry spoke.

"Clay Graham."

Slowly, Stevie turned and faced Terry. Like his eyes, his face was lifeless, an emotional blank slate, as if the name meant nothing to him.

The look concerned Terry. *Does he even know who I'm talking about? Or is he just playing dumb?*

Anger crawled up Terry's back, raising his hackles. He needed to keep himself under control. If he pulled the gun and put a round in Stevie's face, he would not get the answers he sought.

He decided to try another question.

"What about the names Luthor and Chet Morgan? You know them?"

This time, Stevie's eyes darkened with a knowing stare.

Your past just caught up with you, you son of a bitch.

"Yeah. You know who they are," Terry grumbled.

"Gone be!" Stevie barked. "No nittin' no."

"Ah, cut the shit," Terry replied. "We're past that part now. You might not remember my brother's name or his family, but you know who Luthor and Chet Morgan are."

Terry lifted his shirt and pulled the gun out.
"Let's step inside, so we can have a little chat."

<u>TWENTY-SIX</u>

Miller and Ross sat across from Sgt. Dan Harper in his office at the Mercersburg Police Department.

Sg. Harper was in his late fifties with a salt and pepper mustache and dark wavy hair that had begun to gray at the temples. His naturally gruff voice and lined, weathered face betrayed the times he lived in.

He appeared more suited for the Old West than today's modern world.

"Did this caller say anything else?" Miller asked after Harper was done explaining the call he had received earlier that day.

"No. Just that I needed to contact you with this information."

"And whoever called you believed that these three men—Stevie Boyd, Luthor and Chet Morgan—all had something to do with the murders of the Graham family?"

"And that they were involved in two robberies—the Quick Fill and the First National Bank of Gettysburg."

"Do you know any of the names mentioned?" Ross asked.

"Just one. Stevie Boyd. He lives about ten miles outside Mercersburg, in his momma's old place. The guy is pretty messed up in the head. Has a problem with his speech, thanks to his mother, Bobby Jean, beating him for years."

Harper paused as a memory played across his face with revulsion, deepening the lines.

"Bobby Jean was a bitter person. Her husband walked out on her when she was eight months pregnant with Stevie, leaving her to deal with everything. Told her he was going for a beer and never came back. She took all her resentment out on Stevie by beating the boy.

"After we got him out of the house and a medical examination was done, it was discovered that Stevie had sustained severe head trauma. From the years of abuse, his speech was affected. Have you ever met someone with Wernicke's aphasia?"

"Can't say that I have," Miller replied.

"What is it?" Ross asked.

"Wernicke's aphasia affects the temporal lobe. Those affected tend to speak in long sentences that make no sense. They add unnecessary words or even create made-up ones.

"It's found commonly in older adults who've had a stroke. However, it can occur in younger people if there was severe head trauma, like Stevie sustained from his mother's abuse."

"What happened after he was taken out of his mother's custody?" Miller asked.

"He was put into the foster system. Bounced from family to family, between stints in juvie, until he was eighteen. Bobby Jean willed her house to him before she died. I guess it was the only good thing she'd ever done for the boy." Harper's eyes fell away, and in them, there was a look of pity for Stevie Boyd's situation.

"What was he in juvie for?" Ross asked.

"Just a few petty things: breaking and entering, loitering. He stole a car once and was charged as an adult which landed him in a real prison. But since Stevie's been out, he's kept himself out of trouble."

"Fill us in on the facts, as you know them, about the robberies—both at the Quick Fill and the bank in Gettysburg," Ross said.

"Neither job was a spur-of-the-moment thing. That much we're sure of. Our belief is that they had been casing the places out before the robberies occurred. We believe they hit the Quick Fill between ten and eleven p.m. because it was the store's slowest hour of the evening.

"Two guys entered the store. One took the register while the other stood guard by the door. The third guy waited outside in a blue sedan. But that night, things didn't go their way. From what the only survivor, Horace Gillbanter, said, one guy was giving all the orders. He demanded the cash from both the registers and the safe.

"But while the employees told him they could not open up the safe because they didn't have the combination numbers, Tamika Jackson entered the building. She was shot dead as soon as she entered the store by the guy guarding the door. Guess they didn't want to leave any witnesses after that, so the guy doing all the talking shot the two employees.

"Horace Gillbanter survived. He laid on the floor until they left but was able to see a blue sedan fleeing the scene just before he lost consciousness."

"Any surveillance footage of the crime in progress?" Ross asked.

"No. The Quick Fill was still using VHS to record their surveillance footage. The tape was stolen from the deck."

"You ever connect Stevie to the crimes?" Miller asked.

Harper shook his head.

"Never had a reason to look at him. Until today when I got that phone call. But it's questionable that Stevie had any involvement in the robberies anyway."

"Why?" Ross asked. "You already said he had committed petty crimes before. He could've advanced his career."

"I know Stevie well enough by this point to tell you he can't even get work pushing a broom. He collects metal and sells it to a scrapyard to make a living—calls himself Boyd's Salvage, though I'm not even sure it's a registered business.

"He doesn't have the mental capability of pulling something like this off. Besides, these guys worked as a team. A unit."

Harper continued, glancing from Miller back to Ross.

"The video footage from the First National Bank of Gettysburg shows two guys enter, both wearing masks and wielding shotguns. They were a proficient crew that knew what they were doing and how to handle themselves in the situation.

"Same M.O. as the Quick Fill job—one took the registers while one guarded the door, while a third guy waits in the car outside."

"Were there any fatalities with the bank job?" Ross asked.

"No. They were in and out in minutes—five grand richer."

"Any of the money recovered?" Miller asked.

"Some of it turned up at two local casinos. We believe they were trying to wash the bills so they couldn't be traced. Stevie wouldn't have the forethought to do something like that. No, these guys were professional criminals."

A thought occurred to Miller.

"Can Stevie drive?"

"Sure. He has a pickup that he collects scrap with. He's all over town, looking for junk."

"Sergeant Harper, my partner and I uncovered a new piece of evidence this afternoon, just before you called me. We were able to get a license plate number for a blue 1988 Oldsmobile that we can place in Hickory Falls the night of the Graham murders, and only four days after the robbery of the Quick Fill here in Mercersburg. On our way over here, we ran the plate and got a hit."

"Oh?" Harper sat up in his chair and stared at Miller with a hard look etched into his skin, deepening the lines on his face into fissures.

"The car belonged to Dave Lieberman. We were able to contact Mr. Lieberman, who told us he junked the car nine years ago and dropped it off at a small salvage yard in Mercersburg."

Harper straightened in his seat with unease.

"Boyd's Salvage, to be more specific," Ross said.

"Stevie Boyd might not be able to plan and pull off a robbery, but if he can drive, then maybe he was the third guy behind the wheel of the blue sedan—the same blue sedan that was registered at the Twin Pine Motel four days later."

<u>TWENTY- SEVEN</u>

"Sit your ass in that chair and don't move, Stevie."

Terry shoved Stevie into the recliner. It almost toppled, but Stevie caught himself on the wall before it went over. He watched Terry step in front of him with the eyes of a man who didn't understand right from wrong.

There is something mentally wrong with this guy.

"I'm going to ask you some yes or no questions. All you have to do is nod for *yes* and shake your head for *no*. Understand?"

Stevie's eyes drifted to the gun in Terry's hand, still retaining that vacant, incoherent gaze of a man who isn't all there mentally.

Terry couldn't allow Stevie's mental disabilities to deter him from what he came there for. The thought of smacking Stevie around crossed his mind, but he couldn't bring himself to lay into him. He wasn't that much of a bastard.

Still, he needed Stevie to understand that he meant business and placed the .357 to Stevie's forehead.

"Do I have your attention now?"

Stevie nodded vigorously; his eyes filled with such fear they were as wide as saucers.

"Good." Terry pulled the gun away and stepped back, the barrel still trained on Stevie.

If he tried to move or reach for something to bring Terry harm, he wouldn't get far without catching a bullet.

"Nine years ago, were you in Hickory Falls?"

Stevie nodded. His scared eyes moved around the room, looking for a way out.

"Did you meet up with a girl?" Terry continued.

Again, he nodded.

Yes.

"Was her name Ruby-Lee?"

Yes.

"Did you meet her at a bar called Red's?"

Yes.

"Who were you with?"

Stevie went to reply, but Terry held up his hand before he could speak. Stevie would jabber something nonsensical that Terry would have to decipher. He did not have time for that and rephrased the question.

"You were with two other men, correct?"

Yes.

"Were their names Luthor and Chet Morgan?"

Stevie lifted his shoulders.

Don't know.

"You don't know who you were with? Or you don't want to tell me?"

Stevie shrugged.

He's protecting his buddies.

"Okay." Terry took a step forward, cocking the revolver. "Remember who you were with now?"

Stevie held his hands up and cowered into the chair like a dog that didn't want another scolding.

"Luthor and Chet Morgan, were they with you?"

Stevie nodded.

Yes.

Inside, Terry felt a burning hot acid pump from the dark hollow of his heart. He wanted so badly to pull the trigger, to end this sorry excuse for a human being's life right there.

Stay calm. Stay in control until you get everything you came for.

"One of you three shot my brother, his wife and daughter. Was it you, Stevie?"

No.

"Chet?"

Stevie shrugged.

Don't know.

"Did Luthor shoot them?"

Stevie shrugged again.

"Oh, so we're back to this." Terry turned to the television. The baseball game was still on. Philly was beating Pittsburgh 5-3. He squeezed the trigger.

The gun erupted inside the small house with a deafening blast and the television exploded with a shower of sparks, glass, and plastic.

Stevie jumped from the chair and bolted for the door. But Terry grabbed him by the back of his shirt and thrust him back into the recliner.

"You're not going anywhere. Not until you tell me everything I want to hear."

Stevie was like granite, petrified with dread; his fingers dug into the recliner's plush arms.

"Was it Ruby-Lee who mentioned my brother to the three of you?"

Stevie seemed perplexed by the question. His head tilted to the side, and his eyebrows nearly touched with confusion.

"Was it Ruby-Lee who told you my brother had money and that he'd be a good person for the three of you to rob?"

No.

"Someone else in town then?"

No.

"Then how did you find my family? Why did you kill them, you son of a bitch!"

Terry grabbed Stevie by the shirt collar, and pulled his skinny body nearly out of the seat. He jammed the .357 under his chin.

"Why? Tell me!" Terry screamed into his face. He could feel himself losing control. The rage was taking over.

Stevie was shaking his head back and forth frantically. His eyes were bugging out of his skull, pleading with Terry not to kill him.

"You went to their home and took them at night, hoping to get money from Clay's business. Only there wasn't any money. He was broke.

"Once you found out, Clay was just buying time, hoping for a miracle to save him and his family, you guys executed them in the car. Isn't that right?"

No. No. Stevie shook his head with quick movements.

"You couldn't leave any witnesses because of your previous robberies. So, you shot them and got the hell out of town. But you couldn't get far because of the weather and stopped at the Twin Pines Motel to hole up for the night."

"No," Stevie said. "Not us do killin' nobody. Car there to get new."

Not us do killin'. Car there to get new?

Something bubbled up in Terry's brain that he did not want to accept. Stevie repeatedly shook his head no at his questions, even after being threatened.

Was there the possibility that Stevie, Luthor, and Chet Morgan had nothing to do with the murders? If it wasn't them, then who could it have…

No. It has to be them. They were in Hickory that day. Ruby-Lee confirmed it. And I'm sure I saw their car at the gas station and again by Clay's store. They have to be involved. They have—

Terry didn't get to finish his thought.

Stevie's left hand shot up and caught Terry's right wrist, slapping the barrel of the gun out from under his chin. Before Terry could comprehend what was happening or correct where the gun was aimed, Stevie threw a right hook into Terry's left side.

Fire erupted inside Terry. His breath shot out of his mouth in a long, wet gurgle. Blood was forced up from somewhere inside and coated the back of his mouth with that awful coppery taste he had come to loathe.

Terry grabbed at his side and staggered past the recliner, trying to pull a breath. Pain seized his insides. With his mind focused solely on the internal agony and the absence of oxygen in his lungs, Terry did not see Stevie rising out of the chair behind him until it was too late.

He tried to turn and bring the gun up, but Stevie was faster, more agile, than the lumbering, ill hulk that was Terry Graham.

Stevie kicked out. His foot connected with the gun, knocking it out of Terry's grip. It hit the floor with a *thud* and slid out of sight.

Stevie charged at him, throwing a left, right, left combo like a pro boxer.

Terry tried to move, duck, and defend himself, but Stevie landed two blows—one to Terry's meaty gut and one to the right side of his jaw—that knocked Terry off balance.

Stevie drove Terry back into the wall beside the door. Hanging pictures fell from old nails and crashed to the floor, the glass frames shattering.

Stevie clawed at Terry's face, tried to drive his fingers into his eyes, in his mouth, up his nose. He pulled at Terry's beard, his ears and hair, trying to drag him off balance by twisting him this way and that.

The thrashing caused the flesh to rip apart from the stitching at Terry's hairline and a slow blood stream began running down the side of his face.

Terry fought Stevie off as best he could, but he knew it was a losing battle. He was beginning to grow lightheaded. The lack of oxygen to his muscles and brain caused his vision to come and go, like turning a light switch on and off in a dark room.

The taste of copper in the back of his throat was so strong and thick that it was gagging him, causing him to cough; blood spittle erupted from his lips and dotted Stevie's face.

He felt his left leg grow weak under his weight, suddenly as stable as a limp noodle, and he went down to one knee, gasping for breath.

When Terry looked up, all he saw was Stevie's crooked-tooth smirk. It was a look unlike anything Terry had seen on someone's face before—the grin of a crazy person who was enjoying watching him suffer, watching him struggle to pull a breath.

Fear sliced through Terry.

And just before he passed out, he understood with perfect clarity that he had underestimated this man.

Despite his mental incapacities, Stevie was capable of inflicting extreme violence onto his fellow man.

TWENTY-EIGHT

The Mercersburg PD assisted Miller and Ross by providing them with an office to run background checks for Luthor and Chet Morgan, while Sg. Harper drove out to Stevie Boyd's place to pick him up and bring him in for questioning.

Miller pulled their criminal records from the NCIC—the National Crime Information Center, an FBI database.

Ross dug into their background—their juvenile records had not been sealed by the courts as they should have been. It was an oversight of the judicial system but the break Miller and Ross desperately needed.

Miller wasn't completely sold on these men being responsible for the murders of the Graham family. Out of the blue, an anonymous caller gives them a lead just as they are turning their focus entirely on Terry Graham. Someone was to throw them off their trail, Miller felt.

Is it Terry?

Once Miller and Ross compiled their information, they began reviewing it.

Luthor Morgan was forty-eight years old and currently lived in Jackson, about an hour east of Mercersburg. Chet Morgan was forty-six and lived closer in Akersville.

Their list of criminal offenses was a mile long, all stemming from a traumatic childhood.

According to juvenile records, their parents, Mike and Kora Morgan, two longtime drug addicts, had verbally and physically abused both boys until their deaths in November of 1985 from a lethal dose of heroin.

Luthor was ten and Chet eight. Authorities suspected the lethal dose had been administered by a third party by the amount in their systems, according to the coroner's report.

At one point, the police seriously considered Luthor or Chet as possible suspects—maybe they even conspired together to off their worthless, abusive parents.

Violence begets violence, Miller thought. But the DA at the time, after learning what the boys had been through, decided he did not want to pursue such an accusation against two abused children living in a hellhole.

For the first five years as wards of the state, they were fostered together, but in 1990, they were separated and sent to different foster homes. Miller assumed this was done to make adoption easier.

By his early teens, Luthor was already sliding into the criminal world. Petty crimes like pickpocketing and shoplifting, the latter of which landed him three months in juvie before being released back into the system.

In the meantime, Chet Morgan found himself arrested after he vandalized a change machine and stole fifty bucks from a local arcade. He spent a year in juvie before he was placed with a new foster family.

Both brothers would go in and out of foster homes with no adoption attempts. They were damaged kids.

And no one wants a damaged kid.

By 1992, Luthor, now eighteen, was on his own. He quickly turned to full-time theft. His M.O. was breaking into homes in the middle of the night, tying up the homeowners, and then robbing them.

Once he was out of foster care, Luthor brought his brother into the fold. Together, they started hitting convenience stores, laundromats, and gas stations before being apprehended after they pulled off their biggest job. A jewelry store heist, where they left with about twenty thousand dollars in merchandise only to walk right into police custody when leaving.

Someone in the jewelry store had activated the silent alarm.

Both Morgans were sentenced to twenty years in prison. Both were model prisoners and neither had offenses while incarcerated. Early parole was granted in 2012 with two years of probation.

After their probation was up in 2014, they fell off the grid. While searching the prison records, Ross had cross-checked to see if they had done time with Stevie Boyd, but to no avail.

"Stevie Boyd's time was spent in Franklin County Jail. Both Luthor and Chet did time at the Federal Correctional Institute in Loretto, Pennsylvania."

Something burned in Miller's mind. Maybe they were looking in the wrong place, or perhaps they were not connected through the prison system at all.

"Harper said that Stevie Boyd was in the foster system. So were Chet and Luthor Morgan. Maybe that's their connection."

"I'll look into it."

Miller's cell phone buzzed on his hip. Trisha was calling.

"I need to take this." He stood and left the room.

"Hey, Trisha, can you hold on for a moment?"

"Sure. I guess."

Miller exited the building and made his way to a secluded spot across the parking lot to talk to his ex-wife out of earshot.

"Okay. What's up?"

"An officer is coming over tomorrow morning to take Luna down to the station for processing. The McCalls are actually going through with this. What are you doing about it, Henry?"

Fuck me! Miller pinched the bridge of his nose. There was a lot on his plate right now. Luna's problem needed to be dealt with immediately.

"I'm working on it, Trisha."

"Fix this."

"I will. I will."

Miller had wanted to question the kids Luna claimed could verify her side of the story. The truth would exonerate her. That was the legal way to handle the situation.

But with the Graham case now moving like a freight train, he didn't have time to question those kids. He needed to go straight to the source and cut the head off the snake before this went further.

"So help me, God, Henry, if this ruins Luna's life, I will never forgive you."

"Trisha…" He heard the plea in his voice and hated how whiny he sounded, how weak and useless it made him feel.

"Don't 'Trisha' me. Get off your ass and help our daughter."

The line went dead.

Miller wanted to scream at the top of his lungs and punch something in frustration, but what good would that do him? By letting his anger fuel him, he'd probably break his fist.

He wasn't Terry Graham. He kept his emotions in check.

He returned inside.

"Everything okay?" Ross asked, looking up from what he was working on.

"Sure."

Ross noticed the despairing tone in Miller's voice.

"You sure?"

"Yeah." He forced a smile. "How are you making out?"

"Nothing yet. Still searching."

"Keep at it."

Miller sat down at the desk. An idea of how to deal with Luna's predicament itched his skin like a rash.

He didn't like it and did not want to go this route to solve the problem, but what choice did he have? His daughter's future was on the line. Miller needed to get the McCalls to reconsider pressing charges.

Maybe the McCalls have a few skeletons in their closet.

Miller knew if he ran a search on the NCIC, for dirt on either of the McCalls that he could use against them, it could easily be traced back to him. His name would be all over this thing.

But, if he played his hand smart, there might be a way for him to get Luna off the hook, while covering his tracks simultaneously.

"Can you look someone up for me, since you're still in the system?" Miller asked Ross.

"Sure? What's the names?"

"Earl and Rose McCall."

"Who are they?"

"Just some bad apples that I've been watching over the years."

Ross understood. He had his own set of criminals he had arrested and checked in on occasionally, making sure they were still on the straight and narrow. He typed the names into the computer.

Miller watched the look of surprise on Ross's face when the search resulted in an arrest record for Earl McCall.

"This guy's a peach," Ross said with disdain.

"Yeah. Earl McCall's a real winner," Miller replied, trying to hide his eagerness to know what Ross found.

"Says here Mr. McCall's been arrested three separate times for domestic abuse. First two times for slapping his wife around. The third time, the most recent, his daughter. Did six months in county this year. Just got out last month."

Miller stood and came up beside Ross. He quickly read over McCall's rap sheet on the computer, caught his current address, saw his mugshot.

He had a pug-like face, pushed in, stubby, with beady eyes set deep into his skull. His hair was styled in a mullet, making him look like the white trash he was.

Seeing this man caused something malevolent to stir uncomfortably inside Miller, like a monster that had long lay dormant had just awoken. He knew what needed to be done.

"How do you know this guy again?" Ross asked, looking at Miller with skepticism.

Miller ignored the question and said, "I need to take care of some personal things. Can you handle this by yourself for a few hours?"

"I guess. What's up? You sure everything's okay?"

Miller stood and headed for the door.

"Everything's fine."

When Miller pulled to a stop two blocks from the McCall home, the sky still had just a faint touch of blue. The neighborhood had already grown dark, and the maple trees lining the sidewalks kept the light from penetrating onto its streets and lawns.

Miller scanned the darkness looking for signs of life— someone walking a dog, taking out the trash, or just fiddling around in their garage. He saw no one. *Good.*

He would need the anonymity the darkness provided him.

Reaching up, he turned off the interior light so when he opened the door, the light would not come on. He did not need any lookie-loos seeing him.

Stepping out of the car, the humidity rolled over him, and he instantly began to sweat. He reached across the center console and pulled out a black hooded sweatshirt, feeling the weight of the blackjack – a leather-bound bludgeoning device filled with lead shot - inside the front left pocket swinging like a pendulum.

He slipped the hoodie on and reached inside the right pocket and pulled out a pair of black gloves. He strained to pull the gloves over his sweaty palms.

Miller eased the car's door closed without it making much more than a *click* in the hot, still air and started for the McCalls' home.

Miller stopped and studied the split-level rancher before he approached. The living room lights were on, and a rather large man with dark hair sat on the sofa, sipping from a bottle of Rolling Rock. It was Earl McCall.

He had ditched the mullet for a buzz cut, which made him look even more like the quintessential abuser he was.

Miller felt irritation warm him. After learning of McCall's abuse of his wife and daughter, he felt what he was about to do was better than the man actually deserved.

Stuffing his gloved hand into the hoodie's pocket, Miller pulled out the blackjack wrapped in a black ski mask. He undid the mask from around the blackjack and slid it over his face. The heavy fibers were scratchy and made his flesh itch. He smoothed it down with his hands and scratched at his cheek.

Moving up the dark pathway to the house, Miller flexed his hand over the blackjack's handle. Oddly enough, he felt no heart palpitations, no anxiety.

There was only an earnest calm inside that felt right, fitting even.

He rang the doorbell and sidestepped into the shadowy flower bed beside the house. A moment later, Miller heard footsteps nearing the door.

The porch light snapped on and the door opened. McCall stepped out onto the stoop with a disconcerting look, trying to figure out who rang the doorbell.

Stepping out of the vale of darkness, Miller reared back with the blackjack and swung it across McCall's right knee. The man's knee buckled under his massive weight, and he let out a gritted-teeth whimper before falling from the stoop and into the dew-covered grass, clutching his leg.

Miller jumped from the flower bed and charged at McCall, who saw him coming.

His eyes widened in stunned panic, and he opened his mouth to try to call out to someone in the house, but Miller brought the blackjack around in an underhanded swing, catching him across the jaw before he could say a single word.

A sickening, dull, crunching sound of lead shot meeting bone and flesh, and a muted, pain-filled, liquid-like grunt cut across the dark lawn.

Blood spewed from McCall's mouth and dotted the driveway some ten yards away, and he dropped onto his back in the grass.

Miller kneeled down beside him with his hands draped over his knees. Thick black blood leaked from Earl's mouth and Miller saw he had broken several of the man's teeth; they hung from his gums by the thinnest threads of bloody flesh.

"Listen up, asshole," Miller spoke, keeping his voice just above a whisper.

McCall tried to say something, but his words became choked on the blood in the back of his throat. He coughed.

A tooth shot into the air and landed in the center of his forehead with a *tick*.

"Tell Regan she better come clean with what really happened at the soccer field to the cops. Tonight. If she doesn't, I'm coming back to knock the rest of your teeth out until she does."

Miller stood.

"Understand?"

McCall nodded eagerly. *Message delivered.*

"Don't make me come back, Mr. McCall."

As Miller disappeared into the night, Earl McCall began to sob like a baby.

TWENTY-NINE

The scent of burning wood came to Terry as he surfaced from the black world that had held him prisoner.

How long was I out? Terry didn't know.

Slowly, he tried to peel his eyes open, but his eyelids felt heavy, weighted down. He stirred and realized he was lying on a hardwood floor.

Where am I?

A voice spoke, slowly, as if the speaker were talking with a mouthful of mud.

"Think he's comin' to, Stevie."

There was someone else there with him, besides Stevie.

Who? Terry felt his innards shudder.

Footsteps neared, kicking dust up Terry's nose. His eyes snapped fully open, and he recoiled from the dust; it smelled musty and rotten, as if laden with decay. He rolled onto his back, trying to decipher his surroundings. It took his eyes a moment to focus.

He was in a small, shabby, one-room cabin. A single bulb overhead was the only illumination source, powered by a generator. Its hum cut the sticky night air somewhere not too far away.

There was little inside except a wooden table and a cot along the far wall.

A hunting cabin, Terry realized. It was hellish hot inside. The dust and dirt clung to him, his perspiration turning it to mud across his hairy arms and face.

"Welcome back, hoss," the slow voice spoke.

Terry snapped his head in the direction of the voice.

A bearded man about Terry's height stood by the table, watching him with fascination. He wore faded blue jeans that met a pair of well-worn cowboy boots. A black belt with a steer skull belt buckle held his pants up.

The dark brown and blue checkered button-down shirt, with the sleeves rolled to the elbows, was stained with sweat around the collar and under the arms.

And the tan Australian bush hat rested low on his head, concealing his eyes.

Behind him, the cabin door was open. Stevie was outside throwing logs onto an already vigorous fire. The flames were higher than the cabin's roof.

Terry tried to move but realized his hands and ankles were bound with rope.

"You ain't going anywhere, hoss," the slow voice said.

He started across the small space, his boots clicking dully on the wooden floor. Terry inched himself up against the cabin's wall.

The cowboy kneeled beside him and pushed the brim of the hat up. He had the blackest eyes Terry believed he had ever seen in a man. He studied Terry with a quizzical expression as if none of what was happening made a lick of sense.

"Who are you?" the man asked.

"Terry Graham."

"You say that as if your name's supposed to mean anything to me."

"It should," Terry replied.

He looked past the cowboy to Stevie, throwing another log onto the fire. Sparks jumped; the flames grew brighter, hotter.

The man looked over his shoulder, following Terry's gaze.

"Stevie told me what happened at his place."

He turned back to Terry. "Told me you were there to question him about those jobs we pulled a few years back."

Terry said nothing.

"You mind telling me why you're so interested in us all of a sudden?"

"Fuck you!" Terry spat.

The man seemed to consider Terry's remark before he spoke.

"He said you were looking for us."

Terry eyes narrowed sharply on the cowboy. He was talking to one of the Morgan brothers, he figured.

"So, which one are you? Chet or Luthor?"

"I'm Chet."

Terry's hands shot up from his lap, his fingers hooked, clawing at Chet's throat. But Chet quickly, easily, stepped out of Terry's reach, and Terry fell over onto his stomach.

Dust kicked up again, got into his throat, causing another coughing fit.

"Shit, hoss. You don't sound so good. You ill or sum'in?"

Terry used his fingers to inch himself back to a sitting position against the wall. Sweat rolled down his forehead, bringing bits of dirt with it that worked their way into his mouth. He spat onto the floor.

"Or sum'in," Terry wheezed.

Chet studied him for a moment before he spoke.

"So, here's the deal, hoss. You can tell me what you know, how you found us, and who else you told. If you're honest with me, I won't have to hurt you too badly. I'll shoot you through the head and throw you on that farr out there. I promise it'll be quick. Painless. You don't…"

He moved over to the table and lifted a hatchet; its sharp blade gleamed under the single light in the ceiling.

"I'm going to start by taking your fingers. Then, if you still won't talk, I'm going to take your toes. And by that point, if you're still quiet—which I believe you won't be—I'm going to take you apart limb by limb until there's nothing left of you but pieces to throw on the farr. Got it?"

His voice was calm, smooth, unfazed by the viciousness of his words.

Terry tried to swallow, but his throat was bone dry. He got the feeling Chet had done this sort of thing before.

"What's it going to be?"

"Do your worst," Terry replied.

He was done fucking around with these hillbilly assholes, and he wasn't about to cower to their demented demands.

Fuck 'em, I'm in the pale light anyway.

A smile slowly spread across Chet's face.

"Ooooh, a tough guy. I was hopin' you was going to say that. Stevie!" He turned to the door. "Get in here."

Stevie dropped the log he was about to toss on the fire and entered the cabin.

"Jeah?" Stevie asked.

"Get the fat boy on his feet and bring him over to the table."

Stevie crossed the room and reached out for Terry. Terry tried to fight him off, tried to squirm and thrash away from the hands grabbing at him.

But Stevie was too fast and quickly shot behind Terry, wrapped his forearm around Terry's neck, and squeezed, nearly cutting off his air intake.

Despite his slender frame, Stevie hoisted Terry to a standing position with little effort. He pushed him towards the table, where Terry saw his .357 revolver, along with a sawed-off double-barrel shotgun resting on top.

Just before they reached the table, Stevie kicked the back of Terry's left knee, knocking his leg out from under him. He went down. His chin clipped the side of the table.

A flash of white light erupted behind his eyes.

Before Terry knew what was happening, he was again being hoisted up. This time Stevie bent him over the table and then came around to Terry's right side and pressed all his weight on Terry's back, holding him in place across the table.

Out of the corner of his eye, Terry saw Chet. The hatchet rested on his right shoulder.

An ungodly fear shot through his veins, causing his blood to run cold.

"We can still do this the easy way, hoss. All you have to do is tell me what I want to know."

"I'm dying anyway," Terry panted.

"Whatever you do to me will be easier than dealing with cancer treatments. You'll be doing me a favor."

Chet snickered.

"You really are a tough sumbitch, ain't ya?"

Terry said nothing.

Chet looked at Stevie. "Grab his hand."

Stevie reached out and took hold of Terry's right hand.

"Spread his fingers apart."

Terry instantly made a tight fist. But Stevie began working his fingers into Terry's closed hand, prying his fingers apart one by one until he had ahold of Terry's thumb and pinky finger, and spread Terry's hand out flat on the table.

"Last chance, hoss," Chet said, taking a wide-legged stance. He spun the hatchet around three hundred and sixty degrees, a move that looked as cool as it was deadly scary.

"Which finger should I take first?"

"Just leave the middle one," Terry said through gritted teeth. "So when I kill you, I can still say *fuck you* in sign language."

Chet snickered, and his eyes flicked to Stevie.

"Hold' em still, Stevie."

Chet slowly raised the hatchet back over his right shoulder. The sharp blade again caught the light and gleamed.

Terry swore the hatchet's blade was curved into a smile, looking forward to tasting his blood. He tried to pull away, but Stevie's weight prevented him from moving.

Then, in one fluid-like movement, the hatchet fell.

Terry's heart jumped into his throat and the hatchet embedded into the table with such force that the legs lifted off the floor, even with his weight on it.

Terry didn't feel anything at first. He stared at the hatchet, its blade embedded between his right index finger's first and second knuckle.

When Chet yanked the hatchet free from the wood and Terry saw his blood squirt from the severed digit and across the table, he felt a jolt of electricity shoot up his arm and strike his brain.

A sickening quiver crept over him, and he felt the color quickly drained from his face. His mouth began to water like he was about to puke, but nothing came up, because there was nothing in him to come up.

"Wanna talk now, hoss?" Chet asked. "Or should we continue?"

Terry barely heard him. He could only stare at his finger, lying like a meaty chicken wing on the table.

"No? Okay. I guess we'll take another finger then."

Terry couldn't just let them take him apart piece by piece. He had to find a way out of this. His eyes moved to the shotgun only inches away.

But it might as well have been on the moon. He had to get free of Stevie first.

Then an idea struck Terry just as Chet raised the hatchet back over his shoulder.

"I'll talk," he screamed. "Just stop."

"Smart man," Chet said, lowering the hatchet to his side.

Terry felt Stevie's grip lessen and the pressure of his weight ease off his back. He drew a deep breath that filled his lungs. The air burned, and he coughed.

"How'd you find us?" Chet asked.

Terry lowered his cheek onto the cool surface of the table. He drew slow, even breaths as he watched his blood drip between the slats of the homemade table and drop to the floor below.

He needed to draw one of them in closer.

"Well?" Chet barked.

Terry's mind was misfiring like an unbalanced engine, and his eyes were as heavy as pig iron. He could feel his body careening off the cliff of consciousness and into a black abyss.

It would be so easy for him just to take that step and let it take him down into the darkness where there was no more pain. So very easy.

But he couldn't allow his body, or his mind, to drift off into Never, Never Land.

Wake up, Clay's voice shouted in his head, snapping Terry back from the brink of blissfulness that his body craved.

Terry began to whisper.

Chet looked at Stevie, confused.

"You hear a goddamn word he's saying?"

Stevie shook his head and leaned in close, so close Terry could feel his hot breath on the nape of his neck. Terry knew the time was right.

Now or never.

Terry snapped his head backward into Stevie's nose. He felt a soft crunching on the back of his skull as the cartilage collapsed and broke.

Stevie screamed, grabbed his face, and fell to the floor, kicking and screaming like a toddler throwing a temper tantrum.

Knowing he had no time to waste, Terry lunged for the shotgun. Chet did the same but was a moment too slow.

Terry grabbed the shotgun, just before Chet could. He brought it around and cracked Chet across the right side of the head with the small but heavy steel barrel.

Chet's head snapped to the left, the bush hat tumbled to the floor, and his eyes went googly and wet; the hatchet slipped from his hand and bounced onto the table with a heavy *thunk*.

Terry reared back and hit Chet again with the barrel across the face. This time, Chet fell to the floor so hard the cabin shook.

Rising from the table, the shotgun now in his left hand, Terry saw a movement to his right. When he turned, Stevie was climbing back to his feet. He held his hands over his face.

Blood leaked through his fingers, ran down the tops of his hands and forearms, and dripped off his elbows onto the floor.

Terry pulled the two hammers on the shotgun. Stevie froze.

On the floor, Chet moaned. He was already trying to get to his feet, using the table to pull himself up. His right hand was pressed to the side of his head where a fleshy open gash bled profusely.

"What are you waiting for, Stevie? Kill the sumbitch!" Chet screamed.

Terry looked back to Stevie, who was already in motion, running at him. There was a look of pure evil in his eyes, eyes that only wanted to see Terry's violent demise.

Terry squeezed the first trigger. The shotgun erupted and the buckshot tore through Stevie's right leg, taking it off just below the knee.

Before Stevie could process what had just happened, before he could even feel the pain of the amputated leg, Terry squeezed the second trigger.

The shotgun spat fire again, and the buckshot vaporized Stevie's head into a red mist. His headless body lurched forward and fell to the floor with a wet spat, twitching.

"Stevie!" Chet cried. "Oh, God, Stevie!"

Terry turned to the table and dropped the empty shotgun, the barrels still smoking. He picked up the hatchet and put it between his knees, blade up, and began to saw through the rope around his wrists. Blood from his missing finger dotted the floor between his boots.

Taking the hatchet in his left hand, he quickly freed his bound ankles. He stood, turned back to the table, and grabbed his .357.

"Take it easy, man," Chet said, holding out a bloody hand in front of him.

"Just like you took it easy on my brother and his family when you put them in a car and shot them in cold blood?"

"That wasn't us!"

Terry coughed up blood and spat it onto the dirt floor. His lungs burned and ached. He needed to rest and catch his breath before he passed out again. He eased himself down on the edge of the table.

"I know the three of you were in Hickory Falls that day. I know you went to Red's Bar where you picked up Ruby-Lee. Then, you took her to the Twin Pines Motel. What I don't know is why you chose Clay's house?

"But you're going to tell me everything, Chet," Terry spoke through labored breaths.

"We had nothing to do with your family's murders. Honestly."

"You know, we're a long way from civilization. That isn't good news for you right now. I could cut off each one of your fingers and toes until you talk. And if you don't talk by then, I'm going to take you apart piece by piece until there's nothing left of you.

"After I'm done, I'll throw your body on the fire out there."

Chet sneered at him, pale and sweaty. Blood had run into his mouth from the open laceration to the side of his head, staining his teeth. But Terry saw the knowing look in Chet's eyes; that he knew; it was clear the man knew he had no other option but to tell Terry what he wanted to know.

Chet explained how he and Luthor concocted a plan to start hitting banks after they were released from prison in 2014. They needed a getaway driver and a car, so they contacted Stevie, who just so happened to own a salvage yard and had a few old cars sitting around.

They hit two banks before the one in Gettysburg. But the bank jobs brought a lot of news and unwanted police attention. The reward wasn't worth the risk.

So, they decided to rob convenience stores instead.

In and out, quick, and easy. Hit a few convenience stores, get some money, then vanish. After the heat died down, they'd return to hit a few more.

But their newly concocted plan only went as far as the Quick Fill robbery.

"I did a black girl in the Quick Fill job—total accident on my part. I thought she was calling the cops, but she was just looking at her phone when she walked through the door. After that clusterfuck of a job, we needed to put some distance between the cops and us. But there was a problem."

"What problem?" Terry asked.

"The car."

"The Olds?"

Chet nodded.

"It was all over the news. We needed to ditch it. We knew a guy who could fix us up with a car. That's why we were in Hickory Falls. To get a new car."

Terry ground his teeth together. He couldn't believe what he was hearing, but he needed to stay the course.

He needed to know every detail of what had happened that night.

"We get to Hickory Falls in the morning and meet our guy at his garage. He tells us that there's a hang-up with getting us a clean car, but that it will be there by that evening, and we're to come back when he calls us.

"He then tells us to go to a bar called Red's, talk to the bartender, and he'll fix us up with drinks and anything else we need until the car's ready."

"Who was fixing you up with a car? I want his name," Terry asked.

Chet's eyes flipped to the floor, deciding whether to tell Terry what he knew. When he said nothing, Terry lifted the .357 and pulled the hammer, getting Chet's attention.

"Jeff Lincoln. His name is Jeff Lincoln."

Terry's grip on the gun tightened. *That lying son of a bitch.*

"So, what then? You headed to Red's?"

"Yeah. The place is a real dive bar. But they had beer and liquor, so we didn't really care all that much. Anyway, this bartender comes over and greets us.

Luthor tells him what Jeff said, and the bartender is more than happy to comply. He invites us over to the bar for drinks, chats us up, tells us about his Christmas Eve Party that evening and how we should attend.

"Then, this girl comes in. She goes to the bar, orders a drink. Starts making small talk with Luthor and me. She's dancing around her intentions, but we both knew what she was after."

"Her name wouldn't be Ruby-Lee, would it?"

Chet spat a bloody wad onto the floor.

"Yeah, I believe that was her name." He ran his hand over the back of his mouth and continued.

"She more or less begs Luthor and me to take her to this motel."

"The Twin Pines?"

"I believe that was the name. It's a couple of miles east of town, out in the middle of nowhere, right off the highway?"

Terry nodded.

"Then that's the one." Chet spit again.

"Luthor asks me what I think about picking up this broad. I'm down for it—I've always been hornier than a hound dog. So we make the deal. But here's the thing, we didn't pay the girl."

"What do you mean?" Terry asked.

"She made us pay the old guy—the bartender."

Terry stood from the table.

"Why did she make you pay the bartender?"

Chet lifted his shoulders.

"I guess he was her pimp or something? How the fuck should I know, man—they're your people."

"Not my people. Not anymore. Go on."

"So, we get out to the car with the girl when Luthor realizes that he didn't pay for all three of us. Stevie was okay with it. Whores were never really his thing—he always liked to watch."

Chet's eyes shot to Stevie's headless corpse on the floor; it had long ago stopped twitching and now lay still. When he looked back to Terry, he ran his tongue over his bloody teeth. Terry cringed.

"Luthor offers her twenty bucks extra if Stevie can watch. She agrees. We got to the motel and stayed there until the evening. Around eleven we headed back to the bar."

"Was she with you all night?" Terry asked.

Chet shook his head.

"No. She was too fucked up to be useful by the time we left the bar. It had started to snow heavily, so we decided to call it a night and parted ways and returned to the motel to wait for Jeff to call us about the car. He never did.

"Wake up the next morning to hear on the news about the murders in town, and the police are on the lookout for a blue sedan."

Anger seeped over Chet, and his face darkened.

"Jeff set us up, man. We gathered our shit together and hightailed it out of there. Dumped the car in some abandoned quarry not too far from the motel and hitched a ride to the nearest town with a bus station, and parted ways until the heat died down."

Everything was coming at Terry so fast he was having a hard time comprehending it all.

"You expect me to believe all that?"

"It's the truth. We had nothing to do with those murders. I swear to God. I've done a lot of bad things in my life, but we didn't do them."

If Stevie and the Morgan brothers had nothing to do with Clay, Claire, and Sidney's murders, and Jeff had set them up to take the fall in the murders, what was the real reasoning?

"What now, hoss?" Chet asked.

"I can't just let you walk out of here. There's blood on your hands—Stevie's blood—and I can't let that shit go. He was my brother from another mother, know what I mean?"

Terry looked at him and squeezed the trigger.

THIRTY

Miller was on his way back to Mercersburg. His mind was caught in a dreamlike rift that kept replaying over and over behind his open eyes.

He saw himself back at the McCalls' home with Earl McCall at his feet, bleeding and spitting teeth; tears streaking his puffy red face.

The only difference between the waking dream and reality was when Miller turned to leave, Luna stood there. His daughter's eyes were locked onto him with a horrid gaze, seeing not the man she loved and adored but the monster he had allowed himself to become.

Fear of him, of what he was capable of, danced in her eyes.

His cell phone rang.

"Miller," he answered, trying to shake the images from his mind.

"I got something." It was Ross. He sounded tired, but the excitement nearly hid the fatigue in his voice.

"What?"

"I found the connection between Stevie Boyd and the Morgan brothers. They were fostered by the same two people—a Greg and Marcie Page."

"Fantastic work, Ross."

"That's not all. There was a fourth boy."

"Okay?" Miller didn't see how that made much of a difference, but he let Ross continue.

"Jeff Lincoln."

Miller sucked in a gulp of air. Pieces were starting to reveal themselves.

But how do they all fit together?

"Are you sure?"

"Positive," Ross replied.

"Also, we got the prints back on the box. One set belongs to Ruby-Lee, and the other *is* Terry Graham's. I've already talked to Garcia. He wants us to pull the Morgan brothers and Stevie Boyd in for questioning, as well as Terry Graham and Jeff Lincoln.

"These could be the accomplices Terry worked with."

Something wasn't making sense. Why would Terry ask Jeff Lincoln, a man he'd just been in a fight with a day prior, to help murder his family? Could it have been a ruse, set up to throw everyone off?

Miller didn't want to speculate. *Follow the facts.*

"How'd Harper make out with Boyd? Was he able to bring him in?"

"No. Boyd wasn't there when Harper arrived. So, he staked an officer at Boyd's place to pick him up when he comes home. I also sent the local PD to Akersville to pick up Chet Morgan, but like Stevie, he wasn't home.

"I say we shoot for Luthor Morgan. We can bring Terry Graham in after we talk to Luthor. I'm not concerned about Lincoln at the moment; he has no idea we're looking at him, so he's not a flight risk."

"Agreed," Miller replied. "Where are you?"

"Still in Mercersburg."

"I'll swing by and pick you up on the way to Luthor's home. Contact the local PD in the area and have them on scene to assist."

"Coordinating it now," Ross said.

It was past five that morning by the time Miller and Ross got to Jackson.

Jackson was a small, one-street town with homes on both sides. There was no traffic at that hour of the day, and no one was out walking the streets.

As they neared the end of town, Miller saw a police cruiser parked along the sidewalk. Ross eased the car to a stop behind the cruiser and they got out and walked up to the police car. Two officers with the Jackson Township Police waited inside.

"You Troopers Miller and Ross?" the driver asked.

"Yeah."

"That's your boy across the street." The driver pointed to a two-story white home.

The lights were on inside, but Miller could not see anyone moving around. He wondered what Luthor was doing at the moment, not realizing what was coming his way.

"What are your names?" Miller asked.

"I'm Stapleton. This is Hacke," the driver said, hitching a thumb at his partner. "How are we going to handle this?"

"Discreetly," Miller said. "We don't need to tip this guy off that we're here. He's deadly. Might be armed. Ross and Hacke will take the front."

Miller looked at Stapleton. "You and I will go around back and make sure he doesn't try and run once we make ourselves known."

Stapleton unlocked the .12-gauge shotgun from its gun rack and stepped out of the car. Hacke did the same, and the four of them started across the street.

Ross and Hacke quietly went up the porch steps to the front door, while Miller and Stapleton moved up the driveway to the rear of the home.

Miller noticed a detached garage about twenty yards from the house with a dusk-till-dawn lamp attached at the peak.

Coming to the rear of the home, they found a smaller side porch leading to another door. Here, light splashed through the rear door's window onto the wooden floor of the porch.

With Stapleton behind him, Miller eased up the porch steps delicately, not wanting to tip anyone off inside to their presence.

Moving to the door, he looked through the window and saw a bald man with a long, gray goatee sitting at the table drinking a glass of milk and eating a protein bar. He wore shorts, a cutoff t-shirt, and flip-flops.

He was a big guy with a massive, well-built body and arms that could rival Ross's.

Miller heard Ross pound on the door. He tensed. It was about to go down.

Luthor Morgan looked over his shoulder at the pounding. He grew rigid, the muscles in his arms tightened with unease.

"Luthor Morgan. This is the state police," Miller heard Ross's muffled voice say.

"We need to speak with you."

Luthor shot to his feet, knocking the chair over as he did. He hurried to the counter, yanked open a drawer next to the sink, and lifted out a .9mm Beretta.

"Gun! Gun!" Miller screamed, reaching for his own sidearm, just as the first crack of gunfire split the quiet morning.

THIRTY-ONE

He was leaking blood all over the place.

Terry kneeled by Chet's dead body, took a piece of the man's shirt, and ripped it free. He wrapped the torn cloth around his missing finger, looped it into a knot, and pulled it taut with his teeth.

His nerve endings were on fire; pain seared with each heartbeat.

He turned and looked at the carnage left in his wake.

But he couldn't allow himself to focus on what he had done. Terry supposed he would have to deal with the ramifications of his actions at some point.

The mental trauma of taking two lives would surely follow days and weeks after this was all over—if he lived that long.

But for the moment, Terry felt nothing inside but an empty dullness. He was thankful for that.

Later. Deal with it later.

Now he had to get going, had to put this place behind him, like a dream that slowly faded the further you got from sleep.

Snapping out of his head, Terry began to pat Chet's body down and found a pack of cigarettes and a Zippo lighter in his right breast pocket. He pulled a cigarette from the pack and lit it.

The nicotine hit his bloodstream like a tidal wave, and he felt his head become fuzzy.

Stepping out into the humid morning, Terry drew a deep breath of smoky campfire air that burnt his nostrils. It was funny how everything seemed refreshed in one's senses after a life-threatening incident.

It had happened twice to Terry in two days.

Finishing the cigarette, he flicked it into the ever-growing fire. To his left, he saw his pickup. Beside it was Stevie's truck.

After killing him, he figured Stevie and Chet had planned to dispose of his truck somewhere nearby, where it would never be found.

He could see nothing beyond what the fire illuminated; the woods were too thick and dark.

How deep am I in? Terry guessed he was a few miles from the nearest road. Chet and Stevie wouldn't have wanted anyone to see the pyre or hear them torturing him.

Moving past the hot fire, Terry went to Stevie's truck.

He opened the door and began to search through the cab for anything useful. He found an extra box of shotgun shells for the double-barrel in the glove compartment, rope and other tie-downs under the seats.

Taking the shells with him, Terry returned to the cabin. He sat the shells down on the table and picked up the sawed-off shotgun, cracked it, dumped the spent shells, slid two fresh ones in, and snapped it shut.

Just in case anyone else shows up before I can get the hell out of here.

Back outside, the heat from the fire was now so intense Terry felt it singe the hairs on his arms. It had grown above the cabin, the flames snapping and lapping at the nape of the roof.

Embers floated up into the sky like fireflies in the night. With the heat and the dryness, it would only be a matter of time before the whole place went up, maybe the entire forest.

Terry needed to get going.

He quickly moved past the giant inferno and got into his pickup. The keys were still in the ignition.

He fired up the truck and pulled on the lights, which illuminated an impassable dark forest before him.

There has to be a road out of here.

Backing the truck around, the lights caught a clear path cut in the woods. It wasn't a road, per se, but it appeared to be passable to get the truck through.

Good enough.

Terry hit the gas. As he sped away, the first embers began to settle on the roof of the cabin and smolder.

<u>THIRTY-TWO</u>

Miller hit the porch floor just as two bullets ripped through the door, shattering the glass window and splintering the wood, dusting him with shards of both.

A thundering *boom* quickly followed from Stapleton's shotgun, which took most of the door off throwing shards of wood, glass, and metal everywhere.

Rolling on his back as three more shots zinged above his head, Miller crab-crawled backward on the porch, toward steps on his elbows. He saw Stapleton using the wall of the house for cover.

When the shots stopped, Stapleton peeked out around the side. He brought the shotgun up and fired a second round into the house that exploded something wooden inside.

Two rapid *pop pops* from the handgun were the response. The bullets hit the wall in front of Stapleton, causing him to jerk back around the corner for cover.

Miller heard more gunfire erupting from inside the house. He suspected Ross and Hacke had breached the front door and were working their way through the house to Luthor.

Stapleton looked around the wall and said, "You're clear, Miller. Move. Now!"

Miller rolled and pushed himself to his feet and ran for the steps. He heard another round fired from inside and felt a bullet whiz by his head, hitting the dusk-till-dawn light above the garage, exploding the bulb.

A second shot quickly followed. This time, Miller felt the bullet tug at his shirt, knocking him off balance.

He stumbled to the porch floor just before reaching the steps. Miller's heart raced. He was fully exposed. Another well-placed shot would surely end his…

"On your feet!"

Stapleton had moved from his safe spot behind the wall and stood at the base of the porch steps. He reached out and began to pull Miller toward the steps, out of the line of fire.

Three more shots broke the quiet. Stapleton's body jerked this way and that as the bullets tore into him.

Large, red flowers burst from his chest; blood flew across the steps, dotted the railing. Stapleton fell back into the driveway.

Miller turned. Luthor was in the process of swinging his gun at him. If he didn't act, he was as good as dead.

With his gun aimed between his knees, Miller opened up. The shots were wild, erratic. He wasn't firing to hit Luthor but rather putting down cover fire for himself.

Three of his bullets embedded themselves in the wall beside Luthor. The fourth caught Luthor in the upper right chest. Blood blew back onto the wall behind him.

He screamed, grabbed the wound, and fell from Miller's sight.

Now! Move!

Miller threw his feet over his head, tumbled backward off the steps, and came down hard onto his hands and knees in the driveway.

He shot to his feet, firing his last three rounds at the house, before ducking behind the wall, where Stapleton had safely been only a moment ago.

He was gasping for air, his entire body electrified with adrenaline, so much so that his hands were shaking.

Two more shots rang out. Bullets whistled past and off into the darkness somewhere.

"Put your gun down, Luthor!" Ross hollered from inside the house. "We just want to talk."

"Fuck you!" Luthor screamed back.

Three more shots split the night, echoing across the town.

"We can still resolve this. No one has to get hurt," Ross called back.

Too late for that. Miller looked down at Stapleton. There was no rise and fall of his chest, no movement at all.

Peeking around the corner, he saw Luthor was on his feet and had propped himself up against the wall. Blood streamed down the front of him from a black hole in his upper chest, covering him in a thick sheen of liquid crimson.

Luthor ejected the magazine of the Beretta and checked his rounds. Miller had no idea how many shots had been fired, nor if Luthor had more ammo nearby.

He knew he couldn't take a chance and rush him head-on. That was a bad idea that would result in his own death. He also wanted to avoid killing Luthor, even if the heartless bastard deserved it. They needed to speak with him.

They needed to apprehend him alive if they could.

Miller ejected the empty magazine and slid in a fresh one, with hands so jerky that it took him two tries to get it right. He holstered the gun, bent and reached for the shotgun still in Stapleton's hand, and pulled it to him.

He stood back up against the outside wall of the house.

"Luthor, this is your last chance," Ross screamed from somewhere inside. "Come out with your hands up. Now!"

Miller peered around the corner. He watched Luthor shake his head and knew, from the crazed look in his eyes, that there was no way Luthor Morgan would give up without a fight. The man was willing to die to avoid going back to prison.

"Luthor? What's it going to be?" Ross shouted.

Luthor pushed himself away from the wall and opened up again with the Beretta.

NOW!

As Luthor was firing at Ross and Hacke, Miller rushed up the porch steps and into the house.

Luthor never heard him coming over the gunfire. Miller reared back with the shotgun and clipped Luthor at the base of his skull with the stock.

He went down like a rock onto the floor, out cold.

Miller quickly kicked the gun away from Luthor's hand, while reaching for his handcuffs. He pulled Luthor's wrists behind his back and slapped the cuffs on him, making sure to squeeze them extra tight.

"Suspect's secure!" Miller screamed. "But we have an officer down!"

THIRTY-THREE

When Terry got back to Hickory Falls, dawn had broken.

The sky was a blueish-pink color; wisps of clouds stretched past the mountains and kissed the morning horizon. It was beautiful. A great day for the truth to come to light, Terry believed.

Soon it would be over, and everyone in Hickory Falls would know what really happened.

He pulled into Lincoln's gas station and killed the engine. There were lights on inside the garage, but the business was not yet open to the public.

Stepping from the truck, Terry noticed how cool the morning was.

The humidity that had made the week so sweltering and miserable had finally given way to crisp, fresh air, after the rain yesterday afternoon.

Turning back to the cab, Terry lifted the sawed-off shotgun from the bucket seat. Pain throbbed up his right hand and into his arm and shoulder.

He looked down at his missing finger; the makeshift bandage was soaked through.

He tightened it with his teeth. Pain seared.

Slamming the truck's door moved the garage entrance, where a CLOSED sign hung in the window.

Through the window, Terry saw Jeff working on a dual-axle Dodge Ram pickup truck in Bay 1.

He rapped on the glass.

Jeff looked up from the engine; his face took on a perplexed gaze, as if he were surprised to see Terry there that morning.

Putting the wrench down on top of the front left fender, directly beside the engine housing, Jeff turned and started to the door.

Terry slid the shotgun behind his left leg, blocking it from view as Jeff neared.

Spinning the lock, Jeff pushed the door open.

"Terry? I thought you were in the hospit—"

He stopped talking when he noticed the blood on Terry's clothes and the bandaged right hand.

"What… happened to you?"

Slowly, Terry brought the shotgun up and stuck it under Jeff's chin. The mechanic instantly grew stiff and sucked in an audible breath that caught in his throat.

"Step back inside, Jeff," Terry said quietly.

He lowered the shotgun and poked Jeff in the belly, forcing him back into the shop. Terry stepped in, pulled the door closed behind him, and spun the lock.

"Look, Terry…" Jeff's eyes drifted down to the shotgun's half-dollar-size black holes aimed at his chest.

He gulped.

"I don't know what you've heard, but it's not true. I didn't have anything to do with what happened at your place the other night."

"All that stuff about becoming a new man you fed me the other day… it was all bullshit."

Terry jabbed the shotgun into Jeff's belly, forcing him back against the Dodge Ram.

"No more lies, Jeff. You knew the Morgan brothers and Stevie Boyd. That's why they were in town on Christmas Eve. But what I cannot figure out is why you set them up to take the fall in my family's murders."

"Terry, you… you don't want to do this." Jeff stammered. He looked at the shotgun.

"I know you're not a killer."

Terry cocked the double-hammers. Jeff's eyes grew large and round, and a visible tremor passed through his body.

"Chet and Stevie thought the same thing. They were wrong."

Terry watched fear shoot through Jeff like a shock wave, contorting the muscles around his mouth and eyes with the realization that Terry was fully capable, and willing, to do the same to him.

"How'd you know them?"

"We're brothers."

"Brothers? You don't have any brothers, Jeff. Do you take me for a fool?"

"No. It's the truth. Luthor, Chet, Stevie, and I were all fostered by the same couple. Luthor and Chet were only there about a year before they were transferred to another place.

"They were always in some kind of trouble and were bounced around from one foster house to another, when they weren't locked up in one of the juvenile penitentiaries.

"About ten years ago, I found Stevie on Facebook. I was looking up parts on Marketplace for an '85 Camaro I was restoring when I stumbled upon Boyd's Salvage. I sent the salvage yard a message, looking for the part I needed.

"Come to find out was Stevie's business. He and I get to chatting and it turns out, he had kept in touch with Luthor and Chet. We set up plans for the four of us to meet.

"It was the first time I'd seen them in over twenty years."

"Why'd you set them up, Jeff?"

"Two days before Christmas Eve, I got a phone call from Luthor. He tells me he, Chet, and Stevie are in a bind. The cops were after them because they shot two people while trying to rob the Quick Fill—came right out and told me—and asks if I can secure them a car because the Olds they were driving was hot.

"I told Luthor to give me a few hours and I'll call him back if I find one."

"But there never was a car, was there?"

Jeff shook his head.

"No. Like you said, it was a setup."

Jeff looked at Terry's blood-soaked clothing. His eyes rose to the shotgun, to Terry's missing right index finger leaking blood through the bandage. He swallowed, and his throat made a dry grinding sound.

"This was all your fault. You know that don't you?"

"Because of the fight and what I said that night to Red outside afterwards? That my brother and I were going to buy the hardware building and drive him out of business?"

"That's only part of it."

What's that supposed to mean? Terry went to ask, but Jeff continued talking.

"Red couldn't allow you to buy the building before he secured the money himself. If you did, and succeeded with the microbrewery, especially with Clay and Claire's help, he'd be forced to close his bar."

"Was it Red's idea or yours to pin the murders on Luthor, Chet, and Stevie?"

Jeff hesitated to answer. He seemed to sink inward as if a great burden pressed upon his chest.

"Talk, asshole!"

Terry shoved him back into the pickup. Jeff hit the truck's front fender with such force it dented it in. He nearly lost his footing, but he gripped the inside of the engine housing, next to the wrench he had laid there, to keep himself from falling.

"It was Red's," Jeff replied, pulling himself standing.

"I went to Red to see if he knew anyone locally looking to get rid of a car. He always had an ear out for those kinds of things. He asks me why. Stupidly, I told him. That's when the idea struck Red, I believe. However, he didn't plan this alone."

"What do you mean?"

"By the time I was brought in, Red had already been talking to someone. He wouldn't tell me who."

"And you went along with it?"

"I needed the money Red was offering. I had my own string of bad luck. My garage was going under, and what money I was making, I pissed away drinking."

Terry looked away, tried to swallow, but his throat felt thick. Everything was his fault.

He had set things in motion by losing his temper and shooting his mouth off.

It was never about Clay, Claire, and Sidney, Terry realized.

It was about me.

No. Terry had not pulled the trigger. But he might as well have.

Still, something bothered him. It was what Jeff had said: *That's only part of it.*

Terry felt something bigger was at play. And Jeff was still keeping secrets.

Terry turned to ask another question but before he could get the words out, Jeff's hand shot off the pickup's fender toward Terry's face. In it was the wrench he had left there moments ago.

Terry tried to duck, but the tool caught him on the left shoulder, bounced off, and clocked him on the jaw. He staggered back from the blow.

Jeff sprang forward, the wrench raised over his head, poised to come down into the middle of Terry's skull.

Terry looked up just as Jeff brought the wrench down in a wide arch. He quickly sidestepped. Jeff's momentum from the swing pulled him past Terry.

Terry spun on his heels and swung the shotgun's barrel across Jeff's kidneys.

Jeff screamed, grabbed his lower back, and went down onto the dirty, oil-stained floor. Terry kicked the wrench from Jeff's hand. It slid across the garage floor and down into the oil pit in Bay 2.

Stepping forward, Terry shoved his boot on Jeff's neck, pushing him back to the floor, causing his eyes to bulge with fear, and pressed the shotgun's barrels against Jeff's nose, laying it flat against his face.

"We're going to go have a chat with Red. Find out the real reason why my family was murdered. And who this mystery person is."

THIRTY-FOUR

Miller watched the medics roll the stretcher carrying Officer Stapleton's body past him and load it into the ambulance. A tightness gripped Miller's throat, and tears stung the backs of his eyes.

Stapleton had saved his life. Had he not acted, Miller knew he would have been the one being rolled into the ambulance.

"You okay?" Ross asked.

Miller nodded, quickly composing himself.

"Luthor say anything?"

"Nah. He knows to keep his mouth shut until he's lawyered up."

Miller turned and looked down the road. Townspeople had gathered on the sidewalks to watch.

He wondered if any of them knew a killer had been living amongst them. *Probably not.*

"Garcia's on his way. So is the governor. They're going to want to know why this turned into a shit show," Ross said.

"He opened up on us. What choice did we have?"

Ross nodded.

Miller's cell phone began to ring.

He answered it.

"Meet me at Red's Bar." It was Terry Graham.

"Just you. No one else. Got that?"

"Terry, what's going on?" Miller asked.

"Red's Bar."

"I'm in Jackson. It's going to take me some time to get there."

"Then you better hurry before the shooting starts."

"Terry—"

The line went dead.

THIRTY-FIVE

"Get out," Terry ordered Jeff once Miller pulled into the parking space next to him in front of Red's Bar.

"And don't even think about running off, or I'll fill you with buckshot right here in the middle of town, got it?"

Jeff nodded and quickly exited the pickup. Terry followed, keeping the shotgun trained on Jeff as he did.

Behind him, he heard Miller approach.

"What's this, Terry?" Miller asked with an apprehensive tone. He looked worn down, haggard, with heavy eyes that held a deep sorrow; a look Terry had not seen before on Miller.

But if Miller's appearance was a shock to Terry, Terry's blood-covered clothes and the missing index finger of his right hand, leaking a stream of thick red from the makeshift bandage, downright horrified Miller in return.

"Terry, what the hell happened to you?"

"Never mind that now. We're all going to walk into Red's and clear this shit up," Terry grumbled, followed by a cough.

"Put the gun down," Miller said. "Let's talk about this."

"We will, Miller. But inside. This is how it has to be." Terry stepped forward, grabbed Jeff by the shoulder and thrust him toward the bar.

"Walk!"

"Okay! Just take it easy with that thing, Terry," Jeff cried.

"Terry, what the hell happened to you?" Miller asked again, watching the blood leak from the tourniquet and dot the ground in a line pattern that resembled paint dripping off a brush.

"Who hurt you?"

"I found Chet Morgan and Stevie Boyd. They tried to carve me up out in the woods."

Miller was silent for a moment. His eyes darted back and forth, trying to understand what was happening.

"Did you hurt them, Terry?"

"They ain't here, are they?" Terry replied bluntly. He poked Jeff in the lower back with the shotgun. "Move!"

"Let's stop this before anyone else gets hurt. Before this goes any further," Miller pleaded.

"No. I'm clearing my name. And we're going to find out why this shithead and Red Keller, along with someone else, conspired to murder my family."

"I'll tell you everything I know," Jeff said, looking to Miller.

"Please, just get me away from this psycho."

Jeff went to move past Terry toward Miller, but Terry pushed him back.

"No," Terry said quietly.

"I need to hear why they killed my brother and his family, straight from their mouths. I need this, Miller. I need to know the truth."

His eyes rose to Miller. "So do you."

Miller said nothing.

Terry turned, took hold of Jeff, and pushed him through the door into Red's Bar. Jeff tripped over his own feet and fell onto the polished wooden floors.

Terry stomped in after him.

He had not been in Red's since December of 2015 and he now noticed all the updates that had been made inside. They infuriated him. The entire place was more or less his idea, right down to the microbrew beer taps lining the bar; stolen from him by a greedy man.

"Red!" Terry screamed. "Get your old ass out here."

"Terry, stop this!" Miller protested, coming through the door behind Terry.

Terry ignored him.

"Red!"

The door to the kitchen opened, and Red came out.

The shock at seeing Terry standing there, blood-covered, with a shotgun trained on Jeff was enough to drain the color from his face.

"Take it easy, Terry. Just relax," Red said, moving slowly closer to the bar.

Terry pulled Jeff to his feet, dragged him across the floor, and threw him against the bar. Jeff groaned through his teeth upon impacting the wooden surface.

Terry swung the shotgun around and aimed it at Red's face, his fingers on the triggers, ready to empty both barrels into him. There was nothing left for him now but pain and suffering—the cancer ensured that much, sealed his fate.

It didn't matter what happened. This was his last stand, his last moment to get the truth about that night.

"Why'd you do it, Red? What was the real motivation to murdering Clay and his family?" Terry asked.

"I don't know what you're talking about," Red replied, looking Terry up and down.

"Tell him, you dumb asshole! He's as crazy as we believed he was. He'll shoot us both. He's already killed two people," Jeff shrieked.

"Tell him, or I'll tell them what I know."

"You shut your mouth!" Red growled. "If you know what's good for ya."

"Keep quiet!" Terry snapped at Red. He nodded for Jeff to continue. "Go on."

"It was never just about Terry going into business with Clay and Claire. The entire plan was to get back at Terry from the start," Jeff said, glancing at Miller.

"Who else was involved?" Miller asked.

"Don't you say a word, Jeff," Red snarled.

Jeff glanced at Red, who bristled with anger. The old man slowly shook his head in a don't-you-dare-tell-them way.

Jeff turned back to Miller and said, "There were a handful of us."

"Names?" Terry growled, followed by a cough.

"How do the Morgan brothers and Stevie Boyd fit into it all?" Miller asked.

"After I got a call from Luthor about fixing them up with a new car, I told Red about it. Red devised the plan to let Luthor, Chet, and Stevie take the fall for the murders. I called Luthor back and said I had a car for him, and they should meet me at my garage.

"When they arrived, I told them the car wasn't ready, but I would call when it was. I sent them down here, like Red told me to.

Red fixed them up with drinks, food, and with Ruby-Lee—who Red brought in.

"Her role was to take them to the Twin Pines Motel, so there would be a record of them being in town. Afterward, she was to bring them back to the Christmas Eve party at the bar, allowing everyone in here that night to get a look at them."

"Rudy-Lee knew about the murder plot?" Miller asked.

"Yes."

"Why?" Terry asked. "I was never anything but kind to her."

"Money, man. She was a greedy whore."

"But why frame Terry?" Miller asked. "You already had three men to take the fall."

"The plan was never to frame Terry. It was always about hurting him. But Ruby-Lee fucked up."

Jeff looked at Terry.

"After the party, she was supposed to return to the motel with Luther, Chet, and Stevie, make sure their attention was on her while Red and I went to the Grahams' house.

"After it was done, the plan was to make our way out to the motel and plant the shotgun in their car, while they were distracted. The following morning, Ruby-Lee was supposed to make that call and report that she heard gunshots in the Graham Video parking lot and give a detailed description of the men she saw and what they were driving to the police.

"We staged the scene to look like a botched robbery, to make it appear a part of the recent string of crimes that reported seeing a blue sedan. But by the time Ruby-Lee got back to the bar with the guys, she was already drunk. She was useless at that point.

"Red told her to go up to his place to sleep it off. He couldn't do anything to her in the middle of the bar with everyone around.

"The next morning, after it was done, Red woke her up and told her to make the call. Except when she called, she was still drunk, and forgot two crucial details—to describe what they looked like and what model of car they were driving.

"There was nothing Red could do, since she was on a recorded line. Afterward, he beat her so badly she couldn't show her face in public for over a month—that's why they had a fallout.

"But even though Ruby-Lee screwed the pooch, it ended up working out in our favor. With her vague description of what she claimed she saw, everyone began to assume Terry murdered his family because of his reputation."

Terry looked back to Miller. Miller appeared ashen and shaken by what he had just heard.

"Who pulled the trigger?" Terry asked.

"It was Red!" Jeff was quick to say.

"We forced our way into your brother's house. Made Clay and his family get into the Jetta. Red rode in the passenger seat while I followed behind in my truck.

"We made Clay drive to the video store, and Red shot all three of them inside the car."

"And Ruby-Lee? Was that Red too?" Miller asked.

"I don't know. But it wasn't me!" Jeff eagerly said.

"Red phoned me at my garage. Said there were two new state police detectives snooping around and if they questioned Ruby-Lee, she'd fold on us. Said we needed to get rid of her. Maybe it was him."

"That's why you were so agitated when I came to speak with you," Terry said.

"At first, I thought it was just because I was there, but that wasn't it at all. You were concerned the troopers, or me, were going to find out what really happened."

Jeff nodded.

"After you left, I called Red back and told him you were also snooping around and that you knew it was Ruby-Lee who reported the murders. He told me we needed to back you off, too.

"So, I rounded up Ike Arnold and Colin Baker—both of whom were more than eager to help since they ran into you in the square the other day and had some sort of squabble, plus Colin wanted payback for the broken arm nine years ago.

"We went out to your house, set your barn on fire, and beat you up, hoping you would leave well enough alone. Maybe just leave town once and for all."

"You're both under arrest," Miller said, looking Red in the eyes now. "Put your hands on the bar, and don't move."

Miller took hold of Jeff, spun him around, and planted his face on the bar while he pulled his hands behind his back to cuff him.

"Terry, lower the gun."

Terry gradually let the shotgun fall. Then he remembered Jeff had said Red was talking to someone else.

"Who else?" Terry asked Red.

Red did not meet Terry's intense gaze, cutting through him like a hot knife.

"Jeff told me there was someone else involved. I know it wasn't just Ruby-Lee, she wasn't smart enough to put all this into motion. Who else were you talking to, Red? Who else helped? Was it Daniel? Thompson?"

Miller finished cuffing Jeff and looked to Red.

"Your turn, Mr. Keller."

Miller stepped back, placing his hand on his sidearm again. "Come around the bar, slowly, with your hands in the air, sir."

Red's eyes fell to the bar. He was lost somewhere in his mind, weighing his options.

"Who!" Terry hollered.

"Tell him!" Jeff said. "Or I'll tell him who you were talking to, Red."

Red's eyes rose, and they locked on Jeff with deadly intent. In that moment, Terry knew everything was about to go south.

Red's hand shot up from under the bar. In it, he held a .38 Special revolver. He aimed the gun at Jeff's face.

Jeff's eyes widened in terror, and his mouth fell open to scream, but Red pulled the trigger before anything could come out.

The shot was like the snap of a firecracker going off inside the bar.

The bullet went through Jeff's open mouth and exited out the back, showering the floor with blood. Jeff's head jerked back violently, and his eyes rolled up into his head, just before his body crumbled in on itself, like an accordion, to the floor.

Before Jeff's body hit the floor, Red brought the .38 around at Terry.

Terry tried to get the shotgun up before Red could level the .38 on him.

But Red was faster.

The .38 was only inches away from Terry when Red squeezed the trigger and the gun went off.

Terry felt the bullet enter his body just below his right shoulder. It felt like someone had run a hot poker through him; his insides lit up and the right side of his body went completely numb, which caused his grip to loosen on the shotgun.

It fell from his right hand, bounced off the bar and hit the floor butt-first, causing the weapon to discharge.

The buckshot erupted from the shotgun, tearing through several bar chairs, and ripped half of the polished wooden bar away in a large chunk that looked like a giant had taken a bite out of it.

Shards of wood and metal blew everywhere.

Red had fallen into the wall of liquor behind the bar. The blast had stunned him, but he quickly shook his disorientation away and stepped up to the bar. He brought the .38 up and aimed it at Miller, who was crouched down with his face covered with his hands.

Terry saw what was about to happen. Miller was as good as dead. Red had him in a dead-bang shot.

Like shooting a duck in a barrel, just like Clay, Claire, and Sidney had been.

Bleeding from the gunshot to the shoulder, and unable to move his right arm—something felt broken inside and wiggled and popped in and out of place with each little movement, sending intense pain flairs through his upper body—Terry threw his shirt aside and wrapped his left hand around the butt of the .357 and went to pull…

But the revolver's hammer caught on his jeans.

"Miller!" Terry screamed, hoping to get his attention before Red unloaded on him.

But Terry's scream to warn Miller drew Red's attention back to him. Red quickly swung the .38 around, while Terry was still trying to pull the .357 free.

A smirk grew on Red's face when he realized the gun tucked into Terry's jeans was caught.

"For Melissa," Red whispered, just loud enough that only Terry could hear.

The words caught Terry by surprise, stopping him cold, as his mind tried to quickly process what they meant.

And then it hit Terry why his family had been murdered, and who else was involved.

Red pulled the trigger for a second time. Another *snap* broke the air.

The second bullet entered just below his right nipple with enough force to violently throw Terry back into the wall.

The air was driven from his lungs, and hot blood kicked into the back of his throat, along with small fleshy bits of soft tissue that reminded him of the texture of liver meat on his tongue.

Pain seized his entire body.

Cupping his hand over the blood bubbling from his chest, Terry staggered forward, still trying to pull the .357, but his legs stopped working, as if an off switch had been flipped, and he collapsed to the floor.

Miller shot to his feet, pulled the Sig, and fired two rounds in rapid succession. The first bullet struck Red just below the throat.

The second round hit him center mass, went through, and exploded a liquor bottle on the shelf behind.

The force of the bullets drove Red back into the wall of alcohol. Bottles fell from their shelves and crashed to the floor. He stumbled forward into the bar, blood leaking from his fishy lips.

He tried to lift the gun again, to take aim with a limp wrist at Miller.

Miller fired a third round, catching Red between the eyes, He dropped dead over the bar.

Quickly, Miller crossed the room, grabbed the gun from Red's dead hand, and threw it away.

Terry knew by the time he hit the floor on his side that he had been mortally wounded.

Blood filled his mouth, but he could no longer taste it.

A gurgling sound seeped from the hole in his chest that was bubbling oxygen-rich blood as he struggled to pull a full breath.

The right side of his chest felt like it had collapsed, and a heavy weight was pressing down upon him, making it nearly impossible to breathe.

Terry knew this was it. He was dying.

"Just lay still, Terry," Miller said, kneeling beside him with concern set deep in his eyes while pulling out his cell phone to call for help.

But it was no use, Terry knew.

He could feel his heart slowing, the coldness of death creeping over his body.

As Miller went to dial 9-1-1, Terry slowly reached out with a bloody hand and stopped him from making the call.

Miller locked eyes with him, shocked by his actions.

Terry slowly shook his head.

"Terry…" Miller tried.

Terry felt his eyes growing heavy. So very heavy.

His breathing, his heartbeat, it was all slowing to a crawl. He just wanted to go to sleep now, forever.

That was all right with him.

Miller took Terry's hand and held it close to his chest.

"Doesn't… look… like I'm dying alone… after all," Terry whispered.

"No, Terry. I'm right here with you."

But Terry wasn't talking to Miller, and he followed those he saw, those he loved, into the pale light.

THIRTY-SIX

One Week Later

Miller studied himself in the mirror. He was dressed in a black suit and tie for Terry's funeral.

He supposed he looked as good as someone could for such an occasion. He was about to head out the door when Trisha called.

"I was just calling to let you know that after further investigation, and Regan's statement to the police that she provoked the fight and slapped Luna first, all charges against Luna have been dropped, along with the lawsuit."

"Good to hear," Miller replied.

"I don't know what strings you pulled, Henry, but I'm glad you did. You really came through for Luna."

Yeah, I'm a real saint.

His mind flashed back to Earl McCall laying in the grass bleeding and crying. His actions haunted him; what he had done, what he had become to save his daughter.

How he had deceived his partner into running their names through the police database to cover his own ass.

Thankfully, the latter hadn't come back to bite him; either of them. He wasn't proud of himself, and worried if he had become that man twice now, was it possible for him to become that man again.

"How's Luna doing?" Miller asked, trying not to think about who he really was inside.

"She's fine. You want to talk to her?"

He did. But he was running late and needed to get going.

"I'll stop by later if that's okay with you. I'll take Luna out for ice cream."

"That's fine with me. And I'm sure, Luna would really like spending some time with her dad."

"Okay. Talk to you later."

"See ya."

Miller went to hang up, but Trisha called out to him before he could.

"Oh, Henry."

"Yeah."

"You're a good father. I know I should tell you that more often."

Trisha's statement touched him, but it didn't ease his mind that he had gone to extreme lengths to receive such praise from his ex-wife.

Terry was laid to rest in the Mt. Hope Cemetery next to his family. Miller was one of three people to attend the burial. No one else from Hickory Falls bothered to show up.

He wondered if this was because most were still in shock once the truth was revealed that Red Keller, Jeff Lincoln, and Ruby-Lee Huckster conspired to murder the Graham Family.

Or were they too ashamed to show their faces, knowing they had all been willing participants to believe what they wanted to about Terry Graham, instead of using reason and judgment.

Miller didn't know either of the women who came out to pay their final respects to Terry. A red-headed woman with pointy glasses openly wept into a napkin as the casket was lowered into the ground.

Another woman, who looked thin and maybe ill, threw roses on top of the coffin once it was settled on the bottom.

"Rest well, Terry," said the flower woman. "Karl wishes he could be here for you. But I get the feeling, he'll see you soon enough. As will I."

The weeping woman stepped forward, scooped up a handful of dirt, and dropped it onto the casket. Then, using the damp napkin again, she dabbed at her red eyes.

"You still owe me a dinner, Terry." This brought a smile to her face as if she found comfort in knowing she and Terry would be reunited someday.

Miller wanted to ask how they knew Terry. What he had meant to them since they were the only people there, outside of himself, but he decided against it.

He left them alone to have their private moments of mourning.

He stayed until the gravediggers began to shovel dirt back into the hole, wondering if Terry could rest easy now knowing the truth was finally revealed.

That he was not the monster everyone in Hickory Falls thought him to be, but a tormented soul that had been exploited for a personal vendetta.

Miller had made his way to Fifth and Main where he stopped at the red light. Looking over to what used to be Graham Video, where this long nightmare began nine years ago, he was reminded of something Jeff had said: *It was never just about Terry going into business with Clay and Claire. The entire plan was to get back at Terry from the start.*

But getting back at Terry for what?

There was another, much richer layer, that Miller couldn't see.

Jeff told me there was someone else involved, Terry had said to Red, trying to get him to cough up another name.

But as a last ditch effort to keep the secret, Red shot Jeff Lincoln, silencing him just like he had Ruby-Lee—the .38 Special Red used to murder Jeff was the same gun used to silence the woman.

Miller supposed it didn't matter to Terry now. Those directly responsible for the murders of his family were dead.

In the end, Terry could rest easily knowing he was able to clear his name.

But I can't, Miller thought dourly.

His cell phone rang. Ross was calling.

"Where are you?" Ross asked, sharply.

"Still in Hickory Falls. Why? What's going on."

"Miller, we got something interesting here," Ross said with excitement in his voice.

"The records from Ruby-Lee's burner phone came in. Most of the numbers belonged to her clients, except one."

Miller sat up straight in the car's seat. His heart palpitated and his hands grew clammy with sweat.

"The number 717-555-8585, it belonged to Pastor Garland."

Miller felt his chest grow tight.

"Are you sure, Ross?"

"Positive. I'm on the way to meet you in Hickory Falls, along with backup."

The light turned green, and Miller cut the wheel hard to the left and made a U-turn in the middle of the intersection, much to the chagrin of other motorists who blew their horns, shouted obscenities, and flipped him off.

"Miller, what's going on?" he heard Ross ask.

He stomped the gas pedal to the floor; the engine roared as he sped up through town and into the roundabout and pulled longways in front of the church.

"How long before you get to the Zion Methodist Church?"

"Ten minutes."

Miller disconnected the call and jumped from the car and ran up the steps. Pushing open the doors of the sanctuary, he started up the center aisle, toward the pulpit where Pastor Garland preached to his flock.

He remembered what Terry had told him that morning in the hospital.

They were constantly being spoon-fed a lie from a master manipulator high on his pulpit, and they all lapped it up like babies.

It was easier to believe it than to accept the truth.

Lifting his eyes, Miller's gaze fell onto the large golden cross that hung above the church, in front of the stained-glass window.

Just below the intersections where the cross met were three words:

His Holy Sanctuary -HHS.

Miller felt his blood pressure rise. *HHS. Side entrance – 9* had been the text message sent to Ruby-Lee's phone.

He turned away from the pulpit and made his way to the double white doors that led back to the offices. Pulling them open, it was quiet in the hallway and there wasn't a soul around.

In the middle of the hallway, he noticed the EXIT sign they had passed under when Mrs. Hardy led them to the conference room. Moving to it, he pushed the door open into a small alley, just big enough to get a car into.

It was the same place Terry had said he picked up Melissa. And it was the same place Pastor Garland had met Ruby-Lee, he supposed.

"Can I help you?" a voice boomed to Miller's right.

Miller spun, throwing his jacket back, and placing his hand on The Sig.

Pastor Garland stood at the end of the hallway. He looked perplexed to see Miller standing there.

His eyes slowly traveled to the gun and then rose to meet Miller's hard gaze once more.

"You're under arrest, Pastor," Miller said. "For the murders of Clay, Claire, and Sidney Graham."

"Please, come into my office, my son, so we can talk."

"No more talk, Pastor. No more lies."

"Please." Garland stepped back from his office door, inviting Miller in.

"I will explain everything. There will be no need for you to use violence in here."

He looked down at the gun once again before turning to go back into his office.

Miller pulled his hand away from his gun and reached into his pocket and pulled out his phone. He opened the voice recording app and hit the RECORD button.

Then, he started up the hallway and entered Pastor Garland's office.

Garland was sitting behind his desk with his hands folded. A friendly smile rested on his face, making him appear like he was about to counsel a member of his congregation who needed spiritual advice.

"Have a seat, Detective."

"I'd rather stand."

"Suit yourself."

"Ruby-Lee texted you. We were able to trace the messages back to your phone. Did you have her killed, Pastor?"

Garland smiled as if it were an answer. Miller continued.

"You had Ruby-Lee silenced, after she came to see you. She knew the truth about why the Grahams were really murdered. Did she threaten to speak with us? Or tell Terry the truth about why his family was murdered?

"The plan was never to frame Terry. It was always about hurting him."

"Don't you dare speak *his* name inside these walls!" Garland shouted, nearly rising out of his seat.

"I will not tolerate it and I've warned you before."

"Save your rhetoric for someone else," Miller shot back.

"The four of you cooked this entire plan up after Jeff got the call from Luthor Morgan. For Red Keller it was to make sure his future in the town was secure with the purchase of the hardware store.

"For Jeff, it was about saving his garage and getting back at Terry after their fight. For Ruby-Lee it was purely money.

"But you, Pastor Garland, it was about your daughter, Melissa. You wanted Terry to pay for Melissa's death, and when the opportunity presented itself, you jumped at it."

Pastor Garland said nothing.

"But you didn't do this alone. You needed to make sure Terry looked as guilty as possible, especially after Ruby-Lee messed up the 9-1-1 call. That call had to disappear, just like the Claims Adjuster's report because they would have excoriated Terry."

"Sheriff Daniel's contribution to the cause. I told you, I thought he would have made a great husband for my Melissa, and he was more than willing to go along with everything if it meant seeing Terry finally pay for killing Melissa," the pastor said.

Pastor Garland closed his eyes and took a long breath.

Miller spoke again.

"Except you knew the reason Melissa was with Terry that night. You knew because Terry told the police the truth, and I suppose Daniel told you. Still, you couldn't accept, refused to believe that your daughter was in love with someone of Terry Graham's standing.

"So, you used your influence as the town's pastor to manipulate everyone into believing that Terry might have murdered your daughter. No other reason why your Melissa, you angel, would be with *swine* like Terry Graham unless he forced her into his car.

"And they ate it up like dogs."

"The Bible teaches us *an eye for an eye and a tooth for a tooth.* I wanted every eye and every tooth. And believe me, I had been trying to come up with a plan for years to get back at *him.*

"Then one day Red Keller of all people comes to me; says he's heard through town gospel that I sought retribution to the man who caused Melissa's death. Seemed Red Keller and I had a common enemy that needed to be dealt with.

"Red tells me he needs *him* and his family out of the picture—he doesn't say why, and I didn't need to know—and he's figured out a way to do it that can satisfy both of us.

"He begins to tell me this story about these three men who were involved in a recent robbery and double murder at the Quick Fill over in Mercersburg. They're on the run from the law, but need to get rid of the car they were seen in.

"Turns out they were coming to town to secure a new car from Jeff Lincoln, who knew them since they were children. Red says they are the perfect people to pin the murders of the entire Graham family on.

"But here's the thing, Detective Miller, I didn't want to see *him* dead. I wanted *him* to live the rest of his life, never knowing who murdered his family or why—Purgatory, in a way. Just like I had been living. I wanted to ruin *Terry Graham's* life, just like *he* ruined mine. *He* took part of my family, so I wanted to take part of his."

Pastor Garland paused, composed himself.

"It wasn't until after the deed was finished that I enlisted Sheriff Daniel's help to hide Ruby Lee's—that Jezebel—call. She almost spoiled our plans because she was too hungover to stay on script. We were scared this was going to come back on us.

"So, I went into damage control. Started preaching that Terry was an evil man, who not only murdered my daughter, but his family too. It easily took hold around town, especially after all the work I had already done to convince everyone he was responsible for Melissa's death."

"Keep repeating the lie until it becomes truth."

Garland said nothing.

"Get on your feet. You're under arrest," Miller said.

Miller cuffed Pastor Garland and led him outside, just as three state trooper vehicles pulled up to the church. Ross stepped out of the first cruiser, his stare fixed on Miller and Pastor Garland with a mix of pride and dismay.

He started up the steps and stood beside Miller.

"Go arrest that piece of shit with a badge, Sheriff Daniel. He was part of this too," Miller snarled.

"You're sure?"

"Got the full confession from Garland himself right here." Miller reached into his pocket and pulled out his phone and hit the STOP button.

Ross smiled.

He turned and headed back to the cruiser and took off with a patrol trooper driving toward the sheriff's department.

Around the square, townspeople were coming out to see what was going on.

Shock set on their faces to see that their pastor, the man they had listened to, believed, and worshiped with, was being led down the church steps in handcuffs.

Miller could feel every eye on him as he placed Pastor Garland in the rear of the police cruiser and slammed the door.

What their pastor had done would be exposed.

The truth would finally set the community of Hickory Falls free from the lie they had come to believe.

THE END

Westley Smith had his first short story, "Off to War," published when he was just sixteen. Recently, he's had short stories featured in *On the Premise*, *Unveiling Nightmares*, and *Crystal Lake Entertainment*. He was the runner-up contestant in the *Alfred Hitchcock Mystery Magazine's* "Mysterious Photograph Contest," where his name was featured in the magazine. He sold his debut thriller, *Some Kind of Truth*, to Wicked House Publishing. His forthcoming thriller, *In the Pale Light*, will be published with Watertower Hill Publishing for a summer 2024 release. He is also the author of two self-published horror novels, *Along Came the Tricksters* and *All Hallows Eve*. Visit Westley at www.westleysmithbooks.com

This work of fiction was formatted using 11-point Times New Roman font for the body, "Acme Gothic Extrawide" font for the Cover, with 1.15 line spacing, on 55lb cream stock paper.
The page size is mass market paperback 5" x 8".
The custom margins are industry standard, 0.5" all around, and 0.625" inside, with no bleed, and 0.0" gutter. The margins are "mirrored."
The book comprised of 42 different sections, with different odd and even pages, and different first page of section.
Headers and footers are standard.
The cover is full color paperback in a glossy finish.
The binding is 'perfect.'

www.ingramcontent.com/pod-product-compliance
Lightning Source LLC
Chambersburg PA
CBHW032109310726
48972CB00001B/154